What the critics are saying...

4 ½ Stars! "This third installment in the "*A Storm for All Seasons*" series is phenomenal. So emotional and gripping, you're on the edge of your seat worrying what will happen... Once again, *Ms. Burton's* amazing talent shines through. Don't miss "*A Storm For All Seasons – Winter Ice*". You'll never look at the weather in the same way again." ~ *by Susan Biliter ECATAROMANCE*

"*Winter Ice* is a joy – it starts out with a 5 alarm sexual encounter and the intensity never fades. It's sensual and action packed with a surprise or two to keep the readers interest until the last page. I couldn't put this one down!...*A Storm for All Seasons Book 3: Winter Ice* is a sizzling sexy read with depth of characters that will make you want to read it again and again. It's a keeper." ~ *by Patrice Storie JUST EROTIC ROMANCE REVIEWS*

5 Blue Ribbons! "*Winter Ice: A Storm for all Seasons,* the third in Jaci Burton's Storm series maintains the high level of intensity in her previous books in the series. Magic abounds not only in Sophie and the Storm family but also in the relationship between Sophie and Logan. The attraction between the two sizzles both in an out of the bedroom and *Ms. Burton* is a master at setting the pages on fire with lush sensuality while still telling an intriguing story... *Winter Ice: A Storm for all Seasons* is another awesome story by *Ms Burton*; I can't wait to read her next installment in the Storm series" ~ *By Brenda Edde ROMANCE JUNKIES*

Kaitlyn and Brett are terrific characters who complement each other very well. It is absolutely fascinating to watch them dance around each other as they attempt to deal with their feelings. The sex scenes are graphically detailed and hot enough to boil water… The pain and anguish the main characters must deal with tinges the plot with a poignancy that is very touching. This is a terrific book! It is not the first book I have read by *Ms. Burton* and I hope to read many, many more in the future. She is an extremely talented author who never fails to keep me on the edge of my seat. I highly recommend *Spring Rain* to other readers who enjoy contemporary storylines about love and magic. ~ by Susan White JUST EROTIC ROMANCE REVIEWS

ICE AND RAIN

A STORM FOR ALL SEASONS

JACI BURTON

ELLORA'S CAVE
ROMANTICA PUBLISHING

An Ellora's Cave Romantica Publication

www.ellorascave.com

Ice and Rain

ISBN # 141995301X
ALL RIGHTS RESERVED.
Winter Ice Copyright© 2004 Jaci Burton
Spring Rain Copyright© 2005 Jaci Burton
Edited by: Briana St. James
Cover art by: Syneca

Electronic book Publication: May, 2005
Trade paperback Publication: November, 2005

Warning:

The following material contains graphic sexual content meant for mature readers. *Ice and Rain* has been rated *E-rotic* by a minimum of three independent reviewers.

Ellora's Cave Publishing offers three levels of Romantica™ reading entertainment: S (S-ensuous), E (E-rotic), and X (X-treme).

S-*ensuous* love scenes are explicit and leave nothing to the imagination.

E-*rotic* love scenes are explicit, leave nothing to the imagination, and are high in volume per the overall word count. In addition, some E-rated titles might contain fantasy material that some readers find objectionable, such as bondage, submission, same sex encounters, forced seductions, etc. E-rated titles are the most graphic titles we carry; it is common, for instance, for an author to use words such as "fucking", "cock", "pussy", etc., within their work of literature.

X-*treme* titles differ from E-rated titles only in plot premise and storyline execution. Unlike E-rated titles, stories designated with the letter X tend to contain controversial subject matter not for the faint of heart.

Also by Jaci Burton:

Contents

Winter Ice

Dedication

To everyone who believes in the magic of love.

To my editor, Briana St James, as always…thank you for giving me the freedom to create the characters and worlds that live inside my head.

To Patti and Puawai for your advance read and invaluable assistance in shaping this book.

To Missy for all that you've done for me. I'm forever thankful.

And to Charlie, who has a magic about him that calls to me in ways I could never explain. We share a destiny. I love you.

Chapter One

Even in the heat of fucking, Sophie felt the chill Logan emanated. Despite the sweat pouring down his brow, the keening wails coming from the woman's mouth as Logan fed his cock to her pussy, he was cold, distant, removed from the experience as if it was an out-of-body event.

Sophie hid in the corner of the darkened alley, mesmerized by the sight of Logan's thick cock thrusting and withdrawing.

The beautiful redhead he was fucking didn't seem to notice the faraway look in Logan's eyes, but Sophie saw. And wondered why.

She wondered a lot of things. Like what Logan Storm, CEO of New Orleans' fanciest hotel, was doing in a dark alley in the French Quarter at midnight. He was casually screwing the woman with such disinterest he might as well be making out a business agenda.

Sophie felt it all, though. Every stroke of his shaft, every kiss, every caress, everything the redhead experienced. The woman was heated past the boiling point. Logan gave it to her with an icy calm.

Yes, he was definitely cold. At least with the woman. He wasn't giving all of himself, almost as if he'd removed himself from the passion. Yet underneath she felt his heat—so why was he holding back?

"Fuck me, Logan," the redhead cried. "Give me that legendary cock of yours. Hard and deep, baby."

Logan grunted, but didn't speak, just rammed his shaft in and out of the woman's dripping pussy. Sophie's cunt contracted as if Logan's shaft had speared *her* swollen and aching slit.

What brought him out this time of night? This was her area of town, the alleys and streets she haunted. Definitely not a place she imagined Logan Storm frequenting. He had a fine hotel, and he lived in the penthouse apartments above it. Surely he didn't need to have sex in an alley.

Maybe he was hiding out, attempting to be anonymous, thinking no one would see him here. Though Sophie had recognized him right away. Who wouldn't? His face graced the cover of many New Orleans' magazines time and time again.

Then again, it was Mardi Gras, and pretty much anything happened in the French Quarter during this time of year. Winters were relatively mild in New Orleans, and Mardi Gras brought out the tourists and the locals alike.

But a big business mogul fucking a woman in an alley? Now that she hadn't expected.

Yet here he was, in the last place she'd ever thought she'd see him. Men like Logan didn't travel in the same circles as she did. No, it was highly unlikely their paths would cross here. Although she'd known they were destined to meet, and soon. The visions had been growing stronger lately.

Their meeting had been preordained. She just hadn't expected it to be like this. Not here, and sure as hell not like this.

Fate sure was funny at times.

The cool February wind shifted, swirling around her feet and lifting her skirts. The bells on her ankle bracelet tinkled in the breeze.

Logan looked up and turned his sharp gaze to her.

Too late to slip away in the shadows. He'd seen her.

Now what? The polite thing to do would be to leave, go back where she'd come from, and allow Logan and the woman their privacy.

But something in his cold stare compelled her to stay put. A challenge there, perhaps? Maybe a trace of heat? A connection? She'd certainly felt it, an invisible line tying her to him. Did he feel it, too?

He hadn't spoken, and the redhead couldn't see her. Logan's body was between Sophie and the woman's head. Though Sophie could lean to the side and see the woman's torso, could see Logan's long cock piercing the folds of her pussy.

Not that it was necessary for her to see. She felt every single one of Logan's thrusts as if he were fucking her instead.

Her lips parted as she sucked in a breath of the crisp, wintry air. Beneath the thin peasant top her breasts swelled, her nipples aching to be free of the confines of the material. Juices poured from her slit, soaking her thighs with the cream of arousal.

In her mind, Logan was fucking her. In her heart, she wished for it to be so.

Soon, it would be.

As if he'd heard her thoughts, he frowned. She held his gaze and drew her hands up to her breasts, massaging them, caressing the taut nipples through the thin cotton.

He inhaled sharply and grabbed the redhead's buttocks, lifting the woman's skirt even higher over her hips as he drove deep and fast, relentless in his punishing thrusts. The redhead cried out and wrapped one leg around Logan's hip.

"*Mon Dieu*, Logan. Fuck me harder! Make me come!" the woman begged, bucking her hips and grinding her pussy against his pelvis.

Logan seemed impervious to the woman's pleas, his gaze still riveted on Sophie. Something compelled her, some calling from Logan. Mental telepathy? She didn't know what it was, only that it had to be answered. The urge had grown too strong. She couldn't resist sliding her palm over her belly and lower, lifting the ankle-length gauze skirt to her thighs, desperate to massage the ache between her legs. The agony of arousal called to her and she needed relief only an orgasm could provide.

Her hand became Logan's hand, her fingers Logan's shaft as she slipped them between the moist folds and plunged them inside her cunt. Her soft walls quivered, then squeezed her fingers as if they were welcoming a hard cock.

She wished.

Panting, already near a blistering climax, she kept her focus on Logan. His cold blue eyes pierced her, held her captive, demanded her satisfaction as if her pleasure drove him.

Wordlessly, he commanded her and she followed his thoughts, driving her fingers deeper, faster, searching out her clit with her other hand and circling the distended nub, the explosion growing closer and closer.

The redhead screamed, and Sophie leaned her head against the cool brick wall, needing support as her legs trembled and nearly buckled. Logan continued to pound his cock into the whimpering woman, harder and faster.

As if the redhead didn't exist, as if Sophie was responsible for his gratification, he nodded to her. She let the floodgates loose. Her climax ripped through her and she bit down on her bottom lip to keep from crying out. Logan tensed, then groaned and uttered a string of curses as he came. She'd never experienced anything more erotic than having Logan's clear blue eyes focused on her as he came inside another woman.

She felt it all, the spasms of his cock, the trembling of his arms as he held the woman tight, the taste of brandy lingering on his lips as he bent to take the woman's mouth. She felt every single movement as if he was touching her.

She'd never climaxed so strongly from her own hand.

Spent, she could only lean against the building, watching the heat disappear from Logan's eyes. He stepped back, removed the condom and righted his clothing as the woman smoothed her skirt over her hips.

The redhead smirked, pressed a kiss to his lips and caressed his cheek. "You are an animal, *mon ami*. I can't believe you agreed to fuck me out here."

"This place is just as good as any other," he replied, no warmth or emotion in his voice. "Besides, you wanted it this way."

The redhead caressed his cheek. "*Oui*. And you know exactly what I want, *cher*."

Sophie was relieved that Logan's body hid the redhead from view. The last thing she wanted was to embarrass the woman. Then again, if the woman had been worried about discovery, she probably wouldn't have screwed Logan in a public place.

"I need to go," the woman said, squinting to read her watch in the soft light of the streetlamp.

Sophie shook her head, surprised that both of them would consider what had happened as more like a business meeting than a heated exchange of passion. That was the problem. Logan didn't *feel* the heat with that woman.

Because he'd been with the wrong woman.

"Later, *cherie*," he said, and Sophie inhaled the husky tones of his voice. A mix of Cajun, French and downright sexy, his voice enticed her. Just as she always knew it would. She'd been hearing it in her visions for as long as she could remember.

The woman walked toward the main street. Sauntered actually, her hips rocking back and forth. No doubt for effect. But Logan wasn't watching. He'd turned and trained his glowering gaze on her, instead.

She waited as he approached.

"Enjoy the show?" he asked, the sarcasm evident in his now cold voice.

"You know I did."

He crossed his arms across his broad chest, one side of his mouth curling in a sardonic smile. "Glad to be of…assistance."

"I want to see you again," she blurted, knowing that if she didn't do it now, the opportunity might be forever lost.

He arched a raven brow. "I don't think so, *cher*."

"You don't understand. We share a destiny."

She expected anger, not the loud roar of laughter as he tipped his head back and howled into the night. When he dropped his gaze back to hers, bitter cold emanated from his icy blue eyes. "Did my mother send you here?"

Before she could respond, he held up his hand. "Don't answer that. I already know. Look, I enjoyed your masturbation performance, and I'm glad I could help get you off. But that's the end of it."

He didn't know. How could he? Although, she'd always thought he would be aware of her, just as she'd been aware of him. Maybe he did, and was fighting their connection. She wouldn't be at all surprised. "You will come see me." She pulled her card from the pocket of her skirt and held it out to him.

Logan shook his head. "Not a chance in hell, sweetheart. This game is over."

When he refused to take the card, she dropped it on the ground, the wind flipping it toward his shoe.

"You *will* come to me, Logan," she said, then turned and walked away, knowing that nothing she could say or do at the moment would convince him. He'd have to mull it over first. Then disregard the pull he felt for as long as he could.

But it wouldn't do any good.

Soon enough, he'd show up on her doorstep. He wouldn't be able to help himself.

* * * * *

The woman's sultry voice lingered as Logan watched her walk away, admiring the soft sway of her hips that was completely natural, rather than the affected swivel Vivian presented him as she'd left.

You will come to me.

Bullshit. No one told him what he would or wouldn't do. Even if that someone was a gorgeous gypsy of a woman, with waist-length hair the color of a cloudless night and eyes a vivid violet that seemed to sparkle like flowers under a bright sun. Even if she did have buttery soft, mocha skin that he could already feel gliding over his body despite the fact he'd never once touched her.

She was too young for him anyway. Couldn't be more than her mid-twenties, about ten years younger than him. Even so, her eyes belied her age.

An old soul, his mother would say.

Speaking of his mother, Logan would bet anything that his meddling parent had sent the woman. If there was one thing Angelina Storm never tired of talking about, it was the destiny of her children.

That supernatural crap might have worked on Aidan and Shannon, but it held no appeal to him. He had no destiny, no woman he was "meant" to be with. That was all magic, and he wanted nothing to do with magic, especially not the kind that lived within him.

He'd controlled it for thirty-five years and he'd damn well keep it at bay forever. Whatever the mystery woman wanted would have to remain a mystery.

The cool wind fluttered her card against his shoe. He would not pick it up, no matter what.

But it called to him. Dared him to take a look.

Ridiculous.

Okay, maybe just to see what it said, then he'd tear it up.

The background of the business card was the same color as the woman's violet eyes.

Her name was Sophie Breaux. He snorted at the verbiage below her name.

Psychic Readings, Fortune-Telling, Tarot Cards and Mystical Spells.

A fucking fortune-teller. A carnival sideshow meant to bilk unwary travelers with mind tricks and voodoo mumbo jumbo.

Did she think he'd run to her so she could tell his future? What kind of idiot did she take him for?

Obviously a big one, considering she'd seemed so confident that he'd be showing up on her doorstep soon.

Yeah, he'd show up all right. When hell froze over. He ripped the card up and tossed it into the wind, then shoved his hands in his pockets and moved down the alley, forcing his thoughts back to Vivian, the redheaded siren who'd tried her best to fuck his brains out.

They'd been casual sex partners for over a year. Suited them both fine to keep things impersonal. Vivian was a divorcée with a ton of alimony coming her way each month. The last thing she wanted was her very rich ex-husband getting wind of her having a relationship, since he was still possessive as hell over her.

And if she pissed off her ex, he might not be so generous with the money he tossed her way each month. Vivian valued her ex-husband's money much more than she craved a relationship. So they kept things physical. Occasionally, Vivian liked to be naughty and do it in public, though she always pretended to be shocked by it.

Location didn't matter to him. A fuck was a fuck. Sex alleviated the tension and allowed him to focus on business the rest of the time without having to worry about a woman's feelings. That's why he and Vivian got along so well.

The last thing he wanted was an emotional involvement with a woman. Not with what he carried inside him. No way would he fall in love. It was fine for the rest of the Storms, but love wasn't for Logan.

He'd been told before that he was cold as ice. Unfeeling. Lacking emotion and warmth.

Exactly the way he wanted to be. In control.

He turned and headed back to the hotel, confident that he was in charge of his destiny. When he was younger, he'd struggled against the magic, hating losing control over himself.

It took a while, but he'd mastered it, pushed it deep within. As long as he remained cold, removed from anything emotional, the magic stayed hidden.

He was no freak, no sideshow spectacle for people to wonder about, to point and laugh at, or even worse—to fear. He wanted to be a normal, human male living his normal, human life. And he didn't need love and all the ties associated with it to enjoy his life. All he wanted was to be...ordinary.

Sophie Breaux was the opposite of ordinary in every way. He'd bet a million she was as fake as any illusionist. A mistress of tricks and chicanery.

A con artist.

No way was he going to involve himself with someone like her, even if she had made his blood boil in ways he considered both good and bad.

Bad, in that for a moment there, he'd felt the magic churning to life. Good, in that watching Sophie bring herself to orgasm gave him the best sex he could remember. When she touched herself, it was like he'd been fucking her instead of Vivian.

Which was all his imagination, brought about, no doubt, by the concept of having a ménage à trois in the alley. Sure, he'd had his cock in Vivian, but he'd also had the pleasure of enjoying a superb mind-fuck with Sophie. He'd been so in tune to her scent, the slight sounds she made while she pleasured herself and the way her body shuddered in climax.

Yeah, it had been good, for a onetime thing. His connection with her had been sexual, and nothing more. The reason it had been so good was just the mental and visual associated with doing it in public and having someone watch. Watch, and get herself off at the same time. His cock twitched to life again visualizing Sophie's pussy, her dark, swollen pussy lips moistened with the cream of her desire. God, he could even smell her scent—a sweet, musky perfume that had sailed across the alley on the wind.

It had been damn good.

But it would never happen again.

Just like seeing Sophie Breaux. Never again.

Chapter Two

"Mr. Santiago, if you look at what The Rising Storm offers, I'm sure you'll agree it's the best hotel for the price and will provide your clients a fantastic stay during the convention."

Logan waited for the man's response to Aidan's pitch, familiar with the game Santiago played. They sat near the window inside a small café in the Quarter, the midafternoon sun casting its warming light across them.

Santiago was a shrewd businessman. Logan had worked with him in the past. Santiago always tried to finagle a bigger discount than Logan was willing to give. Which was why he'd accompanied Aidan and Lissa to this meeting today. More business was always great, and booking a big convention like Santiago's company had every year would definitely be worthwhile. But he wasn't going to give it away for free, either. Bringing Aidan and Lissa in meant more allies in his corner, and the hope he could eventually turn this pain-in-the-butt client over to them in the future.

"Now, about this discount," Santiago started, and Logan fought the urge to roll his eyes. Same thing every year. They'd argue back and forth, Logan would give him the discount he wanted, and Santiago would want one penny more off that.

Which, of course, he'd agree to, since Logan knew exactly how to deal with this man. Soon, hopefully, so would Aidan and Melissa. Then he could ignore the multimillion dollar cheapskate in the future.

He'd tuned out Santiago, well-versed in the man's argumentative nature, and turned his attention to the window. A colorful skirt caught his eye as it sailed past the window, the familiarity of it making his heart lurch in his chest.

He could swear he heard bells tinkling around her ankles.

Sophie. With that long raven hair flying in the breeze, it could only be her.

A rush of sensation came over him, a feeling of desire so intense it was all he could do to remain seated. The urge to go after her was strong, almost as if he was in a trance and some unknown force pulled at him. Something too strong to resist. God knows he tried, but he couldn't even turn his head to listen to the conversation at the table. His focus was on Sophie. He needed to go to her.

Now.

"Excuse me for a minute," he mumbled, not even looking at his tablemates. He rose and hurried out the door in her direction.

His feet moved of their own volition. He didn't even know where he was going, only that he had to get "there".

"There" turned out to be *Cosmic Connection*, just on the outskirts of the Quarter. He opened the door, his senses assaulted by the scent of patchouli and cinnamon.

Incense burned in small jars on top of all the glass display cases. The shop was tiny, jam-packed with all kinds of voodoo and magic things. Tarot cards, crystal balls, beads, incense, candles, books of spells, magic wands, just about anything imaginable.

What the fuck was he doing in here, anyway?

A beautiful young woman with strawberry-blonde hair approached, her amber eyes showing intense interest. When she smiled, she lit up the room. "Hi. I'm Samantha. Can I help you with something?"

He stared at her, but for some reason he couldn't find his voice. Probably because he had no idea what he'd even say. "I...I..."

Great. Now he was babbling.

"Hey there. I'm Joshua. You looking for something? Or maybe someone?"

He turned toward the sound of a male voice behind the counter. A tall, well-built guy in his mid-twenties with wavy brown hair approached him. Logan shook his head negatively, not sure how to answer.

And he hadn't even had alcohol with lunch.

Suddenly the colorful skirt he'd spotted at the restaurant breezed through the hanging beads separating the main shop from another room. The skirt was attached to the object of his search.

"Sophie," he managed, finally able to find his voice long enough to utter her name.

She smiled and her violet eyes seemed to dance with light. "Logan."

He picked up her scent, similar to the sweet patchouli fragrance of the shop. Only muskier, more sensual, like the woman wearing it. When she moved, bells jangled around her wrists and feet.

At a loss for words, he could only stare at her, oblivious to the other man and woman in the shop.

"We need to talk," she said, slipping her arm through his and leading him into the other room. He turned to offer an apology to the others for being so rude and not speaking, but what was he going to say? *Sorry, I'm in a trance right now?*

She sat him down at a square wood table centering what looked like a sultan's palace. Soft pillows in jeweled colors brightened a small beige couch against the wall. Tapestries of faeries and dragons decorated the walls, and the only light came from the fifty or so candles scattered throughout the room.

Hell, it was sexy in here. Exotic, sensuous and inviting. Despite not knowing what compelled him to come, he relaxed. Possibly because of the beautiful woman who graced him with a warm smile, though his thoughts about her were anything but relaxing.

"I'm so glad you came. I knew you would."

He started to object, but then she reached for his hands, sliding her palms over his fingers. He jerked as a shot of pure electricity soared through his body, hardening him in an instant.

Damn! What the hell was that?

She massaged his fingers lightly, and he began to breathe heavily.

"I need to tell your future," she said, her voice soft and raspy. The kind of voice a man wanted whispering in his ear when his cock was buried deep inside her. The kind of voice that a man would love to hear begging him to fuck her harder, faster. Logan shifted to accommodate his erection, mentally damning himself for the weakness that had suddenly surfaced within him.

"You don't know my future," he objected, starting to feel ridiculous for even being in this place.

"Oh, but you're wrong. While I don't know it all, I do know some things. That's why I wanted to see you again. I have something to tell you. Something urgent."

This should be good. "Okay, go ahead."

The smile left her face. "Your family is in danger."

Priceless. "Really."

She nodded. "Yes. Grave danger. Unfortunately, I don't know the time or place it will occur, but something bad will happen very soon."

Could she be more vague? He almost laughed. "That's not telling me much, *cher*. Easy to see how you could successfully predict the future with information like that."

"I knew you wouldn't believe me. You'll just have to trust me. You must be on your guard because you are the catalyst. Somehow this revolves around you."

"Okay, I have a question."

"Sure."

"Do people actually pay you money for this crap?"

He expected her to be angry. Instead, she nodded and smiled. "Actually, they do. Because I'm always right."

He pulled his hands away and crossed his arms. "What do you tell them? That someday they're going to die? That the stock market will go up one day and down the next? That the local candidate running for office has a 50/50 chance of being elected over his opponent?"

This whole fortune-telling thing was ludicrous, and he wasn't going to stay here a minute longer. He stood and headed toward the exit.

"Logan, wait!"

She rose and approached, stopping inches away from him. Tilting her neck back to meet his gaze, she said, "Please trust me on this. I've had visions about you...very strong ones. You and I are fated to—"

"Hang on a second. Fated? Like destined?"

"Yes."

"Holy shit!" He couldn't believe it. How could she do this to him? Dear God, how old did she think he was, anyway? "My mother put you up to this, didn't she? First the thing in the alley, and now this."

"Your mother? I don't know your mother."

He wasn't buying her confused frown. "Sure you do. Petite woman, busybody. I'll bet she convinced you that you and I shared some kind of fate, right?"

Sophie shook her head. "No, Logan. I've never met your mother. Sometimes you have to take things on pure faith."

He laughed. "Faith? In you? I have no more faith in you than the phony fortune-teller at a carnival midway, honey. Now if you'll excuse me, there's someplace I need to be."

Like at the business meeting he'd left abruptly. How the hell was he going to explain leaving like that?

Maybe he needed a vacation. The stress was getting to him.

He moved to leave, but she reached out and touched his arm. He looked at her, refusing to believe the vulnerability in her beseeching gaze. "Please, Logan, you don't know how important this is. You must be on your guard."

Tired of this ridiculous game, he grabbed her arms and hauled her against his chest, ignoring the feel of her full breasts pressing against him. "The only person I need to be on my guard against is you." He pulled his wallet out of his coat and slammed it on the table. "People like you are driven by this," he said, pointing to the leather billfold stuffed with greenbacks.

"I don't want your money, Logan," she whispered.

"Bullshit. That's the only thing people like you want. Money. Greed and opportunity are your companions. I don't know what kind of game you and my mother have concocted, but I'm not going to play. Understand?"

She shook her head again, her eyes wide pools of purple, darkening with desire. Her body flamed to life like an inferno, burning his hands with her heat. He quickly dropped his arms to his sides, still feeling the scorching fire she emanated.

"I know why you're doing this," she said. "You're afraid of the feelings I bring out in you."

He arched a brow, unable to believe her arrogant conceit. "I don't feel a damn thing for you."

"You're lying. To me and to yourself. I can feel what you feel, Logan. I know, because I have the same need. We *have* to be one. It's fated."

Boiling anger raged within him. He hated being manipulated. "No, sweetheart. We don't *have* to be anything. We're not *going* to be anything."

"I won't give up on you, Logan. You need me. And I need you."

When her lips parted and her tongue flicked out to lick her bottom lip, he lost it. Well and completely lost it. Fury mixed with desire and he could no longer separate the stronger emotion. All he knew was that he had to touch her.

Right now.

He absorbed her gasp when his mouth descended over hers.

Sophie fought for breath under Logan's punishing kiss. He meant to hurt her, to frighten her, but he'd failed. Instead, the warm cream of her desire spilled onto her panties and her nipples hardened as he pulled her closer. His heart beat as frantically as hers, and she wound her fingers into the soft darkness of his hair, tangling her tongue against his and drinking in his groan as his fingers found her hips.

He rocked his erection against her mound and she cried out into his mouth as shooting sparks flamed her cunt. She was throbbing, aching, desperate to feel his hard shaft buried inside her. That night in the alley had filled her dreams for a week now, making her want with an intensity that kept her awake nights. She'd brought herself to orgasm after orgasm visualizing Logan fucking that redhead, until the images blurred and the redhead became her. Yet she was never satisfied. That lingering desire blasted full force now, and she whimpered when he squeezed her buttocks and pulled her tighter against his hard-on.

Desperate to feel him, she reached between them and palmed his cock, rewarded with a muttered curse that tore from his lips like an accusation. She didn't care. She knew his desire, knew he'd dreamed of her the same way she'd dreamed of him. He could deny it all he wanted to, but the fact was, they *would* make love someday.

And if he wanted it right now, she'd give it to him. She didn't want to wait another minute.

He moved one hand over her hip and rib cage, then settled on her breast, easily finding the distended nipple through the thin cotton of her blouse. When he rolled the bud between his fingers, she cried out and arched her back, needing more of the sweet torment.

Goddess, she could come right now just from him petting her nipple.

But then a shock of cold air swept into the room, a frigid breeze blowing out half the candles. Logan stepped away and she opened her eyes.

The heat that had been there seconds ago was gone, replaced by the icy chill of his anger.

"You aren't my type, Sophie. We have nothing in common. You don't have a damn thing I'm interested in. Leave me alone." Turning quickly on his heel, he strode through the beads. She followed, trying to calm the raging desire that hadn't yet abated.

She'd known this wasn't going to be easy. Why she had thought he'd come in here today and take her words as true had been nothing more than wishful thinking on her part.

But she wouldn't give up. She couldn't. His life and the lives of his family depended on her persistence.

Her gaze swept to Samantha's wide-eyed look of surprise, then over to Joshua's glare. Logan paused, nodded curtly to both of them and left the shop without another word.

He'd left without believing in her.

But she wouldn't think of this as a failure.

After all, he *had* come here, had heard her calling to him.

This was just going to take time. And she'd take whatever time necessary to assure his safety. It was her destiny to do so.

Chapter Three

Logan stormed out of the shop and ran smack into Aidan, who smiled and arched a brow.

"Did you have some urgent need to have your fortune told? Maybe a burning desire to buy some tarot cards?"

Shit, shit, shit! This he did not need. He tried to brush past Aidan, but his brother wouldn't allow it. He grabbed Logan's arm. "We took care of Santiago, so you don't have any reason to hurry back. We really want to hear this story."

Logan looked behind Aidan to see Lissa standing there, her eyes as wide as saucers.

She probably thought he'd lost his mind.

She was probably right.

"I don't want to talk about it," he said.

"You don't have to. We'll just ask the beautiful woman behind you."

Logan turned to find Sophie standing in the doorway. She stepped toward him and handed him his wallet.

"You forgot this. I'm glad I caught you before you left." She turned to Aidan and Lissa and smiled, holding out her hand. "Hello. I'm Sophie Breaux."

The day had just gone completely to hell. Aidan and Lissa waited expectantly. Christ, he didn't want to do this!

"Sophie, this is my brother Aidan and his fiancée, Melissa."

"Call me Lissa. I love your shop. I've passed by it many times, but haven't had a chance to go in. All this magic stuff intrigues me," she added, winking at Aidan.

Sophie beamed. "Thank you! Please, come inside and let me show you around."

Before he could object, and really, what would he have said to Lissa anyway, she followed Sophie inside, leaving him standing there with Aidan.

A very curious Aidan, knowing his nosy brother.

"Well?"

"Well, what?" Although there was no sense in playing dumb.

"Who's *la belle jeune fille*?"

"Just a woman I met."

Arching a brow, Aidan said, "She doesn't really look your type."

Logan didn't even know he had a "type". "I'm not dating her, Aidan."

"Then what are you doing with her?"

"Nothing."

"Didn't look like nothing to me. C'mon, *mon frere*, you don't just date women. And you sure as hell don't take off in the middle of a business meeting to follow a pretty skirt. So, give me the details."

"She's nobody. Nothing to me. I met her a week or so ago and she thinks she can con me."

"Con you. How?"

"Aidan! Do you know what Sophie does?"

Logan turned at the sound of Lissa's voice. She was grinning and tugging at Aidan's hand.

"No, *cher*, tell me what Sophie does."

"She's a fortune-teller. And a damn good one, too."

Aidan smirked at Logan and then grinned at Lissa. "Oh yeah?"

"Yes. You should see the stuff in her shop. And she comes from a long line of voodoo priestesses."

Voodoo? Logan didn't know that. Priestess? Sophie?
Bullshit.

"Voodoo, huh?" Aidan said, shifting his gaze to Sophie.

"My grandmere was Lisette Pilar," Sophie added quietly.

Lisette Pilar was a very famous Creole woman whose
voodoo magic was legendary in New Orleans. Which didn't
mean a damn thing as far as Sophie's legitimacy as a fortune-
teller. Logan turned away, refusing to notice the way her dark
lashes swept against her sculpted cheekbones when she bowed
her head.

As if she was embarrassed. The woman was one hell of an
actress.

"It's all for show," Logan said.

Lissa's eyes widened. "Are you kidding me? It is not. She
told me things that…"

"What? She told you what?"

Lissa blushed. "Trust me. She's the real deal." Quickly
turning away from Logan's glare, she looked at Aidan.
"Anyway, wouldn't she be great as entertainment for the Mardi
Gras ball at the hotel?"

Aidan pursed his lips. "An authentic voodoo priestess? In
full costume?" His eyes gleamed and he grinned.

Lissa nodded. "Exactly. We'll make the patrons pay a
bundle for her services. Sophie will get a cut, and the rest will go
toward the children's charity fund."

Damn. Charity. Leave it to Lissa to let her heart bleed all
over the street.

"Bad idea," Logan said.

"Great idea," Aidan countered. "I love it. Sophie, you
interested?"

Sophie looked from Aidan to Logan. Logan hoped the
frosty look he leveled at her would dissuade her from doing
something really stupid. Like agreeing to perform at the ball.

Her full lips curved in a soft smile. Clearly, she wasn't the least bit intimidated by Logan's trademark glare. "I'd be honored to participate, as long as you don't pay me anything. I'd love to contribute to the children's charity fund," she replied.

"Wonderful!" Lissa exclaimed. "Aidan, come inside the shop and look around with me. I have so much to tell you."

"You two go back inside," Aidan said. "I need to talk to Logan for a minute. I'll be right there."

After the women left, Aidan turned to him. "Okay, now don't give me the crap you did before. Tell me what Sophie is to you."

Logan jammed his hands in his coat pockets. "She's nothing to me. I told you that already."

"If she's nothing, why did you leave the meeting and follow her? And why did you let her tell your fortune?"

"I don't want to talk about this. She's a fraud, Aidan. I don't want her at the ball. She'll embarrass the family."

"First off, she's gorgeous and she'll draw a crowd. Second, if Lissa says she's legit, then she is. Lissa would never put the business in a compromising position and you know that."

"Sophie's a con artist. She'll rip everyone off. All she's after is money."

"If that's the case, how come she returned your wallet? And shouldn't you look inside to make sure all your money's there?"

He already knew it was, which was why he hadn't checked. "I have another meeting. I don't have time for this. I don't want Sophie at the ball."

Before Aidan could respond, Logan turned on his heel and stormed down the street, feeling more than a little ridiculous for causing this ruckus.

Jamming his fingers through his hair, he focused his gaze on the Rising Storm and quickened his step, muttering to himself along the way.

"Voodoo priestess, my ass. What a bunch of crap. Why the hell did I have to follow her? I need a goddamn vacation."

This entire debacle was Sophie's fault. He wished he'd never met her that night in the alley. And he sure as hell shouldn't have kissed her inside the shop.

Her taste still lingered on his lips. Both sweet and spicy, like the woman he couldn't seem to get out of his mind, no matter how hard he tried.

* * * * *

Sophie grinned and waved Lissa and Aidan off. After they left, she turned to find two sets of very curious eyes staring at her.

"What?"

Samantha grinned. "Nothing. Just…well, nothing." Sam turned away and headed into the storeroom, leaving her to deal with Josh. And she could already guess how that was going to go.

"Don't start with me, Joshua."

Josh shook his head, his dark brown hair slipping down over his forehead. "You're way out of your league, Soph."

She approached him and reached out, brushing his hair away from his face. Josh was like family. They'd known each other…forever. Since they were kids. He used to spend all his afternoons with Sophie and her aunt, making fun of their spells and magic.

She loved Josh. Always had. Just not in the way he wanted her to. That she couldn't help.

"I appreciate you looking out for me, *mon ami*. But I know what I'm doing."

"Famous last words," he said, shrugging. "I don't know why you always think there's something better out there for you. Why can't you…"

His words trailed off, but she knew what they were. "Josh. You know why."

His brown eyes turned nearly black, frustration evident in the way he clenched his fists at his side. He'd always held his anger in check around her, no matter what she said to him. But she felt it, simmering just near the surface of his emotions, ready to boil over.

Why couldn't he find a love of his own? Josh was so handsome. Tall, muscular and fit, with dark eyes that spoke of sensual depths that most women would swoon over.

But Sophie wasn't one of those women. She'd tried with Josh, but he had always felt like family to her. Or something. It just hadn't felt right, and she'd told him that as honestly and gently as she could. Josh had accepted it, reluctantly, but had continued to be her friend.

"I love you, Sophie."

"I know." She always hated this part of their conversations. They'd had the same one for years, and she always gave him the same answer. "I love you, too."

He arched a brow. "But."

Nodding, she grinned. "But not in that way. We're not destined, Josh."

"Destiny is bullshit. You make your own," he mumbled, moving off to open a new box of inventory.

Someday, maybe Josh would find his destiny with the right woman. But that woman could never be her. With a heavy sigh, Sophie stepped into the small room where she had told Logan's future.

Or at least part of his future. She inhaled and closed her eyes, feeling his presence, his unique scent, bits and pieces of his aura still clinging to the room.

Clinging to her.

He was part of her, whether he liked it or not.

It was only a matter of time until he saw what she saw, until he knew his destiny.

Even she didn't know all of it, just shadows and partial visions. Enough to know they were meant to be together.

Soon enough he'd figure that out.

Chapter Four

If the stars were aligned and today was Logan's lucky day, Sophie wouldn't show up at the ball tonight.

He paced his suite, stopping for the fifth time in front of the mirror to adjust his bowtie.

He hated tuxes. Hated dressing up, hated this part of his job.

But it was a necessity for goodwill and good business.

The door to his suite slipped open and Aidan walked in, dressed in the same type of monkey suit.

"I hate fucking tuxes," Aidan mumbled, jamming his hands into his pockets.

Logan grinned. "My thoughts exactly. Where's everyone else?"

"Lissa, Shannon and Kaitlyn are in the ballroom already, squealing over their respective dresses."

Logan rolled his eyes. Females and their idiosyncrasies were so foreign to him. He never tried to understand how their minds worked. And having two sisters hadn't helped one bit over the years. If anything, they only confused him more. "Where's Max?"

"Doing a little PR work in the office. He said he'd be late."

Max Devlin, Shannon's fiancé, was as much a workaholic as Logan. Except when Shannon crooked her finger. Then he dropped everything and went after her like a dog scenting a bitch in heat.

Logan smirked. Not too far off the mark, actually, considering that Max was a werewolf.

His future brother-in-law a werewolf. And he thought *his* family was unusual. Would they ever have a normal life? Then again, the fact that Max was lupine didn't seem to bother Max at all. He was strong, capable, enjoyed his life and didn't let his unusual abilities affect the way he lived.

Why couldn't he do that, too? Why was it so fucking hard to accept who he was?

"Sophie's here."

Logan cast a sharp glare at Aidan. "I thought I made my wishes clear on that."

Aidan grinned. "We ignored you. Rather, the girls ignored you. Once Lissa told Shannon and Kaitlyn about her meeting with Sophie, there was no changing their minds. It's a done deal."

Figured they'd ignore him. After all, Logan was only the CEO. No one needed to listen to his directives, right?

"Might as well get down there, then." At least he could keep an eye on her, make sure she didn't slip her slender hand into a number of New Orleans' richest pockets, all of whom would be in attendance tonight.

The ballroom was packed. This was one of Mardi Gras' biggest parties, part of the grand celebrations of Carnival.

Logan spent a few minutes greeting the guests, then wandered around to find his sisters.

Kaitlyn was, as usual, fretting over minute details of décor and food. She hugged him when he came up to her.

"Have you tried the hors d'oeuvres yet? I'm not sure I selected the right ones."

He shook his head as he watched her wring her hands. "Would you relax? Everything is perfect."

"Marcel is an idiot."

He laughed. She was always fighting with the head chef. They had never seen eye to eye on menu selection and preparation. If Kaitlyn had her way, she'd cook every meal for every guest at the hotel herself. "Yes, he's an idiot. What did he do this time?"

"Substituted one of my recipes and decided to change the main course. I swear if I had another chef, I'd fire his ass on the spot."

Logan kissed Kaitlyn on the forehead. "That's your area, *cher*. You do whatever you think is right. But you're not going into the kitchens yourself."

She pursed her lips into a pout. "I'll figure something out." Shaking off whatever bugged her, she grinned. "You look very handsome tonight. And Sophie is a charm, Logan. Wherever did you find her?"

His smile died at the mention of Sophie's name. "I didn't find her. I don't even want her here."

"For heaven's sake, why not?"

Shannon sidled next to Kaitlyn. "Sophie's delightful. I don't understand."

It was a conspiracy of estrogen. He couldn't win. "Never mind. How's everything going?"

The light shimmered against Shannon's red, sparkling gown. "Great, of course. The casino's filled to capacity, we sold out of tickets for the ball, and Sophie is already dealing with a long line of patrons wanting their fortunes told. She's going to make us a ton of money for the charity. And she's still refusing to let us pay her for her time tonight. Which means everything we make from her fortune-telling will go to the charity."

She probably had an ulterior motive for giving up her fee. "I'm going to go talk to the mayor. I'll catch you later." He turned away, irritated that every conversation lately seemed to include Sophie.

She was set up alongside the wall in a booth decorated in vibrant silk drapes of purple, green and gold, a canopy and curtains to keep it private and intimate.

Sophie was the center of attention, dressed in a shimmering top of gold that draped off her shoulders, revealing cleavage that any man would want to slip his hand inside. Her full skirt matched the colors of carnival and glimmered against the soft lights of the ballroom. Long hoop earrings brushed against her jawline, and bracelets with bells jingled at her wrists.

The dark tinge of her skin highlighted her vivid violet eyes. Her full lips were made to suck a man's cock. Logan's dick took notice of that instantly, twitching to life at a most inopportune moment.

Adjusting his tightening pants, he approached, winding his way through the throng of people who should definitely know better than to buy into the bullshit of magic.

He peered through the side slit of the canopy. At least he'd managed to find the mayor, who was currently sitting across from Sophie while she thoroughly examined his hands.

No doubt checking his fingers for diamonds and his wrist for a Rolex.

Logan moved his way up front, just in time for Sophie to stand and step outside the curtains with the mayor. She looked up at him, offering a half smile.

A jolt hit him hard and he connected with her, exactly the same way it had been that night in the alley and that day in her shop. He tried to tear his gaze away, but found himself unable to.

His thoughts drifted to satin sheets, naked bodies writhing together, and a full, soft mouth closing over his rock-hard shaft.

She blinked and her eyes widened. When she flicked her tongue over her upper lip and swallowed, he knew then that she was aware of what he was thinking.

"Logan! How are you?"

He shook off the connection and smiled at the mayor, engaging the excited man in conversation.

"Sophie is a delight! What a coup to have her here tonight. She's brilliant, Logan. And genuine, too."

The mayor patted him on the back and moved away, leaving him standing across from Sophie.

"Would you like me to tell your fortune?" she asked, her gravelly voice making him itch to take her mouth in ways he had no business thinking of right now.

Or ever.

"I think you've already told me all I need to know."

She shook her head, her dark hair falling over her shoulder, one slender strand dipping into the generous cleavage between her luscious breasts.

He wanted to reach for that strand and caress the plump flesh that contained it.

"I haven't even begun to tell you what you need to know."

"Oh, and what does Logan need to know?"

Logan whipped around at the sound of his mother's voice.

"Hello, Mother," he said, kissing her on the cheek.

She smiled at Logan. "*Bon soir, mon fils.*" Turning to Sophie, she said, "This must be the Sophie Breaux my daughters have been telling me about."

Sophie rose and hurried over to his mother, enthusiastically shaking her hand. "*Bon soir, Madame Storm. Comment allez vous?*"

"*Je suis tres bien*, Sophie, *merci. S'il vous plaît, appelez-moi* Angelina."

"*Merci, Angelina*," Sophie replied.

His mother glanced over at him. "Leave us for a few moments, Logan." She practically pushed him out of the draped room, then shut the curtains.

What the hell was that all about? He didn't believe for one second that his mother didn't know who Sophie was. Maybe she'd finally seen through Sophie's charade and was going to lecture her privately. Or throw her out of the place completely.

He should be so lucky.

Too curious to walk away, he lingered, talking to the people in line. Important people. Rich people. People prominent in their community.

All of them lining up to hear their fortunes told by a two-bit phony.

He shook his head, unable to fathom the attraction to magical bullshit.

After about five minutes, his mother pulled the curtain aside and motioned the next person in line to go in, then linked her arm within Logan's and walked with him through the crowds.

"I need a drink," she whispered.

He turned his head and regarded her. Angelina Storm was a beautiful woman. No matter how old she got, Logan would forever see her as youthful, exuberant and vibrating with *joie de vivre*.

But right now her normally dark complexion had gone pale.

"What's wrong?"

She feigned a smile he knew wasn't sincere. "Nothing's wrong. I'm thirsty."

"Is it something Sophie said?" He stopped and glanced toward the tent. "I can ask her to leave if she upset you."

His mother patted his arm. "She did no such thing. Now quit worrying and go get me that drink."

Deciding not to press her right now, Logan led her to the bar and handed her a glass of champagne. She downed it in a few gulps while he stood by, shocked speechless and desperately wanting to know what happened when his mother had spoken to Sophie.

When she finished, she set the glass down on the bar, kissed him and said, "Bring Sophie to the house for dinner on Sunday."

"Huh?"

"Oh look. There's Maria Dupree'. I really need to speak with her. Five o'clock Sunday, Logan. Don't be late. Ta-ta."

Ta-ta? That was it? Bring Sophie to dinner, and she leaves?

Was he fucking dreaming the past week of his life? What the hell was the matter with everyone? Was he the only one to see through Sophie to the fraud she was?

"*Vous êtes ainsi baisé, mon frère.*" Aidan stepped around him to the bar, grabbed two glasses of champagne and winked. "See you and Sophie at dinner Sunday."

Yeah, he was screwed all right. Aidan's laughter echoed in Logan's ears long after his brother had sauntered away.

* * * * *

Logan didn't look happy.

Did the man walk around with a perpetual frown? Sophie watched his determined approach with a mix of trepidation and intense, feminine interest. She even sighed appreciatively.

How could she not? He was beautiful, walking toward her with a stealth-like grace that caused her heart to tumble and her pulse to skitter.

She looked around, expecting to find at least the clean-up crew taking down the tables. There was no one left in the ballroom but her and a man who didn't look one bit happy.

"Stay away from my family," he said as soon as he stopped in front of her table.

She blinked. "Excuse me?"

"You heard me. I don't know what kind of game you're playing, but you're not going to play it with my family, or with my business associates."

"I was invited here tonight by Lissa."

"I don't care. I don't want you around my family."

"You don't want me around *you*, is what you really mean." She turned to finish packing the boxes containing the tools of her trade. "Really, Logan, you might as well get used to the fact that

I'm in your life now. As I mentioned before, we're destined to be together, and there really isn't anything you can do about that."

Too afraid to look up and see his angry reaction, she kept her head focused on the box, waiting for him to fire back a retort.

But he didn't. For awhile, she wondered if he'd turned heel and left the ballroom. If it wasn't for the fact she was so in tune to him, she'd think he'd done that very thing.

But he hadn't. She heard his breathing, smelled his unique scent, felt the vibrations of mixed emotions emanating from him.

"Get out of my life, Sophie, and stay out."

With a sigh, she folded the flaps of the box closed and turned to him. "I can't. You need me."

He jerked the table away so quickly she barely saw it. In an instant he had pulled her forcefully against him, his fingers biting into her upper arms.

"Get this straight, Sophie. I don't need you. I didn't before I met you, and I don't now. I will never need you or the brand of *magic*—and I use the term loosely—that you bring. You're nothing but a fake."

His anger should have frightened her. His insults should have angered her. His hands grasping her upper arms should have, too. Instead, they had the opposite effect, because she knew he'd never hurt her. Her body heated, her skin flushing, her panties moistening with a quick flash of desire for the man who was trying to freeze her out of his life.

"I understand this is difficult for you, Logan. After all, you don't really know me that well, and yet I know you better than you know yourself."

"You don't know a goddamn thing about me."

She took in his breath as it wafted across her face, delighting in the smell of cinnamon and fine brandy.

"Why are you fighting what's between us? Don't you feel it?" She reached up and covered his hands with hers, knowing that as soon as she did the jolt would hit them both.

He felt it, too. She knew he did. She could tell by the way his eyes quickly widened, then narrowed and darkened. "Stop that."

"I didn't do anything."

"Yes, you did." He dropped his hands from her arms, but she refused to let him walk away. She held tight to them, feeling the energy increase.

"I'm much stronger than you, *petite fille*. Don't fuck with me."

"Perhaps it's you who wants to fuck with me, but you're afraid to lose some of that careful control you possess."

His eyes narrowed, his voice deepening. "You couldn't handle me if I really let go."

She sucked in her lower lip to keep from blurting out that she wanted him. Desperately wanted him, in a way even she didn't understand.

She wasn't promiscuous. In fact, she could count on one hand—okay, three fingers—the number of men she'd been with sexually. The last one had been two years ago.

This wasn't just about having a sexy hunk of man fuck her until she screamed, although that would be a nice side benefit.

No, her relationship with Logan went way beyond the physical.

But right now, she craved the physical. And it was a place to start.

"Try me."

Chapter Five

Logan stilled at Sophie's words.

"You might not like it if I try you," he shot back, waiting for her to run, to shrug him off, do anything besides stand there with an eager expression on her face.

But God knew that was exactly what he wanted to do. He wanted to try her every way imaginable. His body ached to be inside her...now. No preliminaries, nothing else but sinking his already hard cock deep inside her tight cunt.

He balled his hands into fists, mentally tamping down the primal urges that compelled him to take her. Take what she so obviously offered, then walk away from her completely.

Treat her like shit, and discard her.

Dammit, he'd do exactly that.

He crushed her against him, watching as her eyes widened and she gasped, hoping he was frightening her and she'd run like hell. He tightened his arms around her back so she couldn't get away, then bent and took her full lips, thrusting his tongue inside her warm, wet mouth.

Any minute now she'd be revolted by his combination of passion and ice. He felt it coursing through him, the cold chill despite the feverish heat the touch of her lips gave him.

But she didn't run. She didn't try to get away. Instead, she whimpered into his mouth and wrapped her arms around him. Her breasts crushed against his chest and the points of her nipples scraped the thin material of his shirt.

He moved her backwards, keeping his mouth fixed on her lips, tangling his tongue with hers. When he had her back against the paneled wall, he ground his hard-on between her legs.

She moaned and clutched his shoulders, licking at his tongue as if she were desperate for a taste of him.

Her heat overwhelmed him, ignited him, threatening to melt his protective iceberg. That he couldn't allow.

A swirl of cold air encircled them. He'd warned her that she wouldn't be able to handle him unleashed. He had to freeze her now.

If only to protect himself from her fire.

Sophie tore her mouth away from his and leaned her head back, making eye contact.

"You can't chill me out, Logan. I'm on fire for you."

His breath came out in a rush when she palmed his erection, cupping him possessively and sliding her hand up and down over his hard cock.

"You're on fire, too," she whispered, rubbing her palm over his throbbing shaft. "Don't you realize how connected we are? When you flame, Logan, I burn. Hot, like an inferno."

Ah, fuck it. He couldn't get rid of her no matter how hard he tried, and he no longer even wanted to try.

"Is this what you want?" He pushed away from her, ripping down the zipper of his pants and pulling out his shaft. He stroked it slow and easy, taunting her.

Her eyes darkened a deep purple and she licked her lips, a silent invitation.

An invitation he could no longer resist. He moved to the chair where he'd tossed his coat, folded it over and put it on the floor in front of him.

"Get on your knees and suck me, Sophie."

Her cheeks flushed and she dipped to her knees, reaching eagerly for his shaft.

Slipping her fingers underneath, she cupped his balls, cradling and massaging them lightly as she fit her lips around the swollen head of his cock. She kept her gaze focused on his face so that he could watch her.

Watching her lips close over his cock was the most erotic thing he'd ever seen. He groaned and tangled his fingers in her hair, finding the clip and releasing the dark waves that spilled into his hands.

"Like silk," he murmured, though he wasn't sure if he meant her long, glossy hair or the slippery tongue laving the side of his shaft.

She sucked him masterfully, taking him deep into the back of her throat, then teasing him by withdrawing and stroking him. When she licked the droplets from the tip, the milky fluid gathered on her tongue before she swallowed.

His gut clenched at the beauty of her mouth surrounding him. He could watch her do this to him for a very long time; could spend hour after hour letting her pleasure him and then taking his time to please her, too.

But this wasn't a relationship, he reminded himself. They weren't a couple, and he wanted nothing to do with her. Sophie and he were not meant to be together.

He was trying to drive her away, not think about how they could do this forever.

Quickly withdrawing from her mouth, he grabbed her hands, forcing her to stand.

"I wasn't finished," she said, her throaty voice filled with passion.

He didn't answer her, just tugged down on her skirt until it puddled on the floor.

She wore a flimsy scrap of material for panties, a golden, lacy thong that did little to hide her bare pussy.

The exotic perfume of her scent surrounded him, the sweet smell of her arousal like an aphrodisiac to his senses. He bent over and removed her panties, wanting, desperately to linger at her sex and taste her.

But he refused to allow the intimacy of pleasuring her that way. It was too…personal, and he needed to keep this as impersonal as he could. But damn, he wanted to tease her a bit, take her sweet flavor on his tongue and drive her mad for hours. Instead, he stood and reached for her buttocks, grasping them in his hands and hoisting her up and against him. She wrapped her legs around his waist, the contact immediate and electric. Grinding his pelvis against her protruding clit, he thrust inside her pussy, drinking in her soft cries with a deep kiss.

Her tight cunt squeezed him, milked him, urged him to come hard and deep. A heady mix of patchouli and cinnamon washed over him as if she'd purposely released her scent. He drove harder this time, and her moans grew louder, her face flushing. Pushing her back against the wall so he could free one hand, he jerked her top down and exposed her full breasts. Large, dark nipples pebbled under his searching gaze, and he couldn't resist dipping down and taking one tip in his mouth. He sucked it hard, pressing the nipple between the roof of his mouth and tongue.

The overpowering combination of her taste and scent drove him to fuck her harder, faster, deeper.

"Yes, Logan, fuck me like that," she cried, rocking her hot pussy against him, squeezing him with her tight muscles, pouring her juices all over his aching balls.

"You want more?" he asked, clenching his jaw tight, trying to hold back the impending torrent of come.

"Yes! *Mon Dieu*, yes! Give it to me, Logan! Now!"

He'd wanted this from the moment he'd seen her in the dark alley. Though he'd been fucking another woman that night, he'd wanted Sophie, imagined how hot and tight her cunt would be.

He was right. Her gravelly plea stripped away his control. He let some of the magic loose, holding a tight rein on the majority of its power. If he let it all go at once, neither of them would survive it.

The room covered in frost, ice pellets began to fall, and the water in the glasses around them froze solid.

A bitter wind blew through the ballroom, but did nothing to quench the heat that Sophie's body, her cries, her spasming cunt had fired up inside him.

Her orgasm tore through her and she screamed in ecstasy. Her body tensed, tightening, then quaking uncontrollably. Strange, unintelligible words spilled from her lips.

Suddenly, the ice melted around them, the water became liquid once again and the room dried and warmed.

The heat surrounding Sophie was forced against him, within him, and a raging orgasm soared through him.

Shocked, he could only roar as his release took over. He drove hard one last time and spilled his seed deep in her core.

It wasn't until he could breathe again, until he could focus on the here and now, that he realized he hadn't worn a condom.

Fuck. Shit. Sonofabitch.

He *never* fucked a woman without wearing protection. Yet with Sophie, being skin to skin with her had seemed as natural as breathing.

She lifted her head, tangling her fingers in his hair. "It's all right," she whispered. "You don't have to worry. We're both protected."

He didn't know how she was aware of his thoughts, and couldn't muster enough energy to ask. Nodding, he still felt more vulnerable than he wanted to, especially with her. The last thing he'd do is give her power over him.

Disentangling himself from her sweet, hot body, he retrieved her panties and while she dressed, righted his clothing. Now that he'd separated from her, whatever weird connection they had before dissipated, allowing him to recover his senses. He felt much more comfortable now that his protective outer shell was once more upon him.

Anger filled him. Anger at himself for being weak where Sophie was concerned. Anger at her for whatever magic she possessed, for weaving some kind of spell over him.

Logan was a born cold-hearted man. And he'd learned a long time ago, that the best defense was a good offense.

Releasing the knotted tie that seemed to choke him, he leered at Sophie, his gaze raking over her breasts and hips. "Great fuck, wasn't it?"

Her cheeks still flushed with passion, she blinked and shook her head. "Excuse me?"

"Sex, Sophie. It was great. You're good. Damn good. Thanks."

Regarding him warily, she stayed silent for a minute. No doubt trying to figure out a way to get out of the room with her dignity intact.

Ignoring the knot of guilt forming in his stomach, he firmed his mental resolve to treat her like a tramp, refusing to believe the shocked, innocent expression on her face.

"I don't understand, Logan. What we just did was..."

"Fucking great. I know. We do have chemistry. No denying that." Taking a quick glance at his watch, he grinned and asked, "Need help with that box?"

She looked confused. "Huh? Oh. Ohhh! I get it now! You're trying to brush me off. To protect yourself."

The woman was too goddamned insightful for his liking. "I don't need to protect myself from a little sprite like you, Sophie. But I do need to get upstairs and do some work before a big meeting tomorrow. So, if you don't mind..."

She gathered her box and hefted it into her arms, shaking her head. "I know the way out. Thanks."

Finally. He was growing more uncomfortable by the minute. The stupid, emotional part of him wanted to apologize for acting like a prick. No way was he going to let that part out.

She started toward the double doors leading to the lobby, but stopped and turned, her skirt swishing around her ankles, bells jingling at her wrists and ankles.

"Logan?"

He was ready to accept her anger at his treatment of her. Hell, he deserved at least that much. "Yeah?"

"Don't forget to pick me up on Sunday for dinner at your parents."

She grinned, turned around and headed out the doors.

"Well, I'll be goddamned," he said aloud, his voice echoing in the now empty ballroom.

What the hell was it going to take to drive her away? He'd fucked her, then he'd insulted her, basically treating her no better than a one-night stand, and still she smiled at him, seemingly eager to see him again.

On Sunday. When he had to pick her up and take her to dinner at his family's home.

Maybe she wasn't going to be as easy to get rid of as the other women in his life had been.

Time for him to develop a battle plan, because it sure as hell appeared that dumping Sophie was going to be one hell of a battle.

* * * * *

Instead of heading straight home, Sophie stopped at Samantha's house, knowing that her friend would be up doing what she loved to do most.

Cooking.

She knocked on the door to the tiny house Sam had inherited from her parents, stepped back and inhaled.

Cookies. Her mouth watered and she laughed when Sam opened the door.

White flour clung to the center of Sam's tiny nose.

"What?" she asked, brandishing a wooden spatula like a weapon.

"Flour. Nose. You busy?"

Rolling her eyes, Sam scrubbed her palm over her face and motioned Sophie inside. "Very funny. You know me, Soph. I'm never busy."

"In other words, you're cooking up some magic potions. Eye of newt, wing of bat?"

"You're just full of jokes tonight, aren't you?" Sam said over her shoulder as she headed back to the kitchen. Sophie followed, snatching a freshly baked cinnamon cookie and slipping onto one of the barstools in front of Sam's baking island.

Sophie took a bite, her lips curling in a satisfied smile as the flavors overwhelmed her senses, making her think of home, family, and utter contentment.

"What brings you here so late?" Sam asked.

"Logan Storm," Sophie managed, her mouth full of cookie.

"Ah. That's right. You worked their Mardi Gras party tonight. What happened?"

"We had sex in the ballroom of the Rising Storm."

Arching a brow, Sam asked, "Really? In front of all those people?"

"No! It was later, after the ball was over and everyone left."

"Hot! Okay, so now what?"

Sophie grabbed milk from the refrigerator, poured herself a glass and snagged another cookie on her way back to the barstool. "I don't know what happens now. He seemed to be really into it, you know? Not just physically, either. There was a definite emotional connection. But after, it was like a wall slammed down between us and he was his normal, cold and remote self again."

"You know he's just trying to protect himself from you, right?"

"That's what I think, too."

Sam slipped the next batch of cookie dough into the oven and grabbed a chair. "You got to him, Soph. Big time."

"You think so?"

"I know so. That was easy enough to tell when he followed you to the shop. And you know something else, he got to you, too."

"Not really. I mean I enjoyed the sex, of course, but I'm mainly concerned about the visions and dreams. I just want to help."

"You want a lot more than just to help his family, honey. You want Logan."

"That's not it at all."

"You're lying to yourself."

"Am not."

"This is like being kids again and arguing over Barbie dolls."

"We didn't argue over Barbie. We argued over Ken," Sophie said, remembering their childhood fondly.

Sam grinned. "True. But I still think there's more to your feelings for Logan than just a need to figure out what danger his family is in. Allow your heart to open, Soph. You'll see."

"Think you know everything, don't you?" she teased.

"You know I do," Sam answered with a wink.

"Witch."

"There you go, stating the obvious again"

By the time Sophie had slipped into the driver's seat of her car and headed home, she felt much better. Talking to Sam always helped.

Sam had insights as keen as Sophie's. Only Sophie couldn't see as far as her own heart. So she had to rely on Sam to point out what she couldn't see by herself.

Was she more involved with Logan than she thought? There was no doubt she'd felt the connection between the two of them, but she assumed it was because of her visions.

The fact he was attractive and desirable didn't hurt, either. Despite the fact she didn't engage in casual intimate encounters with near strangers, she'd done it with Logan.

Okay, so what? She was a grown woman now. What was wrong with a little sex between two consenting adults?

But was there more to it?

She'd been so focused on getting Logan to listen to her pleas about the danger his family was in that she hadn't taken the time to assess her own feelings about him.

The way he'd made love to her—fast, furious, almost in anger—had touched her in ways she hadn't expected. She'd fought through both his anger and his magic and had reached him on an even plane where both of them had felt the reality of the experience.

Even now she could still feel him inside her, a part of her in ways that had nothing to do with her visions, and everything to do with her heart.

A heart she'd have to guard very carefully around Logan Storm.

Chapter Six

Logan headed up the long gravel driveway leading to Sophie's place. He quickly scanned the directions she'd given him, shaking his head as he stopped in front of a dilapidated old trailer. It looked to be at least twenty years old.

And tiny.

Jerking the car into park, he threw open the door and walked toward the front step.

Two cracked cement steps led to the yellow aluminum door. The screen was lying half open, having obviously been ripped.

Nice place. Maybe she was hoping to land a rich guy and move up in the world.

He rapped twice on the thin metal door and waited.

He didn't have to wait long. She opened the door and stood aside for him to come in.

"You're right on time. Welcome to my home."

The inside was nothing like the outside. Candles were lit everywhere, giving off the same sensual patchouli and cinnamon scent as her shop. Bright colors from throw pillows and blankets lifted the mood of the place. Shades were open, sunlight streaming into each and every room. It was bright, colorful and homey.

Flowers bloomed healthy and vibrant in various pots throughout the house. Sophie led him from the small living room into the equally tiny kitchen. It was clean and smelled like citrus. Her bedroom was very small, including the bed, but a colorful quilt and a row of colorful plants along the windowsill brightened up the room.

"It's small, but it's home and I love it to death. I know that's silly since it's not much…"

"You have a beautiful home, Sophie." Surprisingly, he meant that. The place was a dump on the outside, but welcoming on the inside. For some reason that meant something to him.

"Let me go get ready. It'll only take me a second." She turned and stepped through the multicolored beads separating the kitchen from the bedroom.

Logan stood in the living room and listened to the sound of rustling clothing. And bells. Like the bracelets she wore around her ankles and wrists. Something about those tinkling bells was surprisingly arousing.

She hummed while she dressed, an upbeat oldies tune that made him think of summer, of being young and carefree.

He jammed his fingers through his hair. Hell, had he ever been young and carefree? Had there ever been a time when he wasn't worried about his magic, how he appeared to others? As soon as he had been old enough to recognize that he had powers, that he was "different" than the other kids his age, he'd pushed his magic as deep inside himself as he could, and fought to keep it there.

Kids were so cruel. They'd pick on anyone who wasn't "normal". And he was as goddamned abnormal as they came.

Was there a time he hadn't tried to mask who and what he really was?

At least with Sophie he never had to do that. She somehow knew of his magic, and because she seemed to possess some of her own, whatever weird powers he had inside didn't seem to matter to her at all.

The beads flew to the side as she stepped through.

She'd pulled her hair up into a high ponytail, showing off sculpted cheekbones and smooth, perfect skin.

How could someone wearing faded blue jeans and a loose, white sweater look so damn sexy? He'd taken her so fast the other night he hadn't had time to explore and taste her. A compelling urge came over him. He wanted to undress her, revealing every inch of her body slowly, then lick her from her neck to her toes.

Sophie's gaze met his and she stopped, her eyes widening.

She knew what he was thinking. He could tell by the dark blush staining her cheeks. Did she feel the same intense desire? His cock rose and pressed against his jeans, clearly outlined for her to see.

He should turn away until he got his unruly libido under control. But he didn't. Instead, he waited until her eyes traveled down to his crotch.

When she looked up at him again, she smiled.

Shit. The sensuous curl of her lips only made his hard-on worse. This was going to be one hell of a long day.

"Why are you doing this?"

Frowning, she asked, "Doing what?"

"Coming to my parents' house today."

"Because your mother invited me."

"That's not the only reason and you know it. Give it up, Sophie. I'm not interested in having a relationship with you."

Her smile died. "I'm doing whatever is necessary to protect you and your family, Logan. I wish you could see that."

"I see plenty. What I see is you trying to wriggle your way into my family, thinking you can tap into some of our fortune." He advanced on her, stopping only inches away. "It's not gonna happen, sweetheart, so you might as well quit now."

He refused to be swayed by the hurt look in her eyes. She was the best con artist he'd ever come across.

Her smile returned, but the pain in her eyes remained. "If there's nothing more you'd like to say, we should probably go so we're not late."

Irritated beyond the ability to think straight, Logan turned on his heel and mumbled, "Fine."

She followed him out to the car and slid in the passenger side, buckling her belt and looking out the side window the entire trip.

Although he didn't know her that well yet, what he did know proved that it was uncharacteristic of Sophie to be silent. He knew why, too.

He'd wounded her with his words.

And he fucking hated that he felt guilty about it.

Too bad. He'd said nothing that wasn't true. She *was* a fraud. He knew it, and she knew it. She was just frustrated because he, unlike everyone else, hadn't been fooled by her.

The show of hurt feelings was just an act, like everything else.

She was *not* hurt!

* * * * *

Sophie forced back the moisture welling in her eyes, resisting the urge to put her face into her hands and sob.

She wasn't a baby and wasn't about to act like one. So Logan didn't believe her. She'd known that would happen. Convincing him was going to take awhile. Until then, she had to remain strong and not let him push her away. No matter how much he tried to hurt her, she would not waver from her goal. Her beloved Aunt Janine would never forgive her if she let her emotions get in the way of seeing a vision through to its conclusion.

She missed her aunt, though she still spoke with her. But it wasn't the same. Channeling the dead wasn't as easy, or as fulfilling, as sitting down across the kitchen table and looking at that person eye to eye. At most she'd be given brief glimpses into Janine's spectral aura, but they were mainly thoughts and feelings, not actual words.

Still, those forces continued to guide her. Her mother, her aunt, and those who had come before. They kept her strong.

And focused.

Which is what she had to be now. She couldn't afford to involve her heart in matters having to do with Logan.

Yeah right. Too late for that.

Despite his icy wall, there was a vulnerability about him that touched her deeply. She sensed that he wanted to love, but he didn't trust. And he'd have to learn to trust in love before he could truly experience it.

Love? Who said anything about love?

No. No way was she falling in love with Logan. She'd guarded her heart, made sure that she'd do her duty to him and his family and not get involved.

Liar.

Oh hell. Despite her own internal warnings, it had already happened.

And now that it had, she was bound and determined to be the woman to win his trust…and his love.

A definite risk to her heart, but who was she to attempt to defy fate?

They drove well out of town and into a densely forested area. The Storm house sat back from the road, down a long paved driveway.

The house was charming in its rustic simplicity, and she couldn't wait to go inside and explore.

"Oh, this is a beautiful home, Logan!" Without thinking, she grabbed his hand when he came to her side of the car to open the door and let her out. And she refused to let go of it as they walked toward the house, even though Logan's narrowed gaze indicated he didn't want to be holding onto her in any way.

Too bad. She was much too excited to pay attention to his frosty mood.

When they walked inside, Logan had to let go of her hand because she was swept into the room by Shannon and Kaitlyn and dragged into the kitchen, where a horde of family members were present.

She was introduced to Galen, Angelina's husband, a huge bear of a man with an Irish lilt to his voice and the most beautiful green eyes she'd ever seen. She also met Shannon's fiancé, Max Devlin.

Whoa, now there was a man with magic.

They sized each other up in a matter of seconds. It didn't take her long to sense that Max was lupine. He grinned and nodded knowingly when they shook hands, obviously as aware of her power as she was of his.

From what she sensed of Max in those few brief seconds, Shannon was one lucky girl.

Every single one of them made her feel welcome. At home. As if she was family.

All except Logan, who kept his distance, eyes narrowed as if he expected her to slip some of the family silverware into her pockets.

Determined to ignore his glaring looks, she decided to simply enjoy his family's company and forget he was even there.

The house smelled of Cajun spices. Angelina let her help out in the kitchen along with the rest of them. They all worked, either setting the table or fixing drinks. Even the men.

They laughed so much it was just like the times spent with her aunt and her friends. Bittersweet memories washed over her, reminding her that she was truly alone in the world now. Yes, she had Samantha and Joshua, who were more her family than anything. But eventually they'd both marry and have families of their own.

She'd be completely alone, then.

Would *she* ever marry? Would she ever have a family like the Storms embrace her and welcome her into their homes, their lives?

She wanted that more than anything. The scary part was, she wanted it with the Storm family, not just any family.

More importantly, she wanted it with Logan.

But wishing for something and having even the slightest hope of getting it were two different things. Clearly, Logan would never accept her in his life.

No, that wasn't quite true. He wasn't ready…yet. Which didn't mean she couldn't convince him. After all, she had set goals her entire life, and had always worked hard to reach them. Grades, college, her own business—every goal she had attempted she had reached.

Logan was a goal. Or, rather, Logan's heart was. If she put her mind to it and made him see what she saw, he'd come around.

She glanced out the back window, impressed by the massive size of the land the Storm family owned. A long stretch of grass and trees surrounded the fenced property. A narrow path led to a wooden dock where two good-sized boats sat on the huge lake.

"Your home is beautiful, Angelina," Sophie said.

Angelina wiped her hands on a towel and came to the window. "Thank you. We love it here. It's so quiet. In the summer you can hear the cicadas sing and watch the lightning bugs do their dances across the black night."

She loved her trailer, but it was surrounded by nothing but dust, gravel, and a sparse collection of very wimpy looking trees. Here there were fat willows sweeping the ground, so thick you could hide within their branches. She sighed, knowing it did no good to want what she couldn't have.

"I'll have Logan show you around later," Angelina said, patting her shoulder.

"I don't think he'll be very willing."

Angelina gave her an enigmatic smile. "You let me worry about that part. Come, dinner's ready. Let's take everything out to the table."

Chapter Seven

There was too much food. Shrimp, crawfish, rice, beans and plenty to drink to go along with it.

Sophie stared wide-eyed at the plate in front of her, then looked over at Angelina, who'd filled it for her.

"Surely you can't be serious."

"It's not that much, *cher*. Enjoy it."

She ate, her mouth taking in the wonderful Cajun flavors as if it hadn't been fed for months. The Storm family definitely knew how to cook.

"Sophie, tell me a little about yourself."

Her gaze shifted towards Galen's strong voice.

Dilemma. How much should she reveal? She quickly looked to Angelina, who nodded and patted her hand.

"It's perfectly all right to be honest, *ma belle*. No one here will tell your secrets."

Such confidence Angelina had in her family. Sophie felt like this had suddenly become a very big deal.

"I come from a very long line of voodoo priestesses," she started, then paused as she waited for shocked or disbelieving expressions.

Surprisingly, no one batted an eyelash. No one but Logan, who arched a brow as if he was waiting for her to spew a stream of lies.

"Go on," Angelina prodded.

"When my parents died, I went to live with my Aunt Janine, who also practiced magic. She taught me to tap into the resources available to me. Turns out I listened pretty well, so after college I decided to open a shop in the Quarter. My aunt had saved the inheritance money my parents had left, and gave it to me as a graduation gift so I had the capital to fund my business."

"Whoa, back up a second," Logan interrupted. "You went to college?"

"Sure I did."

"Did you finish?"

"Yes, Logan, I finished." Was that a big deal?

"What was your degree?"

"Am I being interviewed for a job? Would you also like to see my résumé?"

Aidan laughed so hard he spit out the piece of bread he'd just taken a bite of.

"Aidan Storm! *Mon Dieu.* Close your mouth!"

"Sorry, Mom," he said, still chuckling.

"No, you're not being interviewed," Logan continued, glaring at Aidan. "Just curious what you majored in."

Sure sounded like a job interview. "Psychology. And since you asked, I also got my masters and Ph.D. And yes, from legitimate, accredited colleges, not internet or mail order." Because she just knew that's what he'd think.

"Holy shit, you're a Ph.D.?" Aidan exclaimed.

"Aidan," Angelina warned.

"Sorry. Again. Shutting up now."

"Good idea," Lissa said, cramming another piece of bread in his mouth.

Sophie laughed.

"You've got to be in your mid-twenties, right?" Logan asked.

"Asking my age is illegal in a job interview."

Now it was Max's turn to choke.

Angelina rolled her eyes. "Boys. Really. Logan, you're browbeating poor Sophie. Leave her alone."

"I don't mind, Angelina." She looked at Logan again and said, "Yes, I'm twenty-five. I graduated high school at sixteen, finished my Bachelor's in two years, my Master's in a year and my Ph.D. the year after that."

"Dayum," Aidan said. Lissa threatened him by holding up an even larger slice of bread.

"Wow, Sophie, you must be a genius. Congratulations."

Sophie blushed at Shannon's comment. "Thank you. I just happened to do well in school."

"Do well?" Shannon exclaimed. "Hell, you're obviously quite gifted to get through school that quickly. I'm impressed."

"I'll be damned," Logan whispered as he stared at the wine swirling around in his glass. When he looked up, Sophie was mesmerized by his crystal blue eyes. They seemed to hold her transfixed.

"You have a doctorate in psychology, and yet you run a cosmic voodoo shop in the Quarter."

"It's not a cosmic voodoo shop. It's what I do and it's a legitimate business. I love my job."

"So, in other words, you could be *really* helping people, using your education and your intellectual gifts to aid those who are suffering, and instead you choose to practice bullshit magic."

"Logan, I'm warning you," Angelina said.

The sky darkened outside as Angelina glared at Logan, a rumble of thunder shaking the floor underneath her. Then just as suddenly, the clouds lifted. Angelina focused again on Sophie. "Why did you open the shop, *cher*?"

Conscious of everyone watching her, she kept her eyes on Angelina. "When I first began to learn about the magic inside me, I toyed with it, trying to figure out what I could do. As a child I was very curious. Then as I got older my magic grew more powerful. I worked on it all the time and discovered I had a knack for foretelling—predicting the future, I guess you'd say. I could 'feel' people. Inside of them. Not only where they'd been, but where they were going." She rubbed her forehead. "It's kind of hard to explain."

"I think we know what you mean," Kaitlyn said. "Our magic is similar in a lot of respects, although I don't think it's as extensive as yours."

"Thanks." What a comfort it was to be around people who didn't think she was some kind of bizarre mutant. At least *most* of the people seated at the table felt that way. "Anyway, I discovered that I could accurately predict the future…at least as it related to people, not necessarily events. So don't ask me the lottery numbers for next week because I don't know those."

Everyone laughed. Everyone except Logan, who regarded her with an expression akin to utter disbelief. She refused to let him intimidate her.

"So you decided to set up your shop so you could tell people their future?" Lissa asked.

"Sort of. I also spent some time interning with a social worker and a practicing psychologist, so I try to blend a little magic and foretelling of the future with practical advice. Some people come to me thinking I can solve all their problems, when telling their future won't help them at all. I keep a list of social workers and licensed psychotherapists that I refer people to if I feel they need it."

"Aha, so in essence you *are* using your education to help people," Max said.

"I'd like to think so. I hope so. There are a lot of very lonely people in the world. People who just want someone to listen to them while they reason out their problems."

"It seems like such a waste," Logan said. "You open up a shop, dole out advice from your crystal ball for a few bucks a pop instead of really helping people."

Undaunted by Logan's viewpoint, she said, "I *am* helping people. People who don't have the money for mental or social health treatment, or those who are too afraid of modern medicine to go to the professionals for help with their problems. Those people are the ones who come to me. And I spend a little time with them, talk out their problems, and by the time I'm finished I can usually get them to agree to seek professional help."

"I think what you're doing is admirable, Sophie," Angelina said. "And you're right. There are those who stay with the old ways. People who need the kind of help you provide. You're not so much telling their future as you are helping them understand how their pasts affect their futures."

Finally, someone understood her. She beamed under Angelina's praise. "Thank you. I don't know about admirable, but it fulfills me, if that makes sense."

"It does."

Satisfied that she'd at least managed to win over Logan's family, she relaxed and enjoyed the rest of dinner, listening to them argue and talk over one another. Logan stayed silent, but at least didn't challenge her further.

So Logan didn't admire what she did. So what? It wasn't like she'd ever needed his approval, anyway. She did what she did because it was her destiny. She had no other choice, and wouldn't change it even if she could.

At least his family had embraced her and didn't ridicule her for what she did.

It was times like these that Sophie wished she'd had brothers and sisters. She regularly shared dinner with Sam and Joshua, but it wasn't the same as real family. Her own family.

An intense longing came over her. The need to have someone to love, and a family that loved her.

The only thing that would have topped off the day would be if Logan had managed to unwind a bit and enjoy himself around her.

That hadn't happened yet. From the looks he shot across the table, it wasn't going to happen at all.

"You have something to say, then say it," she said to Logan, tiring of his glares and shaking head.

"I just don't get it, that's all. You're wasting your life."

Before she could respond, he got up from the table and grabbed his plate, mumbling something about needing air as he headed toward the kitchen.

Sophie moved to go after him, but Angelina laid a hand over hers and shook her head. "Let him be for now, *cher.*"

She nodded. Angelina sent a pointed look to Galen.

"Time for us men to clear the table and leave the women alone," Galen said, getting up and taking plates into the kitchen. Aidan and Max followed him, leaving Sophie with Angelina, Kaitlyn, Shannon and Lissa.

After the men had vacated the kitchen, the women moved in to do the remaining dishes and put the leftover food away.

Sophie worked amiably beside the other women, once again struck with the comfortable sense of family.

Yet the entire time she wanted to go after Logan, to explain to him why she had made the choices that had led her to find him in a dark alley one winter night.

"Be patient, *ma belle,*" Angelina said, taking the plates that Sophie offered and slipping them onto the stack in a cabinet. "Logan is…difficult."

Shannon snorted. "Difficult. Yeah, that's an understatement. Cold-hearted, stubborn, narrow-minded, opinionated…should I go on?"

Kaitlyn laughed. "If you did, we'd be going all night."

"All right, that's enough," Angelina said with a smile before turning back to Sophie. "Now, I'm not sure if you're aware of this or not, but Aidan and Lissa's wedding is coming up in a few weeks."

Sophie's gaze flitted to Lissa. "I didn't know it was so soon. Are you ready?"

Lissa shook her head, her long, blonde ponytail swaying back and forth. "I'm never going to be ready, and yet I'm as ready as I'll ever be. There are so many details."

"Details that I'm attending to, so quit worrying," Kaitlyn announced, wrapping her arm around Lissa's shoulders.

"Oh I know you are, Kait. I'm just getting jittery. My stomach is tied up in knots at the thought that something might go wrong."

Sophie let her eyes drift closed for a moment and let her magic surround her. She wondered if what she had seen in her visions had anything to do with Aidan and Melissa's wedding.

She felt the danger, but still couldn't pinpoint the time period.

"I'd like you to come to the wedding," Angelina announced.

"Oh yes," Lissa exclaimed. "Please come."

Shaking off the visions of impending catastrophe, she shook her head. "Oh, I couldn't. Thank you, but I'm sure you have more than enough people coming."

"Nonsense," Shannon said. "There's plenty of space in the main ballroom at the hotel. We'd love to have you there."

Sophie fought back tears. Silly, it was only an invitation to attend the wedding, and yet she felt part of this family.

Which was a dangerous feeling, because she *wasn't* part of the family. She wasn't Logan's girlfriend. She wasn't…anything to them.

Besides, it wasn't as if Logan had asked her to come with him. What if he had plans to bring another woman as his date? She'd feel awkward, or even worse, hurt. And she'd have no right to feel that way. "I don't know. What would Logan think? You know he doesn't care much for me."

Shannon snorted. "Logan needs a baseball bat to the head to knock some sense into his brain cells."

"Be patient with Logan, *cher*," Angelina said. "He feels something for you."

"No, he doesn't."

"Yes, he does. I know it. I feel the turmoil raging within him."

Oh great. Just what she hadn't wanted to do. Upset Logan, and now his mother. "I'm sorry. I didn't mean to—"

Angelina held up her hand. "Don't apologize. I know you sense something happening with our family. When you told me that the night of the ball, I believed you, because I felt something too."

"What are you talking about?" Lissa asked, her voice shaky. "Something bad about the wedding?"

Angelina motioned them to the huge table in the kitchen. Kaitlyn poured coffee and they all sat, staring at her.

"Go on, *cher*," Angelina encouraged. "Tell them what you know."

She sucked in a breath and said, "That's the problem. I feel danger surrounding your family, but I can't pinpoint a where and when."

"Is that why you sought out Logan?" Kaitlyn asked.

Sophie nodded. "Yes."

"I don't know the circumstances of your meeting, but I know he hasn't been the same since that day he chased after you. Lissa told us about that."

Okay, so maybe they didn't know about the night in the alley. "I've had visions about Logan for months now. He's in my dreams, in all of my meditative visions. But all I sense is danger, and it has something to do with your family. I wish I could offer more, but I feel it's my duty to hang around and see if the images get stronger. I don't know why, but I keep thinking that I might be able to do something to either change things, or stop whatever may happen."

"You've come into Logan's life for a reason, Sophie," Angelina said. "But my son is not easy. He is stubborn, refuses to acknowledge or use his gifts, and claims not to want anything to do with people who possess magic."

"I know."

"But he's conflicted, because he feels something for you."

"I'm sorry, but I really don't think he does." He may have felt a momentary physical attraction for her, but he'd scratched that itch at the ball. He'd been even more distant today, as if he regretted their encounter.

She hadn't, though. Making love with him, even in such a frenzied and passionate way, had been exhilarating. He aroused her in ways no other man ever had. He made her want things no man had ever made her want before.

"It's strange," she admitted, "but I feel that Logan is the man I'm supposed to be with. I know you probably think I'm crazy, but I can't help it." She let out a small laugh. "And of course I had to choose the one man who wants nothing to do with me."

"Don't be too sure of that," Shannon said. "I've seen Logan with women before. When it's someone he doesn't care for, he's solicitous, smiles a lot and is very pleasant. But there's no sincerity behind it. It's just part of his façade. With you, he's grouchy and almost jittery."

Sophie groaned and laid her head in her hands. "Oh great."

"No, that's a good thing," Kaitlyn said, tipping Sophie's chin with her fingers so they made eye contact. "You've gotten under his skin."

"Yeah, I've annoyed the hell out of him."

"You've captured his attention. If he didn't feel something for you, he wouldn't be so upset about it," Angelina said. "You will have to remain steadfast and determined if you want to win his heart, because Logan has built a nearly impenetrable wall around himself. It will take a strong woman to make it crumble."

Like climbing a steep mountain in an icy snowstorm. Nearly impossible to grab a foothold, let alone reach the top. "I've never forced myself on a man before."

"And you won't have to with Logan. You're the right woman for him, Sophie Breaux," Angelina said, her voice softening in a way that made her warm from the inside out.

"Thank you. I hope so. I can't seem to break away from him, despite his protests that he wants nothing to do with me."

"If you want him, kiddo," Shannon said. "And I have no idea why you'd want to put up with a pain in the ass like my brother — then you're going to have to work at it."

Kaitlyn nodded. "And if you're willing to butt heads with him and try your best, we'll do everything we can to help."

"Thank you, but I don't understand why you'd want to help me."

Lissa grinned. "Because we feel you're already family, Sophie. The same thing happened with me. I wanted nothing to do with Aidan, and yet fate continued to toss us together. It took me awhile to accept the inevitable. In fact," she added, sweeping her hand across the table, "they all knew before I did. It's the same with you."

"Very true," Angelina said. "You're the one for Logan. We all feel it. Now you just need to convince *him* of that. If you want to."

She did want to, for more reasons than just her visions.

"I'll give it my best shot."

"Great!" Shannon said. "Then you'll come to Lissa and Aidan's wedding, right?"

She had a feeling they weren't going to take no for an answer. Besides, she was family now. The thought filled her with giddy happiness. "I'd be honored."

"I'm glad," Angelina said, then frowned as she glanced outside the kitchen window at the late afternoon sky. "A big storm is coming. Girls, go fetch Logan and ask him to take Sophie home. The weather is about to take a bad turn."

When the women left, Angelina stood and hugged her. "Tonight will be a turning point for you and Logan."

How did she know that? Sophie hadn't felt anything. "I don't know what you mean."

"Your relationship with him will change tonight, and he won't like it. It may not happen right away, but eventually he'll try to hurt you. He'll do his best to crush your heart so you'll walk away. This won't be easy, but I can guarantee the end result will be worth any pain you have to go through."

"I appreciate that, Angelina, and I'm not afraid of Logan. I feel him inside me, as if he's already a part of me. I have to see it through, no matter the outcome."

She knew it wasn't going to be easy. In fact, she wondered if it wasn't impossible.

But she wouldn't give up on him until she'd tried her best. Yes, her heart was involved, but also the fear that her visions might come true and put his family in danger.

Somehow, whatever the mysterious danger, it revolved around Logan.

She had to make him see what she saw, had to make sure he understood the danger.

He might want to drive her away, but Sophie wasn't a quitter.

Chapter Eight

Conscious of Sophie's gaze on him as he drove her home, Logan did his best to ignore her.

Dinner had been a disaster. They all treated her as if she were part of the family.

Despite his voiced reservations about Sophie, they accepted her. He'd never known his family to be so accommodating to a stranger that he'd warned them about. Couldn't they see through her smiling, friendly exterior into the devious liar she was underneath?

Ph.D., his ass. He'd check on that right away. No fucking way could someone with that level of education be wasting her life practicing voodoo magic.

Did she take him for an idiot?

Yet his family had fallen for her lies. And they were no fools.

He shook his head, more confused than ever, the truth blurring in front of him like the hard rain falling on his windshield. He flipped on the wipers.

"The weather is going to get really bad tonight, Logan."

"It's just rain."

"Are you sure?"

Hell if he knew. To be certain, he'd have to allow his powers to sweep through him. And he'd never let that happen. It weakened him, made him vulnerable, made him appear less than...

...normal.

"It's just rain," he said again.

Sophie pulled her light jacket around her. "It's getting colder. The rain may turn to ice."

He laughed. "Not in New Orleans, *cher*. We don't get ice storms here."

"Never say never, Logan. It does happen."

"Rarely."

By the time he pulled into the gravel driveway in front of her trailer, the rain had turned to sleet. He thought about just letting her get out and see her own way in, but somehow he knew his mother wouldn't approve of less than gentlemanly behavior. Turning off the ignition, he went around to her side and opened the door, then held on to her arm as he led her to the steps. The temperature outside was plummeting rapidly, colder than he could ever remember for winter in New Orleans.

Ducking his head down against the relentless ice pellets, he waited while she unlocked the door.

A goddamned ice storm. Just like she'd said. Shit.

When she had the door open, he started to thank her for coming to dinner so he could make a hasty exit.

But Sophie spoke first. "Logan, please come in with me."

He should have said no. But he didn't. Instead, like a man under some kind of spell he followed her inside, shaking the water from his hair and damning himself for not turning around and walking out right then.

"I'll get you a towel," she said, eagerly shrugging out of her wet jacket and heading into her bedroom. She returned with a towel and a hairbrush, motioning him to sit on the tiny, threadbare sofa.

"I'm fine here. I really don't need to dry off."

"Yes, you do. You're soaked. And the sleet is coming down harder now. So you might as well wait it out. I'll fix us some hot tea."

Grudgingly, he picked up the towel and dried himself off, allowing a bit of his magic out to dry his wet clothes. Sophie put water on to boil, then returned to the living room, dragging the brush through her long hair.

Watching her brush her hair was fascinating, though he couldn't pinpoint why. There was something so incredibly sensual about a woman touching her own hair, especially hers. She ran her fingers down each section, her slender hands smoothing the tendrils into waves. His cock reacted with a sudden twitch. Hell, he wanted her to touch him that same way!

Her hair hung almost to her waist. He could imagine the feel of the silky strands wrapped around his shaft as she bent over him, taking his cock between her full, tempting lips and sucking him deeply.

Now his cock roared to life, hard and pulsing. Despite his vehement mental objections, the damn thing wouldn't lie down and play dead like he wanted it to. His senses filled with her as she walked back and forth, her beautiful ass hugged by the worn jeans, her breasts caressing her sweater. Finally, she brought two cups of tea and sat on the couch next to him.

Her damp skin smelled so much like cinnamon and patchouli, those scents forever a part of his senses now. As her hair began to dry, curls formed from the ends upward.

A sudden desire to take the brush from her hands and finish the job himself had him nearly leaping off the couch. Anything to put distance between his barely leashed passions and the woman creating such havoc to his senses.

She put the brush down and reached for her cup, curling her legs underneath her as she settled in. When she turned to him, her violet eyes questioned, invited him. She licked the flavored tea off her lips. He wanted to follow with his own mouth on hers.

No. Abso-fucking-lutely no way. He had to get away from her, and now.

As nonchalantly as possible, he stood and walked to the small window to look outside. Icicles formed on the bare trees, pellets of ice hitting the roof of his car. Shit, sure as hell was one hell of an ice storm coming down.

"I should go before the weather gets worse."

"The roads are already icy and dangerous." She was silent for a few seconds, then said, "I think you should stay here tonight."

His throat went dry at the thoughts conjured up by her suggestion. "I don't think so. I'll be fine driving home."

"But I won't be. I'll worry about you."

He didn't want her worrying about him. He shook his head, refusing to turn around and look at her. "I hardly need anyone worrying about me, Sophie. I know how to drive."

In fact, he should already be on the road. A few steps and he'd be out the door and away from temptation.

Away from her. Her scent, her mouth, her long, silken hair, her full breasts.

Fuck. He had to go. Now.

He heard her shift and stand, smelled her as she approached him. Still, he wouldn't turn around. He wasn't sure he could trust himself if he looked at her.

Instead of touching him or speaking, she stopped inches behind him and inhaled, then sighed.

Christ, how much was he supposed to endure?

"I know you're aware of me, Logan," she whispered, her husky voice like a caress, torturing his already frayed nerve endings.

"Yes, I know you're there."

"Why won't you look at me?"

How was he supposed to answer that? He could imagine what she would say if he told her he was afraid to.

"It's enough that I feel your presence, Sophie."

"Why do you fight so hard against this?"

"I'm not fighting. I'm choosing."

"I think you've already chosen. You're just delaying the inevitable."

Now he did turn around, his pulse racing as he looked at her. Sophie possessed a beguiling innocence that tore his resolve to shreds. He'd never had to fight desire as hard as he was right now. "I get to choose who I fuck."

"I'm aware of that. As do I. But I'm drawn to you, Logan, in ways that I can't change. And you can't either."

"I don't believe in fate."

"I do. And I know you feel our connection."

"It's sexual chemistry, and nothing more."

She nodded and offered a half smile. "True enough. Biology plays a large part in any relationship. But what we share is much more than physical. Tell me, Logan, do you feel me, even when I'm not around?"

"No," he lied.

"Yes, you do. I know you do." She stepped an inch closer. He resisted the urge to back away. "Logan, please be honest with me, just once."

He should lie to her, but what was the point? In the end, the choice was his to make. And he wasn't going to do what his body screamed at him to do. "I've felt you from the first moment I saw you in the alley."

"And I've felt you. You're in my thoughts, in my dreams at night, and I can't get you out of my mind."

That revelation didn't help one bit. It only made his cock fully hard and strain against his jeans. A visual that wasn't lost on her as her gaze traveled down to his crotch, then back up again to meet his eyes. Heat dwelled within them, blatant desire that only made the situation worse.

"Does it make you uncomfortable?"

What? His dick? Hell yeah, it was uncomfortable. But he knew that wasn't what she meant. "Yes."

"Why?"

"Because everything about you makes me uncomfortable, from the way you so easily crawl into my mind to the way I want you whenever you're around."

He winced as soon as the words slipped from his lips. Shit. He hadn't meant to reveal so much. Normally he was good at hiding how he really felt. What was it about this woman that begged for him to tell her exactly how he felt?

She slid her teacup onto the edge of the counter and stepped closer. No woman would make him run. He could handle his attraction to Sophie without compromising his principles or letting down his guard.

"Tell me how I make your body feel," she said, so close he could reach out and touch the strands of curling hair resting on her breasts. But he didn't touch. Wouldn't allow himself to touch. He curled his fingers into his palms.

This wasn't going to happen tonight!

Sophie watched the war raging in Logan's eyes, and desperately wanted to comfort him, to offer him whatever it took to assuage the torment within him. But she also needed to push him into realizing that what they had went beyond a normal physical attraction.

Again she asked, "Tell me, Logan. How do I make you feel?"

She knew what it was costing him to restrain his urges, both magical and physical. And yet she couldn't stop.

"I don't think you really want to know the answer," he said, his voice deepening, his breath ragged.

"Yes, I do want to know."

He paused for a few seconds, arousal flaming in his eyes, darkening them like the storm had blackened the sky outside. "Hot, bothered, damned uncomfortable and aroused to the point of losing control."

She sucked in a breath at his admission, her body flaming to life with desire more fierce than she had ever felt before. Her nipples beaded under the thin sweater. Logan watched it happen, then licked his bottom lip.

Sophie forgot how to breathe, and forced her next words through the desert in her throat. "I'd like to see you out of control, Logan."

He shook his head. "No, you wouldn't."

She stepped closer, the tips of her nipples brushing his chest. "Yes, I would."

He kept his hands at his sides, but she felt the tightly coiled tension in his muscles. He was fighting it, and she didn't want him to. "Give in to it, Logan."

"You can't handle me out of control, Sophie. I'm warning you. Don't push this."

Oh, but that's exactly how she wanted him. Out of control, both magically and physically. "I can handle more than you think. Give it to me."

His nostrils flared like an animal scenting a female desperate to mate. She was that female, anxious for his touch, for the joining of their bodies, for the magic they could share together. "Don't make me beg."

He clenched and unclenched his fists. His brows knit together in a frown, his eyes cloudy with desire. "If you want this, you'll reap the consequences. I can't hold back once I unleash it."

Wrapping her arms around him, she tilted her head up and offered her mouth to him. "I don't care. I want it all."

With a low growl he reached for her hair, winding it in his fist and tugging hard, tilting her head even further back. Then he bent and took her mouth in a kiss that sent flames shooting through her core.

Her sex was on fire, her pussy drenched with instant arousal. She whimpered as his tongue entered her mouth and licked hers, his teeth raking over her tongue as he sucked it into his mouth.

His body was cool, despite the heat of passion surrounding them. When he pulled away, his breath blew out in a white cloud as the temperature dropped in the room.

But the chill was like icy fire, burning her skin, sending her nearly over the edge before her pussy was ever touched. She held back her own magical response and immersed herself within his, knowing she was experiencing something rare, something that Logan had never shared with another woman.

His fingers were like icicles as he threaded his hand under her sweater, cupping one breast. The heat of her body mixing with the chill of his fingers was more arousing than she ever thought possible. She gasped when he found a nipple and rolled it between his fingers, then plucked at it until she cried out and arched against him.

"You smell like cinnamon," he murmured, licking her neck and nibbling the tender skin. "I want more of you to taste."

He pushed away and reached for the hem of her sweater, tugging it upward and over her head, then casting it to the floor.

The cold air surrounding them froze her, making her nipples tight and hard. He smiled and bent over, taking one bud into his mouth and licking it until she thought she might faint. Then he did the same to the other, not once stopping his hands from their roaming journey over her body.

"Logan, please," she murmured, not even aware of what she was begging for. She just wanted…more.

"Yes, *cher*." He kneeled and reached for the button of her jeans, flipping it open with one move, then pulled the zipper down, kissing her belly as he pulled the denim aside.

His lips were a fire on her belly as he touched her skin. Her womb leapt in anticipation, her pussy trembling with the desire to have him lick her there.

In short order he had tugged the jeans over her hips and down her legs, his hands following the trail of her clothes until he'd tossed them away from her.

Clad only in skimpy white panties, she felt way more underdressed than he. And last time she hadn't been able to see his body. Dammit, this time she would.

"My turn," she said, but before she could reach for him he pushed her backwards, controlling their direction until he had her in the living room. He scooted the coffee table out of the way, his height seemingly overpowering the room, making it seem much smaller. More intimate.

He laid her on the floor and reached for the quilt on the couch, spreading it out and rolling her onto it. Then he just kneeled over her and stared.

"We're doing this my way," he growled, reaching for the button of his jeans. "You need to understand this is just sex, and nothing more."

If possible, the cold wall of protection he'd built around himself was nearly visible. But he put it up in vain. It was already too late for him. He just hadn't realized it yet.

She nodded, resisting the urge to purr with utter contentment. "However you want it."

Chapter Nine

Sophie watched intently as the button flipped open on Logan's jeans, followed by the slow slide of the zipper.

There was nothing sexier than seeing the shadow of dark, downy fur hidden beneath that zipper. But instead of pulling his jeans down, he reached for his shirt and drew it over his head.

She sighed. Pure, feminine satisfaction. What a magnificent body he had. Dark, curling hair spread across his well-muscled chest. His shoulders were broad, his arms defined and strong, his waist tapered and covered with the same dark curls that disappeared into his jeans. Her mouth watered, then went dry as he began to push the jeans off his hips.

The room heated with a warmth borne of heavy arousal. It hung thick in the air as she watched him unveil his nearly perfect body.

His cock sprang forward, hard and pulsing, the veins outlined against the tautly stretched skin of his shaft. The head was purple and engorged, and she wanted nothing more at that moment than to lick away the drops of fluid beading at the tip.

But Logan apparently had other ideas. He crouched down and kneeled between her legs, lifting her foot and massaging the arch. When he drew it upward and slowly took her big toe in his mouth, she arched off the floor, the sensation shooting to her sex as if his tongue had just touched her clit.

He sucked it, licked it, even nibbled a bit, then did the same with her other toes. When he was finished with one foot, he moved to the other.

Sophie dug her fingers into the soft carpet and held on tight, for the first time in her life feeling sensations in her cunt that had nothing to do with being touched there. She'd never realized her feet were erogenous zones.

Or the backs of her knees, which she quickly discovered when he raised her leg and kissed the spot behind her knee. She shivered and moaned, which only encouraged him to linger there until she couldn't bear it.

"Logan, please."

"Not yet. I've wanted to uncover your beautiful body. I have an urge to lick you. Everywhere."

He followed his urge, his tongue laving her skin, moving upwards to her thighs until she was whimpering with the need to feel that hot, wet stroke upon her sex. But he moved over her hips and toyed with her belly button for awhile.

This was torture. Endless, unnerving torment. The more she moaned and begged, the slower his strokes became.

Hell, he hadn't even removed her panties yet, which were now soaked with her arousal.

And if he brushed his hard cock against her leg one more time, she was going to find the strength within her to flip him over on his back and fuck him until neither of them could move.

"Logan, please, just fuck me."

He laughed as he licked her neck, then pulled back and looked at her. "I'm crushed. You're just using me."

Oh dear God. The man actually had a sense of humor. Only right now she didn't find him the least bit amusing. "Not funny. Fuck me, dammit, I'm dying here."

"Well, we can't have you dying, can we? Not until I've had my way with you." He leaned over and captured the hard peak of one nipple in between his teeth, then licked it, over and over again until she was ready to scream.

Maybe he'd stop if she did scream.

For someone who kept a chilly countenance, his body was burning as it rested against hers. She couldn't help lifting her hips and rubbing her throbbing pussy against his strong thigh.

"Uh-uh, *cher*. Not yet." He pushed her hips back to the floor and held her while he laved her other nipple.

This was some kind of game to Logan. Wasn't he the least bit turned on? By his hard cock, she assumed he was aroused, but she swore he'd licked every inch of her skin by now, and she was more than ready for release.

Wasn't he?

The man was simply inhuman.

She shuddered against him, raking her nails over his back when he settled his long shaft between her legs. Kneeling, he teased her panty-clad sex by rubbing the tip of his cock against her. His forearms bunched, the muscles bulging, tightening with the effort of holding himself above her.

"Dammit Logan!" She sensed he liked to be in control, to have the upper hand, even in sex. He'd soon learn that once she wanted something, it wasn't wise to mess with her. She'd had quite enough of this teasing.

She slipped her hand into her panties and caressed her throbbing clit. Logan sat back on his heels and watched the movements of her hand.

He wasn't going to stop her. Instead, he was content to watch. His gaze took her heat level up several notches, reminding her of the way he'd watched her that night in the alley.

The same way she'd looked at him. The same way she'd gotten off while he fucked that redhead.

Only this time he was much closer, and had his cock in his hand, stroking it as she brought herself closer to orgasm.

"Let me see it," he said, motioning to her panties.

"You want them off, you take them off."

His eyes flamed dark and smoky. Reaching for the thin straps at her hips, he tugged hard, leaving nothing left of her panties but a discarded scrap of silk and lace.

The air cooled her hot sex, but his gaze inflamed her.

"Rub your clit for me, baby. Let me see up close how you do it."

She did, anxious to feel the sparks that touching herself would provide. She petted the hardened nub gently, circling one finger around the hood, then pulling it back so she could stroke directly over the pleasure bud. Cream gushed forth as she brought herself ever nearer to the edge of reason.

When Logan slipped two fingers inside her cunt and began thrusting in and out, she knew she was going to lose it quickly.

Unable to hold back, she cried out as the orgasm hit. Her pussy clenched and gushed around his ever-moving fingers. She rode out the exquisite sensation until she was out of breath and shaking.

But still she managed to find the one word that would tell him what she needed.

"More."

Logan sucked in a quick breath, unraveling at Sophie's passion. If he wasn't careful, he could easily be swept away by her fiery nature. That he couldn't allow.

He had a tight leash on his control, but she made him want to break free and let everything out.

His cock thrummed with the need for release, his balls rising tight and hard against his body, filling with the come that he wanted to shoot within her tight sheath.

And he would, but he wanted to delay it as long as possible, knowing that every time he touched her he lost a little more of the hardened exterior he'd spent years perfecting.

The free and easy way she shared herself with him, so totally and without reservation, blew him away. No woman had ever given so much without asking for anything in return.

Logan was afraid he was weakening. He was afraid that he wasn't going to be able to rein in his magic once he merged with her. The last time it had taken sheer force of will, and even at that he'd had to let some of it loose.

She made him want more from a woman than he'd ever wanted before. Why couldn't he just be satisfied with fucking her, getting off, and leaving? What was it about her that drove him to want to give her everything?

Seemingly unaware of his internal torment, she smiled up at him, then sat up and took his shaft between her small hands. She rolled her palms over every inch of him, pulling his cock slowly toward her full, eager lips.

Sweat beaded on his brow and he swiped it away, willing a cold rush of air to swirl around them.

Her eyes widened, and then she smiled as her tongue snaked out and licked away the drops of pre-come that had gathered on the head of his cock.

"Christ, Sophie," he murmured, at once wanting to pull away from her, and at the same time wanting to drive his shaft deep into the moist recesses of her waiting mouth.

Desire won out over common sense when she took him inch by inch between her lips, licking at the skin of his shaft until she couldn't take any more in. Then she held her breath and swallowed him, the gulping action squeezing his cock until he felt the tremors in his balls.

He pulled back, forcing himself to breathe, needing some clarity to think his way through this. The magic boiled to the surface, pushing at him, demanding release.

A release he refused to grant. The only release he'd allow would be the elimination of the pent-up desire he'd felt for Sophie all day and all night. That much, he'd allow.

He cupped the back of her head and fed her his cock. "Suck me, *cher*. Take it all in and make me come."

Eagerly, she complied, until he couldn't hold back the rush of fluid. It catapulted from his cock with a rush, pouring into her eagerly sucking mouth. She took every drop, swallowing, massaging his balls until he had nothing left to give her.

And still, even after he'd withdrawn, he was hard for her.

He hadn't yet gotten what he wanted. To drive hard inside her wet pussy and make her scream.

That was the part he'd held back, this naked, body-to-body coupling that was more about emotion and a sharing of souls than it was about sinking his shaft into a willing cunt and getting off.

She knew it, and she wanted it.

Impossible. He couldn't give her that without sacrificing his control. What she wanted and what she was going to get were two different things.

He poised between her legs, inhaling the sweet musk of her arousal, gazing at the come pouring from her slit.

And he paused, gathering his resolve to hold back.

"Give me everything, Logan," she whispered, as if she knew his every thought.

"Once it starts, I won't be able to stop it," he warned, wanting her to know that what she asked from him might not be what she could handle. "You have to decide, right now, if you can take it all."

"Everything you give me, and then some," she answered, no uncertainty in her voice.

"I'm a cold-hearted bastard, Sophie. I'm incapable of loving you, so if that's what you're after, you're going to be disappointed. All I can offer you is sex."

Without hesitation, she answered. "I'm a grown woman, Logan, and capable of dealing with hurt. If my heart ends up broken, then it's my fault, not yours. But I want it all, and I want it now. Give me what you've never given another woman before."

He'd thought to push her away by telling her that he could never be what she wanted, what she needed, in a lover. He wasn't the candy, flowers and love notes kind of guy. No, that wasn't him at all. More like the fuck and run type. And that kind of man wouldn't suit Sophie at all.

She deserved so much better than him. Why couldn't she see that? Why couldn't she change her mind and make this easier on both of them?

"Please, Logan."

Christ! He should go. But goddammit, he *was* only human, at least most of him was. And what she offered, he could no longer refuse. The last of his restraint torn away, he nestled between her legs, desperate to possess her completely. He slid his finger into her cunt and took her clit between his lips, his body on fire from her heat, her scent, the way she bucked against his mouth as he suckled and licked her.

She melted all over him, juices flowing through his fingers. He withdrew and slid them against her anus, needing to feel this part of her, too. Keeping his mouth firmly against her clit, he broke the barrier of her back hole with his soaked fingers, sliding them into her ass and fucking slowly. Her shrieks of delight as she flew over the edge only propelled him further into a near-delirium of sensation.

Every damn thing she did drove him crazy. The taste of her sweet come, the way her ass squeezed his fingers as she orgasmed around them, the moaning sounds she made when he brought her close to climaxing yet again. He felt like he'd been catapulted into some surreal alternate universe, his sanity slowly slipping away

Withdrawing his fingers, he stepped away from her for the briefest of seconds to clean up, then drew her up and bent her over the sofa.

"Please, Logan, hurry," she whispered on a ragged breath, her passion leaving her drenched with sweat.

Nestling against her fine ass, he positioned his cock and plunged inside her, feeling at once how her pussy clamped down around his cock, milking him, coaxing a response he was more than ready to give.

"Fuck my dick, Sophie," he commanded, reaching for her hips and pulling her back against him as he thrust forward, needing to be embedded deep inside her as if the very act of sheathing himself inside her pussy could protect him from the magic pounding away at him.

She moaned and pushed back, drawing forward then slamming her cunt onto his cock again and again. He held on despite the torrents of wintry air swirling out of control around them. Her tight sheath squeezed him like a vise, milking him, commanding him to pour out everything he had within him.

"I'm coming, Logan!" she cried, then words weren't possible as she screamed and came all over his cock. He jettisoned come deep within her, digging his fingers into her hips as he rode out the frenzy that had overtaken them both.

She collapsed against the couch and took him with her. He turned her and cradled her in his arms, taking deep breaths until the world seemed normal again. Finally, he sighed in relief, satisfied that he'd managed to control the magic.

Perhaps what he thought he'd felt for her had been nothing more than pent-up lust. He had nothing to be afraid of. She couldn't tear away his careful control.

"Come with me," she said, standing and holding out her hand. Curious, he let her lead him into the bedroom.

"Lie down on the bed," she commanded, her voice still husky with passion.

He laughed. He'd finally met a woman whose libido was as strong as his. "You want more?" he asked.

One corner of her mouth curled in a sexy smile. "Oh yes. We're not nearly finished yet."

Now that he knew she posed no threat to him, he was more than eager to continue fucking her until she begged for mercy.

But when he moved to pin her to the bed, she shook her head. "Let me get on top."

Grinning, he lay flat on the mattress and said, "Ride me, baby." His cock rose and hardened to accommodate her. She straddled him, lifting her sweat-moistened hair and tossing it over her shoulders.

Inching upward, her sex brushed his cock. She rocked against his shaft, tossing her head back and whimpering as her hard clit caressed his erection. When she looked down at him again, her eyes were glazed dark with passion. She reached for his shaft and stroked it, cupped his balls and squeezed gently.

"Fuck me baby. Now."

Her gaze burned hot as she straddled his hips and inched down over his cock, embedding him deep within her tight sheath.

"Fuck, that's good," he groaned, lifting his hips and thrusting even deeper.

She let out a hoarse cry when he circled her clit with his finger, gently plucking at the distended bud.

"There is no fear in letting someone love you, Logan," she whispered, bending over him and taking his mouth in a gentle kiss.

He allowed her to penetrate his inner sanctum for the briefest of seconds, which was all it took for her to wrangle her way past his defenses.

Suddenly a light began to glow around her, starting out nearly black and then growing, until the entire bed was surrounded in a lavender glow that pulsed every time she thrust against him.

She moved her hands over his skin, stopping to finger his nipples to hard points. He felt the sensation in his cock and thrust hard against her.

A low, murmuring chant escaped her throat. Words he didn't understand, but knew instinctively were ancient and sacred. Unfamiliar vibrations settled over him, and with each touch of her hands on his burning skin, he felt the warmth of a woman's love penetrating deeply, coaxing the magic free, hovering dangerously close to his heart.

Her body was beautiful bathed in the lavender light, her breasts thrusting forward as she rocked against him. She tilted her head back and rode him as if in a trance, and he was helpless against her power.

Sophie had no inhibitions whatsoever, leaning back and giving him access to every part of her as she continued to ride him relentlessly.

He thought he had the power? Hell, right now he had none. Unable to contain the magic, he had no choice but to let it free. Snow began to fall, slowly at first, then the wind picked up and swirled around them.

His magic needed to fight with hers. He had to show her he wouldn't give in.

Yet she continued to murmur strange words, comforting words, and squeezed his cock with her cunt until he couldn't do a damn thing with his magic, or hers.

Surrounded by a blizzard in her bedroom, she kept them safe within the warm cocoon of her aura.

Her energy began to enter him. Through every pore, she seeped bit by bit within him.

He pulled her close, driving his hips upward as he pierced her with pistoning thrusts again and again. Her tears spilled over his chest as she accepted what he gave her. A cry tore from her lips as she spasmed around him and came, the orgasm so intense it nearly rocked him off the bed. He let go and freed both himself and his magic, allowing a part of himself to enter her. For the briefest of seconds, they were suspended in time, their essence flowing one into the other.

Then it was over, and she collapsed against him. Equally spent, he could do nothing but hold onto her and stroke her back, her hair, and wish to all the heavens that he had never laid eyes on Sophie Breaux.

Chapter Ten

The soft light of morning spilled into Sophie's tiny bedroom. She snuggled close to Logan's warmth, the blanket pulled down to her hips.

He admired the lines of her back, counting every vertebra with his eyes as he memorized her scent and the buttery feel of her dark skin.

Last night was like nothing he'd ever experienced. She'd exhausted him. So much that he'd slept better than he could ever remember. He'd never spent the night with a woman. Too intimate. And yet he'd fallen into satiated slumber with his arms wrapped tightly around Sophie.

He could still feel her pussy squeezing his cock, pulling orgasm after orgasm out of him. He'd never met a woman who could match his passions, and yet she'd been game for whatever he wanted last night, for however long he wanted it.

Like a strange psychic pull, he felt her embedded with him, a connection so close that it threatened to dissolve the wall he'd so carefully erected around his emotions.

No, that wouldn't happen, no matter how much his family liked her, or how much Sophie wanted it.

His life had direction and control. Since he'd met her, everything had begun to dissolve. To warm. Thoughts of her filled his days and long into his sleepless nights. Her aroma filled his senses like a snake charmer's spell. Her dark, exotic looks and her wicked smile called to him, bound him to her in inexplicable ways.

Hell. Everything about her intoxicated him.

Sophie shifted and moaned, scooting closer to his body heat. He pulled the cover up around her and let her move her head onto his shoulder.

Shit. He swore he'd never fall in love, and there was no way in hell he'd ever bring children into the world. A child might inherit his bizarre powers, and he'd never inflict that kind of burden on anyone, let alone an innocent child.

No, he'd remain alone, aloof, and impervious to falling in love.

Besides, Sophie wasn't the woman for him. She was warm, had a generous heart and cared deeply. She'd want a home with a husband who adored her, and probably a ton of kids. He'd have to let her down gently, because he could tell she was falling in love with him.

Dammit, he never wanted this to happen. How the hell could things have gotten so madly out of control so fast?

He hadn't led her on; he'd been totally honest with her about his feelings.

And she'd claimed she could handle it. Now she'd be forced to prove it.

"Don't you ever turn that incredible mind of yours off?"

He looked down into sleepy violet eyes as she smiled up at him. And suddenly found himself unable to speak.

"Good morning. Would you like some breakfast?"

Yes, he did. Starting with her sweet pussy, and moving on from there. His cock hardened against her belly and she grinned. "Or maybe you'd like to put off breakfast for a little while?"

He still couldn't manage words, especially when her head disappeared under the blankets and her hot mouth surrounded him.

No, he definitely couldn't form words then. He could only close his eyes and put off the inevitable until much, much later.

She took him deep, his cockhead banging the back of her throat. His balls tightened with the need to release again, a fact that surprised him despite the delirium of pleasure Sophie weaved around him.

"Suck me, Sophie," he said, clenching his teeth as the pressure built to a crescendo. He dug his fingers into the sheets and held on while she wove a wicked spell on his cock.

Her hair slid across his thighs as she threw off the covers and leaned over him, moving her mouth up and down over his shaft.

Watching his cock disappear between her lips, feeling and seeing the way she swallowed him, had him lifting his hips and driving deeper, wanting more of the torment.

When she cupped his balls and tugged, he groaned, held her head with his hand and shot a stream of come down her throat. She milked him, and he gave her everything he had, finally collapsing back on the mattress and fighting to regain a normal heart rate.

He could grow to like this. Hell, he already liked it. And her. Way too much to let it go on without telling her that it was over.

She looked up at him and grinned, then licked her lips. He shuddered, knowing how much he wanted to fuck her ten different ways. He could spend the entire day buried inside her.

"I need to go."

She frowned. "Um, I was going to fix you breakfast."

He slipped off the bed and reached for his clothes. "No time for that. I have things to do today."

She sat up, her hair falling over her breasts. One dark nipple peeked out between the raven curls, and he quickly turned away. She looked way too damn sexy sitting there with the sheet wrapped around her hips, her lips swollen and moist from sucking him.

"Okay," she finally answered, rising and tossing on a pair of sweatpants and an oversized sweatshirt. She wound her hair up and grabbed a clip from the dresser, pinning her hair loosely.

Fuck, even dressed like that with her hair a tumbled mess she still looked desirable. His cock fired to life again, and he all but ran to the door.

"Logan, wait!"

He cringed, but stopped and turned around. She approached and paused a few inches from him.

"Thank you. For yesterday at your parents. For last night, too."

He nodded, unable to say what he needed to say to her. *Tell her it's over, you moron. How fucking hard is that?*

Instead, he grabbed her and planted a passionate kiss on her lips, then quickly pulled away and stepped outside before he did something incredibly stupid.

Like walking back in there and making love to her.

Forever.

* * * * *

"He hurt you, didn't he?"

Sophie looked up at Josh. "No, he didn't."

She wouldn't let Logan push her away. She wasn't going to leave things between them unsettled, no matter if Logan was avoiding her.

"When did you see him last?" Samantha asked, handing Sophie one of the new crystals they'd received in today's shipment.

"Sunday." Four days ago. No calls, and he hadn't come by. Not that she'd expected him to.

Okay, maybe she had expected him to.

"You slept with him, didn't you?" Josh said, his voice accusing.

"That's none of your business, Joshua."

"Since when? Everything about your life has been my business, Soph. For years. Now you can't confide in me anymore?"

She rubbed her temples, more confused than ever. No man had ever mattered enough to her to withhold how she felt, but she knew if she told Josh about Logan, it would only hurt him more than she already had.

"Josh, look. I know how you feel about me, and I just don't think it's a good idea if I tell you about my sex life."

He inhaled sharply, jaw clenching. "Well, there's my answer, then. You did sleep with him."

Before she could say anything else, he left the shop.

Sophie felt horrible. She'd never led him on, but she still hated hurting him.

"He's working on it, Soph," Sam said, patting her hand. "He told me he's been dating this girl who teaches at the college."

Sophie stared wistfully at the closed door, wondering if she should go after Josh. "Really? He didn't mention her to me."

"And he probably won't. You know how he is—how he's always been. He hides his feelings from everyone, and the one time he—"

She paused, and Sophie nodded. "I know, I know. The one time he bared his heart, I stomped all over it." Burying her head in her hands, she mumbled, "I'm between a rock and hard place with Josh. I don't know what to do to make it right with him."

"There's nothing you can do. He has to find his own way. He's still young, for a man, Sophie. This burning torch he's carried for you since elementary school will pass once he finds the woman of his dreams."

And no one would be happier to see him find a woman who would love him like he deserved to be loved.

"I'll talk to him," Sophie said.

"Do whatever you think is best. Now, tell me what's going on with Logan."

She groaned. "I don't know. Sunday was…magical. Perfect. Hot, passionate, we even shared magic."

"But?"

"But he hurried out of there so damn fast Monday morning that you would have thought his pants were on fire. And I haven't heard from him since."

Not that she'd called him, or tried to see him. She wanted to give him space to think, and maybe that had been a mistake.

"Go after him. You already know he's not going to come to you willingly. If you want him, search him out."

She was just cowardly enough to not want to have the door slammed in her face if she did just that. "I don't know. I haven't had a vision in a few days. Maybe the danger to him and his family was false."

"Maybe you're just a coward and this has nothing to do with the visions and you know it."

Sometimes it sucked to have a best friend who knew her so well. "You're right. But really, Sam, how many times should I let him get close and then run away before I give up?"

"Depends on how you feel about him."

Sam gave her a pointed look.

"I don't know how I feel. No, wait, that's not true. I'm crazy about him, Sam. He makes my heart pound, and oh God the sex is amazing, but there's also something so vulnerable about him, as if he's got this huge fear of not measuring up. It's odd, because that's so not like his outward persona."

"Look. This is going to sound hokey as hell, but I really believe true love only comes around once in a lifetime. And if you don't grab it when you see it, it's lost forever. If you love him, honey, then grab it."

She nodded, contemplating her next move. First she needed to talk to Josh and smooth things over with her friend. Then she'd work on Logan after that.

* * * * *

She found Josh at the park, knowing that when he needed to brood, that was where he'd go. It's where he always ran off to, even when they were kids and his mom had left for one of her overnight or several night jaunts, leaving Josh alone with his alcoholic father.

If anyone needed love in his life, it was Josh. She sat next to him on the bench, not speaking, just staring at the trees and the playground, remembering their laughter, how easy it had been for the three of them to bond as children.

How tight that bond had always been. Until lately.

"Josh, I miss you."

He didn't turn to look at her. "He's going to hurt you, Sophie. You're chasing a fantasy. Logan Storm is never going to give you what you want and what you deserve."

"I wish it were you, Josh. I really wish I could—"

"It's not that," he interrupted. "Not anymore." Then he did turn to her, his eyes the same gentle brown that had made her feel his warmth. "Despite the fact that you and Sam seem to think I'm pining away over you, you're wrong. I've found someone, and I like her. A lot."

She smiled and reached for his hand. "I'm happy for you, Josh. That's all I ever wanted for you. For all of us. To love and be loved in return."

"I know that now. Hey, I'm a guy," he said with a sharp grin. "I like to think I'm irresistible to the ladies. When you didn't want me, I had…ego issues."

Giggling and feeling much more lighthearted than she had in awhile, she asked about his new girl.

"She's a professor at the college. New to town. She's from Nebraska. Such a sweet thing, too, Sophie. You and Sam would really like her."

The animation in his face, the excitement in his eyes, told her she'd gotten her friend back. She hugged him. "Bring her around the shop sometime soon, okay?"

"I will. Now, about you and Logan. You gotta listen to me, Sophie. I only want you to be happy. And pining away for a man who clearly doesn't love you is a lot like...well, a lot like what I was doing with you."

How could she explain that it wasn't the same at all? "I'll give it some thought, Josh." She kissed him on the cheek and headed toward the shop. She had a lot of thinking to do. About what Josh said as well as Sam.

And about what the next step was with Logan.

Chapter Eleven

One week. One fucking entire week and Sophie hadn't called or tried to see him.

She'd seen plenty of *his* family, though. How the hell she got involved in helping with the wedding planning for Lissa and Aidan was beyond his ability to understand.

But, oh no. She wasn't just helping with the wedding, now she was *in* the wedding, too.

Just because one of Lissa's college friends had to beg off due to a difficult pregnancy, leaving an opening for a bridesmaid.

How fucking convenient. And Lissa just had to ask Sophie to take her friend's place. To which, he'd heard, Sophie had readily agreed.

Now he had to avoid his own family to keep from running into her.

Why couldn't she stick to her own life and her own friends?

He knew why. Because she was trying to ingrain herself into the Storm family and become part of them. And nothing he said to his family dissuaded them from accepting her.

"You look like a grumpy, old bear."

He looked up to see Kaitlyn leaning in the doorway. She strolled in and slipped into one of the chairs across from his desk.

"What do you want?"

Her lips curled into a smile. "And you sound about the same. What's wrong with you lately?"

As if she didn't know. "Are you here for a reason?"

"Not that I need one, but yes, as a matter of fact I am. I need you to sign these contracts."

She slipped a folder in front of him. He scanned the contracts and applied his signature, then slid them across the desk. "I have a secretary, you know. You could have just handed these to Delores."

"I could have, but then I wouldn't get to visit with you, since you've been in hiding the past few days. Care to talk about it?"

"With you? Hell, no."

"Want to hear about the wedding plans?"

Like he had a choice? "Not particularly. I know when the wedding is. I'll show up on time."

Rolling her eyes, she said, "There's a lot more to it than just showing up and you know it. The rehearsal dinner is tonight."

"Do I need to be there for that?"

"Logan, you're the best man. Not only do you have to show up for the rehearsal so you know what to do, you also have to give a toast at dinner tonight."

"I'm busy."

"You're being a dick. Now stop it and tell me why you're avoiding all of us."

He shook his head and looked down at his paperwork. "I'm busy."

Kaitlyn crossed her arms. "You're avoiding Sophie."

His gaze shot up at that remark. "No, I'm not."

Relentless, she said, "You like her. Really like her."

"No, I don't. I really don't. And I wish all of you would quit trying to throw us together."

"If you'd pull your head out of your ass, you could see she's in love with you. And the reason you're so grumpy is because you're in love with her."

There were times he regretted working in the family business. This was one of those times. "Kait, I'm not in love with Sophie. In fact, I'd be really happy if I never had to see her again. And the more that the rest of you parade her around in front of me, the worse it's going to get, especially for her."

"Aww, you're trying to spare her from the heartbreak, aren't you?"

"Yes, actually, I am. If you'd let me."

Kaitlyn snorted. "Your ego is as huge as the planet, Logan. How can you let someone down that you've never even given yourself the chance to know? If you did, you'd see what the rest of us see."

He leaned back in the chair. "Okay, tell me. What would I see?"

"Sophie has a beautiful heart. She's kind, unselfish, sympathetic and genuinely honest about every aspect of her life. She accepts those around her, especially us, and you know what I mean by that. Plus, she has a keen insight into human nature and a magic that's as strong, if not stronger, than ours."

That was quite a testimonial, but he wasn't going to bite. He already knew the great things about Sophie Breaux. Didn't mean he had to follow formula and fall madly in love with her.

That, he refused to do. "Which is precisely why she's not the right woman for me. You know how I feel about our powers, Kait. I don't acknowledge them, I don't use them, and I sure as hell don't want to be with a woman who has her own."

"I never knew you to be so afraid, Logan. You're one of the strongest men I know, second only to Dad. The fact you're turning tail and running because a woman interests you...well, frankly, it surprises me."

He refused to allow Kaitlyn to bait him into doing something stupid. "Don't you have work to do?"

"Everything's ready for the dinner." She shook her head and stood. "If you keep acting the way you've been, Logan, you're going to end up alone and miserable. Give Sophie a chance. I know you feel something for her."

Glaring up at her, he said, "Do you know how tired I am of people telling me how I feel?"

She stepped toward him and reached for his hands. "Who and what we are should be embraced and celebrated, Logan. We've been given a very special gift."

"More like a curse."

She hugged him, then stepped away. "There are times I feel very sorry for you, *mon frere*. I love you, and you know that. But you're passing up a chance at love, at happiness. Opportunities like that are rarer than you think. You are as deserving of love as anyone, Logan. Open your heart, before it's too late."

She turned and grabbed the folder off his desk, then left, shutting the door behind her.

Silence surrounded him, her words echoing over and over in his head.

Madness. He dismissed Kaitlyn's lecture. Kait loved the idea of love. She lived for romance and everything magical about it and the family's powers.

That wasn't him, and no one could make him be someone he didn't want to be.

Or feel something he didn't feel.

Returning to his paperwork, he tried to study the budget numbers, but finally gave up.

So his family didn't understand him. No surprise there, since he didn't understand himself.

If he was honest, he'd realize that he'd missed Sophie these past few days. Despite his objective of getting rid of her, the fact that she hadn't tried to see him…was damned irritating.

Several times over the past few days he'd had to stop himself from walking by her shop, or driving out to her place at night.

What the hell was wrong with him anyway? She was doing exactly what he hoped she'd do—staying away from him. And now that she had been, he wanted to see her.

Disgust filled him.

What the fuck was it going to take to satisfy him?

Would he ever be happy?

* * * * *

Sophie took a deep breath and walked into the church, genuflecting and making the sign of the cross with the holy water before walking up the aisle toward the group assembled there for rehearsal.

She still couldn't quite believe she had been asked to participate in Lissa and Aidan's wedding. She'd felt so incredibly honored when Lissa had asked her to step in for her friend who was too ill to make the trip. Lissa had even apologized profusely for asking at the last minute, but Sophie had been thrilled.

She'd never been a bridesmaid before, and was really looking forward to it.

Although walking down the long church aisle right now while Logan glared at her wasn't exactly a great start to the evening.

She hoped she'd dressed appropriately. Lissa had told her they'd be having dinner at the hotel afterward, and it was a semi-fancy event.

Of course, Sophie had nothing semi-fancy in her wardrobe, but Shannon had come to her rescue and loaned her a formfitting cocktail dress. The halter-style dress fit her snugly, though. She couldn't even wear anything underneath it or else lines would show.

Nothing like wearing a dress, high heeled shoes and nothing else. At least she had a long coat on to ward off the chill in the air tonight.

So why was she trembling as she made her way down the aisle?

"Sophie!"

Lissa ran up and hugged her. Shannon followed suit, drawing her raincoat open and whistling. "Wow. Now that dress fits you, honey."

Flushing, she chewed on her bottom lip and glanced at Logan. His gaze raked over her, starting at her face and ending at her feet. She felt the heat from his eyes even though more than ten feet separated them.

Lissa made introductions. Of course she already knew most of the wedding party, since Shannon, Kaitlyn, Logan and Max were part of it. Her partner down the aisle was Brett McGregor, Aidan's best friend from college.

Brett was very attractive, with dark, brooding looks that made her think of Heathcliff from *Wuthering Heights*. She sensed a tortuous soul within him, and felt guilty for her magic invading his emotions.

Sometimes what she tuned into couldn't be helped.

"Nice to meet you, Brett," she said, wondering what it was about him that made him hurt so deeply inside. He masked it well, though, offering her a bright smile that didn't quite reach his whiskey-colored eyes.

"Great to meet you too, Sophie. Aidan didn't tell me I'd be partnered with such a knockout."

Determined not to spend the entire night blushing, she laughed. "Now why do I have the feeling you say that to all the girls?"

"Because he does," Aidan said, peering over Brett's shoulder. "Or at least he did in college."

Brett arched a brow and sniffed, feigning shock. "Have no idea what you mean. But now that you mention it, I haven't hugged your sisters yet."

She grinned as he hugged Shannon and shook hands with Max. Her eyes widened when his hug for Kaitlyn was much more subdued. Kaitlyn cocked her head to the side and studied Brett as he walked away, her brows knit in a tight frown.

Sophie wondered if Kaitlyn sensed the same things within Brett that she had. Kaitlyn seemed very astute and in touch with people's emotions. In that, they were kindred spirits.

But it wasn't her place to pry. She didn't even know Brett McGregor, and she'd make sure to keep her instincts closed where he was concerned. Whatever it was he bore within himself, it wasn't something he wanted people to know about.

She also met two of Lissa's cousins, Sean and Loretta, also part of the wedding party.

"Where are your parents?" she asked Lissa.

"Aidan's mom and dad are picking them up at the hotel. They flew in just this morning."

"How long are they staying?"

Lissa rolled her eyes. "I'm actually surprised they even came, being the busy professional couple they are. They're just going to be here until right after the wedding. Mom has to finish her dress fitting and such, so that's why we're having the rehearsal a couple days before the wedding instead of the night before. So many details and Dad just couldn't get away from the firm soon enough to get them out here too many days before."

"And how are you doing?" she asked Lissa.

"Perversely calm, actually," she said, her gaze flitting to Aidan. "Everything is as it should be."

Sophie felt that, too. "You're right. It's all going to be fine."

Lissa hugged her. "I can't thank you enough for stepping in for Susie. She felt awful about having to drop out, but she's having a really tough time with morning sickness and just didn't think she could handle it."

"It's no problem, as I've told you a hundred times. I'm just honored you thought to ask me."

"Well, you're practically family already, Sophie."

If only that were true. Judging from the daggers shooting from Logan's eyes, she'd never be officially family. She'd done her best to keep her distance from him the past week, despite the intense desire to see him.

Hoping that he'd see the light and come to her, she'd been disappointed when he hadn't called or come by the shop. Her nights had been fitful at best, and she hadn't slept well.

The visions had returned, and were growing stronger. She hadn't shared that with anyone, especially Angelina. The last thing Angelina needed to worry about was some impending disaster right before her son's wedding.

Speaking of Angelina, she strolled through the doors of the church, laughing gaily with a lovely woman about the same age. Introductions were made and Sophie met Lissa's parents.

She'd been there thirty minutes and had spoken to everyone…except Logan, who avoided her like she had some communicable disease. When she moved over to one side of the church, he went to the opposite side.

Really, this was getting ridiculous.

Father John, the parish priest, called everyone to attention and began to give instructions.

"Come on, *belle femme*, let's dazzle them together up the aisle."

Sophie turned and smiled at Brett, then linked her arm in his and walked down to the foyer. Logan, as best man, would be paired with Shannon, the maid of honor. She felt his eyes on her back as they made their way to the church entrance.

Father John explained who would walk first and when, and they began to practice as the organist played music. The men would walk down the aisle with the women, except for Lissa, of course, who would be accompanied down the aisle by her father, while Aidan waited at the altar.

The music began and the parents went down first. Lissa's cousins followed, then Max and Kaitlyn.

Sophie met Brett at the door. He lifted her hand and kissed it, then graced her with a dazzling smile. "Ready, beautiful?"

A quick glance at Logan showed him to be less than pleased with Brett's flirting.

Good. She winked at Brett. "I'm all yours."

They walked slowly down the aisle, then parted as they reached the entrance to the altar. Sophie turned and watched Logan and Shannon walk together.

His jaw was clenched tight and she felt the anger simmering underneath.

But was he angry at her? And why? Because Brett had flirted with her?

Maybe there was hope after all.

Once rehearsal was over, they piled into their cars and headed over to the hotel for dinner.

A private ballroom had been set aside for dinner. She was assigned to sit in between Brett and Max, as they were seated according to their pairings for the wedding. Logan ended up sitting directly across from her at the long table.

Brett held out her chair and she scooted in, trying for a smile in Logan's direction.

Nothing. No smile, barely a nod to acknowledge her.

Yes, he was definitely pissed off.

Well, let him be. She'd done nothing wrong. She'd stayed away from him and he hadn't made a move to see her, which meant he wasn't interested.

And she wasn't the kind to play games to make him jealous, so she was pleasant throughout dinner with both Brett and Max.

"Do you live in New Orleans, Sophie?" Brett asked, refilling her wineglass.

"Yes. I live right outside the city, actually. How about you?"

"Yeah, I live in New Orleans. So, tell me, what do you do for a living?"

She heard Logan's snort and refused to look over at him. "I own a shop in the Quarter. I tell fortunes and provide various items to those who practice magic."

Brett's brows lifted. "No kidding? That sounds great. So, are you magically inclined?"

"You could say so. Do you believe in magic?"

His eyes darkened. "I used to. I don't anymore."

Again, there was the pain she'd sensed within him earlier.

"That's because there's no such thing as magic," Logan added.

Shannon elbowed him in the ribs and Kaitlyn coughed. Sophie didn't respond at all. He was trying to bait her into an argument, and there was no way she'd let herself fall for it.

Fortunately, Galen stood and tapped his water glass with his spoon, gathering everyone's attention.

"To my children, Aidan and Melissa. I wish you happiness, health, and please give me grandchildren before I die."

They all broke out into laughter. Then Logan stood and raised his glass to the couple.

"It is said that love is all sustaining, in both good times and in bad. I know that we've all seen that with the love our parents have for each other. The unconditional love they gave to all of us and have taught us to share with others. May your home be filled with never-ending love, and may the circle of your hearts never be broken."

Sophie was in awe of his words and near tears from the sincerity in his voice. What he'd said felt to her as if he'd spoken from his heart.

Was he acting, or did he truly believe in the power of love? He certainly hadn't yet demonstrated a profound belief in love.

At least not with her.

Maybe that was the problem. Maybe she was the problem. Was she beating her head against an icy, impenetrable wall?

"You're second-guessing yourself again," Angelina whispered when she hugged her.

"Probably. I just don't know, Angelina. He's so...angry."

She shook her head. "A defense mechanism. He's trying to convince himself that he doesn't need you, and to do that he has to find some kind of fault with you. Be patient."

"I'll try."

"Try harder. Go talk to him. You look beautiful tonight."

She grinned. "Thank you. Okay, I'll give it a shot."

Logan didn't see her approach as he listened to Max and Brett engaged in conversation.

She stopped behind him, not sure how to begin or what she'd even say to him.

This was a really bad idea, and she felt stupid.

But then Max and Brett moved away and he turned to her, arching a brow.

"Hey," she said, then mentally kicked herself. *Brilliant opening line, Sophie.*

"Hey. You look...nice."

"Thanks. So do you."

Okay, now they were reduced to polite pleasantries. She had to think of something, and fast.

"I'm surprised you aren't hanging out with Brett. You two seemed to hit it off tonight."

She tilted her head, unsure of what her next move should be. She decided to go with honesty. "Would it matter to you if I did?"

"Do you want to?"

"I asked you first. Would it matter if I did?"

He opened his mouth to speak, then shut it quickly. Finally, he said, "I don't know. Maybe. Brett's not for you, anyway."

"You don't get to decide who's for me and who isn't."

"Trust me, Sophie. He isn't ready for a woman in his life."

"Why not?"

"I can't say. Just trust me. Brett isn't the right man for you."

"Then who is, Logan? Or do you just want me away from everyone you know?"

"Frankly I don't care who you go out with. Just leave Brett alone."

Really, the man was insufferable. "I'm not stalking Brett. I only met him tonight and I was being friendly. Which doesn't mean I want to sleep with him." She stuck her finger in his chest, growing more and more frustrated by her inability to reach him. "But, if I so chose to sleep with him or any other man, it's none of your business."

"Bullshit. I'll make it my business."

Appalled that he'd raised his voice, she quickly glanced around wondering if anyone had heard.

No one had, because they were alone.

Not good. And this was going nowhere fast. She grabbed her purse and coat and headed for the door.

"We're not finished," he said, walking after her.

"Oh yes we are. I'm not going to stay and listen to you insult me, ignore me, then tell me you have a say-so in what men I have in my life."

"I just told you to stay away from Brett."

She stopped and glared at him. "Something you have no right to do."

"I don't want to see any of my friends hurt."

"Do you really think so little of me? Oh, what's the point? You go live your life, Logan, and I'll go live mine. Just stay the hell away from me."

She'd never been so insulted, or so angry. Logan really thought she could do harm to one of his friends. And the whole topic was ridiculous anyway, since she had no attraction or interest in Brett, anyway.

Logan went after her and grabbed her arm, then pulled her toward the elevators. She tugged away from him, but he reached for her again, determination evident in the steely strength of his hold on her upper arm.

Anxious to avoid a scene, she allowed herself to be led along, but whispered her displeasure. "What do you think you're doing?"

"There are a few things I want to get straight with you before you leave tonight."

Chapter Twelve

Logan slipped a key into one of the private elevators and pulled her inside, pressing the button for the penthouse suite.

"I'd really just like to leave now."

"No."

She tapped her foot and crossed her arms, waiting silently while the elevator made it to the penthouse floor. He got out, she didn't.

"Get out, Sophie."

"No. I'm going home." She pressed the button for the lobby, but he stepped back inside and stopped the door from closing. Grabbing her hand, he dragged her off the elevator, his fingers like a steel band around her wrist as he led her inside his suite.

She stood just inside the door as he flipped on the light, then inhaled sharply as she surveyed his apartment.

Wow.

It was huge, and opulent. Fully furnished with antiques of dark cherry wood and rich carpeting like a blanket under her feet.

She was way out of her league here. She couldn't even make herself step out of the foyer and into the living room.

"Quit standing there like you've never seen a penthouse before. It's just a place where I stay because it's in the hotel."

He stepped to the bar and fixed them both a drink, handing one to her as he took a long swallow of his.

Forcing her feet to move, she took the drink from his hand and sipped the brandy, letting it weave a trail of fire into her belly.

"Why am I here?" she asked, desperately trying to understand what he was doing.

He removed his tie and shrugged out of his jacket, tossing them both onto the couch as they stepped into the sunken living room.

She sat on a well-cushioned sofa. Logan positioned himself next to her. Close. So close, in fact, she could smell him, her senses recalling the feel of his skin as he moved against her, the taste of sweat beading on his lip as he took her mouth during a hot, passionate coupling. Her heart began to pound like a driving ocean wave crashing against the shore.

"I just think we need to…finalize things between us. Make sure there's no misunderstanding."

"I agree." She shifted and crossed her legs, then noticed Logan frowning as he watched the movement.

Quickly looking into her eyes, he said, "I want to clear the air between us. I think there are a lot of things that haven't been said, that need to. Especially by me."

"Okay, I'm listening." She inhaled deeply and braced herself, knowing that whatever was coming wasn't going to be pleasant.

Logan's gaze flitted to her breasts, where the deep vee of the halter revealed her cleavage.

This time, his gaze left her breasts slowly, lingered on her neck before meeting her eyes. And this time, his eyes had gone a dark, stormy blue.

In turn, her body began to heat from the inside out. She felt the connection, his growing arousal, and her desire flared to life.

He may not want to be with her, but he *did* want her. That much he couldn't lie to her about. Not when it was so obvious. His erection was outlined clearly against his pants, and she couldn't help the slight smile that curled her lips.

There was nothing more arousing to a woman than a man who clearly desired her. She had no power to make him love her, but she wielded a considerable amount of power as it related to sex.

It wasn't everything she wanted, but it was a start. A very good start.

"Okay, granted, we have chemistry," he said, draining the brandy from his glass. "But…"

She waited, giving him her complete attention. He swallowed, his Adam's apple jutting out as he struggled with the function.

"But, as I was saying…"

"Yes?" She inched closer, closed her eyes, and inhaled his scent. It flowed over her like a warm summer shower. Cool, refreshing, and utterly intoxicating.

"Stop that, Sophie."

Quickly opening her eyes, she asked, "Stop what?"

"Stop doing…that."

"That what?" She'd moved close enough now that their legs brushed. The bottom of her skirt had risen to her thighs. She made no move to adjust it.

He noticed, and swallowed again. Hard.

"Stop…stop…oh, hell." He gathered her in his arms, his movements jerky and rough and filled with desperate passion. A passion he poured into her mouth when his lips ground over hers.

She whimpered and leaned into him, her breasts crushed against his chest, her raging heartbeat keeping time with his.

Sophie moved her arms up over his biceps, feeling the tension, the hesitation, that held him removed from her.

But why? Was he afraid of letting go?

"Don't…hold…back," she murmured against his lips, repositioning herself so that she straddled him.

His eyes had turned dark, icy, filled with a tempestuous storm of emotions as he looked his fill of her. He gripped her hips and thrust upward, driving his erection against her wet pussy.

He shoved the dress over her thighs, over her hips, exposing her naked sex.

"God, I love the way you smell when you're turned on," he said, untying the halter and pulling the dress down. He let his eyes drink in her breasts before taking one hard nipple into his mouth. He swirled his tongue over the inflamed peak, licking at her furiously until she was moaning and tangling her fingers in his hair to draw him closer.

And yet, she still sensed a tension about him.

Her gaze met his. "Logan, give it all to me. I can take it. I need it. Please."

"Anything?" he asked, the heat and promise in his husky voice nearly making her insane.

"Yes. Anything."

With a low growl he lifted her and stood. She wrapped her legs around him and held on tight, breathing him in as he strolled down a long hallway and kicked open a door.

The light came on automatically, soft and muted from the wall sconces.

The bedroom was decorated in golden creamy colors, the bed huge and inviting.

But he didn't deposit her on the bed. Instead, he went into the bathroom and sat her on the expansive marble counter, then flipped on a light.

The room was bathed in mirrors, and she saw herself in various angles.

Logan cast her a hot grin. "I want to watch my cock slide in and out of your pussy. I want everything, Sophie. Are you ready?"

She nodded, her throat gone dry with the thought of what "everything" would encompass. Whatever it was, she'd gladly give it to him.

He stripped the dress from her body, then quickly removed his suit. When he pulled her off the counter, her feet slid into soft, warm carpeting.

Logan took her into his arms and kissed her deeply, his hands roaming over her back. He grabbed her buttocks and drew her against his erection, rubbing his cock against her throbbing clit.

"Logan, please."

"Not yet," he said gruffly. "Watch."

Dropping to his knees, he spread her legs, reaching between them to stroke her slit. Juices poured from her, wetting his questing fingers. He slipped them into his mouth and tasted her, then looked up and smiled.

"Watch me eat you, Sophie."

She glanced at the mirrors, her gaze transfixed as his tongue snaked out and licked her bare sex. When he took her clit in his mouth, she couldn't hold back the whimper of need that filled her.

Being able to see what he was doing took her arousal even higher. Her womb clenched with the need to feel him inside her, to sail over the edge of reason with him.

She stroked his hair, caressing it softly, gently, as his tongue caressed her clit. Resting her feet on his shoulders, she gave him complete access to the most intimate part of her, spreading her legs wide and lifting her hips to feed her pussy to him.

Then she couldn't think any longer, could only watch in rapture as he thrust his tongue inside her slit and lapped up her juices. When she thought she couldn't take any more, he moved to her clit, enclosing his lips around it and sucking the nub into his mouth, at the same time slipping two fingers into her cunt.

"Oh, God, Logan. Oh, God." The first tremors of orgasm built. He thrust his fingers faster and deeper. Her pussy grabbed and held, squeezing them as she fell into oblivion.

She cried out her pleasure and ground her sex against his mouth, offering him her release, which he lapped up greedily.

Before the spasms had completely settled, he flipped her around to face the mirror of the bathroom counter.

Bending forward, she braced her palms on the cool marble, still feeling the aftereffects of her climax pulsing through her.

"Watch," he whispered, then settled between her outstretched legs and plunged his hard cock inside her.

She whimpered, tensed, cried out, then came again at his first thrust.

Snow began to fall. Lightly at first, then harder, cool wind swirling around them as the bathroom became a wintry spectacle of snow, ice and sleet.

Yet she felt no cold, only a blissful relief from the heat surrounding her.

She gasped as Logan filled her, the walls of her cunt clamping down around his shaft.

If she looked to the mirrored side of the wall, she could watch his long cock sliding in and out of her. When he withdrew, his shaft was covered with her slick juices, making it easier to slip back inside, burying himself to the hilt.

Her belly clenched in a spasm of painfully sweet need, the visuals intensifying her pleasure. To be able to see what she felt was an amazing experience. She'd never watched herself get fucked before. It was the most erotic thing she'd ever seen.

Logan reached for her breasts, pinching her nipples, drawing out need that racked her body with spasms so powerful they made her legs quiver.

Who was that woman in the mirror? Her face was flushed, her hair mussed. Snowflakes lay like sparkling glitter in her hair and on her body. It was like being fucked outside.

His face was tight, drawn with intense passion and heat as he drove harder each time. He moved one hand over her hips and lower, teasing between her legs.

His cock filled her, and yet he still slid two fingers inside, pistoning them alongside his shaft, something she'd never felt before.

It felt like two men were fucking her at the same time. She'd never been so filled before, never experienced the heady sensation of having a man's fingers tunnel inside next to his shaft, completely stretching her until she thought she would scream from the exquisite sensations. Her cunt squeezed, her vaginal walls clamping down around his cock and his fingers, readying for a burst of orgasm.

Just as she was primed to fly over the edge, he withdrew his fingers and moistened her anus with her fluids. She glanced at his face, his expression concentrated, determined. He met her gaze and one side of his mouth curled in a wicked grin.

His fingers poised at the entrance to her anus, he asked, "You want this?"

Without hesitation she answered. "Yes."

Logan gently probed the rosette, pushing one finger inside her. She was tight, yet well lubricated with her own juices as he worked his finger in and out, stretching her, readying her. Not once did he stop the thrusting movements of his cock.

The sensation was indescribable as he buried his finger to the hilt in her ass while powering his cock against her in forceful thrusts.

She panted, gripped the sink edge and pushed back against his finger, rewarded with his guttural groan of pleasure.

"Yes, Sophie, I think you like this. Have you ever been fucked in the ass before?"

"No."

"You like my finger in there?"

"Yes," she whimpered, showing him how much she liked it by pushing her ass against his probing finger.

"How about two?"

He withdrew from her anus and reached inside a nearby drawer, fumbling around the condoms until he found the rarely used bottle of lubricant. He spread it on two of his fingers and around her anus, then slipped gently inside her again.

She shrieked and he drove his cock deep. Her legs trembled and she could barely stand.

Still she watched, unable to tear her gaze away from the sight of his cock plunging in and out of her pussy and his fingers disappearing inside her ass.

Snow began to fill the room, creating mini-mountains and slopes along the wall and around them. Thankful for the blissful relief from the burning pleasure scorching her, she scooped a handful and spread it over her breasts, shivering when her nipples puckered.

Logan laughed and did the same, covering his cock with a handful of the white cooling flakes. When he reentered her cunt, she nearly died from the sensations of his cold shaft inside her steaming pussy. She could imagine steam pouring from her as the icicle melted inside her volcano.

Lord, the man made her hotter than she'd ever thought possible.

Now she was filled completely. He pulled his fingers back then thrust again, pushing further and further until he'd slid past the tight barrier, and began to fuck her ass in earnest, rearing back with both his cock and his fingers and driving harder and harder each time.

"Touch yourself for me, Sophie. Let me feel you come."

She reached between her legs and found her clit, circling the bud, swirling her fingers around the tortured button as Logan continued to pummel her with his thrusts.

The tightening began low and intense, then spiraled out of control.

"I'm coming, Logan," she warned, sparks shooting off in her womb as the exquisite sensation burst inside her, flooding his cock and squeezing his fingers as contraction after contraction sent her into a climaxing frenzy.

Tears filled her eyes at the amazing sensations. Logan stopped for a moment, then groaned and spilled shot after shot of hot come into her cunt.

Sophie's legs were shaking, the enormity of what Logan had made her feel washing over her. He withdrew and pulled her into the shower with him, turning on the multiple spraying heads and soaking them both.

He soaped himself and then her, pulling her against his chest and kissing her with heat, with passion, with emotion that brought the tears anew. The slippery soap slickened their bodies until they were gliding against each other, his cock hard against her throbbing sex.

The water turned cold, then icy, as if they bathed in a mountain stream. His hands were icy magic over her breasts, teasing her nipples into tight peaks just begging for his mouth.

Whatever control Logan thought he had over his powers had completely disappeared. Winter surrounded them, and Sophie reveled in it.

Shock filled her as her own desires reignited, and he pushed her against the cool tile wall, lifted one of her legs over his hip, then slipped his cock inside her.

This time he fucked her slowly, his gaze never leaving her face. His eyes grew darker and darker with each climb up the hill of desire.

"Everything, Sophie," he said, dipping down for a kiss, drinking her cries as she climaxed around him, squeezing another orgasm from him as the spasms continued long past the point of reason.

When it was over, he turned off the shower, grabbed one of the oversized bath towels and dried her body and her hair.

The snow was gone, the room enveloped in steamy warmth.

He grabbed a brush and drew it through her wet tendrils, the movements of his hands so gentle over her hair that she relaxed completely. She yawned, finally completely sated.

They stepped toward the bed holding hands, just the way a couple in love would do. Logan pulled the satin coverlet down and slipped underneath the sheets, drawing Sophie against his chest. She wrapped her leg over his hips and within seconds, she was drifting off, more contented than she'd ever been in her life.

She loved him. No matter what happened after tonight, she admitted that she'd completely given her heart to Logan. Nothing would ever change that.

Chapter Thirteen

Sophie weaved her way down the long corridor. A ghostly mist clouded her vision, forcing her to hold on to the wall to feel her way.

She didn't even know where she was going, only that she had to go this way.

Hurry, Sophie.

She heard the words, but didn't know who spoke them. But she knew them as truth.

There wasn't much time.

She made a right turn, then a left. The doors were all white, and the mist prevented her from reading room numbers or even what floor she was on.

Yet she knew where she was going, and followed that instinct.

Her feet were cold. When she looked down, she realized she was only wearing Logan's T-shirt. A hysterical giggle escaped her lips.

What if someone came out of their room and found her like this?

What time was it, anyway?

The pull was stronger now, drawing her toward the end of the hall.

Not much time left, Sophie. Not much time. Hurry.

Faster, that was it. Why wouldn't her legs move faster? She had to get there before it was too late. She had to.

Logan was counting on her. His family was in danger, and this was the moment she'd dreamed of for so long.

Logan, why aren't you here with me? Rubbing her temples, she pushed past the throbbing pain.

Where was Logan?

And how the hell did she get in this hallway?

She swiped at the mist with her hands, as if the very act could clear her vision.

But it didn't.

The floor was cold. Ice cold. Not carpeted. Not comfortable.

And she smelled something. Something that burned her nostrils.

Bleach, maybe?

Her foot connected with something solid, bruising her toe.

"Shit!" Limping along, she followed the trail, refusing to acknowledge the pain in her toe.

Soon, it grew numb, although for some reason she couldn't walk very well.

Straight forward. That's it, you're almost there.

Look down, Sophie. Look down.

She did, but all she could see were the clouds in front of her. Everywhere around her.

Dammit, she needed a fan. Something to blow the white mist away so she could find it.

It.

What was it?

Stop! Now look to your right!

There it was! With a giddy excitement she crouched down and reached for the white box.

No, don't touch it!

Quickly snatching her hands back, she railed in frustration, looking around as if she actually expected someone to be there.

"What the hell am I supposed to do? I have to touch it. I have to stop it."

But nothing was said in response.

Screw it. She was going to find out what it was.

"Stop what?"

Her heart slammed against her chest as the mist cleared and she found herself looking into Logan's confused face.

"Sophie. What the fuck are you doing down here?"

"Huh?" Down where? Where was she? Think, Sophie, think. "I…I don't under…Logan! The box!"

He tilted his head. "Sophie, you were dreaming. Sleepwalking or something. Come on, let's go back upstairs.

His voice was a soothing lifeline, offering her reality and something solid, instead of the dream…

The dream!

"Logan, we have to stop it!"

He gripped her by the arms and hauled her into a standing position. "What the fuck are you talking about? Stop what?"

She tried to pull away, to get to the box. Finally, she heard it. "Dammit, let me go! It's ticking!"

"It's what? What do you mean it's ticking?"

She tried to reach it, but he got to it before she did.

It wasn't even enclosed, just sitting in a plain white box.

And ticking.

"Holy shit. It's a bomb of some kind."

From the hushed tone of his voice, she knew he was right. "Let me see it."

"Fuck no, get back."

She pulled away from him and dropped to the ground. "Don't pull me away! I can stop this!"

"Sophie. Goddammit, we have to get out of here. Christ, my parents, my family is staying here. We have to evacuate the hotel! Now!"

He tried to drag her away. He didn't understand that she knew. She could stop it.

Summoning forth her magic, she pushed him away, putting up an invisible wall so he couldn't try to stop her.

"Sophie! Shit, Sophie we have to get out of here now!"

"No! Don't move!" Without even looking at him, she froze him to the spot.

Thirty seconds. She read the numbers on the clock attached to the bomb.

What was she doing? Logan was right. She didn't know a damn thing about bombs. Her hands began to tremble and nausea rolled within her stomach, threatening to erupt.

Not now. Stay calm. Use your psychic strength.

She heard the voice and nodded, reaching for the wire she knew would be there.

The red one. She had to pull the red wire.

"Sophie! Stop that! Don't touch it, for Christ sake!"

She couldn't listen to him. Closing her eyes and muttering a quick prayer to all that was holy, she yanked the red wire with fifteen seconds to spare.

The clock stopped ticking and she collapsed to the ground, sweat pouring from her body as she realized how close they had come to dying.

All of them.

"It's okay," she managed through shaky breaths as the wall dissolved and Logan dropped to his feet beside her.

She had no strength left. "It's okay, Logan. I stopped it in time."

But she'd almost been too late. "I'm so sorry, Logan. I'm so, so sorry." She'd almost been too damn late to save them.

Blissful darkness enveloped her.

* * * * *

Logan paced the confines of the bedroom, his mother's assurances that Sophie was all right unable to still the anger, the outright fear at what might have happened.

He still didn't understand it, least of all what Sophie had been doing downstairs in the laundry room in the middle of the night. Crouched over a bomb.

The doctor had examined her, pronounced her just fine, but suffering from shock. He'd assured Logan that Sophie would wake soon.

His mother had sat with them for an hour, until he finally convinced her to go back to bed. The rest of the family followed suit.

Fortunately, he'd managed to keep the situation contained. The bomb squad closed the laundry room and removed the box.

He'd answered every question he could for the police, but he had no answers. Tomorrow, the staff would have to be interviewed. He'd given the list of every hotel employee and guest to the police. No one was allowed to enter or leave the hotel until everyone had been interrogated.

Shit. Great PR for the hotel. A bomb nearly exploded. He needed to get Shannon and Max on public relations as quickly as possible. Another mental note to add to the hundreds already fighting for space in his weary brain.

But he still didn't know how a bomb had gotten into his laundry room.

Or who had put it there.

Or how Sophie had managed to find it.

He stared down at her, sleeping like a beautiful angel, her raven hair strewn across her pillow, her lips together in a sleeping pout that he found sexy as hell.

She looked so innocent.

Was she? Or was she as guilty as she'd looked when he'd discovered her downstairs?

Confusion filled him. That, and fear that maybe he didn't want to know the answers she held inside.

She'd tried to stop it, he reminded himself. No matter what, she'd tried to stop it.

Hell, she'd done more than try. She'd done it. She'd known which wire to pull, and she sure as hell was no bomb expert.

Or was she? For all he knew, she was a bomb expert. Or maybe the whole thing had been faked. Maybe the only reason she'd tried to stop it was because he'd caught her in the act of setting the bomb.

Christ, what the fuck did he really know about her?

Not nearly enough. Shit. Not nearly enough.

"Talk to me, Sophie," he whispered, collapsing into a chair next to the bed. "I need some answers. I need the truth."

He needed sleep. And a clear head.

"Logan?"

Sophie's sleepy voice registered and he opened his eyes, wincing at the crick in his neck.

How long had he been asleep?

He blinked, frowning at the full sunlight streaming into the room.

"Hey, you awake in there?"

The sound of his mother's voice registered, too.

She smiled as she entered, then her face beamed as she looked at Sophie.

"You're awake, *ma belle! Bonjour*! We were all so worried about you."

Sophie reached for her forehead. "I get a bit forgetful after…after…"

"A vision?" his mother finished for her.

"Yes. Sorry." She sat up and stretched, her breasts outlined against his T-shirt. Logan tried not to notice.

"Give me a minute and it'll come back to me."

"Nonsense. You have plenty of time." His mother turned to him. "I've ordered coffee and croissants. They're out in the kitchen."

"Thanks, Mom," Logan said, wondering if Angelina had the same suspicions as he had.

His mother sat on the bed. "You saved my family, this hotel, and everyone here. Thank you."

Sophie's eyes widened. "The bomb. Oh my God, the bomb! Is it disabled?"

"Yes, it is. You did it."

"I did?"

"Yes, *cher*. You did it."

Tears streamed down Sophie's cheeks and she threw her arms around his mother. Then they both cried tears of joy.

Logan didn't feel joy, though.

He still had questions. Questions he couldn't believe no one had thought to ask.

"How did you know the bomb was in the laundry room, Sophie?"

She stilled, and both she and his mother turned to gape at him.

"What?"

"You heard me. How did you know?"

"Logan, I've told you about the visions."

"Uh-huh. Which doesn't have a damn thing to do with the fact that not only did you slip out of my bed in the middle of night, but I followed you to the laundry room and watched you disable the bomb. What, did you have second thoughts about blowing up the hotel?"

His mother's eyes turned a stormy black. "Logan Storm! How dare you!"

"Oh come on, Mother," he said, refusing to believe Sophie's wide-eyed look of shock. "Didn't anybody wonder how she knew the bomb's location, or how she knew that pulling the red wire would disable the timer? Or am I the only one who made that connection?"

"Logan, I had nothing to do with that bomb. I wasn't even awake when I went downstairs. At least, not in the way you think. My visions, my magic, told me where it was, led me to it, and showed me how to disable it."

He crossed his arms, more convinced than ever that he was right. "Right. How convenient. Your magic."

"Logan, this is outrageous!" his mother objected. "How dare you treat Sophie this way! She saved our lives!"

"Yeah, she did, and wasn't that convenient? Here she is now, the family hero, ingratiating herself even further with the entire Storm clan. You played it perfectly, didn't you?"

Sophie didn't respond, just stared at him, open-mouthed, as if she couldn't believe what he'd said.

"My family might be blind to your lies, Sophie. But I'm not. In fact, I'm sure the police would like to know what a little bomb-maker you really are."

"Bomb-maker?"

"That's right. You made the bomb. You were going to blow up the hotel, or at least make sure I'd find you just as you disabled it. Yeah, your dramatic show was pretty good. I'll give you that much. But I think you orchestrated this whole thing, from start to finish."

"That's enough, Logan," his mother warned, then turned to Sophie. "Please do not think for a moment that any of us believe what he says."

"It's okay, Angelina," Sophie said, her voice so soft he barely heard her. "I think I know exactly what Logan means."

She slipped off the bed and reached for the black dress. "If you'll excuse me, I'd really like to go home now. Angelina, would you mind calling me a taxi?"

"Of course, *cher*." His mother glared at him, and stormed from the room muttering about how she didn't blame Sophie for not wanting to spend another moment in Logan's apartment.

He stood there, unable to believe his mother was simply going to let her walk.

When she came out of his bathroom, she smoothed the dress and stopped in front of him. "I'll be at my shop if the police are looking to talk to me."

She turned away and left, shutting the door quietly behind her.

His mother hadn't left, though. In fact, his father had entered the apartment and was engaged in quiet conversation with her. Galen looked up and glared angrily at Logan.

"Are you daft, boy? What possessed you to accuse the little colleen of trying to harm us?"

Even his father had fallen for her lies. "The evidence is clear."

"Evidence. Bah! She saved your ass, son. Hell, she saved us all."

"Your father is right, Logan," Angelina said, anger clear in the dark fury of her eyes. "I understand your reluctance to let anyone into your heart. God knows I've tried my best to help you understand and embrace your magic. If you were open enough to the gift you have, you'd know already that Sophie was innocent. We all know it, because we feel it. You keep yourself closed off and remote from us as if we're all lepers and you're afraid you'll be infected. Well, no more, Logan. I'm ashamed to call you my son."

Tears pooling in her eyes, Angelina hurried from the room.

His father stepped toward him and shook his head. "And I'm ashamed to call you a Storm. Grow up, son."

His father didn't leave as quietly. The sound of the door slamming echoed down the empty hallway.

Shit! How had he become the bad guy here?

And he still hadn't gotten any goddamn answers. She'd left fast enough, no doubt because she hadn't developed her lies yet.

Well, he'd see her, and demand the answers he sought.

Because he wasn't wrong here. He wasn't, no matter what his parents said.

Chapter Fourteen

"Good lord, Sophie, you could have been killed!"

"No shit, honey. What the hell were you thinking going after that bomb?"

Sophie looked to both Sam and Josh and shrugged. "I did what I had to do."

She hadn't told them about Logan, about his accusations that she had planted the bomb.

It just hurt too much to even think about it, and yet his angry words resounded over and over in her mind. Swiping away the tears, she tried for a smile.

"Honey, what's wrong?" Sam asked, wiping a tear away with her thumb.

What would she do without her two best friends?

"I...I can't talk about it."

"Come on, Soph," Josh urged, wrapping his arm around her shoulder. "You can lean on us. That's what we're here for."

The tears flowed freely as she allowed herself to feel the miserable sensations living within her. "Logan," she managed. "He thought I did it."

"What?" Sam said, her eyes widening. "That's insane!"

"Why in the hell would he think that?" Josh asked, his words biting, anger evident and growing. "I told you he was an asinine prick."

"Well he did find me in the room with the bomb. And I knew how to disconnect the timer. In some ways I can understand that."

"But if he loved you, if he knew you like we do, he'd know there's no way you could do something like this," Sam said.

They were right. He should have known. But he didn't believe her, didn't believe in her.

Didn't love her.

Both Sam and Josh accepted what she'd done without asking for explanation. Because they knew her. More importantly, they trusted her.

She'd never had Logan's trust. And she never would. From the first time he'd met her, he thought she was trying to deceive him and his family, and he'd go on thinking that no matter what she said or did.

"I need to go home." She wanted a shower, a change of clothes and needed to spend a few hours letting out the pain she'd been holding inside since she left the hotel.

She stood, but Josh wouldn't let her go. "I'll take you home. Sam, can you watch over the shop today?"

"Of course." Sam hugged her and said, "Go, get some rest. We'll talk later."

She nodded and let Josh lead her out to his car. The drive home was quiet, and fortunately Josh didn't press for details of her conversation with Logan. He followed her inside and said he'd make some tea while she took a shower.

It felt good to wash away the day before, at least physically. Mentally and emotionally...that was going to take some time and effort. Donning a pair of sweats and a loose shirt, she slipped through the beads and curled up on the sofa. Josh had a hot cup of herbal tea ready and sat down next to her.

She sipped the tea, knowing he was expecting her to talk about Logan. But she couldn't. Talking meant thinking about it, and his accusations were still prominent in her mind. What she needed was to push them away, not talk about them so they'd hover nearby.

Josh smoothed the wet tendrils of her hair and pulled her closer. Admittedly, it felt good to be comforted, to know that she had at least two people in her life who truly believed in her.

"I warned you about him," he said, kissing the top of her head.

She let out a small laugh. "That you did."

"I could kill that sonofabitch for hurting you like this, Soph."

Holding the tears at bay, she looked up at him. "I appreciate that, Josh. But I knew what I was getting into with Logan. He was honest with me, told me he didn't trust me, didn't care for me. Yet I stupidly believed I could change his feelings."

"Just because you knew where the bomb was, and how to cut the red wire doesn't mean you planted it there. God, doesn't he know about your magic?"

"I guess not. He just assumed..." Wait. Something was wrong here. Sophie stilled, her mind trying to process what Josh had just said.

No, she was wrong. She must have mentioned the red wire somewhere in her explanations, right? Forcing herself to remember the short conversation she'd had with both Josh and Sam at the shop, it occurred to her she'd never really given details to either of them, and it was way too soon for any police or news reports to be out.

She gently pushed away from Josh's chest and sat up, not wanting to ask the question, not wanting the suspicions that had crept into her mind. "Josh, how did you know about the red wire on the bomb?"

He frowned. "Huh?"

"The red wire. You said that I had known to cut the red wire."

"Right. So?"

"I didn't tell anyone about the wire, or the color. So how could you know?"

He smiled. "Honey, you must have told us. Otherwise, how could I have known?"

"I don't know." She was being silly. What the hell would Josh know about any of this?

"Trust me, Sophie. I didn't know a damn thing. You must have told us."

"I guess so." She rubbed her forehead, a giant-sized headache forming. "I'm sorry, Josh. I'm just wigged out by all of this, I guess."

"Delayed shock, probably. Go get some rest. I'll hang out here and we can talk when you've had some sleep."

She nodded, grateful to have him here watching over her. Climbing into the bed, she pulled her favorite blanket over her and stared out at the bright sunlight pouring through the window.

Figured. She couldn't sleep. She slipped out of bed and peered through the beaded drape. Josh had settled in on the couch, turned on the television and was sound asleep.

Something she should be doing.

But for some reason she couldn't shake the fact that she knew she hadn't mentioned the red wire. Why was she obsessing over this, anyway? She'd known Josh since they were kids, trusted him and Sam above everyone.

It had to be shock.

Still, the niggle of doubt wouldn't go away. Giving up, she picked up the phone in her bedroom and dialed the shop. Sam answered.

"Hey, quick question. What details did I give you about the bomb I found?"

"Details? None, other than you disabled it. And I'm dying to know. Why? Are you ready to tell me about it?"

Her hands began to shake as the realization hit.

No. Oh, God, no.

"Soph? What's wrong?"

She wasn't going to tell Sam about this. Not yet. Not until she'd had a chance to talk to Josh. "Nothing. I'm just tired. I'm gonna get some rest, Sam. Talk to you later."

Before Sam could ask any more questions, she hung up, curled into a ball on the bed and closed her eyes, wishing she could shut out the knowledge that pounded at her.

Josh knew. There was only one way Josh could know.

"Why couldn't you have just left it alone, Sophie?"

She shrieked at the sound of Josh's voice. Quickly sitting up, she saw him leaning in the doorway to her bedroom.

He'd heard her on the phone with Sam!

"Josh, I—"

"Save it," he said, stepping into the room and stopping at the foot of the bed. "You don't understand."

"Don't understand what?"

Jamming his fingers into his long hair, he moved to the side of the bed. "What it's been like to stand by all these years and wonder when you're going to open your eyes and see what's right in front of you."

He crouched on the floor and took her hands in his. His felt heated, hers were like ice.

"I don't understand. Please tell me what's going on."

A madness glimmered in his eyes. Madness, and a dark magic she'd never seen within him before. How could she have missed it all these years?

"What's going on? Sophie, I love you. I've loved you since we were kids. I'm the right man for you, but you keep making stupid mistakes with men who don't deserve you. Then I have to help you pick up the pieces when pricks like Logan Storm stomp all over your heart."

This wasn't the first time Josh had opened his heart to her. "Josh, we've been through this before."

He squeezed her fingers, pain shooting in them as he tightened his grip. She winced, but he didn't notice, his gaze never wavering from her face. "You don't listen, Sophie. I had to do something to save you."

"Save me?"

"Yeah. Logan was all wrong for you. And his family, too. You don't need them. You only need me."

She closed her eyes for a second, summoning the courage to ask the question she was afraid to get the answer to. "Josh, did you plant that bomb?"

He smiled. "Of course I did."

Every drop of blood in her body drained away, leaving a cold emptiness inside. "Oh Josh, how could you? Do you realize what could have happened if that bomb had gone off? Everyone in that hotel could have died!"

He smirked. "I know. That was my intent. That was the vision you've been thinking about." He tried to pull her closer, but she recoiled, scooting away. His hands clenched into fists. "Soph, you have to know that I didn't plan on you being there. You know I'd never hurt you, honey!"

Nausea rolled her stomach and she wrapped her arms across it, hoping she wouldn't throw up. Tears pooled and splashed onto her cheeks. "I don't understand, Josh. This isn't like you. God, what were you thinking?"

Suddenly the Josh she'd known all these years vanished. He stood, straightening, seemingly growing taller before her. Light shone in his eyes. Evil light that seemed to travel slowly from him to her, reaching out in ways that made her fear him for the first time in her life.

"You really have never taken a look inside me, Sophie. All these years, and you never bothered to figure out who and what I am. It's about damn time you opened your eyes, don't you think?"

No. She didn't want to see, didn't want to know *this* Josh. She wanted the old Josh back, the one who had been her friend for life. Hell, he'd been her family. How could she have been so wrong about him?

How could she not have seen what he was? Where had her magic failed her?

He curled his finger under her chin, forcing her gaze to meet his. "Don't beat yourself up about me, love. You didn't know because I didn't let you know. My magic is much stronger than yours."

That she refused to believe.

"Oh, believe it," he answered as if he'd dipped into her thoughts. "I thought I was exactly what you needed. So I waited. Waited, for you to come to me, to love me. Instead, you told me you didn't feel 'that way' about me. Do you know how hard it was for me not to take you right then and there? To force the issue and make you mine whether you liked it or not? Do you know how goddamned long I've been waiting for you to realize you're meant to be with me?"

His grip on her chin tightened. She closed her eyes and summoned her magic, needing to put a wall between them, to get away from him.

Nothing happened. She tried again, forcing herself to concentrate.

"Give it up, Sophie. Your powers aren't shit compared to mine."

Her eyes whipped open and she glared at him. "You're sick, Josh. You need help."

He laughed and dragged her up against him. "I don't need help, Sophie. I love what I am, what I've always been. And I've given you years to come to me. I'm not waiting one fucking minute longer."

Wrapping his arms around her, he crushed her to him, his mouth descending on hers.

He grabbed her buttocks, grinding his hard cock against her sex. Revulsion filled her.

She gagged at the invasion of his long tongue, feeling his evil entering her. She fought, putting up a wall of resistance, using every aspect of her powers to fight him off.

He growled low in his throat, rocking against her, mimicking the sex act.

Sex weakened a man, no matter whether he was mortal or something else. She couldn't quite put a finger on his evil, but she knew if he pushed her like this, if he tried to rape her, he'd have to give up some of his power.

And she'd continue to fight him. This wasn't the Josh she had known. Whoever he was now, he represented a danger. Not just to her, but to Logan, to the entire Storm family.

To everyone.

Josh had to be stopped, starting with her. And no matter what she had to give up, she *would* stop him.

He might take her physically, but he'd never get what he really wanted.

Her soul.

Chapter Fifteen

Logan fought internal demons as he stood outside Sophie's shop. Passersby bumped him in their hurry to move down the street, but he didn't budge. Just stood there and looked at the store window, wondering for the hundredth time in the past fifteen minutes what the hell he was doing there.

He should just let it go, but he couldn't. There was something about what happened that didn't sit right with him, and he needed answers.

Answers from Sophie.

The bell over the door jingled as it opened. His gaze flitted to the doorway, expecting to see Sophie's face.

But it was her partner, Samantha.

"What are you doing here?" she asked, frowning.

He didn't know. What *was* he doing there?

"You gonna stand there and stare at the window all day or what?

Maybe.

Okay, maybe not. He walked toward her, feeling her heated anger the closer her drew toward the door. "I need to talk to Sophie."

"Tough shit. She doesn't need to talk to you."

"I didn't ask you." He stepped as close as he could without actually touching her. "Get out of my way. I need to talk to Sophie."

"She's not here."

While he admired Samantha's protective nature, she was in his way. "Bullshit. Now move, please, or I'll move you myself."

Heaving a disgusted sigh, Samantha turned and headed back into the shop. Logan stepped in and looked around.

No sign of Sophie. She wasn't there. Obviously she didn't want to talk to him.

Too bad. He moved through the beaded entrance to the magic room, but it was empty, too.

So was the storeroom.

Hell, she really wasn't here.

"Where is she?"

"You lost the right to know anything about her when you accused her of trying to blow up your hotel. Were you born a moron, Logan, or did you have to work extra hard to perfect it?"

"Look, Samantha, I can appreciate your 'protect the friend' persona, but I really need to talk to her. So cut the crap and tell me where she is."

"She's with Josh," Samantha said, a perversely satisfied smirk on her face.

"Josh. That...boy who works here?"

"If you say so. But then again, she's with him right now, not you, and he'll take good care of her. He always has and always will."

Always has and always will. Logan shook the feeling of dread from his head. Bullshit magic anyway. "Never mind, I'll find her later."

"Not if Josh has anything to say about it."

He pulled hard at the front door and stormed out, heaving a breath as he stood at the sidewalk trying to get his bearings.

Something was wrong.

Danger.

Help me, Logan, please.

Logan flinched as pain rocked his stomach, fire burning within him.

Shit! What the hell was going on?

Something *was* wrong.

With Sophie.

She was in danger.

How the fuck he knew that to be true was beyond his ability to even want to fathom. But he knew it.

Trouble.

Josh.

Her trailer.

Goddamit! He tore down the street and jumped into his car, throwing it in gear and speeding away from the curb as if his life depended on it.

His didn't.

Sophie's did. He had to get to her trailer fast.

* * * * *

Sophie finally managed to summon enough magic to fling Joshua away from her.

But he only laughed.

"Nice try, babe, but I'm way stronger than you."

Anger filled her as she leaped across the bed trying to avoid his advance. She summoned up her ancestors. Their strength was needed. She couldn't do this alone.

Please, please help me. I need your power, the power of what is right, what is pure. I need the light of the moon to defeat this darkness, the might of the heavens to send it back to hell where it belongs.

"I'm taking what's mine, what I should have taken years ago." Josh held up his hands. "The fires of hell surround me, their power and might stronger than light."

He had her backed into a corner with no way out. This was really, really bad.

And bad had just gotten worse. Flames shot out from his fingertips, lighting the ends of his hair, and burning his clothes as he burst into an inferno.

The heat blasted against her. The room was so small, the trailer so small.

They'd be toast in no time.

Her blankets blazed, the trail of flames inching toward her.

She closed her eyes, refusing to give in to the fear, knowing she needed her strength now more than ever.

A wall of protection surrounded her, but Joshua's power beat against hers. She had bought herself a little time, that's all.

Very little.

* * * * *

Logan barely tapped on the brakes before he threw the car into park and leapt out. Smoke filtered out through the kitchen windows.

He tasted fear.

And angry hatred.

Time was running out.

He flung open the door and hurried inside. A blast of heat and flame barricaded the bedroom.

Without another thought he called forth the elements, bringing a blinding rain into the trailer, dousing the flaming wall and allowing him entry into the room.

Sophie was in a corner, her face pale, her eyes closed. He sensed her concentration as her magic protected her from the whirling blaze that he assumed was Josh.

The flame turned, angry bursts of fireballs shooting in his direction as loud piercing wails followed suit.

Obviously Josh was not happy to see him. Logan held up his hands and washed away the fireballs. "Let go of her motherfucker — now — and I might just let you live."

A sick, twisted laugh greeted him. "You're too late, Storm. She's mine!"

"I don't think so." Undaunted, he brought his full powers into the fight. Ice, rain, sleet, snow, and biting, arctic winds. Once he'd summoned them all, he stepped into Joshua's circle of fire, determined to come out of this the victor.

The ice of winter mixed with the hottest fires of hell as they battled within an invisible circle. Logan lost sight of reality and his surroundings, concentrating only on making sure he pulled every ounce of magic he possessed into the fray.

Josh was strong. Very strong.

But Logan was strong too, and had years of pent-up magic to release. Anger, frustration and a desperate fear for Sophie's life spurred him on. He hated his magic, had always hated that it made him different. But right now he was damn glad he possessed it, because it just might save them both.

Despite the burning hands reaching for his throat, trying to squeeze his life away, he held on, refusing to give up.

"You sonofabitch!" Josh cried, then the flames surrounding him began to dissipate. Slowly, at first, and then rapidly as Josh became human again and collapsed, shivering as an icy cube surrounded his charred body. He was still alive, barely.

But not for long.

Logan raced to Sophie, heedless of the flames tearing through her trailer.

Whatever barrier she'd put up collapsed as soon as he approached. Her eyes widened and she began to cough, tears streaming down her ash-streaked face as she sucked in the smoke.

Logan didn't pause to say anything to her, just picked her up into his arms and carried her through the fire, dousing it around them with a cold, protective rain.

She hung limp in his arms. As he stepped outside, she closed her eyes and lost consciousness.

He felt her pulse, which was thready, rapid one second, slowing the next. He had to get her to a hospital.

Gently depositing her in his car, he backed away from the inferno that was once her trailer, his fierce anger fading somewhat as he took comfort in the fact that Josh was still inside.

The evil was gone. He felt it. Back to hell or wherever it had come from. Now he had more pressing things to worry about, like making sure Sophie survived.

* * * * *

Sophie woke to the sound of voices. Unfamiliar voices. She was cold, her body trembling violently.

And her throat hurt so damn badly it brought tears to her eyes. The fact she really needed to cough didn't help either.

Forcing her eyes open, she blinked against the harsh lights, taking in her surroundings.

The hospital. Emergency room. A nurse came over and smiled, adjusting the mask that delivered sweet, pure oxygen to her lungs. "Miss Breaux. You're going to be fine. A little smoke inhalation and a few small burns, but otherwise you were very lucky."

Lucky. Right. It all came back to her. Joshua, her trailer, the fact that he was some sort of demon and she'd never, ever known that. How stupid could she be?

Tears pooled and fell and she shamelessly wept for the man who had been her friend since childhood. There had to have been goodness in Joshua. He couldn't have been completely evil, or she would have felt it. She was sure of it. But something happened to him along the way, something that triggered this. Sadly, she knew what it was.

Because she couldn't love him. Not like she loved Logan.

Lying there on the bed and staring up into the lights, Sophie had to smile at the irony. Josh loved her, but she couldn't return that love. And she loved Logan, who didn't love her back.

What a mess.

No, a nightmare.

"You have a few people waiting outside to see you," the nurse said. "Feel up to visitors?"

She nodded while the nurse pressed the remote and moved the bed so she could sit up. Waiting, hands clasped, she wondered if Logan was still here. Her memories were still a little fuzzy, but she did recall him carrying her out of the fire.

Blinking the tears back, she refused to dwell on what she couldn't change.

The curtain drew aside and Logan stepped in, followed by his parents and Samantha. Samantha ran over and hugged her.

"Oh, God, Soph, I had no idea," Samantha said, tears streaming down her face. Her friend squeezed her tight.

Sophie coughed and shook her head. "I didn't, either. None of us did, Sam. It's nobody's fault. Joshua just hid it well."

Angelina pressed a kiss to the top of her head and held her hand. "Some magic is discernable. Some isn't. Your friend was very powerful. You're lucky to be alive."

"I know." If it wasn't for Logan's heroics, she wouldn't be. She turned to him, offering a smile. "You saved my life. Thank you."

His expression was unreadable, but she sensed a tension within him. "And you saved my family's life. I'm sorry I couldn't save your trailer."

She didn't care about possessions. Things meant nothing to her. "Is Josh…"

"Dead? Yeah. And I've talked to the police, explained that Josh set the bomb in the hotel and then went to your trailer and tried to kill you, but we fought and he died in the fire. That's all they know."

She bent her head, studying her fingers, unable to even summon up a happy response that Logan finally believed she hadn't planted the bomb. "Thank you." Then she turned to Angelina and Galen. "I'm so sorry about Josh and the bomb. I had no idea."

Angelina rubbed her arm. "Quit worrying about that, *cher*. Everyone is fine. You meant us no harm, which we knew anyway." She pointedly glared at Logan. Obviously Angelina was still angry that Logan had thought Sophie had planted the bomb. "Now, we want you to stay in one of the suites at the hotel until we can find you a new place to live."

"She can stay with me," Sam said, inching onto the edge of the bed and taking Sophie's other hand.

"No, she stays at the hotel."

They all looked at Angelina. "I wouldn't sleep if I couldn't repay you in some way for all you've been through. We have a doctor on staff at the hotel who can check in on you regularly, and we'll all come and visit."

"Thank you, Angelina, but I couldn't take up space for one of your paying guests."

"Don't be silly," Galen added. "We'd really like you to stay at the hotel."

Angelina nodded. "You'll be pampered. Sam, you can come stay with her. Think of it as a vacation."

Sophie looked to Sam, who shrugged. "Sure, why not? Change of scenery is always a good thing."

"Good. It's settled then. Logan, bring her to the hotel when she's released. Now you rest and we'll get out of here." Angelina kissed her, as did Galen, then they left.

Sam said, "Are you sure this is okay with you?"

Sophie nodded. "It's fine. We'll have fun together."

"Okay, honey. I'm going to go finish up things at the shop. When Logan called and told me what happened, I just ran like hell out of there and only locked the door. It's a mess and I need to close up. I'll pack some clothes. You and I can wear the same stuff until we can get you some new ones."

Sam hugged her, then stopped in front of Logan, taking his hands in hers. "You saved my best friend's life. I'm in your debt."

Logan nodded and Sam left.

Uncomfortable silence filled the small room. Sophie laced her fingers together and stared at them, not sure what she and Logan had left to say to each other.

"The doctor says you can be released in about an hour. I'm going to go make arrangements. I'll be back soon."

She nodded and watched him leave. A strange emptiness filled her.

She'd lost Josh, someone she had thought of as family.

And she never had Logan to begin with, but his polite, amiable manner towards her told her that he wanted nothing more to do with her.

In the blink of an eye, she'd once again lost two people she loved.

Life would never be the same.

* * * * *

Logan had been wrong, on so many counts.

He flipped the cell phone closed and slid it into his pocket, pacing the hallways of the hospital like a caged animal desperate for release.

Yeah, he was desperate to get away all right. Desperate to get away from himself.

He'd been wrong about Sophie's motives, her magic, her reasoning for seeking him out. Then, instead of gratitude he'd accused her of criminal acts. Acts that she hadn't been responsible for.

Which had led her right to Josh. And Josh had almost killed her. If Logan had taken her, claimed her, he doubted Josh would have done anything to stop him. While the bastard was powerful, he wasn't stronger than Logan, and Logan would bet that Josh knew that from the moment they met.

Then again, if it hadn't turned out this way, then his family would have continually been in danger.

What a goddamn clusterfuck.

Which was why they shouldn't be together. He didn't trust her, and didn't trust his own instincts around her. She could have died because he was more worried about protecting his cold heart than he was about protecting Sophie.

That ended here and now. After she recovered, after she'd had some time to rest, he'd go to her, reason with her and tell her they could never be together.

He laughed. Right. Like she'd even want anything to do with him after what he'd put her through. After accusing her of trying to blow up the hotel, she probably hated him right now, which really solved all their problems.

Or at least would solve hers. She needed much more than what he could give her. She needed a man's trust, someone who embraced her magic, the wonderful gifts she gave to those she loved. She'd tried to give those gifts to him and he'd thrown them back in her face.

He didn't deserve her.

If she despised him, she'd no longer insist they were meant to be together. She'd stop seeing him, hounding him, making him want her, need her, desire her in ways he'd never desired another woman.

She'd go her way, and he'd go his.

And he'd never see her again.

Why did that thought offer no comfort?

Chapter Sixteen

Sophie adjusted the pearls around her neck and tried to focus on the bride, not her nervousness at seeing Logan today.

It had been a week since the fire, and she hadn't seen him once. After her release from the hospital, he'd driven her silently to the hotel and delivered her into the arms of his mother. Between Angelina and Sam, she'd kept busy, mostly trying to convince both of them that she was fine and felt no harmful effects from the fire.

Her healing powers were above average anyway, and with the herbs and potions from her shop, the minor burns were already gone.

Yes, she'd lost her trailer and all her possessions, but what did stuff matter, anyway? Although she felt guilty staying at the hotel without paying, something Angelina assured her was no problem at all. In fact, if Angelina had her way, she'd move into one of the penthouse apartments at the top of the hotel.

Permanently.

Which wasn't going to happen, of course. She was surprised Logan hadn't already tried to evict her.

"You're not supposed to be frowning on my wedding day."

She looked up into Lissa's smiling face. "I wasn't." At her pointed look, she said, "Okay, maybe I was. And you're right. How are you feeling?"

Lissa grinned. "Ready as I'll ever be. Lord, this has been a whirlwind. I'll just be glad when it's over. I'm ready for some warm sand, ocean-lit water and five days worth of sex and mayhem."

Sophie laughed, her heart filled with joy and love for Lissa and Aidan. Much as she'd rather begin the process of distancing herself from this family she'd grown to love, today was not the day.

Regardless of Logan's determination to keep his distance, they'd have to occupy the same space today. She had to deal with it, he could too.

"You look beautiful."

"Thank you," Lissa said, a blush staining her cheeks.

Lissa was gorgeous in her full white gown; satin, pearls and tulle took up at least half the room. Her blonde hair had been swept into an updo, and small ringlets framed her face. Her blue eyes sparkled with love, brightening her whole face. Truly, she was a beautiful bride. "Aidan is one lucky man. I hope he never forgets that."

"Not that we'd let him," Shannon said, coming up and giving Sophie a quick hug. "And you don't look too bad yourself."

Sophie laughed. She actually felt pretty today. Being in the company of the Storm family always made her glow with happiness. Besides, who wouldn't feel gorgeous in the bridesmaid's dress? Off-the-shoulder lavender velvet hugged her body, the sleeves ending in a wide bell at the wrist and the straight skirt slit up one side. She just hoped the low neckline wasn't too low. The long string of pearls dipped into her cleavage. Then again, Lissa picked out the dresses, so they had to be okay. She just wasn't used to showing as much skin as she was in this dress. They'd barely had to alter the dress since she was the same size as the girl who was originally going to be in the wedding.

The next hour was spent in preparation for the event. The church was beautifully decorated, and Lissa peeked out now and then to see the people piling in. Sophie felt way out of her element here, and more than a little nervous at seeing Logan again.

Finally, it was time. They gathered in the lobby of the church. Bridesmaids, groomsmen and Lissa's father all arrived.

Sophie caught sight of Logan and her breath halted. Lord, he was beautiful in a tux. The man looked like a born and bred aristocrat no matter what he wore, but when he dressed up like this, he literally took her breath away.

As if he felt her staring at him, he turned his head. He didn't smile, didn't frown, his expression giving nothing away of his feelings.

He'd gotten pretty good at masking them, too, because she couldn't feel him. Maybe too many other emotions swirled through the lobby right now.

It didn't matter anyway. Today was Lissa and Aidan's day, and she'd simply have to push her feelings for Logan aside.

The music started and the long walk down the aisle began.

"You ready, partner?" Brett asked as he stepped next to her.

Refusing to dwell on the pain, she smiled brightly. "Ready as I'll ever be."

The wedding went off without a single mishap. The glowing white aura around Aidan and Lissa was so bright she almost had to turn away. Love filled the church. Sophie shed a few tears as Aidan and Lissa recited their vows, promising to love each other forever.

She couldn't help but glance at Logan while those words of love were exchanged, wondering why commitment came so easily to some while it was so incredibly difficult for others. In her heart, she knew she and Logan belonged together. But she couldn't do anything about the fact that he didn't return her feelings.

Unrequited love sucked. Even though Josh hadn't been who she thought he was, she felt a new sense of empathy for how he'd felt about her. He had loved her, back when he was a different person, and she hadn't been able to love him back.

Would she feel this miserable for the rest of her life?

Shaking off the melancholy, she smiled brightly when Father John pronounced Aidan and Melissa husband and wife. Aidan swept his new bride into a passionate kiss, lingering so long that Father John had to clear his throat to pull them apart.

"Ladies and gentlemen," Father John announced. "I'd like to introduce you to Mr. and Mrs. Aidan Storm."

A huge round of applause echoed throughout the church. They stayed afterward and took what seemed like hundreds of pictures. The entire time, Sophie felt Logan's gaze on her, yet she refused to look at him again.

What was the point? After the wedding reception she'd go back to her job, find a new place to live, and start her life again. She wasn't the type of person to pine over someone who didn't care for her, and there was no reason to beat her head against an impenetrable wall.

She'd tried to win his love, and failed. It was time to move on.

They left the church and rode in limos to the hotel. The main ballroom was decorated in lavender and cream, paper bells, balloons and streamers draped along the rafters and walls. The band began to play as Aidan and Lissa entered. Sophie walked in with Brett, and they were required to dance the first official bridal party dance.

Brett held her close, smiling at her the entire time. Yet she sensed turbulent emotions flowing through him. Happiness, yet a tragic sadness that tugged at her heart.

"You like weddings?" she asked.

He shrugged. "They're fine for other people. How about you?"

"Yeah, I have to admit that I really do like them. But I'm a sucker for romance."

Brett laughed. When he laughed, he relaxed, and some of that dark aura that surrounded him dissipated. She wished she could help him, but there never seemed to be a right time to ask him what made him seem so unhappy on the inside.

Quit trying to save everyone, Sophie. You can't do it. Leave him alone.

Deciding to take her own advice, she let Brett whirl her around the dance floor and tell her jokes. Laughing out loud made her feel much better anyway.

* * * * *

"Logan, you're squeezing the breath out of me!"

Logan blinked and looked down at a glaring Shannon. "Sorry."

He'd been so busy keeping watch over Sophie and Brett that he'd hardly been aware he was dancing with his sister. The way Brett held her close, the easy way he made her laugh out loud, shouldn't irritate him.

But it did. Big time.

"Why don't you just go talk to her? Ask her to dance."

"She's dancing with Brett."

"So what? Go cut in. You two have unfinished business."

He rolled his eyes. Like every member of his family hadn't already told him that. Twice. "Leave it alone, Shannon."

"Oh, please. Look who's talking. As if I'd had any choice when the family was trying to push me into Max's arms."

"Seems to me I recall you going quite willingly."

He winced when she stomped on his foot. "Dickhead."

"Love you too, sis."

She laughed. "Seriously. You love her. She loves you. You belong together. What's the big damn deal?"

He turned his gaze from Sophie to his sister. "I hurt her, Shannon. Do you know how much I hurt her by not believing in her? What kind of a man does that make me? Do you think she even wants me in her life after the things I said to her?"

"We women can be extremely forgiving. Look at all of us. We love you, despite the fact you're an overbearing, cold-hearted, anal-retentive pain in the ass."

He arched a brow. "You're so sweet. Stop. I'm blushing."

Grinning, she said, "That just means I love you and you know it. Now quit acting like such a baby and go talk to her."

"When I want advice, Shannon, I'll be sure not to ask you. Now let it go."

She shook her head. "You're going to end up old and alone, Logan. And cranky as hell. I swear to God if you get any grouchier with old age, one of us will have to smother you in your sleep."

"Ah, nothing like seeing my children get along so well."

Logan turned to his mother, who looked radiant as usual. "Shannon started it."

Angelina laughed. "Uh-huh. I'm cutting in."

Shannon stepped back. "It's not going away until you deal with it, Logan," she said, then headed toward Max, who grinned at her approach. His mother slipped into his arms.

"Want to talk about it?" she asked.

"Does it seem like I want to talk about it?"

"No. Which means you should. At least to me. I know how you feel, Logan."

He started to object, but it was pointless. His mother knew how each of her children felt. All the time, every day, year in and year out. It was damned disconcerting not to be able to hide anything from her. "Doesn't matter how I feel. Or how she feels. It's not right, Mother. Despite what you say, we're not meant to be together. We share no destiny, and if we did and you set this entire thing up between the two of us, it was only because you sensed the danger to our family. I give her all the credit for saving us, but there was nothing else between us."

Angelina frowned. "I set this…wait a minute. What are you talking about?"

He whirled her from the room and out into the lobby, taking her aside. "Look. I know that you and Sophie cooked this whole thing up. You arranged for us to meet because you got some wacky vibe that she and I were meant for each other."

"I did not."

Exasperated, he said, "It's okay. I understand why now, though I didn't at the beginning. You know how I feel about the magic, Mother. You know I don't want any part of it. Look at the havoc it created. Look at what I did to Sophie."

Angelina crossed her arms and tapped her foot. "You think I put you and Sophie together? Well, you're wrong. I met Sophie for the first time the night of the Mardi Gras ball. And yes, at that moment I sensed your destiny, but not before then. As far as your magic, it creates no havoc whatsoever. Only your bullheaded refusal to accept who and what you are generates problems in your life, Logan. I'm sorry you're ashamed of us, but we are who we are and can't change that."

"Wait a minute. You didn't orchestrate my meeting with Sophie?"

"No."

"Then how…"

"Perhaps she knew where to find you. Perhaps you called to her in a way that had nothing to do with manipulation and everything to do with the fact that you were destined to meet, destined to fall in love, and destined to spend eternity together."

He felt the tension boiling within his mother, unable to recall ever seeing her this angry.

"Pull your head out of your ass and grow up, Logan. You aren't the only one in the world learning to deal with magic. Most of us get past it and learn to accept who we are, learn to embrace the wondrous gifts God has bestowed on us. You seem to be the only one fighting it, and it's way past time. Accept it, or not, it's up to you. But I'm tired of placating you and trying to apologize for giving you this gift. I won't do it any longer."

Tears welled in her eyes. He reached for her but she pushed away from him and fled down the hallway to the elevator.

He stood there, stunned and unable to move.

What the hell had he done? He'd alienated his family, especially his mother, the woman he loved more than anyone else in the world. Had his refusal to accept his magic hurt her that badly?

He stepped outside the hotel and took a walk along the river. The night was cool and foggy, yet he didn't even feel it.

It had never occurred to him that his mother might be hurt by his refusal to acknowledge his power. How the hell had it taken him so long to see that?

He knew why. Because he'd spent most of his adult life running from who he was, trying to hide the fact that what lived inside him was a gift from both his parents. Instead of thanking them and celebrating his power, he'd led his mother to believe he was ashamed of the entire family.

And his tunnel vision had extended to Sophie, who had never done anything wrong. She'd offered him kindness, magic and love, and he'd tossed them back at her as if her gifts meant nothing.

Fuck! What the hell was wrong with him? He was thirty-five years old and hadn't learned a goddamned thing his entire life. The truth had been there, staring at him, since he was a kid, but he'd stubbornly refused to see it.

His mother was right. It was time to grow up and face his responsibilities.

Time to open his mind and his heart to the possibilities around him, before he lost everything he loved.

He went in search of his mother. She'd reentered the reception and was busily playing hostess, making sure all the guests had been warmly greeted.

"Mother, may I have a moment?" he asked.

She looked at him warily, but nodded, allowing him to lead her to the corner of the room.

He could have spent an hour apologizing for being an asshole for thirty-five years, but he knew they'd have more time to talk later. Instead, he did the one thing he knew would convince her of his sincerity.

Letting the magic surround him, he created a tiny ice sculpture and placed it in her hands. Two lovers were intertwined in a loving embrace on a crystal rock. They looked a lot like him and Sophie. "You were right."

Smiling at her stunned expression, he kissed her on the cheek and went in search of the other woman he loved.

Chapter Seventeen

Sophie warily watched Logan's determined approach across the room. She maneuvered herself a bit behind Kaitlyn so he wouldn't spot her.

"He already knows exactly where you are," Kaitlyn said, moving away so that Sophie was once again in Logan's line of sight.

"I don't want to talk to him."

"Yes, you do. And that's what scares you."

She turned to Kaitlyn and shrugged. "What else is there to say? Is he going to apologize? That's not what I want. He might even tell me to stay the hell out of his family's life."

Kaitlyn took her hand. "He's not going to say any such thing. And if he did it wouldn't matter. You're family to us, Sophie. Whether Logan pulls his head out of his ass long enough to realize that or not doesn't matter. You'll still be a part of our lives."

Her soul warmed at the acceptance she'd received from the Storm family. She'd miss them, but there was no way she could continue to be around them if Logan wasn't in her life.

And no way was Logan going to be in her life. He'd made that abundantly clear to her.

"I'll bet you that he does want you."

"You're on. No way could he ignore me like this unless he wanted me out of his life."

Kaitlyn waved her hand. "Logan doesn't know what he wants unless you bash him upside the head with a two-by-four."

Sophie laughed. "I'm not the bashing type. I tried and failed, and I'm not going to ask for his heart again."

"You won't have to."

She whirled around, heating in embarrassment as she found Logan standing in front of her. Obviously, he'd heard what she said.

Idiot. When would she learn to keep her thoughts to herself?

"Excuse us, Kait," he said, taking Sophie by the hand and pulling her onto the dance floor.

A slow, seductive jazz song began to play. Logan wrapped his arms around her and pulled her against him. Unless she was determined to cause a scene, Sophie had no choice but to dance with him. Her heart began to pound when he rested his palm on her lower back.

He smelled so good, looked so fine, this just wasn't fair! How would she ever get Logan out of her mind, her heart, her very soul?

"You look beautiful."

Comments like that didn't help at all. "Stop playing with me, Logan. Please."

He frowned. "I'm not playing with you, Sophie. You do look beautiful."

"You can't turn on the heat and charm one minute, then freeze me out the next. I'm sorry, I just can't deal with this any longer."

She pushed firmly at his chest, disentangling herself from his embrace. With as much dignity as she could muster, she hurried from the ballroom and ran toward the elevators, mindful of people watching her.

But she had to escape. She couldn't deal with this any longer. Pain stabbed at her, regret filled her, and the sense of loss nearly sent her to her knees.

Logan caught up with her just as the doors were closing. He slipped inside the elevator, inserted his key and pushed the button to his suite.

"Go away," she said, refusing to let him see her with tears in her eyes.

"No. I'm not going away. Not until you listen to me."

When the doors opened to her floor, Logan moved in front of them, blocking her exit.

"Let me go."

"No. Come up to my suite with me."

She crossed her arms and shook her head. "No."

"Yes."

She pushed past him, but a wall of ice appeared in the doorway. Turning her head to glare at him, she said, "Remove it."

"No. You won't cooperate, so I'm kidnapping you."

The doors closed behind him, and Sophie figured she'd just let him get out at the penthouse, then she'd ride back down to her floor.

She wasn't going to continue this charade with him. After completely ignoring her, now he wanted her attention? And they said women were difficult to understand.

When the doors opened at the penthouse floor, he took her hand. She pulled it back. He reached for her again, but she pushed at his chest. "I'm not going with you, Logan."

"Yes, Sophie. You are. We have unfinished business, and by God we're going to finish it tonight."

Before she could object he'd tossed her over his shoulder like a sack of grain.

"Put me down, Logan!"

He didn't answer, just moved to his suite and slid the key in the lock.

He didn't put her down when he walked inside and shut the door, either. Instead, he moved into the bedroom and placed her on the bed.

"What? You want one last fuck before you tell me to get lost? I'm not *that* easy, Logan."

"No, in fact you're one of the most difficult women I've ever known."

Ha! He thought *her* difficult? He should have been looking in the mirror when he said that. "This is ridiculous. Why prolong this? It's over. You've made that more than clear enough that even a fool like me can see it."

She started to scramble off the bed, but his words stopped her.

"I was afraid."

"What?"

"I was afraid. Afraid of myself, my capabilities. Afraid of your magic, too. Mostly I was afraid of how you made me feel."

Instead of bolting, she sat. "Go on."

"I was also so afraid of losing you that I walked away." He ran his fingers through his thick, dark hair. "I've screwed up my whole life, Sophie. I've been afraid to use my magic, afraid what would happen if I found a woman to love. And when I found her, I hurt her, badly."

Sophie's throat went dry. "I'm not sure I understand what you're saying, Logan."

"Of course you don't understand, because I'm not very good at this."

"You're not very good at what?"

"At telling a woman that I love her. I've never done it before."

Her entire world turned upside down. Her chest tightened. How could sweet words of love hurt so damn bad? "You...you love me?"

Logan kneeled beside the bed and took Sophie's hand, cradling it between his palms. "Yes, Sophie Breaux. I love you. I have never loved another woman before, so this is unfamiliar territory for me."

She knew the feeling. "Logan, I—"

"Wait. Let me finish first. When I met you, you stunned me. Your sexuality, your free spirit, your acceptance of who and what you were. All of those things were polar opposites of me. I purposely kept myself removed from romance, from love, because I was afraid of falling in love with someone, then bringing children into the world who would inherit my powers."

"Your powers are magical gifts, Logan."

He nodded. "I finally understand that. But I didn't before. And there was no way I would allow someone into my heart. Then I met you."

The way he looked at her melted her from the inside out. Heat, passion, those things she loved so much about him, but also something new in his eyes that she hadn't seen before.

Warmth. And love.

"I love you, Logan Storm. I've loved you since before I met you, when you were nothing but a vision in my dreams."

"I know you do. And I'm not worthy of your love. But if you'll give me a second chance, I will right all the wrongs, and spend the rest of our lives trying to make up for hurting you."

She kneeled and opened her arms. Logan pulled her tightly against him, crushing his mouth to hers. He stole her breath with a kiss that poured out his heart to her. She accepted it willingly, feeling his powers mingle with hers.

When they broke apart, she searched his face, touching his jawline and tracing his lips. "There is nothing to forgive. You needed only to realize who you were."

"And I hurt you during that journey."

"I'm strong, Logan. I can take it."

"I hope so. I'm not easy to get along with. I can be cold, forgetful of others' feelings."

"Tell me something I don't know," she said, grinning and kissing him.

"Marry me, Sophie," he said. "Teach me how to be a good partner. Help me learn about my magic, and give me children before I'm too damn old."

She laughed. "Gladly. Would you like to start on the children part now?"

His gaze went from hopeful to smoldering in an instant. "Hell, yeah. Let's make some babies, *cher.*"

Clothes were removed quickly, her dress floating to the floor to rest on top of Logan's tux. When they came together, their naked bodies touching, Sophie soared, feeling the magic leave her body and swirl in the air above them. It mixed with the heady frost of Logan's powers, and she blinked as the first snow crystal fell against her face.

Laughing, she reveled in the storm of flakes falling around them, realizing it meant a release of Logan's inhibitions about his magic. She wasn't cold at all, in fact she was heating up steadily by the second.

It came down harder and faster until the room was blanketed in a winter wonderland. Sheets of snow piled against the walls. The furniture surrounding them dripped in icicles as the snow continued to fall so heavily she could barely see Logan.

She pulled him on top of her, loving the feel of his body covering hers, their skin touching in every place possible. Cold mixed with heat as they slid over each other, their breath a thick fog as they stared into each other's eyes.

"I missed this, *cher,*" he murmured, nuzzling her neck with cool, tingling lips.

She shivered at the contact of his tongue against her skin. "Me, too. When you're not around, I feel cold."

He raised up to gaze into her eyes. "You'd think you'd feel cold when I'm around."

"Oh, no, Logan. You bring warmth to my life."

An indescribable emotion showed in his eyes. "I love you, Sophie. Thank you for not giving up on me so easily."

Reaching up to caress his face, she said, "I couldn't. I wanted you, and I felt we belonged together."

"You're much better at this than I am."

"I'll teach you everything you need to know."

"You do that."

Laughing, he reached for a pile of snow and covered her breasts. She squealed and tried to move away, but he pinned her arms, watching the snow melt, drawing her nipples into tight peaks. She shivered with delight and waited impatiently for his mouth.

Shock made her tremble at the first contact of his heated lips against her icy nipples. Where once he was cold, he now burned her alive.

He slipped his knee between her legs, his cock brushing her aching sex. She arched her hips toward him, needing him inside her more than she needed a breath. "Please, Logan, hurry."

"Ever feel something cold inside your hot pussy?" he asked, bracing his arms on either side of her and rocking against her clit.

Showers of pleasure rained down on her body. "No."

"Good." He slid into her, his cock like solid ice.

Sophie gasped at the sensation of cold within her heat. Her juices melted all over his frigid cock and she cried out as an orgasm tunneled through her, leaving her trembling.

"Damn, woman," Logan muttered. "You're so fucking hot on my dick." In response, he thrust hard and deep, pulling out and thrusting again, taking her back to a frenzied state of arousal.

Wrapping her legs around his waist, she fucked his shaft, grabbing it, squeezing it, its frigid temperature slowly warming until he was burning her on the inside. She was going to come again!

"Not this time, *mon amour*. This time, let's make you wait a bit."

She could have sobbed when he withdrew from her, but then he pulled her off the bed, dragging her into the living room.

"Logan, where are we going?"

"You'll see." He took her to the chair built for two, a wider version of a single, well-cushioned recliner. "Bend over."

He directed her to lay her stomach over the top of the snow-covered cushions. Grateful for the cooling relief of the icy flakes, she braced her hands on the arms of the chair and waited while he probed between her legs. Anticipation filled her and she rocked back, searching for his body.

"Beautiful, baby. Just beautiful," he said, then settled firmly against her and drove his cock deep.

She couldn't help it. The position was so intense and allowed him a deeper penetration than anything she'd ever felt before. She screamed, digging her nails into the cushions of the chair as he rocked against her. She met his thrusts with equal fervor, lifting her buttocks to drive her pussy harder against his cock.

"Keep doing that and I'm going to come," he said, his voice tight with barely leashed control.

"Then come in me, Logan," she pleaded. "Come now."

"Touch yourself for me, Sophie. Let me feel that sweet cunt squeeze the life right out of my cock."

She did, sliding one hand between her legs and massaging her clit with rapid strokes. Coupled with Logan's pistoning thrusts, she was close. So very close.

In the back of her mind was the thought that they could make a baby tonight. What better way for two people to share their love?

"Harder," she moaned, needing more. She quickened the strokes along her clit, reaching further to feel his shaft pulling out and sliding inside her again. It was wet with her cream, her juices flowing over his balls and between her legs.

"Ah, yes, touch my cock, Sophie. Feel how wet you make it."

He joined her, tangling his fingers around the shaft, sliding them inside her to couple with the driving thrusts of his cock. Then he took the juices from his fingers and spread them between the cheeks of her buttocks, working his finger slowly and gently into her anus.

Sweat poured off his chest, spilling onto her back and mixing with her own heated perspiration.

In response to her heated state, Logan called forth a new deluge of icy rain, hammering it over their bodies in cooling relief.

"So hot," he murmured, tunneling his finger all the way into her ass. She closed around him, squeezing him, but he was relentless, driving in and out of her anus while his shaft continued to pummel her repeatedly. "So fucking hot."

A strong gust of chilled wind swirled around them, pellets of ice dropping onto her back, cooling her fiery skin.

This was either heaven or hell, and she no longer cared. Her womb clenched in spasms, driving her climax and shattering her last vestiges of control.

"I'm coming, Logan!" she cried, wanting him to come with her.

He reared back and plunged deeply inside her once, twice, three times. Then he stilled, letting her ride out her orgasm while he spilled his seed inside her.

The ice stopped falling, the wind died down, and Logan's heated body rested on top of her back. His heart pounded a staccato beat against her, mirroring her own rapidly panting breaths.

When reality came back to her, he straightened, turning her around in his arms and kissing her with love, passion, and a promise that tasted oh-so-sweet on his lips.

"I hate to tell you this," he whispered against her lips. "But we're supposed to be at a wedding reception."

She laughed. "Oh yeah. I somehow forgot about that. You think they'd miss us if we didn't come back?"

"Probably. But I'd rather stay holed up in here the rest of the night and make love to you."

She closed her eyes, absorbing the love that he now gave so freely. When she opened them again, she reached for his cheek and caressed it softly. "I'd like that too. And we will. But let's go downstairs and celebrate with your brother and your new sister-in-law."

They cleaned up and dressed quickly. Sophie stood in the bathroom fixing the tendrils of hair that had come loose. When she looked in the mirror, she couldn't believe her own face.

A blush stained her dark cheeks and her eyes were filled with liquid warmth.

She felt almost giddy, like a child who'd just been given a wonderful gift.

Logan held her hand as they took the elevator downstairs to the lobby and made their way to the ballroom. He didn't let go even after they walked through the double doors to the reception.

Sophie watched the people looking at them. Some arched brows in surprise, some just grinned. Especially his family, who surrounded them when they got to the table.

"So, my brother finally grabs a clue," Shannon said, squeezing his arm and kissing his cheek.

"Apparently," Logan said, seemingly not the least bit insulted.

Angelina and Galen nodded at both of them, their faces shining with happiness.

Logan picked up a glass of champagne. "While I have you all here, I have an announcement to make. I'm only saying this in front of family right now, because this is Aidan and Lissa's day, but it's important for you to know."

He paused, looked at Sophie and said, "I love this woman, with all my heart. I've asked her to marry me and she's foolishly agreed to put up with me for the rest of her life."

"About damn time," Aidan said, clapping his brother on the back and reaching for a glass of champagne.

Congratulations were offered and they drank a toast to the newly engaged couple.

"Welcome to the family, Sophie," Angelina said with a fierce hug.

"Thank you." She fought back tears of joy, her heart swelling so much that she felt it might burst inside her.

After they celebrated with a drink, Logan pulled Sophie onto the dance floor and held her close, his lips pressed to her temple as they danced to a slow, romantic song.

"I'm never letting you go, Sophie," he said. "I have a lot to apologize for."

She pulled back so she could see his face. "No. No more apologies. Today we start fresh, okay?"

He paused, then nodded and smiled. "Okay. Tomorrow I'm going to pick out a ring that'll knock your socks off."

She laughed and shook her head. "You knock my socks off."

"You're not wearing socks, but I'll be happy to knock off this dress and show you how much I love you."

The fires of desire burned hot as she looked into the eyes of the man she loved.

"Forever, Sophie," he murmured against her mouth, teasing her bottom lip with his tongue.

"Forever, Logan," she replied, grateful to the heavens, to the magic around them, and to destiny, for bringing her the man of her dreams.

Spring Rain

Dedication

To my wonderful friend Lora Leigh. I can never thank you enough for your insights about this book. You made it better, and for that I'm eternally grateful. Your friendship and counsel mean more to me than anything.

To all the readers who asked about Spring Rain, and who have commented on the Storm For All Seasons series, I thank you from the bottom of my heart. Your enthusiasm keeps me excited about my work and I'm thrilled you've enjoyed reading this series as much as I've enjoyed writing it.

To Mel and Patti, who always read for me and tell me what they think. Thank you for taking the time to read my books and give your opinions.

To my editor, Briana St James, for everything you've done for me.

For Aidan and Lissa, Max and Shannon, Logan and Sophie and finally, Kaitlyn and Brett—thank you for the wonderful adventure. I'll miss you all so much!

And, as always, to Charlie, for giving me the time to do what I love, for encouraging me, editing for me, and most importantly, for loving me. I couldn't do this without you. I love you.

Chapter One

Kaitlyn Storm felt like a voyeur.

Standing outside Belle Saisons, Brett McGregor's art gallery, she watched him through the picture window, her heart climbing into her throat and nearly strangling her. He stood with his back to her, leaning over the counter talking to Marie, the receptionist. Tailored black slacks hugged his firm ass, the white shirt clinging to his muscular back. Her throat went dry. She licked her lips, suddenly very thirsty. Only one thing could quench her thirst. One thing she couldn't have.

Why did he always make her feel like she was seventeen again, tongue-tied and in the first throes of lust? That was a long time ago.

But the feelings had never gone away. Just looking at him tightened her nipples and made her wet. She should have long ago outgrown her teenage crush. After all, he'd married someone else, though he was a widower now. But he had been and always would be a friend of the Storm family and her brother Aidan's best friend, too.

He was also the one man she'd wanted with a hunger that refused to dissipate, despite the years and life events that had kept them apart.

He'd kept them apart, but she never could figure out why. Even at seventeen she'd tasted the hunger in his kiss, the way he'd crushed her against him in desperation, as if he wanted to devour her right on the spot. But then he'd pushed her away, and had left. Married someone else. Even six years after the accident resulting in his wife Amanda's death, he still avoided her.

She shook her head and forced the unwanted thoughts away. Business. She was here on business and nothing more. Lusting after a man who obviously didn't want you was a lesson in futility.

He walked through the double doors leading into the gallery. Inhaling sharply to calm the butterflies in her stomach, she swung open the front door, the soft tinkling of the little bell a welcoming reminder of the many times she'd heard that sound over the years. Recognizing Marie at the front desk, she waved and stopped there first, engaging the woman in quick catch-up conversation before heading back toward the gallery.

She moved through the double doors and down the long hallway toward the gallery. Polished wood floors shone like brand new, the white walls deliberately stark to take nothing away from the art hung there. She paused to examine an oil painting of her favorite French Quarter patisserie. Art was her passion, the only thing other than her job as Events Coordinator for the Rising Storm Hotel that made her breath catch and her heart race.

This painting caught her eye more than others. The sharp reds and whites of the awning sparkled under a midday summer sun. Casually dressed patrons sat at tiny round tables. Matching black wrought iron chairs peppered the fenced-off exterior the occupants of the chairs sipping *café au lait* and eating French confectionaries that made her mouth water. She imagined that first bite into her favorite warm pastry, powdered sugar flying off the flaky crust and into her mouth. Sweet, warm filling would burst from the center of the confection and slide over her tongue, the molten, sugary cream like an orgasm for her taste buds. She sighed, licked her lips and made a promise to herself to eat there tomorrow morning.

"Makes you hungry just looking at it, doesn't it?"

Startled, she whipped around at the sound of Brett's deep voice.

No, it wasn't the pastries. *He* made her hungry, made her pussy weep with need, her womb tighten, her nipples harden and her mouth water for a taste of him. Ten-year-old memories of being hauled against his chest and kissed with a passion she hadn't known existed still flamed so deep it was like she'd been branded. His one kiss had burned a memory into her brain cells that refused to go away.

How could it? Some men exuded sex. Brett McGregor was one of them. And he teased her with it, tantalized her with potent male sexuality that he held just outside her reach, dangling it like the proverbial carrot. Pretended he had no sexual interest in her when she knew damn well he did. Men like him should be outlawed.

And she had no business staring at him this way, had no business allowing her body to light up like a bonfire just from looking at him.

Then again, *he* had no business being so damn sexy he took her breath away. He had no business letting his dark brown hair grow a little too long, making her itch to brush it away from his face. He had no business having eyes the color of aged whiskey, the kind that burned a hole through a woman's clothes when he looked at her. He had no business having a perfect six-foot frame chiseled in all the right places. He had no business making her crazy like this for all these years.

She was getting tired of playing this game.

Using her anger as a shield, she arched a brow. "Well, you're still alive after all," she said, forcing calm into her voice, pasting a polite, businesslike smile on her face.

He arched a brow and offered a half-smile. "Was there ever any doubt?"

Even his voice sounded like sex by candlelight.

"You've broken three appointments in the past two weeks. The art council fundraiser is drawing near and I need your input, since you are the fundraising chairman and in charge of this event."

"Isn't that why I hired you in the first place? To take care of all the details so I wouldn't have to?"

Cheap shot, but she wasn't going to fall for it. "Yes. But unless you want me to make up the guest list for you among other things I have no business doing, you'll give me some of your time."

"Blackmail? Kait, I didn't know you had it in you." He arched a brow and offered a half-smile, that boyish grin never failing to have a profound effect on her libido. Her heart fluttered and her nipples hardened. She pulled her jacket across her breasts.

Really, Kaitlyn, you've got to get a grip.

"Come on. We'll talk in my office." He motioned her toward the open doorway down the hall, forcing her to step in front of him, directing her by resting his hand on the small of her back. She shivered, tendrils of desire snaking up her spine. She hurried forward, breaking the contact, wondering if he did that on purpose to unnerve her.

As she moved ahead of him, she wondered if he watched her ass when she walked like she watched his? If he did, would he get hard like she got wet? God, did she really want to know the answer to those questions? Staying focused on business was difficult enough.

She stepped into the office, sat and watched as he rounded the desk, unable to resist a quick peek at his ass.

"You really don't need my input for all that stuff," he said, seating himself. "I write the checks. You do all the detail work. That's why I selected the Rising Storm for the fundraiser. You're the best event coordinator in the state, Kaitlyn."

She wasn't about to let his compliments sway her. "There are things you need to decide, Brett. I have a list. A really long list. The menu hasn't been selected, nor have the hors d'oeuvres. You need to choose one of the three champagne choices I faxed over last week and give me a final head count so I can make the table arrangements. You still haven't selected what music you'd like to have, or where you'd like the auction items displayed. I don't have a list of items being auctioned. And I'm not going to make those kind of monetary or event decisions without your input. So I'd suggest, if you really want this fundraiser to happen at the Rising Storm, you'd better clear your calendar for the next two weeks. We have a lot to do."

He grimaced. "I knew I should never have agreed to chair the art council fundraising committee."

"So not my problem. We're stuck with each other." Why did she have to work with Brett? She'd just gotten to the point where she could exist knowing he lived in the same city, and fortunately they only ran into each other on occasion. But the next two weeks would be a lesson in self-discipline for her. Unless she decided to chuck all efforts at being polite and straddle him across his chair, rocking her pussy against him until he grabbed a freaking clue that she wanted him.

His half-lidded eyes and full lips both compelled and frustrated the hell out of her. For years he'd given her mixed signals, just like he did now. He avoided her like the plague, then turned those sexy brown eyes on her like he wanted to eat her alive. Then again maybe it was all in her imagination.

"I can give you this now," he said, handing over a printout. "This is the inventory list of the art we'll be showcasing."

Grateful for the distraction from her thoughts, she reached for the list, trying to calm her trembling hands. Arousal was beating her down, making her weak and jittery. God, she really needed sex. Too bad the one and only man she craved it with wasn't the least bit interested.

She scanned the list, unable to mask her surprise as she read it. "Brett, there's nothing of yours on here."

He looked away for a moment, his jaw clenching before he relaxed and turned back to her. "I don't paint anymore."

She shivered at the cold tone, but refused to let him freeze her out. "Again, why not?" She knew she should let it go. Why did she even care anyway? But she couldn't. Not when there was even a tiny glimmer of hope left.

He inhaled sharply and shot her a glare. "I'm too busy running the gallery."

"You've owned this gallery since you graduated college, Brett. And you used to be able to do both. That's a flimsy excuse if I ever heard one."

"Let it go, Kaitlyn."

She ignored his angry tone, beginning to feel the frustration that always came up when she was around him. "I'm not going to let it go. I love your work. Everyone loves your work. Hell, even you love it. Or you used to." Maybe that was the problem. Maybe he didn't love it anymore. No. That she refused to believe. Brett exuded passion, in both his work and the way he looked at her. He always had. She still saw it in his eyes, flaring with heat whenever he shot her a glance.

He might not want to want her, but he *did* want her. And she knew he felt the same way about his art.

His lips tightened as fury flared in his eyes, then disappeared just as quickly. "Art isn't something you just do because people want you to." He stood and stepped to the door, the light and passion gone from his eyes, replaced by a void of dead space that she knew she couldn't reach. "I'll make myself available whenever you need me."

"Right. Just like you've been making yourself available since we started this project." Since he'd first kissed her ten years ago. Yeah, like "available" was even in his vocabulary. He'd long ago put a Do Not Trespass sign on his heart. Then again, when had she ever obeyed the rules?

"I said I would and I will." He leaned against the doorway, a lazy, bored expression on his face as he waited for her to leave.

She'd just been dismissed. But instead of anger, pain lanced her heart. She rose, knowing she'd continue to fight this war with him, but realizing she hadn't won this round. God, she hated always being on the losing end with Brett. "Fine. When can you meet me at the hotel?"

"I'll call you."

"I don't think so. I need a date and time. Now." No way was he going to slip through her fingers again.

Sighing, he walked to his desk and flipped open his desk calendar, giving her a few seconds to ogle his butt again. She resisted the urge to groan at her wayward thoughts, careful to have her eyes focused at his eye level when he turned around again.

When he turned, that fire was present in his eyes again, but this time it was checked anger. She knew she pushed his buttons, knew she had pissed him off. But dammit, how could she let him give up something that filled his soul with joy? How could she care about him but allow the light of his soul to wither up and die? She couldn't. She wouldn't allow it to happen.

"I have a meeting here at six. Is seven too late?" His voice laced with sarcasm.

"Seven is fine. How about my office?" She crossed her arms and arched her brow, letting him know that this time she wasn't going to let him evade her.

"I hate offices. How about dinner instead?"

Dinner? Holy hell, where had that come from? He could barely stand to be in the same room with her, and now he'd asked her out to dinner? She almost fell back in shock.

Business, Kaitlyn. It's just business. He hadn't invited her to bed, he'd just taken her up on her dare to make good on his promise.

Okay, she needed to get out of here and settle her nerves, regroup before they met again. "Dinner it is. Would you like to eat at the hotel?"

"That'll be fine." He stepped to the door and opened it. "Now I need to get to work, if you don't mind."

Oh, no. She wouldn't let him hurt her. Refusing to be affected by his coldly abrupt dismissal, she cast him a glaring smile that didn't quite reach her heart and strolled slowly from the office, hoping he lingered in the hall and watched the sway of her ass all the way to the gallery doors.

Round one might be yours, Brett McGregor, but I don't concede defeat so easily. I hope you're prepared for war, because that's exactly what you're going to get.

Brett was transfixed by the sultry motion of Kaitlyn's hips as she walked down the hall, unable to shake himself out of this state of immobility until she completely disappeared through the double doors without another look in his direction.

Dammit to hell! He adjusted his aching crotch and shut the door to his office, sliding into his chair and palming his hard cock through his pants.

She was out to kill him. Not only was she infuriatingly stubborn, she also had to stroll in here smelling like a fresh spring day, the little bracelets on her wrists jingling with a soft melody.

One look at her, one whiff of her sweet springtime scent and he was shaking like a junkie in need of a fix. All he could think about was her. How she looked in her red flowery suit, her full breasts outlined against the jacket. His fingers itched to trace the line of her suit and slide his hands inside her jacket to cup her firm flesh. A few wisps of raven hair brushed against her heart-shaped face, no lipstick marring the perfection of her full lips. His thoughts had gone south and his dick had shot up at the visual of grasping that ponytail while her sweet mouth sucked on his cock.

Even worse was the soft sound of her voice — melodic and incredibly mesmerizing. Five minutes with her and he'd been so rock-hard he'd had to hide behind his desk until he could wrestle control over his libido.

And then she pushed. And she pushed. Like a relentless dog attacking a bone, she gnawed at his patience and growled incessantly until he wanted to cover his mouth over hers just to get her to shut up about the art.

There were things she didn't know. Bad, really bad things about him. Hell, maybe if he told her the truth about the night

Amanda died, she'd turn tail and run. If she knew what was good for her, she would. And that's what he wanted, wasn't it?

God, he was a mess. For ten long years he'd avoided Kaitlyn Storm. He'd forced his feelings for her out of his mind, knowing that if he acted on his desire he'd only bring disaster to her life. She'd been too sweet, too innocent, too blatantly in love with him to ever think of taking advantage of her. Hell, she'd been a kid back then.

She hadn't kissed him like a kid, though. Ten years after their one and only kiss he could still taste her; her mouth fresh and sweet like the first drop of rain after a cold winter, filled with innocence.

Innocence. He snorted and shook his head. He'd been long past innocence by then. By the time he was twenty he was already in deep shit and sinking fast. No matter how much he wanted her, he couldn't have her. Then, or now. If he'd been smart he'd have left Amanda alone too. Married her for all the wrong reasons. And she thought she could save him, just like Kaitlyn thought now.

He was long past saving. And he'd learned his lessons the hard way. He'd never hurt Kait like he'd hurt Amanda. Kaitlyn was a friend. No, more than that. She was his best friend's little sister and that's all she'd ever be.

He might want her until the day he died, but he'd never, ever have her.

"Don't you have a life to go home to?"

She jumped at the voice, so immersed in her work she didn't even know anyone had come in.

"You scared the hell out of me." Kaitlyn glared at her sister, Shannon. She'd have to start shutting the door to her office. Working at the Rising Storm with her sister, two brothers, a sister-in-law and soon-to-be brother-in-law wasn't always a good thing. Being in the same office just gave them carte blanche to bust in on her whenever they felt like it.

"Not my fault you tune out the world when you're working," Shannon teased. She looked the epitome of springtime in her pale green suit tailored to fit her slender body and her shoulder-length blonde hair spilling loose over her shoulders. And of course the pink glow on her cheeks had been present ever since she set up housekeeping with Max Devlin last year.

"I don't have a hot man to go home to like you do," Kaitlyn replied with a smirk. "So I'll just finish up some work instead."

She meant it as a subtle suggestion for Shannon to leave. A suggestion her sister blatantly ignored as she slipped into a chair across from Kaitlyn's desk.

"You'd have a hot man to go home to if you ever stopped working long enough. You're the last one of us, sis."

The last one. Shannon meant the last unattached Storm sibling. Her brother Aidan had married his coworker Lissa only a few months earlier. Shannon was well on her way to making plans for her wedding to Max, and her other brother, Logan, was house-hunting with Sophie.

Kaitlyn was the lone unmatched Storm now. The only one without someone to love. But there was a good reason for that.

"It's not my time yet, Shan. When it is, I'll let you know." The one man she wanted had never wanted her. Instead, he gave her those looks that made her crazy, but always kept his distance. What she wouldn't give for just one night of hot sex with Brett McGregor.

"You're blushing!" Shannon said.

Kaitlyn's eyes widened and she forced thoughts of tangling naked with Brett out of her mind. "It's...hot in here."

"I think 'hot' is in your mind, all right." Shannon arched a brow. "Did you meet with Brett today?"

Damn her sister for being so intuitive. "As a matter of fact, I did. So what?"

Crossing her arms and offering a smug smile, Shannon said, "That's why you're blushing."

"It is not! I told you. It's hot in here."

"Uh-huh. When are you going to see him again?"

"For dinner tonight. But only to go over the list for the fundraiser. I had to agree to have dinner with him just to grab a little of his time. He's been avoiding me."

"And I'm sure you find having dinner with him completely distasteful."

"Let it rest, Shannon. There's nothing between Brett and me."

"But you wish there was."

Damn her, was she a mind reader? Yes, she wished there was something between them, more than she'd ever wished for anything. But the last thing she'd do is give her sister ammunition to tease her with. "Not anymore. I'm not seventeen any longer. I got over my crush on Brett a long time ago."

"You have not. I know you, Kait. I know how you feel about him. How you've always felt about him."

"And you always accused *me* of playing matchmaker? You're worse than I am. There's nothing between us, so let it go."

At her forceful glare, Shannon nodded. "If you insist. So how go the fundraising plans?"

"Pretty good. And with a little input from Brett we should have all the details tied up in a few days. Did you know he's not painting any longer?"

She winced. Damn. She'd just gotten Shannon off the topic of Brett and what did she do? Jumped right back on it. When would she learn to keep her mouth shut? Her family knowing about her desires would only mean trouble.

Shannon frowned and nodded. "I know he quit painting after Amanda died, but I would have thought by now he'd have started up again."

Well, she'd opened the can of worms. Might as well pour them out on the table. "I don't think he's done *any* work since she died. Six years, Shan! That's too long to waste talent like his."

"I agree. But since I don't know anything about artistic inspiration, I can't offer any opinion. I guess he'll paint when he's good and ready to."

"I think he needs a woman in his life." As soon as the words spilled from her mouth, she knew her sister would jump right back on topic.

"You think he needs *you* in his life."

"No, it's obvious he doesn't want me. But I think it's well past time he met someone and started living again."

"Uh-oh. That means you've got matchmaking up your sleeve."

"And that's never a good thing, as we all know," piped in a male voice. Mentally cringing at being caught discussing Brett, she smiled at their brother, Aidan.

Aidan leaned casually against the door frame, his suit coat slung over his shoulder, looking relaxed and happy despite the long day he put in. Kaitlyn surmised that marriage had mellowed him. He'd lost that driven look since he married Lissa. Now he radiated calm, his amber eyes filled with warmth and love for his new wife.

He walked in and settled his long, lean frame in the chair next to Shannon.

Kaitlyn rolled her eyes. She'd never get any work done now.

"Don't you have a wife to go home to?" Shannon asked Aidan.

"Lissa had a client conference on the other side of town this afternoon, so we're meeting here for dinner. Don't you have a fiancé to go home to?" he shot back.

"It just so happens Max is meeting me here for dinner, too. And Kait is having dinner with Brett at Storm Rise."

Aidan looked over at her. "Dinner meeting about the fundraiser?"

"Yes."

"Maybe a little more than that," Shannon added, a twinkle sparkling in her turquoise eyes.

Aidan kept his focus on Kaitlyn. "Something going on between you two?"

She wanted to drop her head into her hands and scream. "Nothing's going on between us. Shannon's just being annoying."

"I am not. You're the one who started talking about finding him a woman."

Damn.

Aidan frowned. "Not a good idea, Kait. He's not ready."

"It's been six years, Aidan," she argued. "He needs to move on with his life. Do you know he doesn't paint anymore?" God, she was all over the place, from finding him a woman to the fact he wasn't painting. Why she tried to hide her feelings from her siblings was a mystery. They could always read her.

"Yeah, I know. Amanda's death hit him pretty hard, especially since he was driving at the time. I really think his love for painting died with her."

She wasn't buying it. She knew the spark still lived within him, the passion to create magic. She'd seen it. She'd felt it. Her own magic was so in tune to everything about Brett that she could even discern his emotions, no matter how hard he tried to appear indifferent. "I'm aware of the circumstances. I just think a new woman in his life would breathe some freshness into his muse. Maybe he'd start painting again."

"Butt out, Kaitlyn. Brett doesn't need your interference."

Aidan had always been protective of Brett. Almost as if Brett had some deep, dark secret that Aidan didn't want anyone to know about. After Amanda died, Aidan had closed ranks around his best friend Brett, refusing to let anyone see him.

Not even Kaitlyn. And she'd desperately wanted to go to him, to spend time with him and comfort him after his tragic loss. But he'd gone into seclusion after Amanda's funeral, leaving the gallery in the hands of the assistant manager for almost six months while he recovered from surgery and grief.

He'd been hurting, but he hadn't wanted her comfort. He hadn't wanted anything from her, in fact became even more distant the years after Amanda's death. But only with her, not with anyone else. If she couldn't read him so well she'd have been hurt by him singling her out. Deep down inside there was a good reason he kept his distance from her, and she knew it had to do with how he felt about her. He needed her more than he realized. He wanted her more than he was willing to admit. And all her talk about fixing him up with someone else was merely a way to cast off suspicion about her intent toward Brett. Her family didn't know that she already had the perfect woman for him in mind.

Her.

"I'm not going to do anything Brett doesn't want me to do, Aidan. I'm not a child any longer and I wish you'd stop treating me like one. Now if you'll both excuse me, I need to finish up some work before my meeting—emphasis on meeting not date—with Brett."

After a few more moments of conversation, Shannon and Aidan both left. Kaitlyn turned her chair and stared out the window at the French Quarter below. No matter what time of year, it was always busy. The sidewalks were filled with lovers linked arm in arm, sharing a secret kiss or ducking into a secluded doorway for something a little more passionate. An ache settled itself in the pit of her stomach, refusing to go away.

She'd been feeling that ache a lot more lately.

Loneliness wrapped itself around her, despite her best efforts to remain upbeat about her life.

She didn't need anyone. Her career as events coordinator kept her plenty busy. Occasionally she dated, but mostly kept those to one or two casual evenings out to a movie or dinner. Relationships just weren't her thing. She'd tried it a couple times, both ending in disaster. Maybe she wasn't cut out for sex and romance.

Her mother strongly believed in destiny, in fate leading you to the one you loved. Though Logan, Aidan and Shannon had fought against it, all three of them had found their soulmates. Kaitlyn knew her destiny, was as sure of it as she knew her magic would never fail her. But lately she'd begun to wonder if maybe she wasn't barking up the wrong tree.

She'd been a virginal but oh-so curious seventeen the first time—the only time—he'd kissed her. At four years older, he was her brother's best friend and her very first crush. He'd told her she was too young for him, but she'd seen the raw need in his eyes when he looked at her; had felt his thick, hard erection straining against his jeans when he molded her body to his and kissed her in a way that left her breathless and wet with desire.

God, she remembered that night like it was yesterday, not ten years ago. No fog of passing years clouded her visions of her first kiss. It was still clear as a full moon night. The way he smelled, the way his muscles strained under her roaming hands, the way his breathing grew harsh and heavy when he tore his mouth away to look at her. His gaze had flamed hot with arousal, speaking to her of needs he couldn't form into words. She hadn't needed words, even then. He couldn't hide that he wanted her as much as she wanted him.

Then he'd pushed her away and told her to find a nice high-school boy to love. That he was too old for her. That he wasn't the right guy for her.

She hadn't wanted anyone else. She'd wanted Brett. But then he'd met Amanda. Within a year they'd married and began to build lives together. The hurt had been unbearable. She'd felt betrayed, as if she'd expected him to wait a few more years until she'd grown up. Convinced her feelings had been one-sided, she'd decided to just be his friend. Though her feelings had never abated, had never lessened, even though she'd tried to move on.

Even after Amanda died she hadn't approached him, adhering to Aidan's wishes that he be left alone. Other than the occasional social function she hadn't seen much of him. And he never brought another woman to any of those functions.

Now, six years later, not much had changed. He still pushed her away and she was still crazy about him.

But she wouldn't give up. They were meant to be together and she could be as relentless as him if she wanted to be. In fact, she'd start tonight. Somehow she'd figure out a way to break through his shell. He needed to paint. He needed to start living again. And he needed to open his eyes and realize she'd been waiting too damn long for him to take what she offered.

Chapter Two

Brett paced the outside of Storm Rise, realizing he had arrived too damn early. How pathetic was that? Not only was his concentration blown all to hell after Kaitlyn's visit, but his mind targeted their next meeting like it was the only thing on his agenda. He scrubbed his hand over his face, muttering to himself about what a fool he was.

You want her. You don't want her. Make up your fucking mind, asshole!

"You look like you could use a drink."

His head shot up at the sound of her voice, his pulse racing and his heart hammering. Shit. So much for self-control. "Hey."

She arched a brow. "Hey yourself. I'm surprised to see you here. Thought for sure you'd blow me off again."

He nearly groaned at the word "blow" spilling from her lips. For God's sake, was he twelve years old?

His cock apparently thought so.

"Funny. Let's go in."

Now if he could just convince his determined dick to ignore the female in front of him, he might just make it through dinner. Trying to find a neutral topic, he looked to her and asked, "Hungry?"

"Ravenous."

Resisting the urge to groan at her choice of words, he motioned her through the doorway of the restaurant, signaling the hostess that they were ready to be seated.

Storm Rise sat on the top floor of the Rising Storm hotel. Three hundred sixty degree views of New Orleans from the floor to ceiling windows meant there wasn't a bad seat in the house. The restaurant was dark and romantic, with soft gray carpet and a dark blue ceiling painted with silver lightning bolts. It was like walking outside in a storm. Water trickled throughout the restaurant through a carefully constructed rock stream that wound around sets of tables.

The hostess sat them at an intimate little corner, a table for two lit only by a small candle centered on the white tablecloth. The rock stream separated them from the rest of the patrons. Total privacy, chairs side by side instead of across from each other.

Great. Just great.

"How about some wine?" she asked.

He shook his head. "Just iced tea for me, thanks. You order what you like."

"I'll have that, too," she said, then opened her menu. "I'm starving."

So was he, but not for food. Did she have to smell so damn good? Like some sweet wildflower scent he couldn't quite put his finger on. No wonder he always kept his distance. It was self-preservation. Being around her was torture and made his balls ache.

He really needed to find a woman who didn't want a relationship and then get laid forty or fifty times. Maybe that would shake his constant fantasies about spreading Kaitlyn out on the table and feasting on her pussy for dinner.

"I brought the banquet list with me," she said as she closed her menu and slipped it to the side.

Finally. Something work-related to take his mind off licking the cream from Kaitlyn's cunt. His cock lurched against his pants despite his desperate attempts to tame his burgeoning hard-on. "Let's go over it."

After ordering their meals, they spent a half hour talking about the fundraiser. Kaitlyn had a great eye for detail, like an artist constructing a painting. From flowers to food placement to strategies for the auction, she had every single event mapped out, assuring the fundraiser would be a success.

Good thing, too, because his mind wasn't on the fundraiser. It was on the little bracelet she wore on her slender wrist. A chain of tiny golden bells that made a soft tinkling sound whenever she moved. He studied her long fingers, imagining them wrapped around his cock and stroking it from base to tip. When she shifted and crossed her legs, he leaned back and caught a quick glimpse of shapely calves. Her skirt rode up and offered him a tempting look at her thighs.

He wanted to bury his head between those thighs, tickle the insides with his hair while he licked her pussy until she screamed his name. By the time dinner came, his shaft was throbbing and fully erect. Thankfully the restaurant had decent-sized napkins to cover his hard-on.

"Brett, are you listening to me?"

Hell no, he wasn't listening. He was too busy concentrating on the twenty different ways he could fuck her and still not have enough of her. He knew this had been a mistake. He should have never agreed to chair the fundraiser once it was determined the Rising Storm would host it. His mood went south in a hurry. "I heard every word you said. Sorry I didn't comment with high praise. Didn't know you needed to hear that."

Her half-smile just made her look sexier, bringing out the flecks of emerald green in her golden eyes. "Am I boring you?"

Fuck. She was supposed to get pissed off at him for his callous comments, not cast him a half-lidded look that made his balls tighten.

"No. I just have a lot on my mind."

"Okay, so if you heard everything I said, what's the answer to the last question I asked?"

Hell if he knew. "Run it by me again."

She shook her head and rolled her eyes. "Artwork."

Here it comes.

"You need to offer something of yours at the auction."

He knew it, he could see it in the calculating gleam in her eyes. "I said no once already, Kait. I don't paint anymore."

Undaunted, she continued. "Do you know what kind of draw we'd get if you added just one piece of your work? When was the last time you sold a painting of something that you created?"

Too many years to remember. He had a few stored away at the gallery, but he wasn't about to drag those out. The reminders of the mistakes he'd made were too harsh. He didn't deserve to paint again. It filled him with life, with excitement and a sense of purpose. He didn't want to feel that good about himself anymore. Not that he let anyone know that. He knew the routine. Positive mental attitude. And that's what he showed on the outside, at least to most people. He used the gallery and its hectic pace as an excuse for not painting. "Kait, I'm warning you. Drop the subject now."

"Or what? You'll spank me for misbehaving?"

Goddammit! He'd just gotten his unruly dick under control. Now it sprang up heavy and hard. Images hit him without warning—his hand reddening her sweet ass with swat after swat, her pussy juices running over them both as he held her over his thighs, the sounds of her moans signaling she really loved the spanking he was giving her.

Shit.

She reached out and covered the top of his hand with hers. A jolt of searing heat shot through his body. "You can talk to me if you'd like. I'm a very good listener."

He focused on her hand over his, on his erratic pulse, his painfully tightening balls. His mind, his body, was filled with her scent, the softness of her skin, the way she moved and talked. God, he had to get away from Kaitlyn and fast.

He'd never had a reaction like this to Amanda. That thought made him feel like shit because he'd never loved her the way she loved him. She'd given him her heart, her trust and her very soul.

In return, he'd destroyed her.

The memories were like a cold rain pouring over him, effectively dousing the searing heat threatening to set fire to his chair.

Never again. And definitely not with Kaitlyn. People like him weren't meant to be with someone like her. He withdrew his hand and reached for his water glass, taking a long gulp in the hopes the ice would chill the remnants of the raging inferno coursing through him.

"What's wrong, Brett?" she asked, her voice dropping to a near whisper as she leaned toward him.

She knew she affected him. The innocent batting of her eyelashes wasn't fooling him one bit. Kaitlyn Storm was shrewd and calculating and what she wanted, she went after with all her might.

She wanted him. If he were a different kind of man he'd have already dragged her out of the restaurant and would most likely have her panties shredded and his cock buried inside her before they ever made it to the car.

But he wasn't a different kind of man. He wasn't the man who should be thinking about sliding his cock inside Kait's hot pussy. He wasn't the man who deserved her passion and her caring.

Cold replaced the once-surging heat inside him. Carefully placing the mask of indifference on, he looked directly in her eyes and said, "Nothing's wrong."

She cocked her head to the side and frowned. "That's not true. There was heat when I touched you. Raging heat. Then, suddenly, an icy chill. I felt your pain. It goes deep and it's raw. Let me help you."

The Storms were a powerful family. Maybe he'd underestimated just how powerful. How the hell she could feel his pain was beyond his ability to understand. Yet she'd pinpointed exactly how he felt. Raw. The only way to fight her compassion was with anger and indifference. "You don't know a damn thing about me, so butt out."

"I know more about you than you think. I know you have an amazing talent you're not using. I know that since Amanda died you've shut yourself off from your friends, from the people who love you. I know there's a need inside you that isn't being fulfilled and I want to help."

He wished he could take what she was offering without a moment's hesitation. She looked at him with a mixture of love and hot desire in her eyes. That look caused a stabbing pain in his gut. Guilt mixed with need and a war raged within him. A few carefully chosen words and he could lose himself inside her.

But that would only ease the pain for a little while. It would come back, stronger next time. And in the process he'd hurt Kaitlyn.

He might be a prick, but he liked to think he had a few redeeming qualities left. And one of those qualities was the ability to push people away. Better to hurt her now than later. "I don't need anything you have to offer, Kait. I lead my life exactly as I want to. Take your bleeding heart and offer it to someone else. I'm not interested."

Kaitlyn sucked in a breath, clenching her jaw tight to keep from blurting out the words that wanted to erupt. God, he could be such a bastard, his words cutting so deep they drew blood. But in her heart, she knew he was deliberately trying to push her away. He hurt so bad that he was afraid he'd hurt her, too. She felt it as if she could feel every one of his emotions inside herself. And she wasn't going to let him do it this time.

Brett needed her. He may not realize it. No one realized it but her. Not Aidan, not Shannon, not anyone in her family. But she knew it. He was a part of her, his pain so raw it nearly drove her to tears. Brett hid something deep and dark inside, allowing no one else to reach in and help him through it.

Somehow she had to force her way past his defenses. If ever a man needed someone to love him, it was Brett. But she had to tread carefully, gain his trust slowly. Otherwise he'd crawl so far inside his shell she'd never be able to reach him.

"My apologies," she said with a smile. "I have a tendency to meddle where I shouldn't. Ask Aidan, he'll tell you."

Relief washed over his face, relaxing the tiny lines at the corners of his eyes. "Aidan says you're a brat."

She laughed. "I don't doubt it. Something about little sisters and big brothers don't mix well. He's a stubborn pain in the ass."

Brett's lips curled into a smile. "I think I might have said those same words to him a time or two in the past."

Once she'd effectively dissolved the tension between them, they made it through the remainder of dinner and the rest of her list for the auction.

"If it's not too late for you, I'd like to stop by the gallery tonight," she suggested. "I want to select a few pieces of art to showcase in the lobby of the hotel to promote the fundraiser," she suggested, careful to keep her tone businesslike. If he had any inkling she had personal reasons in mind, he'd shut her out faster than she could blink.

He might be a top-notch player in the game of hide, but she was pretty damned good at the game of seek. And just competitive enough to be determined to win.

He stood and pulled out her chair. "Good idea. I have some paperwork to pick up before I go home, anyway."

The gallery was only a few blocks from the hotel. The night was warm, that first teasing glimpse of spring just beginning to ease its way into the air. Walking along the sidewalk with Brett at her side reminded her of the scenes she'd viewed from her office earlier today. Only they weren't linked arm in arm like the couples she'd watched. Their heads weren't touching while they shared intimate secrets. And he sure as hell wasn't dragging her into a secluded doorway to slide his fingers up her dress and cop a feel, no matter how much she willed it to happen. A few inches of personal space separated them, but it might as well have been a mile-wide chasm.

Somehow she'd have to bridge the gap between them. Whether he knew it or not, whether he liked it or not, Brett needed her.

Kaitlyn waited while Brett slid the key into the lock on the front door, punched in the codes for the alarm, then flipped on the lights. She stepped in and waited while he closed and locked the door behind them, then followed him through the doorway into the back of the gallery.

"I have several pieces in storage that haven't been put out yet. Those would make good advertisements for the auction since they're on the list of items anyway."

He stepped to a door at the far end of the gallery, unlocking it and turning on the overhead lights.

The storage room was filled with paintings and sculptures, all covered with thick, white dust cloths. Brett began to pull the covers off while she examined each revealed piece.

He'd uncovered two rows and stood there waiting while she looked them over. She looked to him and shook her head. "None of these have what I'm looking for. They're either too modern, their colors too dull or way too abstract. Keep going."

His lips curled in a half-smile before he turned away to pull more covers. She followed along, stopping at each piece and scanning it, imagining how it would look set up on an easel or table in the lobby.

One piece caught her attention and she studied it, moving from one side to the other and then directly in front of it.

"You like impressionist paintings," Brett said from behind her.

She stilled. His breath caressed the side of her neck. Her fingers curled into her palms and she had to force herself to concentrate her gaze on the painting instead of turning to him. "Yes, I do. This one in particular strikes my fancy."

"Why?"

"The blending of colors. The flower field here—" she pointed, "—evokes vivid images of spring when the crocuses and tulips begin to bloom in tandem. It's fresh and exciting and reminds me of my favorite season."

"You have an eye for color," he said. "Mark Algiers is a great artist. New and a little raw, but with amazing natural talent. It's a great choice."

"Thank you." She took a deep breath, intending to whip around and force him to acknowledge the attraction between them. But when she turned to face him, he had already slipped away to remove more coverings.

Slippery bastard. He was avoiding her. That had to mean something. Surely if he didn't care one way or another about her, he'd have no problem standing close. He felt the same sparks of attraction she did, and because of that he didn't want to get close to her.

But why?

Too many questions, not enough answers. She needed a plan. A plan to get them together and keep him close. In the meantime, she viewed several more rows of art and selected a unique sculpture made from wood and copper. The base looked like a flowing stream, then both the wood and copper had been twisted together into a rising spiral to form two lovers in an embrace.

"Like that one?" he asked.

This time she wasn't surprised to feel him behind her. She'd always gotten completely lost in art and tuned out everything around her. "Yes, I do. The lines are sleek and sensual, the lovers abstract and interpretive. It calls to me on an emotional level. I could look at this for hours."

"You do know your art, Kait."

She smiled at the compliment. "As the old saying goes, I just know what I like. When it touches something inside me, I know it's good."

He was silent for a moment, then said, "How many more pieces would you like to select?"

"Probably one more should do it."

She turned around when his cell phone chimed. He slipped it out of his pocket, and spoke briefly. "Client," he said to her. "I need to get something from my office. Keep looking and I'll be right back."

She nodded and turned back to the paintings, slipping along the rows quickly until she reached the end. Or at least the end of what had been uncovered. A row in the very back of the room sat still covered. Curious, she walked over and pulled the cover off one, instantly realizing why he hadn't uncovered it. She pulled the other six sheets from the paintings, recognizing Brett's work instantly.

He worked in both oils and watercolors. She'd never seen these pieces of art before and wondered how long ago he'd painted them. Studying each one carefully, the last one captured her like an arrow to her heart.

It was a woman. Nude and seated facing front, her knees were drawn up toward her chest and her ankles crossed over each other. The side swell of each breast was visible on either side of her legs. Her long dark hair draped over her shoulders and down her arms. Her head was bent so Kaitlyn couldn't see her face.

It was magnificent. The background was a light blue wall, plain and without adornment. A cream-colored sheet lay crumpled on the floor underneath her, making the woman herself the focal point of the painting.

The woman's arms were crossed over the tops of her knees, her delicate fingers pointing down toward the floor. She looked relaxed and utterly beautiful.

She'd always loved paintings of nudes. They were so free, so part of nature and their surroundings, uncaring that their bodies were bared for all to see. Kaitlyn would love to feel that free and unrestrained. The right artist could paint a nude and capture the subject's very soul. Brett's work was like that.

She reached out to lightly trace Brett's signature gracing the bottom right corner of the painting. His work literally took her breath away and yet filled her with a sadness that moved her to tears. She sighed with a mix of contentment and melancholy, desperately wishing she could reach him, to bring him out of whatever shell he hid underneath and open his heart enough to use his gift again. Her magic flowed from her and kicked up a light spring breeze that blew through the closed room. The smell of lavender filled the room.

Damn. Sometimes she had difficulty reining in her magic, especially when she got emotional.

Why wouldn't he paint any longer? More importantly, what would it take to get him to take a brush in his hand and create again?

"How the hell did it get windy in here?"

She whirled around, forcing the breeze to dissipate. "Have no idea. Maybe a gust blew in when you opened the door."

He frowned and entered the room. "There aren't any windows open in…"

He stopped and looked behind her, obviously realizing she'd uncovered his work. When he looked back at her, anger sparked hot in his eyes, turning them nearly black. Instead of speaking, he sidestepped her and jerked the covers back over the canvases.

"Have you decided on a third painting?" he asked, obviously choosing to ignore what she'd done.

"Yes. The nude you painted."

He didn't even turn around. "No."

"It's breathtaking, Brett," she argued, moving with him and helping him drape the sheets over the easels in each row. "I don't understand why you don't want your work shown."

"I'm not having this conversation with you again."

Yes, he most certainly was going to have this conversation again. She'd touched a nerve. Granted, not a happy nerve, but any reaction was better than indifference.

Finishing up the last painting, they came together again at the back of the room.

"Choose another item, Kait. You wanted three, you selected two."

"No, I selected three." She walked away, moving toward his paintings in the back, uncovering the nude again. "I love this painting. I want this one at the fundraiser."

His lips set in a firm, straight line, he shook his head. She felt the temper boiling within him, knew she'd made him angry. But she wasn't going to back away. "You can't hide forever. And you can't walk away from your talent."

Wrenching the cloth from her hands with a violent jerk, he re-covered the painting. "Stop trying to psychoanalyze me, Kaitlyn. I don't need or want your attention. Do you understand?"

Oh, she understood more than he realized. If he thought he'd hurt her feelings by pushing her away, he was wrong. But an idea had formed. Risky, but still might work. "Fine. I'll abide by your wishes." She turned away and selected another painting that had caught her eye. "I'll take this one for the lobby."

His brows knit in a tight frown as if she gave him a headache. She hid her smile. She probably *did* give him a headache. She'd rather give him a hard-on. Why shouldn't he suffer like she did? Even at his worst he made her wet, made her nipples tingle and her pussy clench with the need to feel his hot shaft stabbing inside her until she screamed.

"I'll have these delivered tomorrow."

"Fine." Now it was time to put her plan into action. Praying it worked, she grabbed her purse and waited outside the storage room door while he locked it and led her down the hallway. Before they stepped through the doors and back into the reception area, she turned to him, halting his progress. "I have a question."

His gaze wary, he nodded. "Go ahead."

"Who else paints nudes around here? A good local artist."

"John Grayson and Mitchell Walker do the best contemporary nude artwork in the state."

"Good. Can I get their phone numbers?"

Arching a brow, he said, "I can arrange to have some of their nudes brought in here. You don't need to contact them directly."

Here's where she hoped her gamble paid off. "This isn't about the fundraiser. I've fallen madly in love with that nude you painted in there." He opened his mouth to object but she raised her hand. "Don't bother. I understand you don't want to sell it, but I've always wanted to own a nude. So I've decided I'd like to have one specially created for my own personal gallery."

"I can arrange that for you. Do you have a particular model in mind, or does it matter?"

"Oh, I definitely have a model in mind."

Brett frowned, dread sending his heart plummeting to his feet. He'd had control of this conversation a few minutes ago, certain he'd steered Kait away from dangerous ground. Right now, he had the feeling an earthquake was about to hit. "Who?"

Smiling, she said, "Me, of course. I want to commission an artist to paint me."

He went rigid at the thought of someone painting her nude. Someone besides him. Another artist looking at her body and immortalizing her on canvas. Tension filled every muscle, his headache pounding harder by the second.

Why the hell hadn't she asked *him* to do it?

Because you'd refuse and she knows that, you moron. Still, she'd specifically asked for someone else. Then again, he hadn't given her any reason to think he'd even contemplate the idea.

Jealousy reared up and filled him with irrational anger he had no business feeling. Nevertheless, there it was and he couldn't make it go away. "Why in the hell would you want to do that?"

She arched a brow and crossed her arms. "Is there something wrong with my body? Is it hideous? Deformed? Do you think some artist will lose his lunch if I stripped naked in front of him?"

God, she left him tongue-tied and unable to say what he really felt. He wanted to grab her arms and wrench her against him and tell her in no uncertain terms that no fucking way was another guy going to see her naked. "You know damn well that wasn't what I meant. Quit playing these games, Kait. You don't really want to…well, you just don't want to do that."

Her lips twitched as if she fought a smile. She was enjoying this! "Do what? Pose naked in front of a strange man?"

"Yes." He was drowning here, with no lifeline in sight.

"It's for art, Brett. I'm not posing for a men's magazine. You've painted nudes before. Did you ever get a sexual thrill from it?"

He'd never painted Kaitlyn. Well, that wasn't entirely true. But he'd never painted her while she was in the room naked. God knows he'd fantasized about it, though. Plenty of times. His fantasy of her was vivid enough. Her creamy skin glowing like gold under the studio lights, her body open to his view, breasts full, nipples arching toward the ceiling, long raven hair streaming from the chaise onto the floor, her pussy —

Fuck! His cock stirred, targeting his vision and demanding he go for it. Absolutely not. It wasn't going to happen.

"No, I don't get a sexual thrill from painting nudes."

"Then I'm not the least bit worried about a stranger painting me naked. Now are you going to get those numbers for me?"

Did he have a good reason not to give her the numbers? Other than he didn't want her naked body showing up for sale in some art gallery. But that wasn't his call. Her body didn't belong to him and all his posturing and steaming wasn't going to change that fact.

Ignoring his irritation, he said, "Let's go to my office." He pushed through the swinging doors and jerked the knob on his office door, trying to rein in his temper so that he wouldn't fling the door against the wall. He hated feeling this way, hated the thoughts rambling through his head.

No fucking way was he going to do what his thoughts compelled him to do. That would be disaster.

He reached for his data manager and scrolled through the names, wishing Kaitlyn had never seen the portrait he'd painted. When he walked in and found that one uncovered, he'd damn near hyperventilated. What if she figured it out? What would she say then? How would he explain it? Hell, he couldn't even explain it to himself. Besides, he'd done that painting a long time ago, before he'd met Amanda. Just a spur of the moment thing on a sleepless night. A vision that haunted his dreams for years. He'd tried to exorcise that vision by painting her, but all he'd done was further entrench her in his soul.

It was still his favorite painting.

Stupid, Brett. Really dumbass move on your part. Now give her the numbers and get her out of here before you do something really stupid, like agree to paint her.

"Of course I'd love it if *you'd* agree to paint me," she said.

Oh shit. Hell fucking no! Even if she had given voice to his thoughts, he wasn't going to do it. "No."

He looked up at her and she shrugged. "Just a thought."

"You're Aidan's sister, Kait. I couldn't do that. Besides, he'd kill me if he found out."

"So, he won't find out."

"No It's too…personal." He turned away and stared out the window at the darkness, wishing he wasn't having this conversation with her.

Give her a goddamn name and get her out of here! But then she touched his arm, the heat of her hand searing through his shirt straight into his bloodstream, filling his cock with the need to feel that hand caressing it, stroking it, guiding it to her pussy. He had to fight not to turn around and jerk her into his arms and ravage her sweet mouth.

She tugged on his sleeve, forcing him to turn around and face her. Her eyes were filled with passion and excitement, the green flecks melding together and creating a fire of emerald in her eyes. He wanted to get lost in her eyes, watch them go completely gold as she melted with arousal and need.

"How could it be personal, Brett? There's nothing between us but friendship. And you said an artist has no sexual feelings when he paints a nude. It's just work. I'd be nothing more than a vase of flowers or a landscape you were painting."

She clearly had no fucking idea what she did to him. Just the thought of bringing her into his studio and studying the angles and planes of her naked body got him hard. And not just hard from the idea of revealing her beauty, but excited about taking a paintbrush in hand again after all these years.

He hadn't felt the urge in years, and it shocked him to feel the force of desire roar to life. Not since Amanda died. Nothing. His muse had been dead. One suggestion from Kaitlyn lit the fires of creativity and he was already itching to sketch out her form. This time without having to rely on his own fantasies and imagination.

And that wasn't all he was itching to do with her body.

Big fucking colossal disaster in the making, McGregor. Don't even think about it.

"I really would feel much more comfortable if you painted me, Brett. I don't know those other men. I mean, I really want the painting done, and I'll hire someone else to do it if you really don't want to. But you'd make me feel safe."

Like hell he would. The last thing she should feel is safe around him. If he got her naked he'd ravage her in the first five minutes, bathe his tongue over every inch of her sweet body and fuck her in every way possible until she was too limp to move. There were things he wanted to do to her that she wasn't even aware of. She looked at him with love in her eyes. How easily he could take that love and destroy it. But it didn't stop him from wanting her. How sick was that? Aidan would have to kill him. "I already told you I don't paint anymore."

"Think of it as a favor to me. I've seen the nudes you paint. They're breathtaking. Especially the one you hide under a canvas in the storage room," she said with a tap of her foot.

That painting would never be sold, exhibited or shown in any way. Ever. He'd already made a huge mistake leaving it at the gallery. He'd have to take it home and hide it away where no one would ever see it again. No one but him.

"I've wanted this for a long time," she added.

So had he. Which was why he'd never agree to it, no matter how much she wanted it, no matter how much the desire soared within him.

"Please, Brett."

Kaitlyn wasn't the type to beg. When she wanted something, she went after it with a tenacity that belied her petite, slender frame. But she stood there, her eyes luminous pools of swirling green and gold. She sucked in her bottom lip and clasped her hands together.

God she begged nicely. He wondered if she'd beg for an orgasm just as prettily. He'd like to see her strung up on a rack of intense pleasure, begging him to take her over the edge. The physical need to touch her right now was unbearable.

He balled his hands into fists, mentally tamping down the urge to take her right now. Fuck! Could he spend weeks with a raging hard-on and do nothing about it?

Not a chance. "I'm not doing it, Kait."

He turned away from the crestfallen look on her face and scribbled down the name of one of the artists in his list. "Call Mitch. He'll do a great painting of you."

She lifted her chin, her cheeks pink, obviously embarrassed that he'd turned her down. He wished he could tell her all the reasons for declining her request, but he couldn't. Not without delving deep into his own fears, and that he wasn't ready to face.

Now she was clearly insulted that he wouldn't agree to paint her and there wasn't a damn thing he could say to convince her that he'd just turned down the opportunity to do something he'd wanted to do for as long as he could remember.

She took the card and tucked it into her purse, her tone clipped when she said, "I'll do that. Thanks."

He watched her walk away, forcing himself to remain mute before he blurted out that he'd been wrong to say no, that he wanted to paint her more than he wanted anything else.

But he didn't. Doing what he wanted would be a disaster for Kait. He let her go, mentally damning himself for the self-hatred that consumed him every day.

Mitchell was an honorable artist and a close friend. He'd paint Kaitlyn beautifully.

But Mitchell would never see her soul, her innocent heart, her sweet, spring-like nature. He'd never be able to paint the Kaitlyn that Brett knew.

No one could.

Chapter Three

Two days after her disastrous episode with Brett, Kaitlyn stood in front of his gallery again, trying to calm her nerves by taking a few deep breaths. Her palms were sweating, her heart pounding against her ribs.

Okay, so far this hadn't gone quite as she'd planned. Her original intent to get him to paint was still her number one mission. One way or another, she'd find out tonight if she had any hope at all of succeeding.

She pondered just turning around and going home, and then calling Mitch Walker to tell him she'd changed her mind about the portrait.

Would she really be able to pose nude for a complete stranger? With Brett it was different. She had feelings for him. She knew him, trusted him. The only reason she'd contacted Mitch was because of this really stupid idea that had popped into her head.

Like arranging for the painting to be done at Belle Saisons, thereby forcing Brett watch.

She refused to acknowledge the perverse satisfaction she felt when she'd made the arrangements with Brett. He'd choked for a few minutes, but he didn't have a valid reason for saying no.

So here she was, about to strip naked in front of two men and have her portrait painted. By someone other than Brett. Served him right for turning her away. God, it wasn't like she'd begged him to fuck her, though she figured he'd have probably turned that proposal down too.

Nevertheless, she couldn't stand out here all night and stare through the window. She rang the bell since the gallery was closed. Brett came into view almost immediately, unlocking the door and standing aside for her to enter.

"Hi," he said, his expression wary.

Did he think she was angry at him? No, she wasn't angry. She was hurt, dammit, but she'd die before she let him see that. "Hi yourself," she replied, pushing back her nervousness and affecting her brightest smile. "Is Mitch here yet?" She'd be damned if she'd act like this wasn't what she wanted. She'd put so much enthusiasm into getting naked for Mitch that Brett would wish he'd have agreed to do the painting.

Brett inhaled sharply and nodded. "Yeah, he's in the back getting ready. Go on through."

"Great. I'm really anxious to get started." She was about to say *get naked* instead, but decided against being that vindictive. Though she did pause, turn around and ask, "You're going to watch, aren't you?"

His eyes widened, then darkened, dropping half-closed as he studied her. Her throat went dry and her nipples beaded against her shirt. God, what she wouldn't give for him to give her that look for an entirely different reason.

"Watch?"

"Sure. I don't mind. And frankly I'd feel more comfortable having you in there. You're practically family, you know."

Zing! Got him with that one. He frowned and said, "I'm hardly family, Kait."

"Close enough. You're like a brother to me and I'll really feel much safer having you there to watch." Without waiting to see his reaction, she strolled through the double doors leading to the gallery and beyond.

Familiar with the layout of the gallery, she moved down the hall toward the studio. Sparsely furnished except for a few easels and a raised wood platform about ten feet square, she spotted a man that looked to be in his mid-forties examining the table of paints.

"Hi," she said, strolling toward him. The man lifted his gaze and Kaitlyn was struck by his incredibly sexy ocean-blue eyes. "I'm Kaitlyn Storm."

She heard the door open behind her and knew Brett had just stepped in. Mitch grinned and brushed a lock of shaggy brown hair off his face, his eyes lighting up like a full moon over the ocean. "*Bon soir, ma belle*. Brett didn't tell me my subject was so breathtakingly beautiful."

"Well, thank you, Mitch. I'm so excited you're going to be painting me."

Mitch smiled. "*Merci, ma petite belle*. I'm looking forward to doing you."

He winked and she realized then he was flirting with her! Her gaze shot to Brett. He stood in the background, scowling. Okay, so he wasn't totally immune to her. Hope filled her.

She couldn't resist egging Mitch on just a bit. "And I'm looking forward to having you do me." When Brett coughed, she continued and said, "I took the liberty of checking out your work at the downtown gallery and I'm very impressed. You have a reputation as one of the best artists in New Orleans."

Though Mitch was indeed a fantastic artist, Brett's paintings called to her emotions more. But she wasn't going to say that.

Mitch laughed. "I'd say we'll play some beautiful music together. Why don't you go change into this robe and we'll get you positioned so we can get started?"

He handed her a short red robe made of terrycloth. It looked more like a towel and would barely cover her ass. Great. Then again, she'd have more than her ass exposed shortly anyway.

This was it. She clutched the robe tight in her hands so neither Brett nor Mitch could see her quaking hands.

Posing naked for a stranger wasn't what she'd wanted. But it was clear what she wanted wasn't going to happen. She'd opened her mouth and thrown down the gauntlet, only Brett hadn't picked it up. So now she'd have to live with her choice. And hope that she really did know Brett as well as she thought she did.

She stepped into the dressing area and hurriedly stripped, slipping the robe around her and belting it tight. It skimmed the top of her thighs. She'd have to make sure not to bend over or she'd give both men one hell of a show.

Her blood pounded in her ears as she stepped through the door, her legs so shaky she wasn't certain she'd be able to walk. Mitch and Brett were huddled together in conversation, both of them looking up as she entered.

Mitch tilted his head to the side and scanned her body from head to toe. "Beautiful subject," he said, motioning her to the platform. "Stand up there, disrobe and we'll get started."

She swallowed hard and turned her gaze to Brett, who hadn't moved an inch since she'd walked in the door. The heat from his eyes shot deep between her legs, almost as if he'd physically touched her there. The look he gave her definitely wasn't an impersonal artist's survey. He didn't look at her body, just kept his focus on her eyes. And she couldn't tear her gaze away from him, no matter how hard she willed herself to turn away.

When he arched a brow and glared at her, she wondered if he thought she wouldn't go through with it. Was he challenging her, daring her to drop the robe?

Fine. She might be nervous as hell, but she'd damn well do it. She always finished what she started, and this project was no exception.

Yes, it could be just you and me doing this. But you said no. Keeping her eyes trained on Brett, she reached for the belt, untied the knot, and grasped the lapels of the robe.

"Kaitlyn."

She paused when Brett spoke. "Yes?"

"Are you sure this is what you want to do?"

Her gaze shot to Mitch who'd stopped what he was doing and leaned back against the table, arms crossed and watching them both.

"Yes! Of course it is. It *was* my idea, you know."

When he didn't say anything else, she shrugged and reached for the lapels of the robe, holding her breath and hoping she wouldn't blush from cheeks to cheeks.

"Dammit! Stop!"

She stilled, refusing to hope. Relief washed over her and she sucked in her bottom lip, waiting for him to say something. Waiting for him to say what she desperately wished him to say.

Mitch glanced over at Brett. "Something wrong?"

"I, uh, need to see you in my office, Mitch."

"Now?"

"Right now."

"Sure." Mitch shrugged and turned his head toward Kaitlyn. "I'll be right back."

She nodded, refusing to budge even an inch as she watched Brett lead Mitch into his office and close the door. Now what? Should she wait? Sit? Go change? The look on Brett's face was murderous.

After about five minutes of standing like a statue, she began to feel ridiculous. Belting the robe again, she stepped off the platform and sat down in one of the metal chairs near the easel. A half-dead plant sat in a container near the chair. She reached over and caressed the petals, offering her sympathies for Brett's neglect. She could certainly commiserate with the how the plant felt.

She could hear their voices, but couldn't discern the conversation. Until it started to get louder and louder. Were they arguing? No, it wasn't quite arguing. But she heard laughter. One-sided laughter, and it wasn't Brett doing the laughing.

The door opened and Mitch came out, still chuckling. Kaitlyn frowned as he stepped up to the table and began to pack his brushes and paints into a large carrying case. Her gaze moved to Brett, who stood leaning against the door frame of his office, his expression dark and angry. That tiny flicker of hope surged into a bright light of joy.

"Is there…a problem?" she asked innocently.

Mitch snapped the case shut and looked up at her, a huge grin on his face. "Nope. I've just been fired."

Yes! Affecting a frown, she said, "Fired? I don't understand."

"You will. Later, *ma belle*," he said with a wink, then headed down the hall.

She stood frozen, watching Brett turn and follow Mitch to the door.

Shortly after he saw Mitch to the door, Brett came back into the room. "Get dressed."

"Why did Mitch leave?"

"I told him he wasn't needed. Get dressed."

Despite her joy and relief, she had to see this charade through to its conclusion. "Excuse me? You told him what?"

"That he wasn't going to be painting you."

"I don't understand this, Brett. Explain it to me."

"I don't want him painting you." Then he turned away and fiddled with the paintbrushes on the supply table.

"*You* didn't hire him." She approached the table and positioned herself on the other side, planting her palms on the scarred oak top. "I hired him. You had no right to tell him to leave."

He shrugged but didn't look up. "My studio, so I made the call. It just didn't feel right."

"Didn't…feel…right." Yet he hadn't said why, hadn't said the words she so desperately needed to hear. Joy was quickly replaced by anger. His ambivalence, his refusal to admit how he felt, filled her with frustration. Forcing in a breath to fortify herself, she said, "You allowed us use of your studio. That's where your responsibility ended! This was my call, dammit!"

"Not anymore," he shrugged, his brows furrowed.

Oh, no. She wasn't going to let this happen! "What the hell are you thinking, Brett?"

"I'm thinking that sometimes you don't always make the right choices, Kait. Mitch's work isn't right for you."

On the verge of exploding, she lowered her voice and tried for calm. "You don't get to make decisions for me." Advancing on him, she poked her finger in his chest, ignoring his wide-eyed response. "I'm going to have a painting done. Obviously, not here in this gallery, but I'm still going to have it done."

She knew she pushed him, but God help her, she didn't know any other way to reach him. She wheeled around and headed for the dressing room. Brett followed, grabbing her upper arm and halting her progress. She turned around and glared at him, feeling ridiculous because this argument was turning her on! Her womb clenched in anticipation, her hard nipples scraping the terrycloth robe. What the hell was wrong with her?

"What are you going to do?"

Make you admit you want me. She jerked her arm away. "I'm going to dress and then I'm going to call Mitch back and make arrangements to have the portrait done somewhere else."

"I didn't want him to be the one to paint you."

"Well, why the hell not? You're the one who recommended him!"

He wasn't going to say it, wasn't going to say anything. She'd be damned if she'd play this game with him. Why couldn't he admit that the need to paint was like a demon inside him? Why couldn't he admit to the attraction that had simmered between them for ten damn years? Why did he continue to hold back, making both of them miserable?

She'd had enough. "I'm getting dressed and I'm leaving."

Her hand was on the doorknob of the dressing room when he shouted, "Dammit! I'll do it!"

Did she really hear that? She turned slowly and looked at him. "What did you say?"

"I said I'll do it, goddammit. You win. I'll paint you."

She shook her head and gaped at him, certain she'd misunderstood what he said. "You want to paint me?"

"No, I don't want to. But I will, if only to keep some other guy from doing it. Aidan would never forgive me if I let some strange guy see you…"

"Naked?" she finished for him, cocking a half-smile at his sudden discomfort. And did he really think she was buying his "I'm doing it for Aidan" excuse?

"Yeah. Naked."

"And you think he'll be fine with *you* doing it."

He shrugged. "Like you said before, Kait. I'm practically your brother anyway."

Now it was his turn to smirk. Just like Brett to throw her own words back at her. She didn't know what made him change his mind, but she wasn't about to question it. "When can we get started?"

He blinked, then shook his head. "Tomorrow. I need to get some supplies. And I'm not painting you here. We'll do it at my place."

Her skin flushed at his suggestion of "doing it" at his place. This was just the beginning. First she'd get him excited about painting again. Then maybe, just maybe, she could get him excited about something else.

You're a bad, bad girl Kaitlyn Storm. "I'll go get changed," she said, grinning as soon as she turned her back to him.

Brett watched her walk away, the sexy sway of her backside knotting his balls. The urge to cup his hands around the soft globes while burying his face between her legs was excruciatingly painful.

Goddamn Kaitlyn for putting him in this position. Just watching her pull the sash off that robe, knowing Mitch was standing there watching, had sent him into a fit of jealousy that shocked the hell out of him. Before he knew it, he'd told Mitch he wanted to paint Kait and asked him to back off. Thank God Mitch was a good friend, though he'd had to endure knowing looks and quite a few laughs at his own expense.

Hell, what was he supposed to do? Stand there and watch the woman he wanted disrobe in front of someone else? He might not be able to have her, but he'd be damned if he would allow another man to paint her.

Maybe painting her would exorcise her from his mind. Yeah, right. As soon as he told her he'd paint her portrait, he couldn't believe he'd said the words. Too late to take them back now. He was committed.

Or he should *be* committed, because trying to keep his distance from Kaitlyn while painting her naked body was going to drive him insane.

The door to the dressing area opened and she came out, a contented smile on her face. Of course she was smiling. She'd just gotten what she wanted. Somehow he knew he'd been manipulated by a master.

"I really appreciate this," she said, grabbing her purse and pulling out her keys. "What time tomorrow?"

"Seven."

She nodded and half-turned, then whipped around to face him again. Her eyes were so beautiful, her dark lashes sweeping her upper brow. Excitement lit them up like a twinkling emerald. "I'm so excited, Brett! Thank you so much! You won't regret this."

He already did.

After she left he went into the studio to pick up, then began to shut out the lights. His gaze caught something next to one of the chairs and he did a double take.

When was the last time he'd watered that old plant? Months ago? He didn't remember it looking as vibrant, its thick leaves infused with a dark green color and shoots of new growth sprouting from the center. It even had a few buds. A quick check of the soil confused him even more. The dirt was wet, as if it had just been watered.

Hell, he'd thought that plant was long ago dead.

Kaitlyn was ready—freshly showered, her skin scrubbed pink and glowing. She'd shaved everything and everywhere, both highly embarrassed and incredibly aroused by the thought of Brett seeing her naked. She'd lathered on unscented body lotion, not wanting to annoy him by dabbing on any sultry perfume. She'd even agonized over what to wear, finally tossing on jeans and a lightweight sweater. She wasn't dressing for a date, after all.

Soon enough she wouldn't be dressed at all, she thought with a chuckle.

One step at a time. First the portrait. She just wanted to spend some time with him and talk. Give him a chance to open up to her.

After that she might go for the perfume. But right now she'd keep it business only.

Business only. Yeah right. So why was her heart pounding like a heavy drumbeat during the entire half hour drive? By the time she reached his house she was about ready to hyperventilate and in dire need of a paper bag. Her palms were sweaty and it felt like her heart had changed locations, now residing in her throat.

Calm down, Kait. What will happen is meant to be. She knew that, her mother had always told her about destiny. If she was destined to be with Brett then she would be. If not, then this project was a waste of time.

No, it wouldn't be waste of time. After all, he was going to paint again and that was important. His soul lived at the end of a paintbrush and he needed this to heal. Maybe everyone else tiptoed around him after Amanda died, but it was time he got on with his life. It was time he experienced the joy he used to feel when he painted. She'd seen his eyes light up when he worked on a project. She needed to see that light again.

The one-story white ranch was surrounded by lush green grass. Fiery red bushes lined its stone walkway. Tall willows draped over the top of the tile roof like a blanket, their arms swaying in the slight evening breeze. Lights poured through the two windows on either side of the oak door. A wide front porch housed two comfortable-looking wicker chairs. She paused to turn around, admiring the view of the lake nearby. She remembered Amanda explaining the reason they'd bought this particular house was so Brett could paint the lake and trees while they sat outside in the late afternoon and watched their kids play on the front lawn.

Her chest tightened at the loss of both Brett and Amanda's dreams. She wasn't sure she could ever survive losing the love of her life. The pain Brett must have gone through for all these years made tears pool in her eyes, made her ache with emptiness. Was she wrong to push him to move on? Should she butt out and leave him alone? Her sister would say yes to those questions, but something deep inside her told her that she was supposed to do this. That somehow, she was the catalyst to Brett's return to his former happiness.

Determined, she swiped the tears away, then pressed the bell and waited. She held her breath, convinced he'd open the door, shocked as hell to see her standing there. He probably assumed she wouldn't show up. Or maybe he changed his mind and would ask her to leave.

Then again, she wondered why she was putting so much at stake on this painting?

For Brett and for his future, she reminded herself. If he painted her, he'd paint again. She knew it would work and that's the only reason she was doing this.

Right. And the thought of standing naked in front of him had nothing to do with her nipples tightening.

The door swung open. Brett stood there in worn jeans and a long, untucked black T-shirt that fit like it was molded to his rather impressive chest. She resisted the urge to see how well his jeans molded to his crotch. "Hi."

"Hey. Come on in. Just getting things set up."

She followed him in and shut the door, reminding herself to breathe.

Though she'd been to his house before, it had been awhile. His place was messy. Definitely lacked a woman's touch. Clothes were strewn haphazardly over the two sofas in the expansive living room. Magazines were piled high on the end tables, and the kitchen table was filled with mail and newspapers.

"Sorry it's such a mess," he said, leading her down the hall. "I never think about picking up and it's just me here anyway."

She felt the pain in his statement but didn't comment, knowing Brett didn't like to talk about Amanda.

The last time she'd been here was for Amanda's birthday party, about six months before she died. Kait had always loved this house with its polished wood floors and tall, white columns rising up to the vaulted ceiling in the living room.

His studio was the same way. The floors shined in here as if they'd been recently cleaned, and not a speck of dust littered the wet bar tucked against one wall. Tall white columns rose from the floor, reaching toward the cathedral ceiling like rays of warm sunlight. The only furnishings were one of those antique fainting couches in a dusty rose color, some sheer cloths draped over the back, and an easel propped up next to a roughly hewn wooden table filled with paints and brushes.

"Would you like something to drink?" He stepped to the bar and leaned across it, reaching around on the other side for a couple bottled waters. "I'm, uh, fresh out of wine or beer right now, but I can offer you soft drinks, coffee or water."

"Water's fine," she said, accepting the bottle and twisting off the top. She took a long swallow to lubricate her parched throat.

This was the moment she'd waited for. She'd been dying to get naked in front of him for the past ten years. Or maybe get *him* naked. Or both of them naked. Either way, this was a beginning and further than she'd ever gotten with him before.

"Ready to get started?"

She nodded and clung tight to the plastic bottle of water, hoping he wouldn't be able to see her hands shaking. Whether from nerves or excitement she didn't know.

He led her to the back of the room where a door stood partially open. He palmed the center of the door and pushed, then motioned her closer.

"This is the changing room and bathroom. There's a robe on a hook on the back of the door. Undress and slip that on, then come out whenever you're ready."

She nodded and stepped in, watching him walk away before she shut the door.

He wasn't nervous at all. Then again, he probably wasn't taking this personally like she was. Being an artist meant he sometimes painted nudes. Her standing there buck ass naked in front of him would be no different than him looking at a bowl filled with apples.

No, the only person who thought this was a big deal was her. She turned toward the mirror between the two vanities and began to undress, carefully folding her jeans and sweater and placing them on the counter. When she slipped off her panties, she tucked them into her purse. Something about leaving them on the counter with the rest of her clothes was so...intimate.

Right. I'm sure he's going to run right in and head straight for your panties.

Ugh. Sometimes she amazed herself with her own moronic thoughts.

She grabbed the robe. Mid-length, it was a light cream silk with an attached belt. She slipped it on, shivering as the sleek material smoothed across her skin.

How many other women had worn this robe? Any? Was it Amanda's? When she felt the little scrape against her wrist she realized it was the store tag. She carefully removed it and smiled, realizing he must have just bought it.

For her? Knowing she was coming tonight? Did he think about how she would look in it, knowing she'd be naked underneath it? Soft and sensual, the material stroked her naked body like a lover's caress. She closed her eyes and wished for another kind of caress.

Her reflection in the mirror captured her attention. Her face was flushed, her nipples hard and straining against the clingy silk. The opening of the robe offered a tantalizing view of her thighs, partially gaping open as she turned from side to side, providing a quick glimpse of her bare pussy.

She pulled the clip from her hair and let the long raven locks fall freely over her shoulders and over her breasts. Her eyes glowed a mixture of green and gold. The woman in the mirror looked like a delectable siren. Definitely not like her at all.

Though the robe didn't hide much, she was comforted at having something to wear when she walked out rather than parading out the door stark naked.

"You asked for this," she whispered to the siren in the mirror. "Now go for it."

Brett heard the dressing room door open but didn't peer around the canvas to look. He was occupied with gathering and organizing the supplies he'd need to begin the sketches.

Okay, maybe that wasn't the only reason he hadn't looked. Since she stepped through his front door bringing the sweet scented breeze of spring with her, his senses had launched into libido overdrive. Even dressed in jeans and a loose sweater, her hair wound up and around a little clip, she mesmerized him.

She might have walked through the door dressed, but his mind saw her naked. So did his dick, which was already clamoring for attention in a very uncomfortable way.

If it were up to him, she'd remain clothed. In fact, he planned to paint her with her robe on. His imagination already pictured her body well enough. The robe would at least cover the parts of her he was tempted to touch, lick and kiss.

"I'm ready," she whispered, clearing her throat. "Where do you want me?"

Naked and underneath me. He rolled his eyes toward the heavens and mentally pleaded for strength, then stepped around the canvas and groaned. Fucking hell. The overhead spotlight shined straight down on her, making her look like an ethereal specter come to haunt him.

Not too far from the truth. Her midnight black hair spilled in soft waves, teasing him by resting on her breasts. The robe clung to every one of her lush curves, making him itch to rest his hands on her hips and pull her against his rapidly hardening shaft. He swore he could hear her heart beating, pounding out a staccato rhythm that was way faster than it should be. Then again, it was probably his heart, not hers, jackhammering against his rib cage as he fought the adrenaline rush of arousal.

She tugged on her lower lip with her teeth and tilted her head, exposing a glimpse of the column of her throat.

God, he could paint only her neck and it would satisfy him forever. Slender, the pulse thumping rapidly against her golden skin, he longed to run his tongue over that throbbing vein and lick until her nipples peaked under his questing hands.

Goddamn this was going to be hard.

Correction. It was already hard. Painfully hard. He wasn't sure he had enough restraint to see this through.

"Do you want me to take this off?" she asked, reaching for the satin belt of the robe.

Only if her intent was to kill him.

Death by hard-on. What a way to go. "Leave it on. We'll start with positioning, then some sample sketches to see which placement I like best. No reason for you to be naked for simple choreography."

Or for any other reason. A man could only take so much torture before he broke. Didn't she understand he was trying to keep his distance for her own benefit?

She moved toward him, sliding her hands into the pockets of the robe. The action moved her hair out of the way of her chest, revealing the outline of erect nipples pressing against the silk.

He bit back a groan and decided the best thing to focus on was her face.

Though the look of pure heated desire she gave him didn't help. He was so screwed. What demon possessed him to agree to this?

Think like an artist. Kaitlyn is a subject and that's all. She wasn't the woman ingrained so deeply into his blood that he thought he'd die if he didn't get to fuck her.

"Tell me how see yourself positioned," he said, needing the distraction of art.

She looked to the chaise and tilted her head again, pursing her lips as she studied it. "Reclining, I think."

"Okay. Sit down and I'll work up a few different positions."

He grabbed the digital camera off the table and brought it over to the chaise, setting it down on the floor. He kneeled in front of her, refusing to acknowledge the womanly scent permeating his senses. But she was close. So damn close he could smell her desire, could see the dark shadow between her breasts, the soft fullness of each globe beckoning to his hands, his mouth.

Just a subject. A bowl of fruit.

Uh-huh.

"Lie down on your side and rest your head in the palm of your left hand." He helped position her, moving her right leg slightly forward over the left. The bottom half of the robe parted and he sucked in a breath before hurriedly covering her legs. Too late, he'd already seen the shadow of her pussy.

Bare. Shaved or waxed, he wasn't sure, but the half-second glimpse made him hungry. His jeans tightened and he was thankful he'd left his long T-shirt untucked. Maybe it would cover his erection. He wished he had some kind of magical powers to become a eunuch during the time he was painting Kaitlyn. Would make this whole process a helluva lot easier.

Touching her was agony, but he had to rest his hand on the small of her back to direct her hips forward, and take her hand in his to drape it over her hip. If his gaze lingered a little too long on the sexy swell of her hip, he couldn't help it. He figured he was doing good just keeping his hands to himself. His thoughts were another matter entirely.

Once satisfied and just about hyperventilating with the effort to maintain control, he picked up the camera, stood and shot a few pictures of her, covering various angles to be sure he had as much of a three-dimensional look as possible.

He placed the camera onto the printer docking station, hit the button and grabbed the photos as they spilled through, then carried them over to Kaitlyn.

"You can sit up now. Let's look at these and you can decide if this pose works."

He didn't even look at the pictures, just thrust them into Kaitlyn's hands and sat next to her, studying the front of the camera.

"Wow," she said. "These are really me?"

Amazement and surprise widened her eyes. She had no clue how beautiful she was, how her inner light shone through in simple digital photographs.

Painting her would be a once in a lifetime experience.

"I like this pose just fine," she said, handing the pictures back to him. "What do you think?"

He scanned the photos, already knowing what the camera had caught. The full curve of her hip, highlighted by her slender arm and tapered fingers. The shadow between her breasts as her robe gaped open, the sensual tilt of her mouth as she watched him take the pictures, the ethereal light in her eyes as she watched his every move.

As beautiful as she was, that's what really gut-punched him—the look in her eyes that he could only describe as a hungry craving. He sucked in a breath and went in search of his bottle of water, downing the contents in a few desperate gulps. He'd sell his soul for a stronger drink right now.

Instead, he reached for his sketchpad and turned back to Kaitlyn.

"Lie back down," he instructed, already committing the pose to memory. Repositioning her was easy.

"What are you doing?" she asked when he sat on the floor just a few feet from her.

"I'll sketch you first. It'll give me a clearer picture when I paint."

"Do you need me to slip the robe off now?"

He kept his focus on the sketchpad. "Not yet." Not unless he really wanted to come in his pants.

Mercifully she quieted and he focused on sketching, his hand moving with rapid speed over the paper. He could easily draw her from memory alone, but occasionally looked up to check her positioning. Each time he did, her gaze captured his and he had to force himself to look away.

Before he did something really stupid, like drop the pad, drag her into his arms and taste from her sweet lips until he drank his fill. Though he doubted he'd ever be satisfied once he crossed that line.

The smartest thing to do was make sure he never did.

Chapter Four

When was she going to get naked?

Dammit, she'd been lying here for two hours already, watching Brett sketch, frown, rip the page from the pad and ball it up to toss it behind him, then begin the process all over again. In fact, he barely looked at her; just kept his head down, his eyes focused on the sketchpad.

She wanted him focused on her.

Naked.

Whoa. Hold on there, girl. You're only here to see that he starts painting again.

Right. Nothing like a good case of denial to get a girl through the day, right? She wasn't supposed to want him. This project was supposed to have nothing to do with emotions and desires. But it did. And denying it or trying to rationalize her reasons for being here weren't going to sweep the real reason under the fainting couch.

Okay, so she wanted him. No newsflash there. She always had. From the time she was old enough for her hormones to start raging through her system, her budding womanhood had been directed at Brett McGregor. And no matter that she'd had relationships with other men in the past ten years, her heart had still wanted only one man.

The one man who didn't want her.

Which begged the question of why she was really here. To coerce Brett into painting, or to seduce him into fucking her? If she were honest with herself, she'd say both, with her main intent focused on the latter, not the former.

"Are you okay?"

Her head shot up to find Brett studying her. "Uh, sure. Why?"

"You groaned. Or something similar. Are you cramping up in that position?"

"No. I'm fine. Sorry."

She couldn't believe she'd actually groaned out loud. Then again, she'd never handled frustration with a lot of patience.

Focusing on Brett instead of her stupid internal questions, she frowned, watching as he ripped yet another sheet off the sketch tablet and wadded it in a ball.

"Problem?" she asked.

"No. Just can't get the right angle on this sketch. It's not coming out like I want it to."

She loved watching the intense concentration on his face, wanted to see him that focused on her while he touched her, fucked her, kissed her. The room grew warm, humidity soaking the air. She shook off her magic. "Am I doing something wrong?"

His gaze met hers and she was shocked to see the heat simmering there. She wasn't inexperienced in the ways of a man's desire, and unless she was inserting a little wishful thinking into what she saw on Brett's face, that look of raw need was unmistakable.

Need, and something else. Almost a wistful, painful longing. She felt it, but she couldn't pinpoint the reasons for his pain.

Was he missing Amanda still? Or was it something else?

Need and desire was strong between them. She didn't need magic to recognize the sexual hunger in his eyes. But there was more that he wanted, and that's what she couldn't figure out.

Then again she'd never been able to figure him out. Both aloof and hot as hell, he'd always given her mixed signals, just as he was doing now.

Was it possible he wanted her as much as she wanted him? Or was she seeing only what she wanted to see? Maybe his gaze swept her body from head to toe because that's how he sketched her. Maybe he lingered at her breasts and that spot between her legs a little longer than the rest of her because she hadn't taken the robe off yet and he couldn't visualize what he wanted to?

And why the hell hadn't he asked her to disrobe yet? How was he supposed to paint her nude when he had no idea what her naked body even looked like?

His eyes were still locked on her breasts. They warmed as if they'd been touched by his fingers, and she bit her lip and forced her magic deep within. But damn, a cooling breeze would offer relief right about now. The heat was building, and it wasn't from the room. It was coming from the inside out.

"Brett, are you intending to get me naked anytime soon?"

His hand stilled on the sketchpad, his gaze traveling from her breasts to her eyes. "Naked?"

"Yeah. You know. As in nude, without clothing, bare. The way you're supposed to paint me."

He arched a brow. "I know what it means. It's just not necessary to have you disrobe right now. I don't need you naked to get the positioning right."

Well hell. So much for him dying to see her body. Clearly he wasn't the slightest bit interested. Then again, she did detect a bit of fullness at his crotch. Not that she was staring there or anything, but when her gaze swept between his legs purely by accident, she might have noticed a bulge straining against the crotch of his jeans.

Probably wishful thinking on her part again. She wanted him hard and aching while he sketched her. She wanted his balls throbbing just like her pussy throbbed right now.

Since he'd decided to focus on his paper again, she closed her eyes and imagined him standing, his arousal outlined against the zipper of his jeans, straining against it as if desperate to burst free. His body bathed in the soft overhead light, he'd pull his shirt off, baring his chest and rock-hard abs. A dark sprinkling of hair across his upper chest would call to her, making her want to tangle her fingers in the tiny curls. The top button of his jeans would be undone, a trail of soft, dark fur clueing her in that he wore no underwear.

She'd rise from the chaise and walk toward him, her heart pounding against her ribs as she reached out with anticipation of feeling his heated skin under her palm. When she rested her hand against his chest, she'd feel the rhythm of his heartbeat, the mad thumping beats matching hers.

With her other hand she'd palm his cock and feel him rock his hips against her in silent answer to her unspoken question.

Yes. He wanted her, too.

Unable to wait a moment longer, she'd grasp the zipper of his jeans, tugging it slowly down its tracks, then working her hand inside to wind her fingers around his thick, long, pulsing…

"Kaitlyn."

Her eyes flew open and met his. He was kneeling in front of her, the sketchpad on the floor next to him while he studied her face. The urge to part her robe and slide her fingers over her slick pussy was unbearable. A pulsating ache trembled within her cunt. God, she needed to come. Why hadn't she done that before she'd raced over here tonight?

"How about a break? I think I've figured this out, and with another hour I can have it finished."

"I'm fine if you want to keep going." And going and going and going. Maybe he could start painting her tonight.

"Actually I need to make a call, but I'll be back in a few. Get up and stretch a bit. Use the bathroom if you need to."

So much for her fantasy. Pushing aside the disappointment, she nodded and stood on wobbly legs, her limbs shaky because she was in the throes of a dynamite fantasy and only minutes from climaxing. Her nipples beaded tight against her robe, no doubt quite obvious to Brett.

That is, it would be obvious to him if he'd even noticed. Considering how focused he'd been on his drawings, the chances of him being even remotely aware of her need were somewhere between fat chance and no way in hell.

Well, he might not be turned on, but she sure as hell was. She stepped into the dressing area and shut the door, turning on the water in the sink and sliding her wrists underneath it to cool her heated body. She shut the water off and dried her hands, but the heat still boiled inside her. She couldn't shake her fantasy.

Taking the opportunity of a few minutes of alone time, she conjured a cool gust of wind that entered the room, hoping it would quench the heat rising inside her. Instead, it blew open the robe, the air sweeping against her wet pussy. Her clit was on fire and her cunt ached with the need to be filled.

Staring back at her in the mirror was a woman in an obvious full state of arousal. Her cheeks wore a pink blush, her breasts felt swollen and tender and moisture seeped down her thighs. She couldn't go back out there like this. She'd just have to take care of it right here, right now.

Considering her state, it should only take a minute or two to get some relief. Immersing herself in the fantasy she'd started earlier, confident that Brett was on the phone in his office and nowhere within earshot, she raised her hands to cup her breasts, unable to hold back the whimper as she circled her distended nipples with her fingers.

"God, Brett, why aren't you here touching me?" she whispered, moving her hand between her breasts and then lower, parting her robe and dipping her shaking hand over her bare mound.

"I shaved my pussy for you," she said to her invisible lover. "Hoping you'd want to touch it, pet it, tease it with your fingers and your mouth."

The wind within the room picked up, blowing her hair behind her and nearly knocking her off her feet. She backed up a step and braced herself against the wall as the gusts grew stronger.

"My hand is your hand," she said. "Touch my clit, Brett. Slide your fingers in my pussy and feel how hot I am for you. Hot, slick, ready for your cock."

When she dipped two fingers into her cunt, she moaned, the exquisite pulsing sensation nearly driving her to her knees.

"Fuck me, Brett. I need you to fuck me."

Brett stood riveted outside the dressing room door, his hand still poised in midair where it had been a couple seconds ago. He'd intended to knock lightly and let Kaitlyn know he'd returned, but the sound of a whimper froze him to the spot.

Kaitlyn was talking to him in a voice that spoke of sensual promise, of heated desire. His cock, still semi-rigid despite his every effort to tame the unruly bastard, went to full erection in a millisecond. She spoke in a breathy whisper, urging him to touch her, lick her, fuck her. It didn't take a rocket scientist to figure out what she was doing. She was masturbating in there! Masturbating while fantasizing about fucking him.

His cock strained, pulsing against the zipper of his jeans. He could no more deny the urgent need to come than she could. His mind shot to visuals of her standing in the dressing room facing the full-length mirror, her robe parted, her breasts swollen, her nipples taut and throbbing. Her bare pussy would be glistening with her cream as she traced the outline of her slit, then dipped her fingers inside and began to fuck herself.

Walking away and forgetting what he heard would be the smart thing to do.

Then again, when he had ever been smart? Instead, he unzipped his jeans and pulled out his cock, already heavy and pulsing with the need to give her exactly what she wished for.

How easy it would be to open the door and find her there, her fingers buried in her cunt, her eyes dazed with passion. She'd be too far gone, too in need to offer any protest. He'd go to her, his shaft in his hand just as it was now, letting her watch how he stroked it, drawing his palm from base to tip, squeezing it tight so it would feel like it was buried in her pussy. Her initial shock would be immediately replaced with desire as her half-lidded eyes darkened and she continued to thrust her fingers in and out of her wet pussy, inviting him to watch her pleasure herself.

As he drew closer, now only inches away from her, she'd withdraw her fingers and lift them to his mouth, sliding them between his lips so he could taste her. He'd moan at her flavor; sweet, like fresh honey, and he'd lick off every drop before pulling her fingers away from his mouth and wrapping them around his shaft.

Her small, delicate fingers would be like a vise of fire, singeing his flesh with her questing heat. He bit back a curse as his own hand moved over his swollen cock, drawing ever closer to a blistering climax.

"Oh, God, Brett, yes. Fuck me hard!"

Though whispering, her voice was like a resounding song at full decibel level, driving him to stroke faster, imagining how tight her cunt would be when he shoved her against the wall and grasped the soft globes of her buttocks to lift her.

Her lips would part, an unspoken invitation that he could not refuse. His mouth would crash down hard over hers at the same time he positioned his cock between the soft lips of her pussy and plunged inside.

The gasp he heard through the door would be the same sound she'd utter as he buried himself fully inside her tight sheath. Her pussy gripped him, wanting his come. He held back, gritting his teeth as she continued to ride up and down on his shaft, her tongue dueling with his as they moaned together.

"Oh, Brett, I'm going to come. Please, please make me come!"

She was trying to keep her voice quiet, but it didn't matter. He knew what she was doing, had the image firmly implanted in his mind. He could hear the sound of her fingers thrusting in and out of her pussy, the wet, sucking noises getting faster and faster.

He moved his hand in time to her rhythm, holding back, needing to hear her cries of delight first.

"Yes! Oh yes, I'm coming!"

Her cries were sweet relief as he shuddered, pumped hard then came all over his hand. Hot spurts of white cream poured out of him until he'd stroked himself empty.

He leaned against the wall and fought for breath, wishing he had the guts to burst through the door, take her in his arms and give her what she fantasized about. But he didn't. Wouldn't. She might want him, and he might want her, but their coming together would have to remain in both their fantasies.

Hurrying to clean up the mess he'd made, he righted his clothes just in time to see her walk through the door. Her face was flushed, her lips slightly parted, her breasts still full and luscious, clearly outlined against her robe.

She looked up at him, her eyes widening. "You…been here long?"

He shook his head and buried his gaze in the sketchpad. "Just got back. Sorry it took me so long."

"Oh no problem. Gave me a chance to…rest a little."

He smiled. Rest. Right. What they both did wouldn't garner either of them any rest tonight, he'd wager. In fact, it was all he could do not to blurt out that he'd heard her, that he'd jacked off listening to her sweet cries and whispered words.

Before he did just that, he had to get her out of there. "I think I've got enough to finish the sketch. You can get dressed and we'll call it a night."

She blinked and frowned. "Are you sure? I don't mind staying awhile longer."

If you stay any longer, I'll fuck you before the night is through. "That's okay. I've got other things to do anyway."

"Oh. Okay. I'll just go get dressed and get out of your way."

He turned away from the look of hurt pooling in her eyes, waiting until he heard the soft click of the dressing room door before he tossed the sketchpad on the table and jammed his fingers through his hair.

What in the hell was he going to do about Kaitlyn? How was he going to keep his distance from her, knowing what he knew, hearing what he'd heard?

As difficult as it had been before, the possibility of painting her without wanting to take a taste of her loomed like an impossible task before him.

If he ever needed strength, now was the time.

Because God help her if he touched her. He'd ruin her life, and that he just couldn't do.

Kaitlyn stared out the window of her condo and watched the flurry of activity with a wistful smile. A male and female robin had moved into the small birch tree next to her patio. As they gathered discarded twigs and grass to build their nest, she shook her head at the feeling of jealousy that stabbed her middle.

Even the robins had found someone to love, to make a life with. Her destiny had been pounding away at her lately like an incessant discomfort she couldn't pinpoint. She sensed her time was approaching, that her fated love would soon make himself known to her.

Could it be Brett? After all these years, was it possible she could end up with the only man she'd ever fallen in love with? Hope filled her, but she tamped it down. It wasn't going to happen and all the wishing in the world wasn't going to make it so.

Brett. Oh, God, she'd been so reckless! Embarrassment over what she'd done last night spread heat over her cheeks. What was she thinking, masturbating in his bathroom like that?

Stupid, stupid, stupid!

Even worse, she'd been quite vocal about it. What if he'd walked back into the room and heard her? What if he'd come to the door to knock and discovered what she'd been doing? The thought both appalled and made her cross her legs, clit quivering at the image of him standing at the door listening to her fuck herself.

Would he have been excited? Or disgusted?

Tonight she had to go back there. Brett had called and told her to be there at five this time. A quick glance at the clock told her she had about an hour before she had to leave. Maybe this time she should take out her vibrator and fuck herself to a quick climax before she went over there.

Right. Like that would help. One look at him and her panties would be wet, her nipples erect and her mind rushing through possible scenarios of how she could throw herself at him.

"You're pathetic, Kaitlyn," she said to herself. "Hopelessly pathetic where Brett is concerned. You really need a man."

Someday she'd have to get over him. Asking him to paint her naked had been a stroke of idiocy. She never should have gone down this road with him. But she had and now she'd have to see it through. And hopefully behave herself.

Brett seemed like a normal healthy male. Though since Amanda died she'd never seen him with a woman. Not even out on a dinner date. They traveled in the same social circles, so they ran into each other often. Each time he was alone.

Maybe he didn't want to love and lose somebody again. That seemed like a normal reaction. Then again, it wasn't like Amanda had died recently. It had been six years, and Brett was in the prime of his life.

Oh hell. He *was* prime. Tall, dark and handsome didn't even begin to do him justice. With his great body and sexy dark eyes, he probably made women cream as they passed him on the street.

A shot of pride mixed with jealousy struck at the thought of Brett being ogled by passing women.

"He's not yours, you moron."

"You really need to get another roommate, sis. Talking to yourself is not good."

Kaitlyn jumped at the sound of Shannon's voice. She jerked her chair around and glared at her sister's smirking face. "Dammit, Shan! I have got to get that key back from you. You scared the hell out of me!"

Shannon sauntered in and slipped into the chair across from Kaitlyn's. "Not my fault you're dwelling in fantasyland and didn't hear me come through the front door."

She turned her head away and looked outside, staring at the tiny little buds on the trees. Spring would soon be reborn. A soaring shot of pulsing electricity coursed within her, like an adrenaline rush. She shuddered and turned to Shannon. "I need help."

Shannon's face changed from one of teasing mirth to frowning concern. She reached across the tiny table and grabbed Kaitlyn's hand. "What's wrong, honey?"

"It's Brett."

"Ah. So what's going on between you two?"

"Nothing. Something. I don't know what it is and that's my problem." She extricated her hand and stood, folding her arms across her middle and moving to the bay window to stare outside.

"Okay, I can sense how tense you are. Take a deep breath, calm down and focus your thoughts. Then talk to me."

"He's painting my portrait."

Shannon's brows rose. "Really. So you got him to start painting again."

"Yeah. Reluctantly, but he agreed. Only to save my virtue," she finished with a half-smile.

"Kait, did you ask him to do a nude of you?"

"Yeah."

"That was subtle," Shannon teased.

"Well, I had to do something!" she shot back. Something to get his attention, to make him notice her.

"I'd say that's something. Though I'm surprised he agreed to paint you since he hasn't picked up a brush since Amanda died."

Kaitlyn shook her head. "Oh, he didn't agree, not at first. I had to arrange for another artist to paint me first."

"You'd really let some guy you didn't know paint you nude? You're braver than I am."

"I didn't want to, but when I asked Brett and he gave me a firm no as an answer, I really didn't have any other choice. Then when I started to disrobe, Brett fired the artist and said he'd do it, but only because Aidan would kill him if he allowed another guy to see me naked." Though she was convinced his agreement was based on a lot more than placating Aidan.

"Okay, sounds to me like you got exactly what you wanted. So why are you unhappy?"

"Brett started the painting last night."

"I gather it didn't go well, then?"

"It went fine. Sort of. He didn't paint me, he just did sketches and took pictures for placement. I didn't even get to take the robe off. Maybe he doesn't want to see me naked. Oh, I don't know. Saying it out loud sounds stupid." She shook her head and waved her hand. "Forget I said anything. It's probably just a raging case of PMS or something."

Shannon snorted. "Well, that might be, and it might be something else. Why do you think he made you leave the robe on? Do you think if it had been another model he'd have no problem asking her to disrobe?"

"The thought had crossed my mind. After all, he pushed me away when I threw myself at him before."

"Well, honey, it's a damn good thing he did. You were seventeen and he was nearly twenty-one. Aidan would have killed him. Or Logan would have. Or, God forbid, Dad. It wasn't your time yet and Brett knew that."

"So he told me. I think he just wasn't interested and was letting me down easy by using the age thing as an excuse."

"Are you blind? I see the way he looks at you when you're in the same room. I'm sure everyone else does too."

Kaitlyn turned to Shannon. "How?"

Rolling her eyes, Shannon said, "Like he's Adam in the Garden of Eden and you're the forbidden fruit."

She shrugged. "I think he just looks damned uncomfortable when he's around me."

"Probably because he's trying to hide the hard-on he gets whenever you're within twenty feet of him."

Kaitlyn's eyes widened. "He does not!"

"Like I said…blind. It's obvious he's uncomfortable around you because he wants something he doesn't think he should have."

Could that be true? Did Brett see her as forbidden? And if so, then why? She wasn't seventeen any longer and short of throwing herself on top of him and begging him to fuck her, she'd given him every signal in the world to let him know she'd be receptive. "Why do you think he feels that way?"

"I have no idea. Maybe it's because he's been friends with Aidan for so long that he can't see jumping you and alienating his best friend."

"Or maybe he's flat-out uninterested."

Shannon squeezed her hand. "Trust me, honey. The man is interested. Only he knows why he's holding back. I guess that's for you to figure out."

By the time she arrived at Brett's house, she had nothing figured out, least of all his strange, inconsistent behavior. Late afternoon clouds sailed over the tile roof, obliterating the sun and darkening the skies.

Kind of like her mood. Dark and unsettled, the smell of impending spring rain tingeing the air with a musky scent that dove into her senses and made her tremble with anticipation.

Swirling winds swept around her, whipping strands of hair around her face. The rumble of thunder sounded in the distance.

Despite the ominous threat of a storm, Kaitlyn smiled, closed her eyes and inhaled the crisp scent of spring. Her season, her power, swirling around her, infusing her with its energy.

She was so lost in the sensual delights of spring, she hadn't realized Brett had opened the door until she felt his warm hand on her shoulder. Her eyes flew open in an instant, remnants of her magic still filling the air with its sweet, flowery scent. Brett removed his hand and arched a brow, studying her with great interest.

"Meditating?" he asked.

"You could call it that." Crimson heat flooded her cheeks. Nothing like communing with her element on his doorstep while he watched. "I like spring."

"Obviously." He held the door and she brushed past, electricity pinging as her arm made contact with his chest. Shaking off the vibrations from his touch, she moved into the studio, conscious of his position behind her, once again wondering if he watched her when she walked, if he studied her movements the way she did his. When they entered the room, she stopped and turned, awaiting instructions.

"Go ahead and change while I get set up. I'll begin painting tonight."

"Okay." She hurried into the dressing room, the smell of the spring-laden air still clinging to her skin as she stripped and slid the robe on. Tonight she'd finally get to undress, the thought making her nipples once again pucker against the satin fabric. Her pussy squeezed and pulsed, as if waiting for her to drive her fingers deep inside again, just like last night.

Not this time. Tonight she'd exercise some control. Not a chance would she allow her libido to gain the upper hand like it had yesterday. Cool, calm and collected. That's how she'd present herself to Brett.

Right. Now if she could just figure out how to actually feel that way.

When she opened the door, he was standing next to the easel waiting for her. She couldn't help admiring the way he fit a pair of jeans. Old, tattered and paint-spattered, the worn denim hugged his thighs and rested low-slung over his hips. Tonight he wore a sleeveless white shirt. His hair was a little mussed, quite different than the normally cool and poised persona he presented in business and at social functions.

She kind of liked him mussed. In fact, she'd love to run her fingers through his thick dark hair and make a real mess of it.

God, she was hopeless. Hurriedly crossing her arms over her breasts to hide her painfully erect nipples, she managed a smile and asked, "Should I disrobe now?"

He shook his head. "Not necessary yet. Lie down and we'll get you into position first."

Damn. He really didn't want to see her naked. But why? She'd like to think it was because he wanted her and was afraid he wouldn't be able to control himself, but her lack of ego refused to believe that. There had to be another reason. Maybe he really did think of her as a little sister and the thought of seeing her nude repulsed him.

With her luck, that was the reason. She'd likely spent the better part of her adult life lusting after a man who thought of her as a sister. How disgusting.

He positioned her just as he had last night, then disappeared behind the easel without another word. Just moved her limbs and quickly withdrew his hands as if her skin was on fire and he didn't want to get burned.

She waited, not moving at all, for at least an hour. The only time Brett peeked around the easel was to take a quick look at her, frown as if he didn't like what he saw, then pop back behind the canvas again. She heard the rasping sound of brushstrokes on canvas, but he didn't speak.

Finally she couldn't take it any longer. "How's it going over there?"

"Fine."

Rolling her eyes, she mentally counted the minutes, waiting for him to offer any small tidbit of conversation. Nothing.

"Do you need me to reposition?"

"No."

"Are you always this quiet when you paint?"

"Yes."

Fine. No. Yes. This was great. Then again, what had she expected? *You're a bowl of fruit, Kaitlyn. Remember? An artist isn't going to have a conversation with a bowl of fruit.*

This wasn't going at all like she anticipated.

"Brett."

"Yeah."

"When do you want me to remove my robe?"

Silence.

"Brett?"

"Uh, I'll let you know when the time is right."

Somehow she got the idea the time would never be right. And the longer she laid there, the robe covering her nudity, the more irritated she became. He was an artist. She was a model. She wanted a nude painting, not one with her wearing a robe. Oh sure, he could slap some obscure tits and pussy and vague idea of her body shape onto the canvas, but it wouldn't really be her.

"So what are you doing over there? How can you paint my body if you've never seen it?"

"An artist doesn't need to see the entire subject to create in his mind's eye."

Mind's eye, her ass. This was ridiculous! Now she was certain he would never ask her to remove the robe. Whatever made him hesitant to see her naked was strong enough to allow him to compromise his artistic integrity. Well, that just wasn't going to work.

"I need a break," she announced, irritation evident in her clipped tone. At this point she didn't care how she sounded.

He laid the brush down and stepped out from behind the easel. "Me too. Go ahead and stretch, use the restroom or whatever and I'll make us some coffee."

"Fine." She slipped off the chaise and rested her hands on her lower back, bending backward to stretch the kinks out of her muscles. Brett stepped out of the studio, so she decided to go hide in the dressing area for a few minutes.

She turned the water on and took one of the disposable plastic cups from the unit on the wall so she could get a drink. Taking a spot on the cushioned bench against the wall, she stared into the mirror and made faces at herself.

What a stupid idea. Oh sure, let him paint you. Well, he was painting all right. The problem was, he wasn't painting her!

And exactly what was she going to do about it? She stared at her reflection long and hard, until the image in the mirror arched a brow and grinned. A rather evil little image, actually. She kind of liked it.

Even better, she now had an idea. A rather bold one, but still, a necessity if she was going to push Brett to do what he really needed to do. What she really wanted him to do.

And what exactly was that? To begin painting again, definitely. But there was more than that. Much more than that, and it was about time she admitted it. All the games and denial were over.

Whether Brett liked it or not, when this little game resumed, they'd be playing it according to her rules.

Chapter Five

Brett stared at the thin stream of coffee flowing through the filter into the pot. The ticking seconds pounded inside him like a time bomb attached to his crotch.

Painfully hard for the past hour and a half, he knew there was no way in hell he'd be able to do the painting justice. He didn't want to imagine the color of Kaitlyn's nipples or whether her areolas were small or large, coral, pink or bronze. He wanted to see them. Even worse, he wanted to rim his tongue over the pebbled points and taste her.

He wanted to spread her legs and look his fill of her, kneel between her thighs so he could inhale her sweet scent and touch her silken pussy lips, then lick the length of her and drive his tongue between her drenched slit to sample her cream.

His cock lurched against the zipper of his jeans. He wondered if his hard-on would dissipate if he dipped it into the pot of scalding coffee.

Probably not. He was doomed to an eternal erection as long as Kaitlyn occupied his home. Because he was not going to touch her, and no way would he let her take off that robe.

He set cream and sugar on a tray and poured the coffee into a carafe, then dragged two cups out of the cupboard and carried everything into the studio.

The door to the dressing room was closed, so he laid the tray on the bar. He heard the click of the door and turned toward her. Her cheeks were flushed and she'd brushed her hair so that it shimmered in soft waves over her breasts. The overhead lights made it look as if she wore silvery, moonlit stars in her hair.

His gut tightened. She literally took his breath away and he forced himself to inhale. He poured a cup of coffee, grateful for something to occupy his hands. "Cream or sugar?"

"Both," she said, her sultry voice a vibration in his jeans. His balls throbbed, reminding him of the last time he'd heard that gravelly voice. Last night, on the other side of the dressing room door, while she begged the imaginary him to fuck her.

But it was only in Kaitlyn's imagination that he'd be able to touch her, to slide his shaft between her fiery pussy lips and bury himself deep until they both cried out.

He shuddered and sucked in air, hoping his hands wouldn't shake as he poured the cream into her cup. He handed it to her and poured his. Black, strong, fiery-hot, he didn't care. He needed the jolt of caffeine to slap some goddamn sense into him before it was too late.

"Mmm, this is good," she said, her eyes partially closing while she rubbed her lips together, then snaked her tongue out to lick coffee from her top lip.

Would she moan in pleasure like that if a drop of his come lingered on her lips? She was driving him to the brink of sanity. One more sultry look, or moan of delight, or revelation of an inch more of her skin and he'd fly right over the edge of reason.

Instead, he leaned his arms against the bar and studied the steaming coffee in his cup.

"Brett?"

"Yeah."

"Why don't you want me to take my robe off?"

Shit. He'd always found her honesty and bluntness refreshing. Now he wished she'd keep her curiosity to herself. "I don't need to see you naked to paint you."

"That's a lie and you know it. I've never known an artist to paint a nude with clothing on. Kind of defeats the purpose, don't you think?"

"The painting will come out just fine. Don't worry."

"I don't want it come out fine. I want it to come out looking like me. Exactly like me. You don't even know what my body looks like underneath this robe."

No, but he could well imagine every curve, every line. Her body was burned into his imagination for all time, as it had been from the time she was seventeen and crushed against him in a passionate embrace. Then he'd touched her, memorizing the swell of her hips, the tautness of her butt, the firmness of her breasts. Granted, she'd filled out since then, her curves more like a woman's instead of a teenager's, but his vision of her had grown right along with her.

"I have a good imagination, Kait. I'll do you justice."

"I think there's something keeping you from seeing me naked and I want to know what it is."

Out of the corner of his eye he caught a flash of cream colored silk and tanned leg as she shifted on the barstool. The silk slid down her legs, revealing the tops of her thighs. He swallowed and took a long gulp of coffee, which wasn't doing him a damn bit of good.

What he really wanted was a drink. A stiff, no rocks, no seltzer, shot of whiskey.

No, that wasn't right. What he really wanted was to turn around and finish parting her robe, then take what he'd wanted to take for the past ten years.

Since he wasn't going to experience either the shot of whiskey or Kaitlyn, he'd just have to buck it up and be strong.

"Look at me, Brett."

Unable to come up with a valid excuse not to, he set his cup on the bar and turned around to face her, trying to keep his gaze focused on her face and not on the dark shadow between her breasts, or the fact that the robe had fallen further away from her legs and now covered only a fraction of an inch of her upper thighs. If he looked hard enough, he was certain he could see right between her legs.

Best thing to do was not look anywhere but her face, though that was pretty damned distracting too. Her bottom lip was full and lush and he was dying to run his thumb over it to see if it felt as soft as it looked. Her little upturned nose had a small sprinkle of freckles along the bridge, but it was her eyes that did him in. Shaped like a cat's with a golden green swirl that he could study for hours.

She wore her emotions in her eyes, and right now what he saw in there caused his jeans to tighten rather uncomfortably.

"Why are you afraid of me?" she asked.

"I'm not afraid of you."

"Yes, you are. You have been for years. Whenever the family sees you at social functions, you'll throw your arms around Shannon and give her a tight squeeze. Then when you get to me I receive a brief hug and you pull away like I'm infested with fleas or something. It's kind of disturbing."

Because Shannon really *was* like a sister to him. Kaitlyn, on the other hand, was the woman he'd wanted for as long as he could remember. The only woman, other than Amanda, he'd cared about. He'd already ruined one woman. Hell, he'd killed her. He'd die rather than hurt Kaitlyn.

But seeing the pain swirling in her mesmerizing eyes, he realized that by keeping his distance he *had* hurt her. "I'm sorry. I didn't realize I was so aloof with you."

She shrugged. "It's okay. Just makes me curious. Why?"

"It's…complicated." *Yeah, there's an understatement.*

"Explain it anyway. I'm not going anywhere."

She leaned against the back of the stool, the action causing one side of the robe to slip and bare one well-sculpted shoulder. Her skin was golden tan and glistening with something that sparkled. He wanted to lick her, right there, then move his way over every inch of her body. She made no move to lift the robe back over her shoulder, either. Damn her, didn't she have a clue what she was doing to him?

What happened to him in the past made him stronger, but he wasn't that strong. And she was tempting him. Deliberately. And she had no idea of the darkness that lived within him. If she wouldn't protect herself, he'd have to do it for her. He reached for the top of her robe, conscious of her eyes widening as he slid his fingers between her upper arm and the silk. But when he lifted the material back over her shoulder and covered her bared skin, he caught the hurt pooling in her eyes before she quickly averted her gaze.

Shit. Would he forever make mistakes with her? Why couldn't he make her understand that if he touched her once, he'd want her forever. And that would be the worst possible thing he could do to her.

Kaitlyn stared at the far wall of the studio, refusing to let Brett see the tears gathering in her eyes. Stupid tears anyway. She had no business being upset other than idiot woman emotions. But dammit, when he reached for her, she'd held her breath, certain he was finally going to touch her, slide the robe off her body and bare her to his gaze. Instead, he had redressed her as if she was repulsive and he couldn't bear to look.

She knew he liked the way she looked, so the idea of being repugnant to him didn't fly. He just wasn't interested. That had to be it.

"Kait. Look at me."

How the hell was she supposed to follow through on her plan to seduce him if she let all these self-doubts take control? She was an attractive woman and by God she'd seen the way the crotch of his jeans filled out when looked at her. She gave him a hard-on. Men that weren't interested in a woman didn't get erections just looking at them.

Now or never, Kaitlyn. This is your chance, so go for it. The worst that can happen is he pushes you away again, just like last time.

No, that wasn't going to happen. Not this time. Last time she was a kid. Now she was a woman. A woman who knew exactly what she wanted and wasn't going to take no for an answer. Straightening her shoulders, she turned to face him, forcing a confidence she didn't really feel inside.

She slid off the barstool.

He frowned and scooted away from her. "Things between us…would never work."

Don't buy into it. He's scared. That was easy enough to read from the wary expression in his eyes. Even he didn't believe what he was saying. So she kept moving toward him. "Why not?"

His brows rose in surprise and he shifted away from the bar and headed toward the supply table. "You're Aidan's sister."

She followed. "So?"

"I've known you since you were a little kid."

He reached for the paintbrush, but she pulled it out of his hand and set it back on the table, then covered her palm over the top of his hand.

She breathed him in, the crisp, masculine scent of him, drawing in the musk of desire, letting it fill her completely. When he tried to pull his hand away, she twined her fingers between his, moving them slowly back and forth. "I'm not a kid anymore."

"I can see that just fine. And that's the problem."

Enough of this game. "Touch me, Brett."

He frowned and looked down at her hand. "No."

She managed a half-smile. "You want to. You've always wanted to. I think you're afraid of acting on your feelings for a million different reasons. And none of those are good enough reason not to."

His gaze whipped up and caught hers. It was so fierce, so filled with emotions she couldn't untangle. Anger might be in his heat-filled eyes, but so was desire.

"You have no idea what my reasons are. Stop this, Kait. Right now."

He hadn't turned tail and run for the door—yet—so she took it as an encouraging sign. That and the fact that the crotch of his jeans had started to fill out again. Quite nicely, as a matter of fact. She licked her lips. "You don't really want me to stop, do you?"

Though he'd started to move backwards toward the wall, she stayed in step with him, feeling like a beast stalking its prey. A rather exhilarating feeling, actually. Her nipples tightened and she knew they were visible against the silk from the way his gaze zeroed in on her breasts before he shifted to her face again. "Stop. I mean it. You have no idea what you're doing."

"I'm twenty-seven years old, Brett. I'm not a virgin. I know *exactly* what I'm doing."

His back hit the wall and she stopped, keeping her eyes trained on his face as she reached for the sash of the robe.

"Don't," he warned. "Don't start this."

"It started a long time ago," she said, releasing the ties on the robe and letting the sides fall open. "And tonight we're going to finish it. I'm tired of waiting for you to realize what's between us."

Brett's gaze roamed over her neck and breasts, traveling slowly as he drank in her body from her belly to her sex and down her legs. When he made eye contact with her again, his eyes had darkened and he stared at her with a sexually sinful look. "You have no idea what you're getting into. You don't want a guy like me."

Her lips curled upward. "I do want a guy exactly like you. Despite what you might think of yourself for whatever reason you think it."

He tilted his head and gazed at her through half-lidded eyes in a way that made her heart thump.

"I'm *not* nice, Kaitlyn. Don't ever assume I am. And be careful what you wish for because you just might get it."

With a quick shrug of her shoulders, the robe slipped down her arms and pooled at her feet. Brett sucked in a breath, his chest rising sharply. He stood still for a fraction of a second, then moved forward and bridged the small distance between them.

"I'm warning you. If you continue to push me, I'll damn well take what you're offering."

She rolled her eyes to the heavens and prayed for strength. "Do I have to hit you over the head with your easel? I *want* this, Brett. I want you to take what I'm offering and frankly I'm getting tired of waiting."

Faster than the lightning arcing outside, he reached out, palmed the back of her neck and drew her against him, pinning her tight to his chest. Her heart slammed against her ribs, pounding so hard she knew he could feel it.

"You'll regret this, Kaitlyn. We both will. You don't really know me. There are things you don't want to know."

She tilted her head back and looked into a pool of molten amber. Reaching out, she caressed his cheek, her palm tingling at the soft scrape of his beard stubble. Hurt and uncertainly reflected in his eyes. She'd do anything to take that pain away and free his soul. "I don't care about any of that. Kiss me, Brett. I've already waited a lifetime as it is."

For a second he paused and she was afraid she'd have to resort to begging. She held her breath, knowing this was the moment that could change things between them.

Please, Brett. Don't walk away this time.

When his mouth descended, she sighed in blissful relief at the first touch of his lips against hers.

Finally.

Kaitlyn surrendered to the magic of Brett's kiss. He brushed his lips over hers using what she considered amazing restraint. She'd expected violent passion from him, not this exquisite tenderness that brought tears stinging to her eyes.

Maybe she expected the violent passion because her need for him had gone unrequited for so long she was ready to burst with joy now that she was in his arms. A quaking need built like a storm inside her, ready to break free in a maelstrom of fury to equal the raging tempest outside. But she held it in check, needing to let him take charge.

The warmth and wetness of his tongue elicited a shiver of delight as he traced the seam of her lips, parting them gently to stroke every inch of her mouth with his tongue.

She released the whimper she'd held inside, the beauty of being kissed by him so much more exquisite than she remembered from so long ago.

At seventeen she'd been eager to experience womanly passion, but had no idea what to do with her pent-up sexual desires. As a woman, she wanted to savor every second, burn it into her memory banks so that she'd never forget the pulse pounding feeling of this first kiss.

Because it *was* a first kiss. Before had been clumsy and youthful and over way too quickly. She had thrown herself at him and like the gentleman he was, he had ended it. Now he painted her lips like a master artist, creating a vivid portrait of swirling emotion that made her breath catch and her limbs tremble.

She tasted him, the mixture of coffee and mint making her want to lick at his tongue like a favorite dessert. When she laved his tongue with hers, he groaned and tightened his hold on her.

Magic fought to escape. Thunder crashed louder outside, a spark of lightning flashing out the window and brightening the room with a quick surge of brilliance.

That spark of magic surged within her, too. It drew energy to her and shot out in all directions. She tried to hold it in but couldn't, and realized that Brett was about to get a revelation he might not have expected.

When it surged, she dug her nails into his biceps and shuddered. The magic flamed like a flash of pure sexual heat deep in her core. Brett stilled, groaned, and plunged his tongue in her mouth, darting and withdrawing in the same rhythm he rocked his hips against her weeping sex.

Her pussy quaked and spilled cream down her thighs. She could no longer control the storm raging within her. If he knew what happened he didn't stop, instead moved his hands over her bare skin, stroking her hair, her shoulders, her back, cupping her buttocks to draw her closer against him. Desire coiled tight in her womb, squeezing every ounce of energy from her and directing it to her sex. She whimpered against its power.

Brett spun her around so her back braced against the cool paneled wall of the studio. He slipped his thigh between her legs and nudged it against her sex, drawing a cry from her as her clit exploded with fiery pulsing.

And still, his mouth wove a tapestry of incredible sensation over hers while the storm grew in fury outside.

She hadn't expected this—this unbearable need that forced her magic to swirl around them. Wind picked up and blew in waves over her hot skin, bringing with it the scent of spring flowers. She tensed, waiting for Brett to notice, to say something, to draw back in shock and push her away. But he kept on kissing her and rocking his muscled thigh between her legs until she was certain she'd fall to the floor if he hadn't been holding onto her.

Despite the wickedly sinful sensation of denim against her naked sex, she grew desperate to feel his skin against hers. Reaching for his shirt, she slipped her hand underneath and caressed his taut abdomen, savoring the feel of his muscles jerking in surprise.

"Please," she whispered after she tore her mouth away from his.

He stepped away and drew the shirt off, casting it to the floor, then reached for the button on his jeans. Her gaze was riveted on his movements as he jerked the zipper down, revealing a dark thatch of hair that she wanted to nuzzle against. He drew the jeans down his hips and off, then stepped toward her.

"Wait!' She held out her hand to make him stop. All these years of imagining what it would be like to see him standing naked before her. She had to take a moment and just look at him.

His face was tight as if he struggled to hold onto his control. She knew the feeling. She wanted nothing more than to spread her legs and take his cock between them. But she'd waited ten long years to gaze at his body, and she wanted these few precious seconds.

Exactly as she imagined. No. Better, in fact. His body was tanned, well-muscled, the only evidence of the car accident six years ago the long white scar that ran down the front of his left thigh. He'd broken his leg and they'd put a pin in. She remembered Aidan telling her about all those long months Brett had to hobble around on crutches, then all the physical therapy after that. Now the only reminder was a thin white line. She moved forward and reached out to run her fingers over his broad shoulders and the rounded muscles of his biceps before dipping to her knees to trail her fingertip over the pale scar.

She felt the pain there, drawing in the misery and desolation he'd felt after the accident. She made it a part of herself just as it had been a part of him. Sharing his pain was an enormous emotional shot, but one she could handle. She needed to do this as much as he needed to share it with someone.

His harsh gasp caught her attention. He stared down at her with eyes swirling in darkness, his lips parted and his breathing short and labored. She knew why. Out of the corner of her eye his cock bobbed up and down, calling to her. She wanted to taste him, to envelop his shaft between her lips and savor the flavor of him.

Instead, she pressed a kiss to his scar and ran her tongue along its length, just as she was about to do with his cock. The muscles of his leg tensed and she felt a slight tremble. Could she really excite him that much? What an amazing thing to be responsible for his pleasure.

Turning her attention to his cock, she grasped it with both hands, feeling it pulse against her fingers as she stroked the length of him.

"Christ, Kaitlyn. Do you know how long I've waited for this?"

She didn't answer, just smiled up at him and closed her lips over the tip of his shaft, her tongue swirling over the head to capture the salty taste of him. The flared head heated against her tongue and he jerked his hips forward, sliding his cock deeper and deeper into her mouth. He tasted of need and dark, wicked lust, everything she'd wanted from him for years.

She sucked harder, laving his shaft with her tongue and reaching underneath to cup his balls in her palm, gently squeezing them.

"Oh, shit, Kaitlyn!" he bellowed, driving his cock head toward the back of her throat. She revealed in her power to pleasure him, needing to feel him erupting and shooting his come down her throat. But instead, he reached down and hauled her to her feet, planting his mouth over hers and kissing her with a devastating passion that left her trembling.

She laid her hands on his chest, squeezing the steely muscles there before letting her hands trail down his abdomen. He drew in a harsh breath she wrapped her fingers around his shaft.

"Oh yeah, baby. Stroke it," he urged, his voice as dark as his heavy-lidded gaze.

His command thrilled her, stoked her own internal fires to a raging inferno. Eagerly she complied, caressing the thick shaft from base to tip, savoring how it pulsed with life against her palm.

A part of her couldn't believe she held Brett's cock in her hand, that he was standing before her naked, letting her touch him. How many nights had she dreamed of doing this very thing? Of touching him and taking his cock into her mouth, sucking until he cried out and came.

Now that she had him naked and hard, she intended to fulfill all the fantasies that had gone unfulfilled for too long. Just in case this was the one and only time she'd get the chance.

As she moved her hand over him to caress his taut flesh, she raised her gaze to his. His lips curled in a devilish grin.

"Normally I'd say go ahead, touch and look as long as you like. But *cher*, I need to be inside you and goddamned quick. We'll play later."

Fire burned in his eyes, turning the amber to molten lava. His heat seared her core, her cunt opening, weeping, begging to be filled.

"So turn that powerful magic on us, *ma belle petite sorcière*, and let's make love."

He'd called her his beautiful little witch. God help her but the endearment made her melt. It signaled an acceptance of who she was, when she wasn't sure he was even aware of her powers.

Before she could utter a response, he swept her into his arms and carried her through the studio and back into his house. Lightning sizzled and thunder roared outside, the wind pushing around them with gale force just as it slammed against the windows.

Yet he didn't falter even a step, nor did he ask her to explain why the storm outside the house had moved inside with nary a window open. Being allowed to free her magic made her senses soar with bliss, aligning her with the forces of nature outside and slamming her insides with the need to experience a fury all her own.

He kicked open the door that led to his bedroom and deposited her on the bed. A flash of lightning at the window lit up the room.

The furniture was different since the last time she was here, but she only caught a glimpse of a couple dark wood chests of drawers and the posters on all corners of the bed. She scooted across the comforter and made room for him to join her, holding her arms up to receive him.

In an instant he was next to her, his hips nestled against hers as he drew her to her side and wrapped his arms around her. His cock felt like a burning torch against her belly, hard and throbbing. He took her mouth, threading his fingers into her hair and holding her head in place while he ravaged her lips and tongue with intense kisses. His assault left her mindless and gasping for breath. Her magic pulsed, filling the room with the scent of lavender.

Brett lifted his head, stared at the flowers bursting from his carpet, and turned to her, a smile curling his lips. "That's some interesting magic you have there, Kaitlyn Storm. Is there anything else about you that I should know?"

She wasn't quite sure how to answer that, but he spoke again, this time drawing his hand over her belly and between her breasts. "For instance, if I lick your nipple, will a flower pop out there?"

She giggled, but only for a second because he did just that, his lips covering one taut nipple, his tongue swirling over the aching bud. She arched her back and moaned at the exquisite sensation as he pulled and tugged at the crest until it popped free of his mouth, standing glistening and erect. He leaned over her and took the other nipple in his mouth, teasing it to the same state.

A soft whimper escaped her lips and she moved her hips in a silent signal, hoping he'd take her as she'd dreamt of for so many years. Her pussy was drenched, liquid arousal seeping from her. Instead, he palmed her belly again and shook his head.

"Incredible body. Just as I imagined. You didn't have to worry about me painting you wrong, Kait. I've known every inch of you for years."

"You've never seen me naked."

His gaze moved from her sex to her face, the smile disappearing as he said, "Yeah, I have."

"When?"

"I've dreamed about it."

Her heart clenched at his words. He'd dreamed of making love to her, the same as she had about him? Then why had they spent all these years apart? Why had he married Amanda instead of—

No. She wouldn't go there, it wasn't fair. Back then neither of them had been ready for this. Now? Now she was more than ready.

"I used to dream about you, too."

"Is that right?" But he'd turned his attention from her face to her belly again, sliding his hand over the flat plane and then lower to cup her sex. "I'll bet you had sweet little girlie dreams of lovemaking. My dreams about you were a little...darker."

His hand on her mound was like dipping into a fiery bath. She cried out and rain burst from the ceiling, the light mist tinged with the smell of sweet flowers. Brett didn't even pause, instead slid his fingers lower, circling her clit and slipping one between her throbbing pussy lips to dip inside her cunt.

"Christ, it's hot in there," he murmured, withdrawing his thick finger, only to thrust two of them inside her. She moved her hips against his hand, so close to orgasm she could feel the quakes squeezing his fingers.

"Please, Brett," she whimpered, reaching down to grab his wrist and guide the tempo she needed. "God, I need you inside me."

He gave her exactly what she needed, using his thumb to draw circles around her clit. Searing heat burned her but she still inched closer to the flame, needing what only he could give her. A rush of cream spilled from her again, and he murmured his approval.

"Oh yeah. So fucking hot. I dreamed of touching you like this, to feel the heat that radiated from your body. I knew you'd be hot inside. Hot and creamy."

His words melted her, drawing more juices from her.

"I dreamed of a lot of things," he continued, his fingers continuing to pump inside her. "Hot, wicked, nasty things I wanted to do with you. Can you handle that, Kaitlyn? Can you give me everything I want?"

She couldn't answer him, his words driving her closer and closer to the edge of sanity. But each time she poised near the edge, he slowed the pace, painting her clit with her own juices — soft, swirling caresses over her distended pearl, then moving away as soon as he found that spot guaranteed to catapult her into immediate orgasm. He was driving her slowly crazy, but it was an amazing experience, one she wouldn't miss for a thousand orgasms.

When he moved his hand and rested it on her thigh, her eyes flew open, beseeching him with her gaze.

"Not yet, baby. Answer my question."

Whimpering her frustration, she said, "I want it any way you want it, Brett."

"Oh I don't know about that." He traced wet circles around her belly button, painting her skin with the cream from her cunt. "I want to fill every hole you have with my cock — I want to feel it in your mouth, your pussy and your ass. I want to bend you over and spank that gorgeous ass of yours while I fuck you. I want you to suck me until I shoot buckets of hot come down your throat. So tell me the truth, *cher*. Can you handle me?"

Pitié douce! The way he described what he wanted to do with her was so damn hot she could cry. "Yes!" she whimpered, desperate for him to do all he suggested. "Yes, I can handle it."

"Good."

She sighed in relief when he skated down her belly and cupped her sex again, dipping his fingers inside her and thrusting with renewed precision.

"So wet. You're burning me, Kaitlyn. Now come for me. I want your cunt gripping my fingers when you come. I want to feel what it's going to be like when I fuck you."

This time when he caressed her clit, he didn't stop. Instead, he used one hand to pluck and pet her bud while driving his fingers into her cunt. She lifted her hips and cried out, digging her nails into his arm as she flew into a rushing orgasm that filled the room with a heavy downpour of rain.

Thunder shook the bed, lightning arcing just over their heads. The wind whipped tendrils of hair into her face, but she hardly noticed any of it, too caught up in the maelstrom of orgasm. The pulsing had no more subsided than he was over her, nudging her legs apart with his knee and coming down on top of her.

She was still pulsing when he drove his thick cock deep into her pussy. Her tight channel gripped and sucked him inside. She wrapped her legs around his waist, tears pouring from her eyes and mixing with the raindrops pelting the pillows.

Brett was inside her, one with her, just as she'd imagined all those years ago. The enormity of the moment was unbearable and she cupped his face in her hands to draw him into a kiss.

His mouth ground against hers, his pelvis doing the same against her pussy as he reared back, only to thrust deeper inside her heated core.

This was the magic. Not the thunder or lightning or rain. This moment with this man, she felt the awesome power of destiny, and knew what she had always suspected was true. Brett was her destiny. Time had not changed her feelings for him. They had only deepened. She loved him as much now as she ever had before, with an intensity that both frightened and compelled her. She'd never known feelings like this, had never felt so complete in a man's arms before. He fit her perfectly, inside and out.

"Bring on the thunder, *cher*," he said, slamming against her with savage power. "Come with me and make it pour on both of us."

His balls slapped her ass as he moved with lightning speed inside her. The movements of his pelvis grinding against her clit had her clutching him for support. She felt like she was falling. Slowly, irrevocably sailing over a cliff and he was her only lifeline.

When her second climax hit like a rushing wave, she held her breath and took him with her, holding tight as he poured hot jets of come deep inside her, then collapsed and rolled her over on top of him.

She could stay like this forever, listening to the sound of the retreating storm, his hands roaming featherlight over her back and buttocks. She tried to shift, afraid she was too heavy on top of him, but he held her in place with his hands, continuing to stroke her skin and hair.

The room was totally dry, the blankets bearing no evidence of the earlier indoor downpour. She was certain that at some point she'd have to explain the Storm family powers to Brett. But he hadn't asked, and she was more than happy to wait to explain.

Besides, there was nothing more magical than being in his arms as he held her safe within his embrace. If her life ended right now, she'd die happy. All the years of waiting for love to find her had been worth this one moment in time.

"I hope you're not too tired," he whispered against her ear. "Because we've just started. We have a night's worth of debauchery ahead of us."

She lifted up to look at him, grinning at his mussed hair. His eyes twinkled with devilish delight. This night was just like she'd imagined. "Debauchery, huh? Bring it on."

Chapter Six

Brett stared into Kaitlyn's excited eyes at the mention of the things they had yet to do.

The things they shouldn't be doing. He should have never let her push him this far. Oh hell, who was he kidding? She barely poked a finger in his chest and he crumbled, taking her despite years of self-warnings.

But now he wouldn't think about the repercussions of what they'd done. How could he when a goddess rested on top of him?

God, she was beautiful. Her hair tumbled over his chest, her skin moist with sweat and scented with sex and flowers. The Storms' magic, which he'd known about for years, made her even more special, especially since he took the outpouring of rain, lightning and thunder as a sign that she'd lost all control during their lovemaking. Hell, what guy wouldn't take that as a compliment?

The feel of her breathing against his chest, her body pressed so intimately against him, had him ready again. His cock twitched and began to harden again, rising up between her legs to nestle between her buttocks.

Her eyes widened. "So soon?"

"You have no idea how long I've wanted to get you naked and have my wicked way with you," he teased, taking one of her hands and nibbling on the pad of her thumb.

She shivered and wriggled against him, her wet pussy stroking the top of his shaft. He clutched her buttocks and drew her back and forth, the tiny nub of her clit grazing his pelvis. Once she realized what he was doing, she braced her arms on either side of his shoulders and rocked with him, lingering on the down sweep and enveloping his shaft between the soft globes of her ass cheeks.

Her gaze caught and held his, the intensity swirling in her eyes something he wanted to stop and immediately paint. Just her face and the way her prominent cheekbones pinkened when she was turned on, the way she worried her bottom lip with her teeth when she concentrated, but especially how her eyes seemed to change color from golden to green as he watched.

He wanted to paint her in the middle of a field of green grass, sweeping magnolia trees and wildflowers, her arms outstretched toward the heavens while rain poured over her. Because that's how he saw her right now.

"Tell me what's on your mind," she asked, dragging herself up his chest so that their noses touched. Her eyes crossed and she giggled.

"Do you really want to know what's on my mind?" He wouldn't tell her about how he saw her. That would only make her blush. The best he could do was show her how he felt, because he'd never be able to put his feelings into words.

"Sure I do. I mean, I can certainly feel something down there between my legs. I might know what you're thinking about, but I can't be sure."

His teasing seductress arched a wicked brow and licked her bottom lip, an invitation he couldn't refuse. He cupped the back of her neck and drew her toward his waiting mouth, plunging his tongue inside as soon as lips met lips. Her breath washed over him, as sweet as a stolen bud of spring honeysuckle. She tangled her fingers in his hair and pressed her lips harder against his, lapping at the tip of his tongue until his balls drew up tight and throbbed.

She was sweet spring and innocence mixed with a full-blooded womanly temptress and he wasn't sure which one he preferred. Probably the combination of both, since that's what made Kaitlyn the woman he l—

...lusted after. That was the right "L" word. There was no emotion behind it. He simply couldn't get enough of her.

But he would get enough, and it would have to be tonight. Because there'd be no repeat performance, no doing this again, no chance in hell of this becoming a relationship. He owed at least that much to her, to save her from what would someday be her enormous regrets that this night had occurred. Better to enjoy it while it happened for what it was, which was purely and simply...sex.

Great sex. Phenomenal sex. The kind of sex he'd whispered in her ear earlier, when he'd told her all his deep, dark desires for her.

He cupped her buttocks and rolled her over onto her back, then slid off the bed and dragged her hips to the edge. Her legs dangled over the sides and he picked up one tiny foot, marveling at the bright pink toenail polish on each nail and the delicate silver chain of tinkling bells adorning one ankle. The sounds they made when he moved her leg reminded him of soft, falling rain.

When he kissed her toes one by one, she sighed. When he took one into his mouth and swirled his tongue around it, she moaned, then had the same reaction when he took her other foot and did the same thing. When he scooted between her thighs and blew softly on her wet, bare sex, her head shot up, her widened eyes made contact with his.

"Let me...clean up a bit."

He grinned and held firmly to her thighs, holding her in place. "No. I want to taste the two of us mixed together. You need cleaning up, I'll do it. With my tongue."

"Brett, I really don't—oh, God."

His mouth made contact with the swollen pink lips of her pussy. Her head fell back against the sheets, her fingers curling into the satin coverlet under her hands.

God, her pussy was so hot, so creamy. Both his come and hers dripped from her, reminding him what it had been like to shoot inside her. He licked a few of the salty drops from her slit before plunging his tongue inside to take a mouthful of the sweetest cream he'd ever tasted.

Her hips bucked against his face, little mewling cries escaping her lips. He buried his nose along the side of her clit, licking her cunt and sweeping his head from side to side to torment the little pearl hidden under its protective hood. With great regret he moved away from the tasty juices pouring from her pussy and swirled his tongue around the bud of her clit, coaxing it out from its hiding place. He pressed the flat of his tongue gently over the distended nub, licking in small circles until her knuckles turned white from clutching the covers and she was shrieking louder than the thunder outside.

Along with her cries, his mouth was suddenly filled with the tasty hot cream of her come as she flooded his tongue and rocked her pussy against his face. He smiled against her skin when he felt the mist of a soft rain that seemed to fall from the ceiling, but took it as a sign she was being well satisfied. And that was his primary goal tonight—to satisfy his woman. During the short period of time she was, in fact, *his* woman.

He leaned back and watched the cream pour down the crack of her ass, his cock so damn hard and his balls so filled to bursting that he wasn't sure he could make it another minute before he came.

But he would. Oh hell yeah, he'd make it that long, because he wanted to totally possess her in every possible way. And seeing the river of cream coat the small puckered hole between her ass cheeks made his cock lurch hard against his belly.

He stood and leaned over the bed, pressing a kiss to her mouth. When she licked her own cream from his lips he thought he'd died and gone to heaven. But would she give him everything he desired? "You remember what I told you earlier?"

She frowned. "What was that?"

"About how I wanted to take you in every hole, in every way imaginable."

"Oh that. Yes, I remember."

Her eyes lit up with excitement.

When he pushed forward, his cock teasing her anus, her eyes widened, but not in fear. Arousal turned them a molten gold, the green flecks sparkling like emeralds in her eyes. She planted her feet on the mattress and gave her assent by spreading her legs wide, allowing his cock head to rub against her ass.

He could have come right then, shooting all over her sweet asshole. Instead, he reached between them, sliding his fingers through her cream and drawing it downward to coat her anus. Palming his cock, he positioned it at the entrance to her tiny hole and pushed gently against her, just enough to breach the outer barrier.

"Oh, God, Brett, that feels so good," she whispered, sliding one hand down her belly to cup her sex.

The sight of her fingers teasing her clit was a sweet, torturous pain in his balls. He surged forward again, pushing his cock head against the muscled barrier, keeping his gaze focused on her fingers teasing her pussy lips.

"Yes, that's it," he said, his body taut as he held back the need to drive hard inside her ass and bury himself deep. "Touch yourself for me, *cher*."

Glistening moisture flowed from her pussy and coated his cock head, allowing just the right amount of lubrication to ease past the rigid muscle at her anal entrance. His balls tightened when her passage gripped him and pulled him deeper. He fought for control, firming his resolve to hold back when instinct told him to ram hard, ram fast, and spurt a load of come inside her ass.

Kaitlyn shuddered and reached for his arms, digging her nails into his skin. He stopped, afraid he was hurting her. "Do you want me to stop?"

"No," she whispered, her voice gravelly soft. "Please, more."

Now it was his turn to shudder at her husky plea. He pushed, gently, inch by inch until he was buried to the hilt inside her ass. He paused and closed his eyes, savoring the feel of her vise-like grip around his shaft. God, she was tight. He stilled, waiting for her body to grow accustomed to his thick invasion. When she released his arms and slipped her hand between her legs to draw lazy circles around her clit, he moved again, this time drawing out partially and sliding back in, letting her set the rhythm and the amount of force he used.

"Have you ever let a man do this to you?" he asked.

She shook her head, her eyes glazed with passion. "Never."

Being this intimate with her was more than he could have ever imagined. That she'd never allowed a man to penetrate her here made her gift to him so much more meaningful.

If only he had something to give her in return. But he didn't. Only this one night of passion, this one night where he intended to please her and give them both memories to last a lifetime.

"Play with your nipples, Kait."

She smiled and moved one hand over her breast, using her thumb to strum one nipple back and forth. It peaked and pointed straight up, too delectable to resist.

Bracing his palms on either side of her, he leaned forward and captured the crest in his mouth, flicking his tongue over the bud before closing his lips over it to suckle. Her harsh intake of breath and the quickening movements of her hand between them as she caressed her clit signaled her intensifying pleasure.

A low rumble began, the bed quaking around them. Brett cast his gaze out the window and saw that the storm was long gone. Stars were visible in the night sky.

This storm came from Kaitlyn and he reveled in its amazing power. With every stroke of his cock in her snug passage, the thunder growled, lightning shot across the room, and a stiff breeze gusted, cooling their heated, perspiring flesh.

Her anus constricted around him, waves of gripping pleasure making his balls knot up against his body, readying for release. Brett leaned back and powered inside her. She whimpered and pressed the heel of her hand against her clit and plunged two fingers into her cunt to fuck herself. The smell of sex permeated the air around them, filling the room with a musky scent that made his balls quiver in response. The slick sounds she made as she fucked her pussy with her fingers were the most erotic noise he'd ever heard. For this one moment, she was his. Totally his, just as he'd imagined for the past ten years.

"God, I can feel your fingers in there," he groaned. It felt like another cock rode inside her pussy, pumping in time to his thrusts in her ass.

Her eyes were half-closed, her lips parted as she panted and moaned. She drove her fingers deep, arching her back and crying out as the waves of her orgasm penetrated through to her anus. Lightning-intense heat singed his skin. Along with the pulsing squeeze of her tightening ass it was more than he could bear. He erupted inside her, groaning a harsh curse as jets of hot come sprayed from his cock. Kaitlyn shuddered in the throes of climax, her head tilted back to expose the slender column of her throat.

He could paint her just like this, in the moment of orgasm when her face and breasts were flushed with desire, the hard points of her nipples jutting up, her lips parted as she gasped for air. He'd never seen a more erotic vision in his life. The memory would never leave him.

All too soon the thunder dissipated, the lightning gone, too, leaving behind the sweet scent of wet wildflowers mixed with the smell of hot sex.

When Kaitlyn opened her eyes and smiled up at him, he leaned in and captured her lips in a bittersweet kiss, aware it was getting late, and knowing he'd never get a repeat of tonight. He already missed her taste and the feel of his cock buried deep inside her. But he wasn't ready to let go of her just yet.

"How about a shower?" he suggested.

She nodded and he withdrew, leading her into the bathroom. He pulled her into the shower, the warm, misty spray a welcome relief to his sweat-soaked skin. He washed every inch of her body, savoring the feel of her under his hands. She sighed and relaxed against him as he soaped her breasts, belly and pussy, his cock surprising him by hardening again.

Kaitlyn tilted her head back and smiled at him, then quickly covered her mouth to stifle a yawn.

He could take her all night long, again and again and again until he couldn't get it up anymore. But she was exhausted and he knew it. So he rinsed her off, turned off the shower and grabbed a towel to dry her, then led her back to his bed and slipped under the covers with her. Wrapping his arms tightly around her as she nestled against his chest, he wondered if he'd ever been this content.

Though he already knew the answer. No. From the time he'd met Amanda until the day she died, he'd been a drunk. Hell, he could only piece together half of their years together. The rest was nothing more than a thick fog of semi-memories. He was certain he'd missed a ton of great things.

Stop this. Now isn't the time to think of the past. Not when he held Kaitlyn in his arms for the first and last time.

"Sleepy?" he asked.

"Mmm, a little." She snuggled closer and draped her leg over his crotch, nestling her breasts against his side. He kissed the top of her head and shut his eyes, grateful to have had at least this one night with her.

Now he could paint her portrait while knowing every intimate detail about her, and maybe get through it without wanting to jump her again.

Yeah, right. He would forever crave being inside her again, and he was more than a little afraid that desire would never go away.

Kaitlyn stared across the kitchen table at Brett, pondering his total turnaround in demeanor.

Last night had been all heat and passion. He'd been attentive, loving, and had held her in his arms the entire night. By the time she fell asleep she was convinced their relationship had turned a corner and was headed in the right direction.

But this morning everything had changed. Gone was the warm-blooded lover who'd given her multiple orgasms and the best sex of her life. In his place stood a surly, monosyllabic grouch who barely gave one-word answers to her questions.

Maybe he just didn't do mornings well.

"Are you hungry? I could fix us something for breakfast."

"No."

Don't bother to ask if I'm hungry. "Okay. Um, what are your plans for today?

He looked up from his coffee cup and frowned. "Plans?"

"Yeah. I thought maybe we could spend the day together."

"No."

All right, then. It was clear she wasn't wanted here. She gripped the coffee cup like a vise, not wanting to immediately jump up from the table and run off, but his abrupt dismissal sure made it difficult.

"I'm sorry. I'm preoccupied with a few business matters that'll keep me busy today. I didn't mean to come off sounding like such a prick."

That made her feel a little bit better. "Oh, it's no problem. We can do it another time."

"No, Kaitlyn. We can't."

"What do you mean?"

He stood and poured himself another cup of coffee, then refilled hers. When he sat down, he took her hands in his. "I had a great time last night."

"Me too." She knew there was a "but" coming and felt it stab her middle like the quick jab of a sharp blade. She wrapped her arms around her stomach as if covering it would prevent him from saying the words.

"But, I'm not in the market for a relationship. I had one and it ended tragically."

There it was. And despite her instincts to protect herself, she'd felt every word with a burning pain that pierced her skin. Pushing back the hurt, she wanted to blurt out that not every woman he fell in love with would die so terribly, but held her tongue. Instead, she said, "You can't let the past dictate your future, Brett."

He jammed his fingers through his hair. "It's more than just what happened with Amanda. In fact, one doesn't have anything to do with the other. I'm just not cut out to have a woman in my life."

"You seemed to enjoy having a woman in your life last night." She sounded bitter, but dammit she felt bitter. This wasn't fair!

"I like sex. Hell, I loved the sex we had last night. It was the hottest fucking I've had in a very long time. But that's all it could ever be. I'm sorry if you were looking for more than that."

Pain lanced her chest and she wanted to rub the spot that ached near her breast.

She had no one to blame but herself for this. She'd asked for this by assuming that making love with him meant as much to him as it had meant to her. And she'd been the one who'd pushed for it. He had tried to talk her out of it.

Maybe she should have listened.

Okay, so he was only in the market for casual sex. If that was all she could get, she could live with it. Because she wasn't buying for one second his spiel about just being in it for the physical aspect. That was his pain talking, and his fear of losing someone else he loved. She was patient and was willing to wait it out.

"There's nothing wrong with a little casual sex between two people who have great chemistry, Brett. I'm not...looking for a relationship, either."

Liar. She wanted forever with him.

He arched a brow. "You're not exactly the type of girl who fucks just for fun. I'll bet you haven't had more than a handful of lovers in your lifetime."

He hit that right on the mark. She shrugged. "I'm just not ready to settle down. I enjoy sex, and yeah, I am discriminating when it comes to choosing partners. But after last night, I wouldn't mind a repeat performance now and then."

It cost her dearly to adopt such a carefree attitude when she was breaking inside. But she stood and put her cup in the sink, then approached him. He stared at her, frowning, as if he couldn't quite believe what she'd said. Good. Let him stew on it for a while. She leaned in and pressed a soft, lingering kiss to his lips, winding her fingers down his naked chest to cup his balls and palm his already hardening cock. When she pulled back, his eyes had gone smoky dark.

She grinned and said, "I gotta go. Let me know when you want to schedule another session for...painting." With a wink she turned and left the kitchen, gathered her things and hurried out the door before she did something stupid, like burst into tears.

Brett sat frozen, unable to move after Kaitlyn's warm kiss and questing hands had him hard and shaking with the need to take her right on the table.

Ah, hell. The idea of having casual sex with Kaitlyn made him feel like a prick. He'd take and she'd give and then what? He'd still want more, and he'd end up hating her and hurting her for forcing him to acknowledge his own desires.

That he refused to do. He was never going to subject her to the darkness that hovered just inside him, threatening to return him to the days of alcoholic oblivion.

His alcoholism had caused the death of his wife. God, he'd been really drunk that night. And Amanda had called him on it, demanded that he seek help for his addiction. She'd even tried to take the keys away from him. But oh no, he was perfectly in control and didn't need his wife to drive him home.

Yeah, he was in control all right. He'd controlled the car right down that embankment and hit the tree head-on. And Amanda had suffered irreparable internal injuries that had taken her life, while he'd walked away with a concussion that he'd been too drunk to even feel and a broken leg. He'd deserved much more than that. He'd deserved to be the one to die, not Amanda. He'd deserved to go to prison, and probably would have if the hospital had done a blood alcohol on him. For some reason they never even checked. Of course he'd been stone cold sober by the time they pulled Amanda out of the wreckage. And it had been raining that night so the streets were slick. He told the police he'd lost control of the vehicle on a slippery curve and they'd bought it.

The last words spoken with Amanda had been words of anger. Yeah, he remembered that part all too clearly. "You're going to kill us both, Brett," she'd said, right before he'd lost it.

Closing his eyes and forcing back the gut-wrenching memories, he wished for the millionth time that he'd never touched that first can of beer. Hell, he wished a lot of things. Blamed everyone else for what had been his problem all along.

But he couldn't go back, and he couldn't change what he'd done.

And no matter how long he'd been sober, he'd never take the chance that he could harm someone he cared about.

He'd never hurt someone he loved like he'd hurt Amanda. And despite the fact he hadn't touched alcohol since that black day six years ago, he knew the temptation that lived inside him, knew at any moment he could reach for a bottle and take one giant step back into the days of hell.

If and when that ever happened, he'd make sure he was the only one stepping into that void. Kaitlyn would not be accompanying him on the journey. He'd just have to work harder to push her away.

The sound of the phone ringing jerked him out of his self-torment.

"Hello?"

"Brett McGregor, are you avoiding me?"

Oh, God. Kaitlyn's mother, Angelina. "Now how could I avoid the most beautiful woman in Louisiana?"

"Quit sweet-talking me, you scoundrel. You're as bad as Aidan and I'm immune to the both of you. We haven't seen you around here in months. It's Sunday and we're having the entire family over for dinner. Get your butt over here at five o'clock."

Shit! The last thing he needed to do was see Kaitlyn again. Not until he could put his mind around what he had to do to keep her at a distance. But one never turned down a request from Angelina Storm. She was the closest thing to a real parent that he'd ever had, and she was right. He'd been so immersed in his work that several months had gone by and he hadn't seen the rest of the family. Turning her down would only make her more determined. In fact, he wouldn't put it past her to drag dinner and her entire family to his doorstep. "Yes, ma'am. Five o'clock it is."

"Excellent! I'll see you then."

He hung up and wondered at the sudden invitation. Knowing the Storms and their incredible magic, he wouldn't put it past Angelina to know that something was going on between him and Kaitlyn. He groaned at the thought of a family inquisition, and decided he'd better be mentally ready to handle a barrage of questions.

This wasn't going to be a fun night.

"You invited Brett for dinner?"

Kaitlyn cast wide eyes toward her mother, who blinked back at her with an innocent look that Kait wasn't buying.

"Yes I invited Brett for dinner. Any reason not to?"

Yeah, about a hundred, the least of which was the oh-so sweet soreness that still lingered between her legs. She'd barely gotten out of his house with her dignity intact this morning. Add last night's sexcapades into the mix and this was going to be one uncomfortable evening.

She thought she'd have at least a day or two before she'd have to face him again, so she could figure out her battle plan.

Right now she had no plan, other than hoping like hell her family didn't find out what was going on between them. The last thing she needed was them sticking their noses into her business.

Oh, God, this was *not* good!

"What's wrong?" her mother asked.

"Wrong? Nothing's wrong. What could possibly be wrong? Do you need some help with dinner? How about I set the table? Want me to cook anything for you?"

"*Ma belle*, you're babbling."

She closed her mouth before more idiocy spewed forth. "I am?"

"Yes. Does this have something to do with Brett?"

The sound of a perfectly timed snicker behind her had her blood boiling. Leave it to Shannon to walk in at just the right moment. Or wrong moment.

"You know something," her mother said, eyeing Shannon suspiciously. "Someone tell me what's going on."

"Nothing's going on," Kaitlyn said.

"Brett's painting Kait nude," Shannon said, kissing her mother on the cheek and turning to wink at Kaitlyn. Shannon's fiancé, Max, just grinned and walked by without a word.

Max was a smart guy. Even though a newcomer to the family, he knew when to keep his mouth shut and not get involved.

Unfortunately, both Aidan and Lissa took just that moment to step into the kitchen too. Kaitlyn resisted the urge to turn tail and run like hell.

"Wanna run that one by me again?" Aidan said, arms crossed as he leaned against the doorjamb.

"Yeah, in graphic detail, please," Lissa added with a wide grin, wrapping her arms around Aidan and leaning against him.

"I don't want to talk about this." Kaitlyn turned away and busied herself by stirring the rice on the stove. Her cheeks flamed with embarrassment, her mind scrambling for a way out of this mess. She shot Shannon a vicious glare, but her sister only shrugged and grinned. "You can't keep secrets like that around this family, Kait. You of all people should know that."

"What secrets?"

Oh, God. Logan. This was not good. Not good at all. So much for them not finding out. Damn Shannon and her big mouth!

"Brett's painting Kaitlyn nude," Angelina said.

"Oh, that's sexy." Logan's fiancée, Sophie, would think that. But Sophie was a sensual creature, so Kaitlyn wasn't surprised.

"Really. How…fascinating," Logan said, nearly sending the kitchen into a deep freeze with one glare of his icy blue eyes.

She knew Logan well enough to realize the cool tone in his voice meant he wasn't happy. Too bad. She turned and faced them. "This is none of your business. Stay out of it and for God's sake leave Brett alone when he gets here."

Aidan arched a brow. "Brett's coming for dinner? As your…date?"

She rolled her eyes, seriously thinking about running out the front door and avoiding the mess tonight's dinner was bound to be.

"No. I invited him this morning. Though I didn't know you two had grown so…close," Angelina said, her warm smile not at all comforting to Kaitlyn. When her mother smiled like that, she had something up her sleeve. Like matchmaking.

Maybe Brett would cancel.

"So are you two going out?" Lissa asked, slipping into one of the kitchen chairs.

"No. We're not going out. I wanted to have my portrait painted and Brett's a phenomenal artist. So I asked him to do it."

"And he agreed?" Aidan asked. "That surprises me. He hasn't painted at all since Amanda died."

"I had arranged to have someone else paint me, but at the last minute Brett canceled him and said you'd kill him if he allowed someone else to paint me nude."

Aidan smirked. "He's right about that."

"Besides, we're like brother and sister," Kaitlyn pronounced, hoping that would put an end to any romantic thoughts her family had about the two of them.

Shannon snorted. "Nobody's buying that one, honey. There isn't a soul in this room who hasn't seen how you look at Brett, who hasn't felt the energy between you two. So you can knock off the brother/sister act because it's not gonna fly with us."

Kaitlyn pulled the spoon from the pot and rested it on the holder, then sank into the nearest chair. "I really wish you all would just leave it alone. It's my business. I'm an adult. Brett and I do not have a relationship together. I commissioned a painting. He's the artist. It ends there."

Or at least that's how Brett wanted it to end. She wasn't about to let things lie between them. But she also didn't need her family interfering. They would only make things worse. She knew if they started pushing Brett about her, he'd back off.

"Face it, sis," Shannon argued. "You've been in love with Brett since you were sixteen years old. And you still are. The question is what are you going to do about it?"

"I'm not going to do anything about anything. And I'm not in love with him."

Ignoring her statement, Shannon asked, "Well, then what's Brett going to do about it?"

"Do about what?"

Kaitlyn's head shot up at the sound of Brett's voice. He stood at the entrance to the kitchen, a big grin on his face. The room went silent and his smile died as several sets of eyes zoomed in on him.

Merde! *Just kill me now*! She mentally pleaded for mercy and a quick death. Anything would be preferable to what was about to come.

Brett knew the moment every head turned in his direction that they'd been talking about him. He'd heard the mumble of conversation when he walked through the door and followed the sound, knowing he was always welcome in the Storm kitchen. Then he heard his name.

Now Kaitlyn sat there blushing crimson, and several arched brows and questioning looks were aimed solely at him.

Christ, she hadn't told them about last night, had she?

"Brett," Angelina said, stepping forward to wrap her arms around him and give him a tight squeeze. "It's been too long, *cher*."

He hugged her back and then pulled away to look at her. "And you keep getting younger."

"And you're still full of blarney," she said with a wink. "Come, sit down and relax."

He slid into a chair next to Kaitlyn. "Kait," he said, trying to sound nonchalant even though he felt anything but. God, just looking at her brought back memories of last night. Her pink sweater molded to her breasts. Color rose high on her cheekbones, her eyes sparkling with intense interest. And embarrassment.

They knew. Shit, somehow they knew. Surely she hadn't come over here and told them what happened last night? He knew Kaitlyn would want to avoid her family's involvement at all costs. Though from the color in her face and the warm gold flickering in her eyes, she looked like she'd spent the entire night making love. And he'd like to take her right here and right now, her family be damned.

"Brett." She gave him an artificial smile that spoke volumes about her current discomfort level.

"Shannon told us you're painting Kait nude," Aidan said.

Shit. So much for subtly working that into the topic of conversation. "Yeah. She was rather insistent about that. So I had no choice but to agree. Better me than someone else, right?" He hoped Aidan would see the logic in that.

"I guess so," was Aidan's only reply.

"I didn't exactly twist your arm," Kait mumbled.

"And how's that going?" Logan asked, standing near the stove with his arms crossed.

Logan Storm could intimidate the strongest of men with his icy blue eyes and fierce, chilly demeanor. But Brett had known him forever and wasn't the least bit bothered by it. "We're just getting started, but it's going well. Your sister is a beautiful subject to paint."

"I'll just bet she is," Logan replied, sarcasm dripping off every word.

"Logan, quit being an ass," Sophie piped up. "I think it's sexy as hell that you're painting her nude. And Kait, I admire your bravery. I don't think I could do it. Well, not unless Logan learns to paint."

Brett laughed. "There's really nothing sexual about painting a nude. It's one of the first things they teach in art class. The human body is nothing more than another art form to an artist."

"Brett, can I talk to you for a minute alone?"

Brett looked at Aidan and nodded. "Sure." He knew what this was about. Aidan was going to do the brotherly thing and look out for his little sister. If he'd had siblings, he'd have done the same thing.

Kaitlyn looked pale. Did she think he was going to talk to Aidan about what they did last night? Hell, he wasn't dumb. Painting was one thing. Sex was another. He winked at Kait and followed Aidan out the back door and down the steps.

They walked all the way to the boat dock at the end of the property and sat in chairs overlooking the lake. For a few minutes Aidan was quiet, so Brett just let him ponder his thoughts.

"Have you told her yet?" Aidan finally asked.

"About what?"

"About you, your problem, and what really happened the night Amanda died."

One thing Brett always admired about Aidan was his blunt forthrightness. Granted, his words stung, but he knew the reasons behind the questions. "No, I haven't."

"Don't you think you should?"

"I don't think she needs to know all that just because I'm painting her."

Aidan looked him in the eye. "You know damn well you're doing a hell of a lot more than painting her. The energy between the two of you is seismic. It's clear you're sleeping together, so don't bullshit me, friend."

Though his tone was light, Brett caught the irritation sizzling just beneath the surface. "And you don't approve of that."

Aidan shrugged. "Kait's a big girl. She can make her own decisions about who she sleeps with. I just want her to have all the facts. You owe her that much."

"It's just sex, Aidan. And I'm sorry if that hurts you, but you know I'd never do anything to hurt Kaitlyn."

"And you think fucking her isn't going to hurt her? She loves you, man. She always has."

Brett didn't believe that. She might have thought she loved him when she was seventeen, but she was much older and smarter now. She knew the difference between love and sex. "No, she doesn't. We have a physical attraction and we're having sex. And that's all there is to it."

"I know you as well as anyone ever has, Brett. And I also know you've always had feelings for Kaitlyn. I appreciated you backing off when she fell all over you when she was just a kid, but now she's a grown woman. And I know you still care about her, so don't feed me a bullshit line about how it's just sex between the two of you."

He should have known better than to lie to Aidan.

"Look," Aidan continued. "I'm not going to interfere in your relationship. Just be careful. You know I love you like a brother, but I love my sister, too. I don't want to see her get hurt."

Which confirmed to Brett what he already suspected. He had no business getting involved with Kaitlyn. Even his best friend had no faith in him. That hurt, more than he'd ever let Aidan know.

But Aidan was right. He had no business playing around with Kaitlyn, despite her assurances that she was only interested in sex. He knew her. That wasn't her style at all.

The sooner he removed Kaitlyn from his life, the better it would be for both of them.

Chapter Seven

Kait stared out the back door, wishing she could hear what Brett and Aidan were talking about.

The rest of the family had meandered into the family room to watch television with Dad, leaving her alone with her mother. She knew it was only a matter of time before the questioning started.

Putting a lid on a simmering pot of crab legs, her mother wiped her hands on a towel and sat in the chair next to her. "Okay, while things are cooking we can talk."

Here it comes. "There's nothing going on between Brett and me."

"Yes, there is, *ma petite*. I can feel it."

Kaitlyn rolled her eyes, knowing better than to try and refute her mother's "feelings". The best thing to do was come clean, at least about a few things. Not everything. "We're having sex, Mom. That's all. Just physical, fun sex. We're not even dating." *We're just fucking.* But she wouldn't be so crass as to say that to her mother.

"I think you both feel a lot more than you're letting on. Brett's heart is aching, *cher*. And it's aching for you. But something's holding him back."

"Amanda," she replied.

Her mother nodded. "Partially, but not because of what you think. There's more to it than his memories of her, or his guilt over the fact he was driving the night she died. A lot more."

She frowned. "You know something."

"More a feeling than anything. Besides, it's not for me to say. You'll have to figure that out with Brett."

As if she'd ever be able to figure him out. "He confuses me, Mom."

"I can tell you this," her mother said, taking her hands and squeezing them tight. Kaitlyn felt the strength of her mother's magic, a powerful, positive force entering her. Her mother had always given her strength when she needed it most. "I see a future for the two of you. You are the bright sun in Brett's life. He needs you. But there are dark clouds on the horizon. You're going to have to be strong because he'll fight you."

Oh great. As if she could knock him down and force him to love her. "I don't know if I *can* fight him. He has very sturdy walls built up." Huge, impenetrable walls. Some days she felt like she was trying to kick through steel plate with her bare feet. Useless.

Her mother grinned. "Knock them down, *ma petite*. Knock them down."

Any further discussion was put on hold as Aidan and Brett stepped back into the house. Kaitlyn looked at him, trying to gauge his mood, but he just smiled and went past her into the other room without a word.

The quick look he gave her caused her to worry. Something happened between Brett and Aidan. She felt the tension when they came back in, and neither Aidan nor Brett made eye contact with her throughout dinner. Fortunately, there were so many people at the table no one noticed, and both Aidan and Brett seemed calm, relaxed and both smiled and joked.

She wasn't buying it. Something went on outside. As always, a Storm family dinner was noisy with multiple conversations going on. Now was not a good time to try and figure out Brett's mind anyway. The last thing she wanted to do was try to have a discussion with him while her nosy family was eavesdropping.

Later, after the dishes were cleared, she caught him alone and tugged on his shirt.

"I need to talk to you."

He shook his head. "Now's not a good time, Kait."

"I know that. How about later? I can come to your place."

"That won't work. I have…plans tonight."

A quick jolt of jealousy pounded in her stomach. She brushed it aside. Plans could mean grocery shopping for all she knew. "Okay. Some other time, then."

"Maybe. I gotta run."

Before she could say anything else, he left the room, saying quick goodbyes to everyone. She stood there fuming silently, watching him make a hasty exit out the front door. She tapped her foot and breathed out an irritated sigh, trying not to feel hurt over his dismissal.

So they had hot sex last night. Clearly not a big deal. He'd never made any promises to her, never even wanted to touch her. She'd pushed for it, she'd forced the issue between them.

Now she'd have to live with the consequences. Her heart might be deeply involved, but it was obvious Brett's wasn't.

Brett sat in the darkened bar and nursed a hot coffee, tuning out the sounds of French Quarter revelry and the slurred conversations of drunken patrons.

After he left the Storms…no, correction, after he'd run like hell away from Kaitlyn earlier, he'd driven around and ended up stopping at his favorite bar haunt, not wanting to face the isolation and quiet of his house.

Besides, he liked to come here regularly, to test his strength. The lure of taking a drink was always strong. He knew it would never go away. But the harder he pushed himself and surrounded himself with alcohol, the stronger he felt when he resisted.

Now if only he could draw on that strength to resist Kaitlyn. Making love with her had opened up a Pandora's Box that created havoc around him.

He sighed and signaled the bartender for another cup of coffee.

He'd hurt her tonight by leaving without an explanation. Then again, he needed to avoid her. More importantly, he needed to avoid his feelings for her.

And if there was one thing he was damned good at, it was avoidance.

"Hello, darling. Whatcha drinkin'?"

He turned to the attractive woman sliding onto the barstool next to his. Well, almost falling onto the barstool was more like it. Obviously drunk, she arched a brow and rested her hand on his arm.

"Evening," he said, not wanting to be impolite. The last thing he needed or wanted right now was company. Especially female company.

"Can I buy you a drink?"

Wasn't that supposed to be his line? God knows he'd used it plenty in the past. "No thanks. Just coffee for me tonight." And alone time. He didn't want to rude, but the last thing he needed was a female hovering around.

Then again, maybe that's exactly what he needed. A little distraction to get his mind off Kaitlyn. She wasn't the only woman in the world for him. There were plenty of other available women. He'd just never taken the time or the interest in finding any.

"I've seen you here before. You always come in alone, sit at the bar, and nurse a couple cups of coffee, then leave."

He turned to the blonde. She was about his age. Very attractive with dark green eyes and a gorgeous body that she displayed quite well in a body-hugging, short red dress. "And why are you here alone?"

She grinned and took a sip of her drink. "Nursing a divorce with a couple cocktails."

He laughed. "Sorry."

"Don't be. He's a prick. Cheated on me, then lied about it. I finally had to hire an investigator and, man, did he take some interesting pictures."

Behind the wall of alcohol he heard pain. He knew all about pain, and knew better than most about using alcohol to obliterate it. "I'm really sorry. You're way too beautiful to have a man treat you that way."

"I'll get over it," she said with a half-smile and a shrug. "And I'll get everything, too."

Well, at least she had a sense of humor about it. She was easy to talk to, and right now anything was better than being alone with his own thoughts.

A soft jazz tune sprang up from the jukebox. Brett decided it was time to test the waters. One woman was just as good as another, right? He turned to the woman and held out his hand. "My name's Brett."

"Nice to meet you, Brett. I'm Gail," she said in return, sliding her hand into his.

"Would you like to dance, Gail?"

Her eyes lit up like emeralds and she smiled. "I thought you'd never ask."

Two hours later he had Gail in his car, wondering what the hell he was doing.

No, that's not quite right. He knew exactly what he was doing. Making a huge fucking mistake. Gail was three sheets to the wind, obviously lonely and horny. And he was being an asshole and taking advantage of it. Then again, she'd been the one who suggested they go back to his place.

Only she wasn't the woman he wanted stretched out on his bed, naked and primed for fucking.

"Let's go, babe," Gail said, her legs splayed out in front of her, showing off the tops of her thigh-highs. Her tongue swiped over her full lips and she said, "I'm ready to get these clothes off."

Any other guy would be eager as hell to get her into his house. But his blood ran cold at the idea. Disgusted, he turned the ignition back on. "Honey, I've just made a huge mistake. I'm sorry but I'm going to have to take you home."

Hurt glistened in her widened eyes. "Why? Don't you like me?"

So far tonight he'd hurt two women. Maybe he could go back to the bar and pick up another one, see if he could go for a triple.

Or maybe he could do the right thing and undo the mistake he'd almost made. He turned to her, gently drawing her skirt down over her thighs. "Gail, you're a beautiful woman. You just picked the wrong man for a husband. And what you want to do with me is for all the wrong reasons."

She snorted. "I just want to get fucked."

He smiled and caressed her cheek, well knowing how pain could cause a person to do a lot of really stupid things. "No you don't. You want to hurt your husband."

She pulled the edges of her leather jacket closer together and sniffed. "So, what if I do?"

"This," he said, pointing his finger to her then back to him, "isn't really what you want."

"You have no idea what the hell I want," she muttered, looking down at her lap. "I thought you wanted me."

"Give me your address and I'll take you home. You deserve a lot better than me. You deserve a lot better than your husband. Go get sober and get your life together, Gail. Trust me, it'll be worth it."

After she mumbled her address, she promptly passed out.

Brett found her place, grabbed her keys from her purse and took her inside, depositing her on her sofa. That was as far as he'd dare go. He slipped the door closed and got back into his car, realizing what a mistake he could have made.

No, he didn't just want any woman. And it didn't matter how many women he met, dated or screwed in the future. He'd still only want Kaitlyn.

He was so fucked. If he ever thought he'd been on the road to recovery, he was dead wrong. He had simply traded one addiction for another.

Kaitlyn stood in the dressing room of Brett's home studio, not at all in the mood to pose tonight. Admittedly, she had been surprised when he called her today. After he'd made his escape from her parents' house a couple days ago, she was certain he never wanted to have another thing to do with her. His call and suggestion they meet to work on the portrait tonight had been a total shock.

Once again, she couldn't figure him out. He blew hot and cold worse than a woman in the throes of raging PMS. Her first thought was to tell him he could take his painting and shove it, that she was tired of trying to decipher his ever-changing moods. But since the painting had been her idea in the first place, and it meant he *did* have the urge to paint, she couldn't very well say no.

Now she stood staring at herself in the dressing room mirror, the silk robe covering her naked body. The last time they'd done this, she'd ended up in his bed having the wildest sex of her life. What would happen tonight? Most likely he'd paint her, not say a word, and then send her home.

Fine. If that's the way he wanted to play it. She was tired of throwing herself at him. Or at least that's what she had to keep reminding herself. After all, a little self-respect was in order here. And his brush-off hurt, dammit. She could only handle so much rejection before she had to admit defeat.

Armed with as much self-dignity as she could muster, she opened the door and found him waiting beside the easel, paintbrush in hand. Tonight he wore gray sweats and a sleeveless shirt that showed off way too much of his muscled arms and shoulders.

She decided to ignore him. And since she no longer had anything to hide, she stepped to the chaise, slid the robe off and tossed it on one of the nearby tables. He arched a brow but didn't say a word as she positioned herself on the chaise, then stared at him, waiting for him to start.

Though she did catch the darkening of his eyes, the hot gaze he couldn't disguise before he slipped behind the canvas and began to paint.

Okay, so he wasn't immune. Good. She hoped he suffered terminal hard-ons for the rest of his natural life.

She posed until her body went numb, absorbing the quiet of the room. The only sounds were Brett's brushstrokes on the canvas and him occasionally asking if she was comfortable.

No, she wasn't comfortable. She was naked in front of a man who a few short days ago had taught her more about her own body than she'd ever known. And she still wanted him, wanted his hands, his mouth and his cock on her and in her, painting her body with strokes of utter pleasure.

Her nipples tightened. She knew they were erect but could do nothing to stop her wayward thoughts. The sounds of brush against canvas made her imagine Brett taking the soft paintbrush and stroking it around her nipples, then drawing a swirling trail over her belly and lower. Her clit throbbed as she envisioned him taking that brush and drawing featherlight circles over the tight bud. She moaned, unable to hold it back before it spilled from her throat.

Brett peered around the easel. She met his gaze with one of dark hunger and a need she couldn't deny to herself, let alone to him.

Tension filled the room as he stood and stared at her. Unable to help herself, she rose from the chaise and approached him, her body on fire, torching her from the inside out. Only his touch could douse the flames. Her senses told her he wanted her, but he wasn't moving fast enough for her.

Okay, so she had no self-respect. But dammit, she loved him! And when had she ever given up until the last flame of hope had been doused?

"I need you, Brett."

"I'm painting," he said, his voice low and husky. His words didn't match his voice, or the way his eyes sparked and flamed with the desire she saw evidenced in the erection straining his pants.

"Then paint me." Her hands rose to her breasts, her fingers swirling around the globes. "Take a paintbrush and paint my body, Brett. That's what I've been thinking about for the past two hours."

She watched the bob of his Adam's apple as he swallowed, saw the need burning in his eyes. She reached for him, but he caught her wrist in his hand before she could touch his face.

"Stop."

She shuddered and watched him hurry from the room, then turned away, the heat of desire melting into a hot flush of embarrassment. Once again she'd made an utter ass of herself with him. At least the last time he hadn't run when she pushed. This time he'd left the room.

How long was she going to go on being stupid? She wasn't the kind of woman who threw herself at a man. Ever. Yet she had no shame where he was concerned. What was wrong with her anyway?

Tangling her fingers in her hair, she combed it away from her face and went to pick up the silk robe she'd tossed on the table earlier. She was about to slip her arms into it when she heard Brett.

"Stop."

Clutching the robe in her hands, she spun around to face him, about to tell him he didn't have to worry about her trying to seduce him ever again. But her jaw dropped as he approached.

He held a thick, soft-bristled paintbrush in one hand, a jar of something dark in the other. He set the items on the table and snatched the robe from her hand.

"You won't be needing this," he said, casting it to the floor before walking right past her.

"What are you doing?" she asked.

He didn't answer, just pulled a white sheet from a shelf in the back of the room and laid it down over a foam mat laid out in the center of the floor. Then he turned to her and held out his hand. "Come here."

Too curious to resist, she approached him, surprised when he pushed her gently onto the mat.

"Lie down on your back and don't move."

Her heart pounded as she watched him retrieve the paintbrush and jar. He set them on the floor next to the mat and stood, this time removing his shirt and sweatpants until he was as naked as she was. His cock was already thick with his erection, the ridged veins and flared head an aroused, angry purple. Joy and desire spread through her, filling her with elation and a desperate need to feel his body against hers. He knelt against the edge of the mattress, keeping his gaze on her face while he picked up the jar and unscrewed the lid.

"What are you doing?" she asked.

"Giving you what you asked for."

"And what's that?"

"Painting you."

Oh, God. "What kind of paint is that?"

His lips curled into a wicked smile that devastated her insides. "It's not paint, *cher*."

Not paint? She tilted her neck up to read the label, her eyes widening. "Where did you get *that*?"

"You think I don't have fantasies about you, Kait? That I haven't thought about taking a brush to your skin and painting you, then licking it off inch by inch until you're screaming for me to fuck you? I bought this today. It's amazing how in tune our minds are, isn't it?"

Desire shot between her legs, coiling like a snake in her womb and firing off hot shots of electrical pulses that made juices pour from her pussy.

Chocolate body paint. Good God in heaven, he was going to drive her mad!

Beyond that, hope surged within her heart, pounding away at her until she was forced to ask herself if maybe *this* time he had seen the light. Had he really given up the fight and decided to recognize what was between them?

She pushed the thought to the back of her mind. Now was not the time to ponder their relationship. Not when he dipped the brush into the chocolate and pulled it out, then held it over her belly.

A thin trail of chocolate beaded in her navel before he lowered the brush to her rib cage. The bristles were incredibly soft, not at all what she expected. He drew a pattern across her ribs, then dipped the brush in the chocolate again, this time sweeping it under one breast and drawing a circle around the aching globe. She shivered at the warm chocolate oozing over her skin. When he drew the brush over her nipple, she moaned, her cunt pulsing with the need to feel him inside her. He lingered at the hard tip of one crest, sweeping the bristles back and forth until she wanted to scream.

The chocolate warmed as it touched her body. She flamed when he bent down and covered one crest with his lips, teasing his tongue over the hard bud with light flicks back and forth. When he drew back, he took her mouth, letting her taste the sweet chocolate mingled with his own unique flavor. She slid her tongue along his lips and licked up every drop, loving the texture of his tongue and mouth against hers.

She could kiss him for hours, but he moved away and gathered more chocolate, this time painting down her hips and outer thighs, then curving toward her inner thighs. Her skin prickled with goose bumps, anticipating where he would go next.

"Spread your legs for me, baby," he said, his voice tight. His cock brushed against her thigh, dipping into the chocolate he'd painted there. She shuddered at the feel of him rocking against the thick syrup. His cock was hot against her skin. She wanted to taste him, engulf both his shaft and the body paint together in her mouth.

She was about to lean up and capture his cock in her hand, but Brett took that moment to paint a swirl of chocolate over her clit, the brush teasing the throbbing bud with the softest of strokes. Her head slammed against the mat and she fisted the sheet, letting him brush back and forth over the sensitive bundle of nerves until she couldn't stand it any longer.

"Brett, please."

"You're right. That's enough." He set the jar and brush on the floor and leaned over her his tongue tracing the pattern of swirls, starting with the pool in her navel. He dipped his tongue inside and scooped up the chocolate, swallowing and licking his lips before descending on her ribs.

She was on fire and trembling from the scorching heat of his tongue. Everywhere he'd painted, he licked. From the underside of her breasts to the sharp points of her distended nipples. He lingered at each nipple, lapping at her like a cat given a treat of cream. She tangled her fingers in his hair and held him there while he suckled and nibbled until she cried out, the intensity of pleasure shooting straight to her core.

She needed more. So much more than just kissing and nibbling. She needed to be filled by his hot cock, feel it powering up inside her so deep his balls would bang against her ass. And she needed that now.

"Brett," she pleaded, near breathless with need. "Fuck me."

His low chuckle made her shiver in anticipation. "Not yet, *ma petite sorcière*. I need to clean up this paint first."

He slipped between her legs, capturing her gaze as his hands slid under her buttocks, tilting her sex toward his waiting mouth. He smiled up at her, then blew a soft breath of air against her clit.

In response, her magic fired up and cast a cool breeze over their bodies, ruffling his hair. He grinned and covered his lips over her slit, licking in rapid strokes with the flat of his tongue, lapping up the juices that spilled from her.

His tongue was as soft as the paintbrush, but oh-so much hotter as he seared her sensitized skin with swirling movements that set her right on the edge of climax in mere seconds.

She tensed, wanting to hold back, but the pressure built with each swipe of his tongue over her heated sex. When he slipped two fingers into her liquefied cunt, her pussy went into spasms and gripped his flesh, holding tight while she bucked her hips in a stormy orgasm she couldn't prevent.

He continued to pump his fingers into her while she rode out the waves of her climax. His mouth teased and taunted her clit with light, feathery strokes until she was damp with sweat and drenched in her own cream.

And still it wasn't enough. She closed her eyes and fought for breath, her body quaking with the need to be filled.

Her eyes shot open when she felt a flood of warm wetness over her breasts and belly. Brett leaned over her, pouring the contests of the jar of chocolate onto her skin.

She laughed when he put the jar down and then slid up her body, his tongue tracing a path in the copious amounts of chocolate covering her torso. By the time he was face-to-face with her, his face was dripping in chocolate. It coated his nose, his chin, drops of brown syrup falling from his hair.

He'd never looked sexier. She smiled and reached for his head, cupping the back and drawing his mouth down to hers. His body covered hers, the squish of chocolate oozing down her sides. She devoured his mouth, tasting again the sweet mix of chocolate and Brett.

But the sweetest of all was his hard cock brushing between her folds, seeking entrance to her drenched pussy. She spread her legs and lifted her hips and he drove inside her with one hard thrust. Her whimper was absorbed by his mouth, his tongue tangling with hers as he powered hard against her flesh.

"Oh, yeah," he said, bracing up on his palms so she could look up and watch his cock disappear between her legs. "You like watching, baby?"

"Yes. Oh, yes." In fact, she craved an even better view than the angle he presented to her.

He must have read her mind, because he withdrew and sat up, pulling her onto his lap. "Straddle and fuck me. We'll both watch this way."

She wrapped her legs around his hips and slid down over his cock, the angle enabling her to watch each thick inch disappear between her engorged pussy lips. Feeling and seeing at the same time was heaven. Brett leaned back on his palms and rocked his hips up, his cock appearing and disappearing. Her pussy lips gripped his shaft as he withdrew, as if desperately trying to hold him inside her.

Chocolate ran in rivers down her breasts and belly, dropping onto the sheet and their legs. She didn't care. Her mind and body focused on the exquisite sensations of his cock head striking that sensitive tissue just inside her pussy. Angled as he was, he rubbed her G-spot with every stroke, taking her closer and closer to the edge again. Only this time, she'd wait for him, if she could hold on that long. His cock was so thick, filling her completely, that each thrust brought about a painful pleasure that made her bite her lip and squeeze her buttocks to keep from coming. Brett was relentless, powering in and out with expert finesse, using just the right rhythm to stroke her sensitized tissues into a frenzy.

But as she caught his gaze, saw the desire flaming in his eyes, she knew he was as close to the edge as she was.

"Please, Brett," she whimpered. "Now, please."

"You want my come, baby?" he asked, his eyes hooded.

The floor rumbled as thunder crashed around them. She gripped his arms and slammed against his shaft, needing more pressure, more intensity. "Yes, please come in me."

"Take it, *cher*." He tunneled harder, faster, his cock scraping her clit when he pushed her onto her back without once losing his connection inside her. "Come for me now, Kait."

Scooping her buttocks in his hands, he pushed hard, deep, and she flew into a climax that had her weeping as waves of ecstasy crashed over her. Rain poured down and a gust of wind blew papers all around the studio as the chocolate washed away in the storm. Brett buried his face in her neck and groaned her name, shooting hot jets of come deep into her womb.

Gasping and panting for breath, she held tight to him, savoring the feel of them joined so intimately.

She never wanted to let go. Having him inside her was perfection, the culmination of every dream she'd ever had about the man she loved.

He raised his head and took her mouth in a kiss so tender her heart throbbed with love for him.

"We're stuck together," he said with a grin.

She knew he meant by chocolate, but when he wriggled his hips all she could think of was cock to pussy. "Indeed we are. I like it that way."

"I meant the chocolate."

She giggled. "I know."

"How about a shower?"

"Definitely."

The tenderness Brett showed when soaping and rinsing her convinced her there was something very special between them, that her emotion hadn't been one-sided after all. She shuddered with need and love for him every time his hands touched her skin, every time his dark eyes met hers.

After they dressed, they made plans for him to finish the portrait by the end of the week, right before the fundraiser. Though no words, no commitments, were spoken between them, when she stood at the front door to say goodnight, he pulled her into his arms and kissed her with more emotion than she had ever felt before. She stumbled out the door, more confused than ever.

She was hopelessly lost and in love with Brett, and had no idea what to do about it. He'd never mentioned love to her, or a relationship. Only sex and even that they hadn't discussed. They'd just done it.

She slipped into her car and sat there, staring at the lights inside his house, wishing she were still in there, still making love with him. How easy it would be to forget reality and get lost in lovemaking.

But logic reared its ugly head and forced her to face facts. She was in way over her head with Brett, with no clearer picture of their relationship now than she'd had two weeks ago.

Did he love her? Did he care? Or was she merely convenient, someone to have sex with? Desire was there, of that there was no doubt. But she knew she needed so much more from him than simply great sex.

So much for her grand plan. All she'd done was open her heart to a man she was afraid had no idea what to do with it.

Chapter Eight

Brett stood at the entrance to the *Rising Storm's* Grand Ballroom, smiling benignly and shaking hands with everyone who entered. After all, these people had paid over a thousand dollars a ticket to have dinner and then pay even more money at the auction. The least he could do was smile at them.

The bow tie around his neck felt like a noose. He'd like nothing more than to shed his stupid, confining tux and slip into paint-stained jeans and a T-shirt, then spend the evening in his home studio, just like he'd done the past week.

Of course he'd had company while painting, namely his sexy, constantly naked subject. She'd tried his patience lying there batting her dark lashes innocently while he tried his best to still his shaking hand and subdue his raging hard-on. Some nights he didn't even make it an hour before he threw the brush down in disgust and went to her, dragging her into his arms to spend the remainder of the night making love.

So much for his resolve to push her out of his life. He'd failed miserably, in fact he was pretty certain she was in love with him.

And he knew damn well he was in love with her.

Recipe for disaster. He'd have to put a stop to it. The portrait was finished, and after tonight's event he'd have no further reason to have contact with her.

She'd done a damn fine job putting the fundraiser together. The room was decorated in shades of velvet and gold. Artwork she'd chosen graced the lobby along with a massive sign proclaiming tonight's event. Paintings and sculptures to be auctioned tonight were lined up along the roped-off area between the walls and tables, allowing the patrons to walk up and down the long ballroom and inspect the items up for bid. There was plenty to drink, a smorgasbord of food, and he couldn't wait for it to be over with. Then again, when he saw her walk into his line of vision, he lost his ability to breathe, the last thing on his mind ending the relationship with her. Maybe he could delay the end for a few more hours. He wanted to make love to her one more time.

One addiction for another. One more time would become another one more time, until he never let her go. No, tonight had to be it.

The black dress clung to her body in all the right places. Sleeveless, it was cut in a low vee in front, showing a subtle amount of cleavage. A delicate silver lariat necklace dipped down into the shadow between her breasts.

He tried to swallow, to no avail. When she caught his eye, she smiled. Her eyes glowed like a woman in love. A woman in love with him. His heart lurched against his ribs, his pulse racing as he watched the soft sway of her hips, the dress hugging her long legs and slit up each side almost to her thighs. His gaze followed one slender leg from mid-thigh all the way down, where a tiny silver bracelet called attention to her slim ankle.

Even the shoes she wore got him hard. He wanted to fuck her while she wore only those shoes. Drag that sexy dress from her body and take her up against the wall right here in the ballroom while she wore only those stiletto heels.

God, he was getting an erection in the middle of New Orleans' polite society. The worst part was he didn't think he cared.

"Evening," she said as she stopped in front of him.

Inhaling her scent was even worse. She worse no cologne, just the fresh lavender smell of her shampoo and the natural scent of her body. He fought to clear his throat and find something appropriate to say to her. "You're gorgeous."

That wasn't what he intended to say, but it brought color to her cheeks and a golden glitter to her eyes. She pressed a hand to her throat and smiled. "Thank you. So are you."

He shook his head and held out his arm for her, then guided her into the ballroom. "You've done an incredible job with the fundraiser, Kait. I could never have pulled this off without you."

"That's my job, Brett. But I have to tell you I had fun coordinating this event. I can't wait to see how much money the Art Council makes tonight."

From his knowledge of the net worth of the combined population of the room, he'd wager the council would rake in a bundle.

That was the easy part. The hard part would come later, when this was all over. It was now or never with Kaitlyn. He'd have to make the break with her tonight, or he was afraid he never would. He was weak where she was concerned. He wanted her, of that there was no doubt. But he was starting to need her, to miss her when she wasn't with him, and that wasn't good for either of them.

It was especially bad for her. Because if he didn't let her go, he'd hurt her. Maybe not today or tomorrow, but he knew he would someday. And that he refused to do.

It was going to be damn hard to let her go. Her fresh spring fragrance entered his senses, making him feel like he was standing outside in a meadow filled with sweet lavender.

"I've got to go do a few hostess-type things, but I'll see you around," she said, looking from side to side. Then, with a quick shrug as if she didn't care who saw, she cupped his cheeks and pressed a soft, lingering kiss to his lips that still burned on his mouth long after she'd sauntered away.

After that the night passed in a blur of activities. He talked, pressed flesh, encouraged donations to the Art Council and did his best impression of a fundraising manager. He tried to keep his eye on Kaitlyn, but she was busier than he, coordinating both the food and drink staff and still finding time to stop at every single table and talk up the fundraiser. She wore two hats tonight. One as event coordinator, the other as an attendee, along with her parents.

She was an amazing woman. He loved her.

And he was going to let her go.

Part of him thought it was the biggest mistake he'd ever make. The other part of him thought it was the most noble thing he could ever do for her.

Though he didn't feel very fucking noble about it.

"You're drooling over my daughter."

Brett turned at the sound of a deep voice behind him, smiling at Galen Storm. Galen was a bear of a man who looked just as uncomfortable in his tux as Brett felt in his. His eyes showed a pained expression that was either due to too tight shoes or too many people hovering about.

"You look about as happy as I am to be here," Brett teased.

"Yeah, but I'm not drooling. Though looking at Angelina makes my mouth water."

Brett laughed and followed Galen's gaze to Angelina. She stood next to Kaitlyn, looking more like her sister than her mother. Angelina, like Kait wore black with silver jewelry, their faces lit up as they laughed with each other.

In thirty years or so, Kaitlyn would look just like her mother, just as ravishing as she did right now.

His chest tightened as he watched them together. Galen was a very lucky man. Brett was an idiot to let Kaitlyn go.

"My daughter loves you."

Brett tore his gaze away from Kaitlyn and looked at Galen, affecting a casual smile despite his discomfort at Galen's comment. "Nah, she doesn't love me."

He was hoping no one would see the look in Kaitlyn's eyes, but obviously it was too late. Dammit, this wasn't going to sit well with the Storms when he stopped seeing Kaitlyn.

But hell, it wasn't like he could give her the fairytale romance that her parents had. Galen and Angelina Storm were the model for a couple in love after thirty-five years of marriage. They were the glue that held the family together, and they were the people he'd been most comfortable with growing up, even more so than his own parents. He'd spent a lot of time at the Storm house while his parents were out partying and getting drunk every weekend. Maybe he should have spent more time with the Storms and less with his own parents. Though he didn't blame them for his problems, he couldn't help but feel he'd followed in his parents' footsteps, and not in a good way. They didn't exactly set the best example of wholesome, clean living.

When he was a kid he dreamed about Galen and Angelina adopting him so he could live with a "normal" family. That hadn't happened, and no matter how he wanted to deny it, the lifestyle of his parents *had* rubbed off on him. But he'd also had a choice to be like them or not, and he'd chosen to emulate the worst parts of them. That's what he wouldn't expose Kaitlyn to.

"Kaitlyn's lovely," Brett said. "But you don't have to worry about her and me. There's nothing going on between us."

Galen arched a brow. "Why would I worry? I'd love to see you with my daughter."

Pain ripped through him, the knowledge of how much he was going to hurt Kait as well as her family tearing a hole in his chest. "Thanks. But I think our lifestyles are too different. She's just enamored right now because I painted her."

"Yes," Galen said, coughing uncomfortably. "We won't get into how you painted her. Some things parents don't need to dwell on. Just treat her right, son, and you'll make her happy." He squeezed Brett's shoulder and moved off to join his wife, slipping his arm around Angelina's waist and pulling her against his side.

Kaitlyn beamed as she watched her parents. Brett knew that was the kind of happily ever after she was looking for. A man who could offer her stability and strength.

Brett could offer her neither. And the sooner she recognized that, the better.

The rest of the night went off without a single glitch. Dinner was fabulous and the auction was a huge hit. They sold every item, some for an amount that made even his eyes widen. The Art Council would be able to provide several years funding for grants and projects now. The members of the board congratulated him and said he could be their permanent fundraising chairman if he wanted the job.

When things started to wind down, his tension began to increase. He knew Kaitlyn would expect them to spend the night together, only he wasn't going to give her what she expected.

"Hey there, stranger."

He whirled at the sound of a feminine voice, frowning for a moment until recognition struck. Gail, the blonde he'd driven home from the bar. "Hi, Gail. I didn't see you earlier. Who are you here with?"

Great. A mistake he'd almost made the other night, come back to haunt him.

She grinned and sloshed a little wine out of her glass, clearly as drunk tonight as she'd been that night in the bar. "I'm here with Miles Denton. But he's boring."

Brett laughed. He couldn't argue with her there. He'd known Miles for years. Besides the fact he was a stuffy art snob, the man was at least twenty-five years older than Gail.

"You passed up a really good thing with me the other night. Or at least I think you did. I kind of passed out. What actually happened when you brought me home?"

"I placed you on your couch and left."

Her lips formed a red pout. "That's too bad." When she trailed her finger over his bow tie, he swallowed hard, decidedly uncomfortable with her forwardness. "Maybe we could correct that oversight tonight. After all, you said you wanted to fuck me the other night."

Gail's gaze drifted over his shoulder and her lips tightened. Brett turned his head, his heart slamming against his chest as a wide-eyed Kaitlyn stepped around them. Shit! She'd heard what Gail said, it was obvious. Her face had gone pale, her eyes glittering with unshed tears. Before he could utter a single word, she scooted around them and hurried away.

"Kaitlyn, wait!" He started to go after her but Gail clutched his arm like a lifeline.

"Hey. We were talking."

Trying for patience, he turned to Gail and said, "Let me set you straight. I made a big mistake the other night, thinking I'd use you to forget someone I cared about. I'm sorry, Gail, but I don't want this. And frankly, I don't think you do, either."

She shrugged and drained her glass of wine, nearly toppling off her high heels when she tilted her head back. "I just want to have some fun. Shouldn't I be allowed to have some fun?"

How many times over the years had he used that excuse for drinking himself into oblivion? But he couldn't help Gail with her problem. Only she could do that. Relief washed over him as Miles appeared, shaking his head at Gail's weaving form.

"I think she needs some assistance out of here," Brett suggested.

Sniffing, Miles nodded. "I'll make sure she gets home safely. Really, Gail, must you drink so heavily?"

Miles led her away, Gail babbling and giggling as she leaned against him. Brett shook his head, then immediately turned to search for Kaitlyn.

The room was practically empty now, and she was nowhere to be seen.

She'd heard Gail talk about the other night. God, what she must think of him! This wasn't how he wanted to end things with her. Not with her thinking he was a cheating, lying bastard.

He had to talk to her, had to explain what had been going through his head the night he picked Gail up.

If he could manage to figure it out himself.

Kaitlyn paced the confines of her living room, still seething about that blonde bitch falling all over Brett. Jealousy and hurt mixed together in a powerful concoction of really disturbing emotions. She rubbed her arms, shivering despite the warmth of her sweatpants and long-sleeved shirt.

Embarrassment at her quick exit took a little chill from the air. How old was she, anyway? Sometimes she wondered if she still bore the raging emotions of a seventeen year old. She'd torn out of the ballroom as quickly as she could, unable to face Brett after what she'd heard.

Okay, not her most mature moment, but then again, what was she supposed to do when she overheard that woman say Brett had wanted to fuck her the other night? What other night? Was it during the time period that they'd been…

…No. Brett wouldn't do that. Would he? That didn't seem like Brett at all. She'd been with him damn near every night for the past few weeks, and God knows lately they'd had enough sex to exhaust them into a deep sleep. Why would he go looking for more?

Wasn't she enough for him? What the hell was it going to take to make that man happy?

Maybe more than she could offer. She flopped into a chair and propped her bare feet on the coffee table, an emptiness gnawing in the pit of her stomach as she realized how foolish she'd been. She'd barreled into his life, forced him to paint her, forced him to have sex with her…she'd pretty much forced herself on him in every possible way, despite his continued protests.

He didn't want her. Okay, he wanted to fuck her, but he didn't want her in his life. If he could take up with another woman while still seeing her, then it didn't matter how much of her heart she gave Brett. She'd never have all of his.

The gnawing ache felt like a hole in her stomach. Realization and cold reality chilled the air even further. It was over. She might be dim-witted and obstinate, but even she knew when to throw in the towel.

When the doorbell rang, her gaze flitted to the clock on the wall. It was eleven o'clock. Who the hell could be here? She rose and went to the peephole, mentally cursing when she saw Brett standing there.

Damn. She laid her forehead against the door, not in the mood to talk to him right now. Besides, whatever he had to say wouldn't make any difference. She was finished with him.

"Kait, I know you're there. I can hear you breathing against the door."

She sighed and blinked away tears. Might as well let him in, then. Besides, she had a few things she wanted to say to him, starting with "it's over".

She opened the door and said, "What are you doing here?"

He was still dressed in his tux, though his tie was gone, collar unbuttoned and his jacket was open. And he looked entirely too edible. She was supposed to hate him, not want him.

"I need to explain about Gail."

"No, you don't."

"Are you going to invite me in?"

"I don't think so. We don't have anything to say to each other. I think what I heard made it quite clear."

"You heard wrong."

He pushed past her and left her standing holding the door while he stepped inside and waited for her. She couldn't very well cling to the front door without looking stupid, so she closed it and walked into the living room, chin held high.

She would not cry.

"That day I had dinner at your parents, I went to a bar afterward."

"And picked up a woman." How convenient that he left that part out. No wonder he hightailed it into another woman's arms after the inquisition from Aidan. No doubt her brother told Brett to keep his distance or some other meddling comment. She knew Brett had been disturbed at the house that day, but she'd never wanted him to elaborate on his conversation with Aidan.

"Not really. She kind of picked me up."

Despite her best efforts to control the magic, the temperature in the living room began to drop. She mentally cursed both her powers and her stupid nipples for reacting to the cold. Wrapping her arms around her chest, she glared at him.

He tugged his jacket closer, obviously aware of the deep freeze about to happen in her house. "I never touched her."

"What you do with your personal life is no concern of mine. You made it quite clear early on you didn't want a relationship with me. I didn't listen and I forced you into it."

His lips curled into a half-smile. "You hardly forced me, Kaitlyn."

"You know what I meant," she said, dismissing him with a wave of her hand. She turned and flopped onto the couch, curling her feet underneath her. "You don't owe me any explanations." *Please go, before I say something else stupid, like "I love you or I'm the best thing that could ever happen to you, dumbass".*

"I do owe you an explanation." He slipped onto the sofa next to her. "Gail was drunk. She came onto me."

"And you just couldn't resist telling her you wanted to fuck her. Look, I might be dense, but I have finally grabbed a clue here, Brett."

"No you haven't."

Great. Now he was calling her clueless. "I'm pretty damned smart. I know what I heard, so don't fill me with a line of bullshit."

Brett blew out a breath of cold-tinged air and raked his fingers through his hair. "This is hard to explain."

"I'll bet it is." Hard to make up excuses is what he really meant. He couldn't because there weren't any. Stab, stab, stab. She was bleeding all over the furniture, her soul slowly leaking out her body. Why wouldn't he just go away? She needed a good cry and a dose of amnesia and she'd be just fine.

"I was afraid of you."

She arched a brow, dragging herself out of her self-misery. "Afraid...of me."

"Yeah. Kait, I've known you since you were twelve years old. I've been trying to avoid getting physical with you since you were seventeen. Hell, that first time I kissed you I nearly self-combusted. I had to push you away then and I tried to push you away now. Hell, I'm still trying. That's what I was doing that night at the bar. Gail offered and I grabbed at the chance to be with someone else, thinking I could forget about you."

"Am I supposed to take that as a compliment?"

"Let me finish. I took her to my house but I never touched her. We never even made it out of my car. I was disgusted with the idea of having anyone in my bed but you. I took her back to her place and hadn't seen her again until tonight at the fundraiser. It was a really stupid mistake and I'm sorry I made it. I just wasn't thinking."

"I'll say." She wanted to believe him. She wanted to feel complimented by the fact he needed another woman to forget her. But why did he want to forget her in the first place?

"I'm sorry, Kait. I never seem to make the right choices where you're concerned. And that's what I came here to talk to you about."

Uh-oh. "Fine. Talk."

"We can't see each other anymore. Things between us just aren't going to work."

"I see." How nice of him to make that decision for them both. And how nice to get her hopes up by apologizing and clarifying the situation with the other woman, only to turn around and dump her anyway. "Why did you even bother coming over here, then? You could have left me believing you'd fucked that woman, and you would have been free of me."

"You don't understand."

That did it. She stood and stared down at him. "Do you know how many times I've heard you say that I don't understand? Well, I understand plenty! I understand that I gave you my heart and you stomped all over it. I understand that I gave you my body and you sure as hell enjoyed using it, but it's not quite what you're looking for."

"Godammit, that's not what I said!" He shot to his feet and met her fierce glare with one of his own. "I'm trying to explain something to you and as usual you're not listening!"

"*I'm* not listening? I've been listening plenty. I just don't like what I'm hearing! Why don't you leave?"

Not bothering to do it the normal way, she directed her magic to the front door. A strong gust of cold wind blew it open, crashing it against the backstop. Brett's gaze shot to the door and back at her. "This isn't the way I wanted to end things."

"You don't always get to be the one to choose how it goes. Now get out."

He opened his mouth, then closed it again and brushed past her. She used the wind to slam the door shut behind him, leaving her alone with her own anger and her own thoughts.

The room grew colder and her heart chilled. Even the tears sliding down her cheeks were tinged with ice.

The warmth and renewal of spring had given way to a blast of late winter, cold and fierce and hanging onto her with icy tentacles that wouldn't loosen its hold on her soul.

She shut out the light and headed upstairs to bed.

* * * * *

"So, you just let him walk away, or rather, you just threw him out?"

Kaitlyn scrunched her shoulders, tension tightening her muscles as she frowned at Shannon. "Yes, I threw him out."

"Why?"

"Because he doesn't want to be with me!" God, her sister was dense sometimes. They'd argued about Brett for a week now, Shannon convinced that Kaitlyn should go talk to him.

"I agree with Shannon, Kait. I really think you should see him."

She rolled her eyes, feeling trapped in her own office as Shannon and Lissa browbeat her. "I'm not going to see him."

"I never thought you'd give up so easily," Shannon said, arching her brow in challenge.

Kaitlyn wasn't going to take the bait. "I know when to call it quits. I think I beat my head against the wall plenty with Brett. He doesn't want me."

It took her days to be able to say it out loud. Days of wandering her house all alone, the emptiness inside her unbearable. Now she said it regularly. She had already convinced herself, so she had only the rest of her meddling family to convince.

"Kait, you know how difficult it was for me to come to grips with Aidan's, shall we say, hardheadedness?" Lissa asked.

Shannon snorted. "That's an understatement. Our brother is an arrogant pain in the ass."

Lissa laughed. "Yes, he is. And you love him dearly. So do I. But I had to open my heart and then force him to open his, too. It was a rocky road but it was well worth it."

"I know the feeling," Shannon said, nodding. "Max is a lot like Aidan. Then again, so am I. We butted heads a lot, both wanting control. We had to learn to give a little on both sides to make it work. And believe me, I'm the last person who ever thought I'd give an inch to anyone!"

Kaitlyn smiled at them. "I know what you both went through to find love. But my situation with Brett is...different. I wanted him. He knew I wanted him. He still doesn't want me. What am I supposed to do? Go over to his house with a hammer and beat him over the head until he comes to his senses?"

Shannon and Lissa exchanged glances, then turned toward her.

"Not a bad idea at that," Shannon said with a grin.

"No. Bad idea," Kaitlyn shot back.

"I think it's a great idea," Lissa agreed. "Go talk to him. You two left things unfinished."

"No, we didn't." It was as finished as it was going to get. She'd never put herself through this agonizing hurt again. Someday, maybe, she'd get over him and find a man who wanted her. Really wanted her.

Though even she didn't believe her own denial. They *had* left things unfinished. She was angry and she'd let her anger cloud her normal common sense.

Brett didn't want her. She wanted to know why. She needed to know what it was that kept him from taking that one final step to commitment.

"You still have to get your painting from him," Lissa suggested. "It's finished, isn't it?"

"Yeah."

"Then go get it. And see what happens," Shannon urged. "You'll kick yourself if you don't at least try to figure out where his head is."

They were right. Pride told her to leave it alone, that he'd only hurt her again.

But when had Kait ever let pride stand in her way?

Chapter Nine

Brett sat at the bar in his studio, his hands caressing the cool glass bottle of whiskey. The dark amber liquid had a voice of its own, calling to him to open it, to take one drink, maybe two at the most.

A most familiar voice. It still haunted him after all these years. How many days had he sat here staring at that bottle? Two? Three?

Hell, how many years?

He removed his hands from the bottle and stared at them, willing the trembling to stop.

It wouldn't. It hadn't. Not since he'd gotten that call three days ago from his AA sponsor, telling him the bad news about Frank.

He and Frank had entered AA at the same time. They'd been friends for six years, calling on each other when one needed to talk about how much they wanted a drink. They'd seen each other through the fires of hell and had come out the other side. They'd survived.

And neither of them had taken a drink in six long years.

Until three days ago. Three days ago, Frank fell off the wagon. Only he hadn't just taken a drink, he'd taken a lot of drinks. Then he'd gotten behind the wheel of his car with his girlfriend in the passenger seat and had proceeded to roll his SUV right off the highway embankment.

Frank was fine, just a few bruises. His girlfriend wasn't. She'd be in the hospital a long time. Her leg was shattered.

He hadn't even been able to go to the hospital to see Frank, to ask about him, to be there for him. The whole scenario was way too close to his own life, his own mistakes the night he'd killed Amanda.

It didn't even matter what happened to set Frank off. Brett knew the same thing could happen to him at anytime. On any day, he could open that bottle of whiskey and drink the whole damn thing down in one sitting.

He could hurt Kaitlyn.

God, he missed her. He could still smell her on his sheets when he tried to sleep at night. The studio even held her sweet lavender scent. Not that he'd even tried painting the past few days. The life had gone right out him the night Kaitlyn threw him out of her house. She'd done the right thing. He only wished he could have done the same long before he ever touched her.

The doorbell rang but he ignored it, wrapping his hands around the bottle and holding tight. It was a test. If he didn't touch it, he was somehow perversely comforted.

Or at least that's how it used to be. Nothing comforted him anymore. What he really wanted was to screw off the top and pour a huge glassful, feeling it burn its way down his throat. Then he wanted to keep drinking until he found that oblivion he searched for.

He ignored the persistent knocking. Whoever it was could go away. He hadn't even been to the gallery for the past three days, let alone opened his door to anyone. The last thing he needed or wanted right now was company.

Besides, he wasn't really alone. The demons were here with him. Always here, always a part of him, trying to lure him back to that dark place where alcohol numbed reality and made it so much easier to cope.

He wanted a drink so damned bad it hurt.

But something was different this time. Before, drink had always won out over everything he cared about. His life, his job, his friends, even Amanda. This time it was different.

Yeah, he wanted that goddamned drink. But he wanted Kaitlyn more.

"Brett."

He snorted. Now he even heard her voice. And he wasn't even drunk.

"Your door was unlocked. I hope you don't mind that I just came in but I was worried when I saw your car and you didn't answer."

Ah, Christ. He didn't need this right now.

Kaitlyn read the tension in Brett's shoulders, wincing at being so forward that she would walk in his house. But dammit, her senses told her something was wrong.

He turned around and glared at her. She was shocked at seeing his unkempt appearance. Several days' growth of beard peppered his face with dark stubble. His uncombed hair drifted over his forehead and she had to fight the urge to sweep it away from his face.

"Go away, Kait."

He turned his back to her, wrapping his hands around a bottle of whiskey.

Undaunted, she stepped forward and slid onto the barstool next to him. "What's wrong?"

"Nothing. Go out the way you came in. I'm not in the mood for company."

"Something's wrong, Brett. Please tell me."

He turned his head toward her, pain evident in his tired, hollow eyes. He looked like he hadn't slept in days.

"I'm too busy to deal with you right now. Just leave."

Pushing back the hurt at his words, she said, "You don't look busy. You look upset. Let me help you."

He shoved at the bottle until it slid all the way to the back of the bar. She reached over and grabbed it before it fell onto the floor. Brett shot up and raked his hands through his hair. "Look, dammit. You can't help me. No one can help me. Get the hell out of here, Kait. I mean it."

Now she knew something was wrong. Something serious. Brett had never acted this way. She touched the sleeve of his denim shirt. "I *can* help you if you'll talk to me."

He jerked his arm from her grasp and walked away, pacing the length of the bar. "You've never understood how it is with me. You just don't know. I'm poison, Kait. I tried to keep you away but you just wouldn't listen."

"I care about you. I'm not leaving."

He paused, the hurt in his eyes like a pain in her belly. "See? That's what I'm talking about. I could insult you ten different ways and you'd still stand there and take it. Why? Because you're good. There's a light of goodness shining around you that everyone wants to soak in. Your sweetness, your generosity, all those things you are that I'm not. You have no business wanting to be with a man like me."

Her heart tore just listening to him, the urge to offer him comfort stronger than any anger she might have had. "You're a good man, Brett. I don't understand what you're telling me."

He sighed and leaned against one of the pillars, crossing his arms and leveling a glare at her. "No, you don't understand, because I never told you. Hell, I never told anyone. Only Aidan knows."

Whatever secret he'd been keeping was eating away at him. It hurt her to watch him tear himself up like this. "I can take anything you want to tell me."

"Can you? Let's see if you can handle this. I'm an alcoholic, Kait."

Shock turned her blood cold and she shivered. An alcoholic? How could that be? That wasn't true. She'd have known…somehow she'd have known. "What?"

"You heard me. I'm a drunk. I've always been a drunk and I always will be a drunk. I have been since I was fifteen years old."

"I...I didn't know." Oh, God, how could she have *not* known this? She was supposed to be close to him, yet she never made the connection between him drinking water and tea and coffee all the time to being an alcoholic. Some people didn't drink out of personal preference. She'd never thought twice about it.

How could she know? She'd never seen him drunk. Ever. She looked up at him. "I'm so sorry, Brett."

His smile didn't reach his eyes. "Sorry? Oh, you won't be sorry when you hear the rest. You'll hate me, like you're supposed to. I was drunk the night Amanda died. Too damned drunk to drive, but I did it anyway. The accident wasn't a faulty brake line like everyone was told. I killed my wife, Kait. Now tell me you can take it."

His words were flung at her without caring, yet she knew what it cost him to say them, how much pain he hid behind his statement. He thought he'd killed his wife. God, had he lived with this all by himself for all these years?

She stepped toward him and reached for him, but he jerked away. She stood her ground, refusing to let him push her away this time. "I'm so sorry, Brett. Sorry for you and for Amanda. It was a mistake, and one that cost you dearly. But it doesn't make you less a person."

He snorted but didn't say anything.

"And you stopped drinking. That counts for something." It didn't make her love him less, either.

"You don't understand," he said, advancing on her, his eyes nearly glowing with the pain rushing through them. "I stopped drinking when Amanda died. That's true enough. But I still want that drink. I crave it more than anything. Every morning I get up, I walk in here and take that bottle out, wondering if today will be the day I'll open it up. Because I want that drink more than I want to paint. I want it more than I want a successful gallery."

He stopped and pressed his palms on either side of her, his face only inches from hers. "I wanted that goddamned drink more than I wanted you."

Shocked into silence, she could only look at him, blinking fiercely to hold back the tears at his words. Words designed to hurt her, to get her to call him a bastard and leave. But he'd said "wanted". Past tense. And now it all made sense to her. Her memories drifted back ten years, when he pushed her away and said they weren't right for each other. He'd been an alcoholic even then, though she'd been too young to recognize the signs. He'd hid it so well from her, from everyone.

All those years of hurt, of suffering alone. She wanted to scream her frustration and sorrow for all he'd lost, all he'd had to endure. Dear God, the strength it must have taken him to exist every single day after Amanda's death, to fight his addiction, to conquer it. Didn't he realize how much he'd changed since then?

"Get out, Kaitlyn. You have nothing to offer me. Unless you're offering a bottle of whiskey. That I'd take. Anything else, I'm not interested." He pushed back from the bar and took his seat on the stool, once again staring into the murky amber depths of the bottle.

Did he really think he could scare her off, that her love for him meant nothing? Did he think his shocking revelation would somehow change her feelings for him?

"You don't know a damn thing about me, Brett McGregor," she started, standing and walking toward him. She stopped when he turned around in his barstool to gape at her. "If you think you can make yourself look less desirable by revealing all your dark and dirty secrets, then you've had me pegged wrong all these years."

He arched a brow but said nothing.

"You see, I've loved you since I was too young to even know what these feelings were inside me. I've loved your heart, your talent, the way you made me laugh and yes, even the way you infuriated me sometimes. The fact you're an alcoholic makes no difference to me. The fact you were driving drunk the night Amanda died doesn't matter. You screwed up and you paid the highest price possible. You lost the woman you loved."

She stopped and let that sink in before continuing. "I was going to give you credit for learning from your mistakes, but I don't think I'm going to. After all, you're about to lose another woman you love. Is that what you want to do?"

His face paled. "I don't love you."

This time she placed her hands on either side of him. "Yes, you do. You've always loved me. You loved me when you thought I was too young, and for the past few weeks you've loved me like I never thought I could be loved. Are you willing to walk away from that kind of magic, Brett? Because I'm not."

"You have no idea what you're saying."

She smiled. "Don't I? You haven't touched alcohol since Amanda died. Do you know how much I admire you for that?"

"Don't," he warned, his eyes darkening. "I'm not someone to admire."

"You might not think so. But I do. What you've done requires the kind of inner strength the average man doesn't have. Many would have climbed further into the bottle and never come out. You could have done that too. But you didn't. You made the choice to change your life. Not only change your life, but live, sober, having to face the reality of what you'd done every single day of your life. In my book, that makes you one of the strongest men I know."

"You have no idea how weak I really am," he said, inclining his head toward the bottle over his shoulder. "I take that bottle out all the time and stare at it, so damned tempted to take a drink it drives me to my knees sometimes."

His expression was so desolate, so filled with self-loathing that it nearly crumbled her. "Tell me, Kait. How could you possibly ever want to be with a man like me?"

She'd had enough. She pushed at his chest as she moved away from him, this time venting her ire without holding back. "Aren't you tired of feeling sorry for yourself, Brett?"

"What?"

"You heard me. You're so caught up in the mistakes of your past that you refuse to live the rest of your life ahead of you. You've been so frozen by what happened that it's made you stop living. Is that really what you want? Is that what Amanda would have wanted?"

His lips seamed tightly together, but she saw the glittering of moisture in his eyes.

"You loved her. She loved you. You fucked up in the worst way possible and she died. But she did love you, with all your faults. And so do I. And guess what? I have faults too. I make mistakes too."

"Not like mine."

"Oh, so is this a game now? I couldn't possibly be as bad as you so you can't possibly be with me? Come on, Brett. Grow up, get over yourself and start living again." She went to him, wrapping her palms around his stubbled cheeks. This time, she didn't try to hold back her tears. She let them out, along with the magic that swirled around them in a vortex of flowery-scented wind.

"I don't care that you're an alcoholic. It's part of who you are but it doesn't define who you are. Only you can do that, by your actions. You are worthy of love. You deserve a second chance. Please let me be the one you take that chance with. I love you. I always have."

She inhaled, struggling to say the words through the tears. But they had to be said. She had to issue the challenge this one final time. "Now what are you going to do with that knowledge?"

Brett had to fight for breath. His chest squeezed tight with unshed tears and emotions he hadn't allowed in far too long. Maybe ever. Had he ever had this kind of connection with Amanda? He loved her, of course. But it was a different person who'd loved Amanda. He wasn't that man any longer. He'd never been the same man with her that he'd been around Kaitlyn.

But he'd spent the past six years trying to be the kind of man Amanda would have been proud of. He'd spent a lifetime wishing he was the kind of man Kaitlyn could love.

God, he wanted to take that step with her. He needed her more than he'd ever needed anyone before. And she stood here, right now, offering him everything he'd ever wanted.

"Please don't push me away this time, Brett. If you do, I won't come back."

"I'm afraid I'll hurt you."

Her lips lifted into a half-smile. "You might. And then you might not. We're stronger together than alone. Let me love you. Open your heart to me. I need this. I need you."

A light mist fell over them, making Kaitlyn's face glow as if tiny diamonds sparkled on her skin.

She was magic. Everything about her, from her powers to make it rain and to bring springtime into his life, to the way she loved him without question. Without recrimination or accusation. She loved him, with all his faults and all his demons.

How could he say no to a lifetime of loving a woman like her? How could he deny her what she wanted, even it was a broken-down alcoholic like him?

How could he deny himself the one thing he'd always wanted? For the first time in too many years, hope surged within him.

He stood and moved her back. "Wait here. I'll be right back." He hurried to the storeroom and came out with two covered canvases. He put them both on easels. She frowned as she watched him set them up.

"Come here, Kait."

She approached him, curiosity blending the gold and green in her eyes. He grazed his hand down her cheek. This one time, he could finally give something back to her after all she'd given him.

When he pulled the canvas off the first portrait, she gasped, her hands flying to her cheeks. "Oh my God, Brett!"

Kaitlyn fought to breathe through the tears streaming down her face. She stared at the painting, unable to believe what he'd captured.

There she was, naked and lying on the chaise, just as he'd posed her. But instead of a plain backdrop to the painting, he'd painted the chaise in the middle of a green meadow, colorful wildflowers popping up out of the grass. The skies were dark gray and rain poured down over her, a single cloud parting to shine a ray of light over her body.

He'd captured her magic. He'd captured her heart. She turned to him, at a loss for words, her heart swelling with so much love she thought she might burst. "I don't know what to say. It's breathtaking."

"It's you." He bent and kissed her softly. Her mouth trembled at the first touch of his lips against hers. But then he pulled away and said, "This is you, too."

When he pulled the sheet off the second portrait, she blinked, then cast a frown in his direction. "What do you mean?"

It was the nude she'd spotted in the storeroom. The one that had given her the idea to ask him to paint her.

"That's you, Kait. I painted it when I first fell in love with you, when you were first coming into your maturity as a woman. Now I have two portraits of you, Kait. The young girl I first fell in love with, and the woman I love now."

The dark hair cascading over her body, the delicate arms and fingers posed in front of her, hiding her nudity. Her gaze searched his. "This is me?"

"Yes."

She turned to him and threw her arms around him, capturing his mouth in a kiss that seared her senses. Holding him tight, she was afraid to let go, afraid to believe she could be so lucky.

His mouth was hungry, devouring hers and making her forget all about portraits and the pains of the past. Now was all that mattered. Being in his arms, feeling his hands roaming over her body. He cupped her buttocks and pulled her closer, pressing his erection against her sex until she thought she'd die from the pleasure of it. Sparks of sweet delight rained between her legs.

She tore at his shirt, desperate to feel his skin under her hands. He shrugged out of it and made quick work of his jeans, then pulled off her sweater and slid her pants down her legs in a frenzy of hurried tugs and pulls. His hands circled her waist and he lifted her to the bar, brushing the bottle of whiskey out of the way to plant her butt right in the center of the cool countertop.

She shuddered at the feel of icy cold bartop against her heated, bare pussy.

"Lie down on the bar, baby," he instructed.

Anticipation filled her as she laid back against the countertop, her excitement doubling when he drew her legs apart and swiped his fingers over her moist slit.

"Wet. God, you're always so wet for me, Kait," he murmured, bending his head toward her sex. He licked her center, circling her clit and driving her mad with teasing strokes of his tongue, never touching the tight knot of nerves begging for his mouth. He petted her slit, his thumb grazing her moist pussy lips. When he slipped two fingers inside her and covered her clit with his mouth, she cried out, arching against him, demanding without words that he take more of her, fill her deeper and make her come.

How could a mere few days without him make her so desperately needy for his touch, his mouth, the pleasure only he could give her? How could he turn her into a whimpering, sobbing, wanton who only wanted his fingers in her cunt, his mouth on her clit?

She struggled for control while he painted the tiny pearl with his tongue, swirling in circles until she was sobbing and writhing against his mouth. Her orgasm hit like a shockwave. She lifted her buttocks and crushed her sex against his lips, demanding he suck harder as she rode out the rush of incredible sensation.

He kissed her thigh, holding onto her legs as she trembled in aftershock, then made his way to her mouth, letting him taste her come on his tongue and lips. She licked at him greedily, needing to give him what he'd given her.

He dragged her toward him, lifting her easily and carrying her to the chaise where he'd painted her. She sat and watched, licking her lips in anticipation while he stood in front of her stroking his thick cock.

"You like to watch me touch it, don't you, *cher*?"

"Oh, yes," she said, her gaze lifting to his. "But I'd like to suck it even more."

With a low growl he came toward her, holding her head as she opened her mouth and greedily took him between her hungry lips. Her tongue twined around the thick, hot head of his cock, tasting the salty pre-come that gathered there. She licked the ridged veins on the underside of his shaft, trailing her tongue down the base to capture his balls between her lips. She suckled them gently, grasping his cock in her hands to stroke it upward while she licked the sac underneath.

"Fuck!" he groaned, his hand tightening in her hair. He drew her head back and positioned his cock head between her lips again, grasping the base of the shaft and thrusting it hard into her mouth.

She loved this side of him, the demanding, dominant male who knew exactly what he wanted, who looked to her for his pleasure. She wanted to take him to the same heights he'd led her just now, until his come spurted into the back of her throat and he cried out in ecstasy as she emptied him.

But he pulled away and dragged her up, flipping her over so her stomach was pressed against the back of the chaise.

"I can't wait any longer to be inside you." He positioned his cock between her thighs and plunged home, striking her womb with the depth and force of his thrust.

Kaitlyn screamed at the sweet, painful pleasure, her juices coating his cock, slickening it as he withdrew and powered inside her again. The power of the elements bubbled up inside her, threatening to explode in sweet ecstasy. How could she have lived a moment of her adult life without this man? How could she ever think she would be whole without him? This joining meant everything to her, the feel of him inside her stroking taking her to heights she'd never thought possible. Her body shuddered as the joy of springtime burst within her.

"Make it rain, Kait," he groaned. "Let me feel your magic."

Releasing her power, she inhaled as the scent of lavender filled the room, then lilies, then roses. Such sweet perfume when mixed when the utterly earthy scent of sex. Her womb clenched as he drove deeper powering his cock inside her with unrelenting thrusts. The rumble of thunder was followed by the downpour of hard, driving rain.

The drops sluiced down her back into the crack of her ass and onto his cock. Cool moisture penetrated her as he thrust forward again, striking her G-spot with each forceful stroke. She gripped the edge of the chaise and held on tight, feeling the stirrings of orgasm build within her.

But then he withdrew and flipped her around, pushing her onto her back and covering her mouth with his lips. His tongue slid inside and fucked her mouth, at the same time driving his cock between her swollen pussy lips and burying himself inside her.

Though they'd made love before, this time was different. She felt the release of tension within him, and knew this time he held nothing back. Before there had always been a part of him she couldn't have, a part he kept tucked deep inside. Now he gave her everything, and she took it all in, embracing his essence within her own. An outpouring of love and emotion permeated her senses, and she felt more powerful than she ever had before.

Together they were strong. They could handle anything. Thunder shook the room, the crack of lightning brightening the room like daylight.

His groan made her tremble, his hands tightening as he wound them underneath her to lift her hips and tunnel deeper inside her cunt. She cried out against his mouth, hovering on the precipice of ecstasy before she flooded him with her juices. He jerked and shot hot streams of come inside her, trembling with the force of his orgasm.

Her climax tore a scream from her lips, his fingers biting into her hips as he shook with the force of his own release. She claimed his mouth, licking at his tongue and biting his lower lip as she trembled and quaked through yet another shaking orgasm. Brett held her tight as they rode out the storm together until all that was left were tiny aftershocks.

She closed her eyes and felt the power of his love, knew she had found all that she could ever want, and more. If she died today, she'd leave blissfully happy.

"This isn't going to be easy," he mumbled against her neck. "I'm difficult."

"I know," she said, tangling her fingers in the soft thickness of his hair. "And I love you anyway. And I'm stubborn. More stubborn than you. Which means you'll never get rid of me, Brett. Don't even try. I'm yours forever."

He leaned up and searched her face, his eyes showing a warmth she hadn't seen before. "The best day of my life was the day I found the Storm family, the day I met you. I love you, Kaitlyn. I always will."

"I love you too, Brett. This journey we take, we'll take together. One day at a time."

He kissed her and she knew then they would fight the battle together.

As long as they had each other, the battle was already won.

Epilogue
One year later

Angelina Storm slipped her hand into her husband Galen's, always seeking his power through touch. His magic merged with hers and gave her the strength to keep from sobbing like a baby, something she swore she wouldn't do.

Then again, watching her daughter Shannon take that first dance with her new husband, Max brought a tear to her eye she couldn't hold back.

Her second child had been married today. Logan would be following suit in six months' time, and Kaitlyn and Brett's wedding was only a year away.

She smiled through the pool of tears and looked up at Galen, still so handsome even after thirty-six years of marriage. He still had the ability to make her pulse race and her body think things no woman her age should. Well into his sixties, his raven-black hair was mostly gray now, but his deep blue eyes still sparked her libido and made her heart do flips against her ribs. Sometimes she still felt twenty-five years old and in the deep throes of first love. Then again, why wouldn't she? Galen had been her first and only love.

"Are you crying again, lass?" he asked, swiping away the tear with the pad of his thumb.

"Of course not. Okay, maybe a little bit," she said with a tremulous smile.

"Our babies have grown up."

She nodded, the moment bittersweet. This is what she'd wanted, for all her children to find their destiny in the arms of the one they loved. All four had done it. Aidan and Lissa were expecting their first child in a few months, the glow of impending motherhood lighting up Lissa's face as she stood next to Angelina and reached for her hand.

"Shannon looks beautiful, Mom," she said, her own crystal blue eyes sparkling with unshed tears.

Angelina squeezed her hand. "As beautiful as you looked the day you married my son."

Lissa's face lit up. "I love him more every day. Is that normal?"

Angelina laughed. "Of course. I'd be surprised if you didn't."

"Of course she loves me. I'm damn near perfect," Aidan said, wrapping his arms around Lissa's swollen stomach and leaning his head against hers.

Logan coughed behind her and wrapped his arm around his mother's shoulders. "Full of it as usual, bro."

Aidan arched a brow and grinned. Angelina beamed as her children surrounded her, taking comfort in their strength and the astounding love that flowed from them. They'd all found their happiness despite the difficulties. Their destinies had been hard roads to travel, but each had come through exactly as she'd expected them to — with strength borne of the union between her and Galen.

The wedding dance finished, Angelina applauded and held out her arms for her daughter, resplendent in bright white tulle and lace, her cheeks pink with excitement. Shannon hugged her back, whispering, "Thank you, Mom."

Leaning back, Angelina searched Shannon's face. "For what?"

"For showing me how to love someone. For giving us all an example of what true love is all about. You made it so easy."

Later that evening as the entire Storm clan gathered for an official portrait, Angelina waited behind the photographer while he positioned Aidan and Lissa, Max and Shannon, Logan and Sophie and Kaitlyn and Brett, then motioned for her and Galen to join them in the center of the group.

She looked to all her children and the ones they loved, then turned her gaze on Galen. He slipped his arm around her waist and squeezed. "Who'd have thought we would end up like this when we first met all those years ago?" he teased.

"I couldn't stand the sight of you, as I remember," she said, winking at him.

"Ach. You were…difficult, to say the least. But I have the magic touch and showed you the error in your thinking."

She tilted her head back and laughed. "That you did, my love, that you did." And the end result was the portrait being taken right now. Love and magic flowed from Galen and their children, filling her with peace and contentment. Yes, it had been a rocky start for her and Galen, but she had finally realized her destiny and walked into the arms of the man she would love for all eternity.

The circle was complete and the Storm name would live on in her grandchildren and those who came after that. She and Galen would leave a legacy of love and destiny that she fervently hoped would last for all time.

She leaned her head against Galen's shoulder and smiled as the photographer snapped the picture.

About the author:

In April 2003, Ellora's Cave foolishly offered me a contract for my first erotic romance and I haven't shut up since. My writing is an addiction for which there is no cure, a disease in which strange characters live in my mind, all clamoring for their own story. I try to let them out one by one, as mixing snarling werewolves with a bondage and discipline master can be very dangerous territory. Then again, unusual plotlines offer relief from the demons plaguing me.

In my world, well-endowed, naked cabana boys do the vacuuming and dishes, little faeries flit about dusting the furniture and doing laundry, Wolfgang Puck fixes my dinner and I spend every night engaged in wild sexual abandon with a hunky alpha. Okay, the hunky alpha part is my real life husband and he keeps my fantasy life enriched with extensive "research". But Wolfgang won't answer my calls, the faeries are on strike and my readers keep running off with the cabana boys.

Jaci welcomes mail from readers. You can write to her c/o Ellora's Cave Publishing at 1056 Home Avenue, Akron OH 44310-3502.

Why an electronic book?

We live in the Information Age—an exciting time in the history of human civilization in which technology rules supreme and continues to progress in leaps and bounds every minute of every hour of every day. For a multitude of reasons, more and more avid literary fans are opting to purchase e-books instead of paperbacks. The question to those not yet initiated to the world of electronic reading is simply: *why?*

1. *Price.* An electronic title at Ellora's Cave Publishing and Cerridwen Press runs anywhere from 40-75% less than the cover price of the <u>exact same title</u> in paperback format. Why? Cold mathematics. It is less expensive to publish an e-book than it is to publish a paperback, so the savings are passed along to the consumer.

2. *Space.* Running out of room to house your paperback books? That is one worry you will never have with electronic novels. For a low one-time cost, you can purchase a handheld computer designed specifically for e-reading purposes. Many e-readers are larger than the average handheld, giving you plenty of screen room. Better yet, hundreds of titles can be stored within your new library—a single microchip. (Please note that Ellora's Cave and Cerridwen Press does not endorse any specific brands. You can check our website at www.ellorascave.com or

www.cerridwenpress.com for customer recommendations we make available to new consumers.)

3. *Mobility.* Because your new library now consists of only a microchip, your entire cache of books can be taken with you wherever you go.

4. *Personal preferences are accounted for.* Are the words you are currently reading too small? Too large? Too...**ANNOYING**? Paperback books cannot be modified according to personal preferences, but e-books can.

5. *Instant gratification.* Is it the middle of the night and all the bookstores are closed? Are you tired of waiting days—sometimes weeks—for online and offline bookstores to ship the novels you bought? Ellora's Cave Publishing sells instantaneous downloads 24 hours a day, 7 days a week, 365 days a year. Our e-book delivery system is 100% automated, meaning your order is filled as soon as you pay for it.

Those are a few of the top reasons why electronic novels are displacing paperbacks for many an avid reader. As always, Ellora's Cave and Cerridwen Press welcomes your questions and comments. We invite you to email us at service@ellorascave.com, service@cerridwenpress.com or write to us directly at: 1056 Home Ave. Akron OH 44310-3502.

erridwen, the Celtic Goddess of wisdom, was the muse who brought inspiration to storytellers and those in the creative arts. Cerridwen Press encompasses the best and most innovative stories in all genres of today's fiction. Visit our site and discover the newest titles by talented authors who still get inspired - much like the ancient storytellers did, once upon a time.

Cerridwen Press

www.cerridwenpress.com

THE
☥ ELLORA'S CAVE ☥
LIBRARY

Stay up to date with Ellora's Cave Titles in
Print with our Quarterly Catalog.

TO RECIEVE A CATALOG,
SEND AN EMAIL WITH YOUR NAME
AND MAILING ADDRESS TO:

CATALOG@ELLORASCAVE.COM
OR SEND A LETTER OR POSTCARD
WITH YOUR MAILING ADDRESS TO:

CATALOG REQUEST
c/o ELLORA'S CAVE PUBLISHING, INC.
1056 HOME AVENUE
AKRON, OHIO 44310-3502